Kids
OF CONCERN

By Perry Logan

perrylogan.ca

4THFLOOR PRESS

4thfloorpress.com

ISBN 978-1-988993-35-5

eISBN 978-1-988993-36-2

eISBN 978-1-988993-37-9

Published by 4th Floor Press, Inc.
4thfloorpress.com
1st Printing 2020
Cover Design by Kevin Western
Shervin Communications Inc.
goshervin.com

perrylogan.ca

What started as a dream has become a reality!

I want to thank the following special people who made it come true!

Ron Anderton

for being a sounding board to my ramblings

when I just needed to vent.

Allen Wiebe

To the man who shared his experiences and wisdom that I

needed to hear. He was right every time.

Janine Fulla

for sharing her experiences as a writer and for

guiding me through some interesting challenges.

And my wife **Sandra**

She kept me motivated.

Having good friends and family is what makes life great!

PROLOGUE

The summer of 1993

Gabriola Island is amongst a scatter of islands thirty miles
west of Vancouver's mainland. It was once home to the largest coal-
producing mine on the west coast of British Columbia. While it
was active, Hub City Mining employed five hundred workers and
was a major contributor to the Vancouver Island economy. It also
claimed the lives of nearly fifty miners due to shaft collapses or the
carelessness of workers.

After the mine finally closed in the spring of 1975, Gabriola
Island became a popular camping spot for the locals over in
Nanaimo. The hiking trails and sand beaches made it a great place
to spend time as a family.

Over time Gabriola became the home to a squatter's community
that built shelters out of supplies they salvaged from the decaying
mining buildings. The community grew and their garden harvest
eventually expanded outside of vegetables. Marijuana became a
form of currency on the island. The money earned selling high-
grade weed was then used to purchase the other necessities to live
as castaways.

A street gang of thugs known as the Golden Eagles got wind of
it. They specialized in street intimidation and extortion but had their
hands into anything that made them easy money. They devised a
simple plan to take the pot plants, and as insurance, they would send
three of their toughest guys to beat anyone who got in their way.
How much resistance would a bunch of stoned hippies put up.

The three loaded into a small watercraft and headed towards Gabriola Island. It took less than thirty minutes to cross the Salish Sea and they found a deserted beach.

The commune members had finished a fish-fry dinner and were down on the beach skinny-dipping and getting high. The only one left behind to clean up camp was Mickey, a fourteen-year old Coast Salish runaway. He was a tall lanky teenager with long dark hair braided down his back.

No one was sure if Mickey was the kid's real name and no one cared. He was smart and enjoyed listening to the stories told around the nightly campfire. Everyone on the island was running from something and Mickey was no different. The scar tissue above his eyes and his crooked nose was evidence of a tough childhood.

For the first time in his young life, he felt safe. There would be no more beatings from his abusive father who called him '*boy.*' He had plenty of scars, but he was determined that no one would ever hurt him again.

Once he finished his chores, he headed out for his nightly workout.

A mile past the beach where everyone hung out, there was a stretch of secluded sand that the boat glided up onto. The motor was turned off. Willie was the recruit and he jumped into the knee-deep water and dragged the boat onto the beach. Once it was secured, the other two joined him.

Frank was the leader and lit a cigarette. "Let's go get those plants so we can get back."

Willie was sitting on a rock squeezing the water out of his socks. "What if they're being guarded?"

Frank didn't say anything to the recruit. He reached into his pocket and pulled out a switchblade and hit the release. A four-inch blade snapped to attention.

Mickey paced back and forth and filled his lungs while he recovered from his run. He stood on the cliff and watched the passenger ferry sail into the harbour from Vancouver. One passed every two hours and that's how Mickey gauged the time.

Mickey put himself through an intense thirty minutes of wind sprints. Being physically fit was a priority and once he was done, he began his martial arts training that was designed by his idol, Bruce Lee. When he searched for food one night, he found a magazine in a dumpster with a Lee training insert. He memorized and worked on every move.

When exhaustion finally took over, he let the cool breeze battle the sweat pouring down his back. He was interrupted by the voices directly below. He saw the boat anchored on the beach and watched three strangers disappear into the trees.

He suspected they were here for the plants. He thought about his options to stop them.

Mickey stayed out of sight. He wanted to be sure they were there for the marijuana. He watched from behind a cluster of bushes and they were not happy having to climb up the steep trail. A small pit of nerves festered in Mickey's stomach.

"Hold up," Frank sounded unsure. "Let me look around."

Willie was frustrated. "Do you know where we're going?"

The third member, a big Russian with a tattoo of a rattlesnake on his neck finally spoke. "Are you sure this is where the plants are?"

Frank gave them both an annoyed look. "Shut up and follow me. Those plants are here somewhere."

Neither wanted to be the one to get Frank upset. He had a vicious temper. It was what always got him in trouble and was the main reason he spent time in prison. They moved forward, with Frank leading the way.

"There they are, off to the right," Frank announced triumphantly. "Let's go make some easy money."

Mickey overheard Frank and the pit tightened. His theory was confirmed. They were there to steal the plants. And without any concern for his safety, Mickey stepped out from behind the bush and onto the path. He stood behind them. "Where do you think you're going?"

Not expecting to be followed, the three men stopped. Without knowing what they were up against, they turned slowly to see who was behind them. Frank was the first to lay eyes on Mickey, and when he realized it was just a kid, he regained his arrogance.

"It's an Indian! Where did you come from?" Shouted the man who was more than twice Mickey's age. "Do you live with the freaks, or are you here to rip them off too?"

Mickey remembered what Lee's lessons taught him. He set his feet into a combat stance. His fists were clenched and raised. The pit in his stomach festered.

Frank glanced at his buddies and then glared at Mickey. "Are you here to stop us from doing a little harvesting?"

Mickey said nothing, but locked eyes with the gang member.

Frank recognized Mickey's stance from a movie he saw. "Hey, boys, this fucking Indian thinks he's Bruce Lee."

Seeing he was only a kid, the men laughed arrogantly. The recruit stepped forward. "What are we going to do with him?"

"You're going to beat the shit out of him so we can get to work," was Frank's simple response. "because I want to get back to the bar and have a few beers. You're up."

Willie was confident he could easily take the kid, but before he could raise his fist, his jaw was broken in two places by a powerful and perfectly executed sidekick. Willie dropped to his knees and bent forward so the blood could exit his mouth. He gasped for air between coughs and his eyes started to turn purple.

The two older gang members looked at each other in shocked disbelief. Their arrogance was replaced by anger and a little taste of respect. On the other side, Mickey was filled with adrenalin and he was bouncing on the balls of his feet. He stayed focused on the next fight that he knew was coming. The pit was gone and replaced with a feeling of power he had never experienced.

Knowing he was up, Vladimir stepped forward. He pulled off his black leather jacket and tossed it to Frank. He turned to face the kid. Mickey's fists were already raised, waiting to fight the bigger man.

The Golden Eagles had recruited Vladimir because he was a cruel street fighter. He didn't just enjoy winning fights; he enjoyed inflicting punishment on his opponents.

"Alright, V, kick the shit out of this punk so we can get going," encouraged Frank. "Hurt the little fucker and make him pay for what he did to the recruit."

Vladimir looked at Mickey and gave Frank a confident glance. He flicked out a few skillful jabs and then threw a hard roundhouse that was supposed to catch Mickey off guard and end the fight before it even started. The punch missed Mickey's chin and in response, Mickey swung his foot into Vladimir's knee, connecting solidly and sending a shot of pain up his leg. It hobbled the gang member. Mickey knew he had to take the bigger man down if he had any chance of winning.

Once the pain passed, Vladimir let his anger corrode his judgment. He lunged at the kid and that was a mistake he would regret. Mickey sidestepped and landed a clean punch to the right eyebrow. Blood started oozing out from above Vladimir's eye.

The Russian wiped the blood away with the back of his hand and glared at Mickey. "You piece of shit!"

Mickey stayed calm and readied himself for the next assault.

The damage to Vladimir's knee was evident by his severe limp. The young fighter took advantage of the weakness and sent another sweeping leg kick that found its mark. Vladimir let out a scream of agony. He fell forward onto his knees and Mickey landed a solid blow to the temple. The big Russian was out cold before he hit the ground.

Frank was left speechless. He pulled out the switchblade and kept it hidden in his palm.

Having witnessed the kid's skill, he knew he would need any advantage he could get to stand a chance.

"Who the hell are you, boy?" Frank scowled, trying to distract Mickey as he moved closer, "and where did you learn to fight?"

Before Frank could position himself, the much younger fighter stepped forward and swung a roundhouse kick that missed Frank's head. Although it didn't connect, it got his attention.

"You little fucker," Frank muttered angrily. He released the blade from its case and held it out in front of him. He waved it back and forth. "Other than fear and common sense, what's stopping you?"

Mickey saw the blade and his adrenalin pumped harder, knowing only one of them would walk away. He felt an ease come over him.

Mickey returned to a fighter's stance and for the first time, he spoke as he bounced on his feet. "I guess I have no fear, so let's go, asshole."

Frank stepped towards Mickey, using the blade like an epee. Mickey anticipated the move and deftly stepped to the side. He measured the distance between them, knowing the gang leader would make another attempt. When he did, Mickey took advantage of the opening and threw a straight punch that landed flush on Frank's nose.

Blood spewed out of the shattered nose, but Frank was able to fight through the pain. He lunged at Mickey and pushed him off balance. The kid took a quick step to regain his bearings. They were only a few feet from the cliff.

Both took deep breaths, getting prepared for the next round. Frank knew he had to get close to Mickey if he was to stand any chance. It had to become a battle of strength. The kid was too quick with his counter moves. Frank held the blade in his right hand while he guided with his left.

Mickey shifted left to right, trying to keep his opponent off balance. When Frank stabbed at Mickey for the third time, he was ready and countered with a left uppercut, followed by a right hook that stunned Frank. In a desperate counterattack, Frank lunged at Mickey's legs, but missed. Mickey used the opening to land a downward kick in the middle of Frank's back, knocking the wind out of him.

Instead of inflicting more punishment, Mickey backed away. Frank gasped for air as he rose to his feet. Mickey saw that Vladimir was now conscious and sitting beside Willie. Both men were too wounded to consider interfering. In the split second that he took his eyes off Frank, the more desperate fighter, slashed at Mickey with his knife blade.

Mickey felt the steel slice his forearm. It was a clean cut and painless. Warm blood dripped into his hand and Mickey's expression changed to anger. He was mad that he let his guard down. Mickey instinctively lashed out and landed two quick jabs to the face with his other hand. He followed that with a powerful kick to the groin.

The force of the blow pushed Frank backwards and his feet tripped out from under him, causing him to fall backwards. He disappeared over the edge of the cliff and his screams resonated as he fell to his death on the rocks.

All three were stunned and almost expected to see Frank climb back up. Mickey packed up his few things at camp and left the island that night. He was on the run again.

ONE

The Year is 2012

The British Columbia provincial government announced that after years of internal debate they were putting Gabriola Island up for sale to the highest bidder that also met the environmental requirements. The plan was to recoup the millions the province had spent trying to decide what to do with the island now that it was no longer a mining mecca.

The law firm given the chore of managing the sale was Cooke and Magill, based in Nanaimo. They were responsible for managing the processes and recommending a successful bid to the Land Title and Survey Authority of British Columbia.

On Tuesday, May 1, 2012, Ray Cooke, a senior partner of Cooke and Magill stood at a podium on the ferry dock and announced in front of twelve media members and concerned citizens that bidding on Gabriola Island was officially open and would close on Friday, July 6th, at 3 pm.

Ray Cooke's face bore the usual markings of someone in his late forties, but his short, dark hair showed little grey and his body was in great shape from daily rounds of golf and squash. Now back at his firm he wore a satisfied grin while he stood in the boardroom sipping on twelve-year-old single malt. Across the table, cradling his water, was his partner and lifelong friend, David Magill.

David was the managing partner for the firm. "With the extra work we'll need to hire a new paralegal."

Ray topped up his drink. "Just make sure she's a looker."

TWO

It was July 6th and Ray Cooke was in his office earlier than usual for a Friday morning. It was the last day for anyone to submit a bid for the Gabriola Island lottery. Wearing a new gold tie that was a gift from his latest wife, he looked more self confident than usual. With an expresso in one hand, he flipped through the stack of bids on his desk. He grinned when he thought about the large check someone would be writing in the next week. A check that would include their twenty percent commission, just north of $500 thousand.

Magill walked into Ray's office unannounced and took a seat in front of his partner's desk. He eyed the pile, "Is that all of them?"

"So far."

"How many?"

"Last count, twenty-two," Ray sipped his coffee. "Any plans for your cut?"

Before David could answer, his phone rang. He looked at the display and stood up. "I've got to take this. See you in the boardroom at 3:30."

The receptionist in the lobby was booking a new client when a male courier handed her a package. Without even looking up, she signed for it. It was bid twenty-three and came in just under the deadline. She sent a note that it arrived.

David grabbed the last entry on his way to the boardroom. Ray was right behind him and closed the door. He saw the envelope in David's hand. "Who's that one from?"

"A company called Liberty City," David examined the outside of the envelope, not sure what he was expecting to find. "Never heard of them."

Ray checked the time on his Rolex GMT Master. It was a gift from his second wife for their first wedding anniversary. They never had a second because Ray was addicted to beautiful women. The Rolex was one of the few items he salvaged from the divorce proceedings. "The bidding is now closed."

Now he was forty-eight and remarried for the third time to a twenty-seven-year-old with an amazing body and expensive hobbies. They had met at his country club's annual Christmas party a year earlier, while his divorce from number two was being finalized. She had shoulder-length golden blonde hair with a tantalizing smile that did nothing to discourage his urges. A long white designer dress with only thin shoulder straps holding it in place was the final straw. He had to have her.

Inside the boardroom there was a wet bar in the corner. Ray made his way over and poured himself a two-finger portion of scotch. "What's our next step?"

"It's a little early for a drink, isn't it? We have a lot of work ahead that requires our attention," David stated with a sense of concern. "Is everything okay at home with., Tiffany?"

"Life is good," he took a sip as if he was testing the scotch, "but the girl has a wild side I can't keep up with."

The two had been best friends since middle school when David's family bought the house across the street from the Cooke's. They went to the same schools, played sports together, and eventually enrolled in the same university, where they both graduated with law degrees. But they were two different men.

David scowled at his partner. "How bad can it be having a much younger wife who wants to have sex every night?"

3

"That's not as easy as you might think," Ray chuckled, "and that isn't my concern."

David poured a glass of water from a pitcher on the table. "What's up then?"

Ray swished his scotch around the glass and took another sip before sitting. "Tiffany has expensive habits and it's catching up to me." His cut of the commissions couldn't come at a better time.

They were interrupted when the receptionist poked her head in the door. Ray gave her an inviting smile that David noticed. She delivered a cylinder wrapped in gold paper and silver ribbon. It was obviously a bottle of liquor.

"This just arrived," She returned Ray's smile as she placed it on the table. "Enjoy."

There was no card, so Ray ripped off the wrapping. "Very nice! A bottle of Macallan scotch. I wonder who sent it?"

David wasn't interested. "Let's get started."

Ray grabbed a fresh glass from the bar. "Might as well enjoy it."

"We need to get to work," David reminded him, feeling frustrated with Ray's lack of focus. "Let's start reviewing these packages."

For the next two hours, the room was quiet as they went through the contents of each envelope. By the time six o'clock arrived they had eliminated over half of the bids for various violations. Ray decided he needed a break and walked over to the bar and poured himself a second Macallan. By seven, both men were ready to call it a day. Their reasons differed.

David had chosen a simpler life with his wife, Nina, and their teenage sons. He was committed to be an active part of their lives, while Ray chased a grander existence. But things were not perfect. Three months earlier, Nina had been sexually assaulted in their home while David was at soccer with the boys. The attacker was never caught and the emotional trauma it caused was something David

4

and his wife were working on together. Nina had insisted that no one outside the family and her therapist ever know about it. The police were never called, so the Magill family tried to cope and move on. David never even mentioned it to Ray.

He leaned back in his chair and stretched his arms over his shoulders. "Let's wrap this up and we'll continue on Monday."

"Sounds good," Ray finished his third scotch. "I'm meeting Tiffany for dinner, so I need to get going."

David's cellphone rang. "Excuse me. I'll be right back."

When David left the room, Ray took the opportunity to refresh his scotch without fearing any sarcastic remarks. When David returned, he noticed Ray's new drink but chose not to say anything.

Ray had a sneer on his face. The scotch was working. "Come on, David. We need to celebrate what this means for our firm," he poured a drink for his partner, "and you can tell me who keeps calling that makes you leave the room."

David ignored Ray's last remark but did accept the drink. "I'm meeting Nina at her parents at eight, so let's make it a quick one."

"I have a gorgeous woman waiting for me," Ray boasted, "and a big chunk of prime rib."

David noticed the new scotch bottle was half empty. "Are you okay to drive? I can drop you off on my way."

Ray rejected the offer. "Thanks, but I'm okay. I'm just whipping over to the Barrel and Sword restaurant."

David decided against the drink and poured it down the sink. "I have to get going. Are you sure I can't give you a ride?"

Ray gulped down his remaining scotch. "I'm good. Go enjoy your in-laws."

Ray climbed into his 2012 Red Porsche convertible that he couldn't afford and pulled out of the firm's parking lot. Within seconds he was on the freeway and the 250-horsepower motor pushed the car to a speed of over one hundred and eighty kilometres per hour. Bon Jovi blasted from the stereo and the warm night air whipped through his hair. He was enjoying himself. That was until he saw the red and blue lights flashing in his rear-view mirror.

"Shit!" Ray muttered as he lifted his foot off the accelerator and steered the Porsche off the highway. He under-estimated the distance to the curb and bounced the forty-thousand-dollar car off the curb. The officer pulling in behind took note of his error.

The red and blue lights behind him made Ray start to recognize the seriousness of what he might face. He did a quick calculation of how much scotch he drank and knew he was legally impaired. He reached inside his glovebox and grabbed his registration papers.

The officer appeared at the driver's window, holding a flashlight that he shone into Ray's eyes. "Do you know why I pulled you over?"

"To blind me?" Ray complained before realizing he should cooperate. "I was driving a little faster than I probably should of. I just got this new car and…"

The young officer cut him off. "Have you been drinking tonight, sir?"

Ray hesitated before answering. He thought about his options. His law proficiency was kicking in, but the amount of scotch he had consumed was evident as well.

"I asked you a question," the officer said forcefully.

"No, sir," he lied. "I just left work and I'm heading to meet my wife for dinner."

The officer ordered Ray to open the door. He could smell alcohol and Ray's glossy eyes indicated he was lying. "Step out of the vehicle."

"Am I under arrest?" Ray asked, initially refusing the officer's request.

The officer became impatient. "Have you been drinking?"

Ray reluctantly stepped out on the street and the officer guided him to the front of his car. "Okay, I had two drinks at work."

"So, you lied," The officer wasn't showing any indication he was going to give Ray a break. "Why do you think you can lie to me?"

Panic took over. "Do you know who I am, officer?"

Tiffany sat on a bar stool in the lounge at the Barrel and Sword restaurant sipping on a martini while she waited for her husband. She checked her phone for what seemed like the hundredth time and there was still no message from Ray, who was now thirty minutes late. The jerk better not be at the office with the receptionist.

Tiffany Cooke was blessed with ageless beauty and was aware of the attention she attracted from both the men and women in the lounge. She used her sexuality to her advantage when it got her what she wanted. Like a free drink. The bartender replaced her empty glass with another complimentary martini. All she had to do was let him think he had a chance.

Across the lounge, the evening's entertainer stepped onto the stage to begin his first set. The tall auburn-haired singer strapped on his twelve-string acoustic and stepped up to the microphone. "Good evening and welcome to the Barrel and Sword. I'm Steve and I'm looking forward to entertaining you tonight."

He started his night with an Eagles classic and Tiffany forgot that she was bored. She turned to watch the handsome singer with a rustic tone belt out the lyrics to *Take it Easy*. He looked attractive in his white collared shirt and tight-fitting jeans. She decided her husband was being an ass and Steve might be a lucky guy.

After failing the sobriety roadside test, the officer handcuffed

Ray and put him in the backseat of his squad car. A crowd had gathered across the street to watch the scenario play out. Ray held his head down and wished the cop would start driving. He was humiliated.

Ray was charged with Driving Under the Influence and placed in a holding cell at the local police station. He looked around at the people he was surrounded by and began to understand how much he had messed up.

Ray requested his phone call and was guided to a payphone. He dialed David's number and let it ring. His partner would clear this up. Nina finally answered. "Get David. I need to talk to him now."

"He's with the boys," Nina was agitated he called so late. "Do you want him to call you back?"

"No, I need him now!" Ray snapped.

Nina wasn't a fan of Ray, and it showed in her tone. "Don't be a jerk. I'll get him."

David grabbed the phone. "What's up that can't wait until tomorrow?"

There was a slight hesitation. "I've been arrested."

THREE

Ray paced nervously inside his holding cell and constantly looked at the clock in the hallway. Two hours and there was still no contact from David. And to make things worse, he was now stuck with a new cellmate. The guy was a drunk with a long grey beard and body odor that you get when you haven't washed in days. And he wouldn't stop complaining.

"I caught my girl banging the neighbor," he slurred, "and now I'm facing assault charges."

Ray was impatient. "I really don't give a crap about your problems."

The drunk looked insulted and moved towards him. Ray turned, ready to stand his ground. The last thing he needed was to get into a fight. "Look, I've had a couple shit days myself, so back off."

"What are you in here for? You don't look like a regular."

"I was brought in for impaired driving."

The man rubbed his beard, "That's it?"

"Yup."

David arrived at the police station and was escorted to a small interrogation room where Ray waited. Ray was glad to have some time away from the cell mate. David tossed his briefcase on the table and looked at his law partner, who was now a client.

He listened as Ray tried to justify his situation by shifting the blame on the officer. His list of excuses was long and pathetic. Ray's ego blinded him from the truth. He had a problem with alcohol but was used to getting his way.

"Does Tiffany know you're here?"

"Fuck no," Ray retorted, remembering their dinner plans, "and she doesn't need to. Just get me out."

"You're an idiot! I offered you a ride."

Ray ignored David. "I know I fucked up, so I need you to fix this for us."

David stifled his anger. "What do you mean, *us*?"

Ray looked squarely at his friend. "If I get charged and found guilty, the firm will lose the Gabriola deal and that would hurt both of us."

Ray was shifting the responsibility, as was his manner, and that infuriated David. He masked his frustration. "The police report says you were doing over one-eighty."

"So what?" Ray treated the charge like an inconvenience. "It's only a fucking speeding ticket."

"True." David continued to read the report. "The ticket won't be a problem. It's the impaired charge. Your blood alcohol came in at .14."

Ray leaned back in his chair and rubbed his tired eyes, his frustration starting to show. He needed David to do some legal maneuvering. "What's your plan?"

David closed the file and tossed it on the table. "I don't have a plan. The only chance is we meet with the officer in charge. Hopefully, we can get the DUI dropped or down graded to a simple roadside suspension"

The arresting officer interrupted them when he entered the room. He carried two bottles of water and tossed one to Ray before handing the other to David. "You must be his attorney."

David didn't recognize the young officer and was careful not to be too aggressive. "I was hoping we could work something out with the impaired charge."

"I'm Constable Giles, the arresting officer," he said to David, "and I'm sure you've read the arrest report."

David nodded.

"I can't dismiss the charges. You will need to discuss that with Detective Murphy."

Ray couldn't restrain himself. "Why is there a detective coming? What department is he with?"

"Narcotics," Giles turned to Magill. "He will update you on the charges your client is facing."

"Narcotics?" Ray blurted nervously. "Why a narcotics detective?"

As if on cue, a broad-shouldered man with a well-established beard entered the room. He motioned for Giles to leave. "Gentlemen, I'm Detective Ken Murphy."

Ray looked at him. "Why the hell is there a narcotics detective in here?"

David took control of the conversation. "Sorry, detective, but my client and I are confused. The arrest report indicates this is a simple impaired driving case. What are we missing?"

The detective looked at Ray and then shifted his attention to David. "You're correct, it began as an impaired charge and I'm not concerned with that."

Ray felt a short-lived sense of relief hearing that the impaired charge might disappear. "Then, why are you here?"

FOUR

Detective Murphy took a seat across from Ray and interlocked his fingers. The man had huge hands. "I'm here because we found a kilo of cocaine in your car."

Ray was dumbfounded by what he heard.

The detective studied his reaction. "We got a tip and searched your car."

David challenged the detective. "You decided you had grounds for a search based on an anonymous tip? No judge would ever grant that."

"Never said it was anonymous." countered the detective.

Ray was overwhelmed. "I didn't have any cocaine in my car."

Murphy stood and wandered to the door. "I'm going to give you boys a few minutes while I go make a call. And unless you have a great answer as to why we found that much cocaine in your vehicle, I'm going to be charging your client with possession for the purpose of trafficking."

Murphy closed the door behind him.

Ray looked blindly at David. "What just happened? You know the coke isn't mine."

"It doesn't matter what I believe." David emphasized. "You've obviously pissed someone off if they're willing to lose a kilo of cocaine to get you busted."

"I could sure use a scotch."

David shook his head in disbelief. "It was the scotch that landed you here in the first place, you stupid asshole."

A few minutes later Detective Murphy re-entered. "I need you to stand up, Mr. Cooke," The big detective assisted Ray by putting his hand under Ray's arm. "You're under arrest for the possession of narcotics with the intent to distribute."

Ray started to shake uncontrollably as he was read his Miranda rights. He gazed helplessly at David. "Do something!"

"Go with the detective and I will work on getting you out on bail," David stepped aside as the detective led Ray out of the room. "I'll be back when I can."

David left the police station and climbed into his Lexus. He burst into laughter as he started his car. That couldn't have gone better. David steered his car onto the street and drove away. It was his turn for a celebratory scotch.

FIVE

It was 6 am and the guard made his morning rounds. He slapped his metal baton against the bars to announce his presence and remind everyone just who was in charge. "Rise and shine, assholes."

The loud clang of his baton against the steel bars woke Ray from a shallow sleep. He had spent a humbling night in a holding cell with a man who he hoped was now sober. When Ray wasn't asleep, he had tried to figure out who might be behind the cocaine. He never did come up with a plausible name. Most of his clients were grey-haired men planning retirement and trying to avoid paying taxes.

Ray's throat was parched. "Can I please get some water?"

The guard purposely ignored him.

Ray repeated his request, this time with the threat of a lawsuit.

It was nearly thirty minutes before the guard returned with a small paper cup. He slid it through the bars and when Ray reached for it the guard intentionally spilt most of it on the floor. "Oops."

Ray held his temper and gulped down what was left. "Any word when I'm getting out?"

"I'm just the gatekeeper," The guard sounded disinterested. "You need to talk to your lawyer. Oh wait, *you are* a lawyer, and look at you now."

Ray knew that getting into a verbal exchange with the guard would not improve his position, so he quietly took a seat on the metal bench. His roommate was still sleeping it off in the corner.

David enjoyed a goat cheese and spinach omelet Nina had

made while he read the morning news on his tablet. It wasn't going to be a good day for the image of the Cooke and Magill law firm, but that was expected. Ray's arrest was a huge story on every media source. The headline screamed:

'Prominent City Lawyer Charged with Possession of Cocaine'

David sipped his orange juice, while he read the story in its entirety and thought about his next move. A paralegal was already in the office drafting Ray's resignation letter. The move was necessary, and David knew that his soon to be ex-partner would fight it tooth and nail. He finished his breakfast and kissed Nina on his way out the door. His morning would start with a quick visit to the jailhouse to inform his client his bail hearing didn't go well. He had one stop on the way.

While Ray forced down a breakfast of lumpy oatmeal and the worse orange juice he had ever drank, he wondered what the hell David was doing. He also considered what he would tell Tiffany when he finally saw her.

The guard returned to collect the tray. "How'd you end up in here?"

Ray thought about ignoring him but decided it might be better to play along. "I was pulled over for speeding and now I'm charged with trafficking."

"I didn't know about the drug charges," the guard sounded sympathetic, "and that's heavy."

Ray forced a tired smile. "I'm innocent, but I bet you hear that all the time."

"I do," Laughed the guard. "One question though."

"Shoot."

"With you being a high-priced attorney, why has no one come to bail you out?"

Ray nodded. "That's the million-dollar question."

SIX

David pulled his Lexus into Ray's driveway and Tiffany greeted him at the front door wearing only a satin housecoat and an appearance that confirmed she was hungover. He was in a hurry and after a quick hello, he headed to Ray's office. Tiffany was close behind.

"Have you seen my asshole of a husband?"

David tried not to gawk at her curvy body hanging out of her robe. "You don't know, do you?"

"Know what?"

"He got pulled over for drunk driving on his way to meet you. They searched his car and found a kilo of cocaine. He's been charged with intent to distribute and he's currently waiting for me to get him bailed out."

Tiffany shook her head in disbelief. "Are you serious? How will this effect his job?"

He started looking through Ray's desk. "A little early to worry about his job, don't you think?"

"What are you looking for?"

"The keys to Ray's safe. There's a file I need."

"What file?"

None of your business, is what he wanted to tell her, but instead, he just lied. "It's Ray's copy of our shareholder's agreement. He needs it to qualify for bail."

Tiffany tightened the belt around her robe. "The key isn't in there."

David stopped looking. "Do you know where it is?"

Tiffany walked to a large vase on the windowsill and lifted it enough to pull a gold key from under it. "Here you go."

David went to the safe hidden behind a wall painting. He knew the combination because it was part of the agreement he had with Ray. It was a failsafe in case one of the partners got into trouble or died. He pulled out a manila envelope.

She followed David to the door. "Is Ray getting out today?"

David noticed a pair of cowboy boots that Ray would never wear at the front door. He didn't mention them. "He might be a while."

Detective Ken Murphy was already in his office when David arrived with two fresh coffee. "I took a chance you drink it black."

Murphy gratefully accepted it. "Compared to the crap they make here this is much appreciated."

David took a seat and glanced around the office, which was nothing more than a cubicle with a steel desk and a double-high filing cabinet. "I was hoping we could have a conversation regarding the charges you filed against my client."

"What are you thinking?" Murphy took a careful sip of the hot coffee and enjoyed the flavour. "I'm not sure what I can do for you at this point."

David eased into his strategy. "We both know the cocaine doesn't belong to my client."

Murphy corrected him. "We don't know that."

David shifted his position in his chair. "I've known Ray almost all of my life and he's not a drug dealer. He can be an arrogant ass at times, but he's not peddling drugs."

"Then explain how a kilo of high-grade cocaine got into his car. That amount isn't something regular people have access to," Murphy countered. "It's obvious that your partner has expensive tastes. Does he have any serious debt?"

David remembered Ray's comment in the boardroom. "I can't answer that until I speak with my client."

The big detective grabbed a file from his desk and passed it to David. "You might start by finding out why the car is actually in his wife's name?"

David seemed surprised. "Really?"

"How's their marriage?" questioned Murphy.

David remembered the cowboy boots. "As far as I know, their marriage is good."

"Well, that still might be your starting point," suggested Murphy, "because unless you can convince me otherwise, we're moving ahead with the charges."

David signed himself into the prisoner's visitation area and was escorted to the same interview room from the previous night. He gripped his briefcase tightly to ease his anxiety. He knew the first topic that needed to be resolved was the ownership of the firm. It would be an awkward conversation.

When Ray was escorted in, David was not prepared to see his partner outfitted in prison garb and handcuffs on his wrists. He looked exhausted and other than a brief greeting, David waited until they were alone before they spoke. "How are you holding up?"

"A little hungover, but otherwise I'm fine. Why am I still in this hellhole?"

"I'm working on your bail application, but you're facing some serious charges." David tried to keep the tone positive. "I met with Detective Murphy and at this point, he's not ready to make any kind of deal."

"What is going on?" Ray was frightened. "You know the cocaine isn't mine."

"I do, but unfortunately my opinion doesn't count for much in these circumstances."

David gazed at his partner. "Do you have any idea who would want to set you up?"

Ray shook his head.

David tried to sound compassionate. "Another tough topic we need to discuss is your partnership in the firm."

Ray threw his hands in the air. "Seriously? You want me to give up my ownership in the firm?"

"We have a shareholder's agreement that will be exercised if the firm or firm's business is put into jeopardy by either one of us, David pulled out the manila envelope. "We need to exercise that clause right now if we want any chance of finishing the Gabriola deal."

An expression of disbelief appeared on Ray's face. The events of the past twelve hours were numbing. "I know you're right, but…"

"Look, Ray," David interjected firmly, "I know this is tough for you, but I promise that once we get all of this behind us, I'll reinstate you."

"Okay," he conceded. "What is happening to my life? I haven't even heard from my wife. Does she know I'm here?"

David remembered the cowboy boots. "I saw her this morning and she sends her love."

Ray rolled his eyes. "I bet she does."

"If you can sign these papers then I can get working on your bail arrangements."

"Are you sure this is the only way?" Ray pleaded. "There's nothing else we can do?"

"You have to do this. I need to be able to tell the land commission office that you're no longer associated with the firm in any capacity."

"Okay, I trust you," Ray grabbed a pen, "but when this gets sorted out, we shred these papers, right?"

"Absolutely."

Ray reluctantly picked up the pen. Over twenty years building a law firm and now with one signature, he was signing it all away. He scribbled his name and pushed the papers back. He put all his faith in his *now* ex-partner.

David gathered up the papers. "Okay then, I'll get working on your bail."

Ray gave David a tight embrace. "Please get me out of here."

David stood outside the police station. The Magill Law Firm. It has a nice ring to it.

SEVEN

Ray's cellmate finally woke up after snoring on the floor for what seemed like an eternity. The first thing he did was wash his face in the water fountain and then used his stained shirt as a makeshift towel. Ray was glad he had asked the guard for water.

He shot Ray a bewildered look. "Are you still here?"

Ray rolled his eyes. "In the flesh."

"You must be in some serious shit."

Ray shrugged. "It would seem so."

He took a seat on the bench. "What's your name?"

"I'm Ray," he responded, "and you?"

"Bjorn."

The two men spent a few minutes doing small talk. Ray explained his episode with the cop and Bjorn repeated his story about what was now his ex girlfriend. They both laughed at how stupid they felt.

The guard came around the corner and pointed at Ray. "Your bail has been posted, Cooke. Let's go."

Bjorn leaned over on the bench and pulled Ray by his shoulder. He spoke quietly, but with conviction. "Liberty City."

Ray pulled away and looked at Bjorn.

The guard grew impatient. "Let's go, Cooke."

Ray asked. "What did you say, Bjorn?"

"Pick Liberty City and this all goes away."

EIGHT

It was two o'clock on Sunday afternoon and David sat alone in his office reviewing his schedule for the week. It was busy. Now that he was the sole partner in the firm, he had a lot of work ahead to make the transition smooth.

There was no one else in the building and that was the way it was planned. He had a quick rendezvous with a man who liked to keep a low profile. It was his visitor's idea to meet when the building was empty. He also insisted that the security system be de-activated while he was there. David didn't put up any resistance.

Nina was at yoga and expected him to pick her up after class. She had no idea he was at the office. Her progress since the assault moved slowly. She was in counselling, but he was worried about the long-term impact. He wanted vengeance against the attacker and for the first time he understood what hatred felt like.

David's appointment arrived with a loud bang on the front door that echoed down the hallway. David unlocked the door and let a tall bald man in. The man's face was pale, and he looked like he hadn't smiled in years.

"Let's go to my office," David started walking. "Do you want anything to drink?"

"I just want what I came for." He grunted.

David reached into a drawer and pulled out a thick white envelope. He tossed it on the desk. "There you go. Thirty thousand, as agreed."

The man looked at the envelope but made no attempt to reach for it.

David wanted the meeting to end. "It's all there. You can count it."

"I don't think you're stupid enough to try and rip me off."

David nodded. "I can assure you, I'm not a stupid man."

The man finally grabbed the envelope. "So, tell me. What did your partner do that made you so angry?"

"Does it matter?"

"No, but he must have done something bad because you're sending him away for a long time."

"He deserves every minute he gets."

NINE

After spending thirty-six hours behind bars and facing challenges he had never imagined, Ray needed time to think. All he wanted now was a hot shower and some quality sleep in his own bed. On the taxi ride home, all he thought about was Bjorn and his comment before he was released. "Pick Liberty City and this all goes away."

Who the hell was this Bjorn guy and how did he get into his cell?

The taxi arrived at Ray's house, but he was in no hurry to go inside and face Tiffany. He took a deep breath as he stepped out of the car and wondered what kind of reception was waiting inside. He finally went inside.

He took his shoes off and walked quietly down the hallway to the kitchen. After a walk through he realized Tiffany wasn't home and he was relieved. Some extra time to figure things out wasn't a bad thing. He grabbed an apple and headed upstairs to take a shower.

David steered into the yoga studio parking lot. His phone rang and it was Ray. He didn't want to answer but knew he had to. "Hey, buddy. You home yet?"

"About an hour ago. Can we get together later? I have some interesting things we need to discuss."

"We do need to get together, but I'm just picking up Nina," His wife climbed in the car. "Let's meet tomorrow in the office at nine. We can discuss everything then."

Ray was anxious to talk now. "Okay, I'll see you at nine. Have you filed the shareholder's papers yet?"

"Yesterday, like we discussed."

Ray thought for a second. "Okay, let's talk tomorrow. One last thing, have you reviewed the bid from Liberty City?"

"No," he lied. "Why?"

"We'll talk tomorrow."

Nina leaned over and kissed David on the cheek. "How was your day?"

"Interesting."

Nina snapped on her seatbelt. "I bet it was."

TEN

When Tiffany got home, she purposely went out of her way to avoid Ray's feeble attempt at a hug. It wasn't going to be that easy. She walked past him and into their bedroom. He followed and took a seat on the corner of the bed and watched her change out of a short summer dress into some comfortable shorts and a sleeveless white t-shirt.

"Where have you been?"

"You're a no show at the restaurant, you get charged with impaired driving, and to top all of that, you get busted with a kilo of cocaine in your car," she stated calmly, sounding rehearsed, "and you're asking where I've been? What the hell, Ray?"

"All valid points," Ray conceded. "You know I'm not a drug dealer. I'm being set up."

"By whom?" She knew her husband wasn't a dealer, but he had already been tried and convicted on social media. "You have big-time lawyer friends. Can't they just make this go away?"

"I might have a way out, but I have to meet with David first," Ray put his hands around her waist and pulled her close. "We'll get it figured out."

Tiffany put up little resistance to Ray's advance. Even with all his indiscretions, she was still attracted to him. "You seem awfully calm for a guy out on bail."

Ray remembered Bjorn. "I've had a lousy couple of days. Let's go to bed."

"It's ten in the morning."

"Who cares?"

27

ELEVEN

Ray was up before 6am and after a quick breakfast, he was on his way to the office. He wanted a head start researching Liberty City to find out who they were and how they might be the answer to his freedom. He also needed to find out how he could find Bjorn. He'd start by getting a last name.

When he arrived at the Cooke and Magill firm, everything on the surface seemed normal. He tossed his jacket on a door hook and got to work. It started with a call to the police station.

"Hello, my name is Ray Cooke."

A receptionist answered. She had read the morning paper. "How can I help you, Mr. Cooke?"

"I'm an attorney and I'm representing a client that requires an affidavit from someone who was in your holding cells yesterday," It was a well-rehearsed lie. "I need a last name and contact information."

There was a slight chuckle. "Do you always do your paralegal's work, Mr. Cooke?"

Ray smiled at her quick wit. "Not usually, but I'm in a time crunch, so I thought I would make the call."

She was aware of Cooke's pending charges. Everyone in the building was. "What can you tell me about the person you're looking for?"

"All I know is his first name is Bjorn. He was drunk when they brought him in."

"Let me look." He was put on hold.

After a short pause, the receptionist came back on the line. "I'm sorry, Mr. Cooke, but we have no record of any Bjorn being with us yesterday."

"Are you sure?"

"I'm sure." she confirmed.

He hung up. That wasn't the start he expected. Someone was going to great lengths to screw-up his life and they were apparently well connected. The question that was still unanswered was who and why?

When David arrived to work at nine, he was surprised to see Ray engaged in researching his own defence. David couldn't remember the last time he saw Ray doing real case study work. After grabbing a coffee from the reception area, he joined him in his office.

Ray looked up and smiled. "Hey, David. We need to talk."

"How was sleeping in your own bed again?"

"It was great," he responded. "What's going on with my case? And where are we at with the Gabriola process?"

David let Ray finish before stepping in. "You need to remember that you are no longer a member of this firm. I have to be careful what I discuss with you regarding the Gabriola Project."

"We need to talk about that."

"Talk about what?"

"My involvement in the firm," Ray sounded upbeat. "I might have my problems taken care of."

David was frustrated that Ray was even at the firm. "You're facing some serious charges that won't just disappear."

"They will if we choose Liberty City as the winning bid," Ray stated matter of fact. "That's all we need to do, and my problems go away."

David raised his eyebrows in disagreement. "What has you convinced that's what will happen?"

"A guy I met in jail named Bjorn told me."

"Do you know how ridiculous that sounds?" David tried to

sound serious. "You're no longer part of this firm because you made a stupid decision to drive while drunk. And now you want to make another stupid decision by listening to a wacked theory from some derelict you met in a jail cell? That's not going to happen."

Ray understood David's reluctance, but he wasn't ready to step down. "We have to trust this guy. I don't have a lot of choices. Why are you resisting it?"

"I'm not resisting anything," David stated firmly, "but I'm not risking my career, or the firm, based on a comment from some guy I've never met."

What began as a promising morning had quickly gone sideways, "Okay then, what are you suggesting? Let's start with my ownership in the firm."

David's temper surfaced. He had heard enough. The years of looking the other way were over. "The papers were filed yesterday. You're no longer a partner."

"You didn't waste any time," Ray complained sarcastically. "I don't deserve this."

"Everything is always about what you deserve!" snapped David. "That changes today."

Ray realized any support from David wouldn't be forthcoming. In fact, David was attacking him. "Are you going to help or are you throwing me under the bus?"

"You threw yourself under the bus a long time ago, so don't put this on me," David's eyes boiled with anger. "You expect me to risk everything so you can get a free pass again. Do you even realize how self-centred that is?"

Ray understood David's resistance, but he couldn't figure out where the hostility came from. "Look, you're upset at me and I get it. But this is my life we're talking about. I made a stupid decision to drive, but you and I both know that cocaine isn't mine. So, I'm sorry if you're upset with me, but let's get past it."

"You're sorry?" David laughed to stifle his outburst. "Do I look like I want an apology?"

Ray slumped like a defeated fighter, staring up at the ceiling fan going round and round. "I have no idea why you're so pissed, but whatever it is, we can get through it."

David pulled a USB stick from his pocket and tossed it to Ray. "Plug it in and hit play."

"What's on it?"

"Watch it!" he ordered. "You'll see."

Ray stared at the stick. "I don't get it."

"Plug it in and play it," David pointed at the laptop. "There's a short movie I want you to watch."

Ray had no idea what he was about to see, but he still felt uneasy. He plugged it in and hit play.

David watched Ray's reaction closely. He wanted to witness his expression. "What you're about to watch happened at my house."

The video started with a car driving up to David's house. An unidentifiable person staggered to the front door. It was obvious that the person was drunk, very drunk.

The video switched to a view inside the front entry. Nina was walking to the door. Without any warning, a person burst inside her house and overpowered her. They threw her onto the floor and mounted her from behind. After a dozen thrusts the intruder stood up.

Ray looked at David. "What the hell is this?"

David pointed to the screen. "Keep watching!"

Ray sat with his mouth open, stunned by what he watched. "Did I just see Nina get raped?"

David corrected him. "You just watched *yourself* rape Nina."

TWELVE

Ray was in complete denial. He had known Nina longer than David. He introduced them. "You can't be fucking serious?"

"It was you! And you're going to pay."

Ray was shocked by how easily David accused him. "I'd never hurt anyone in your family. Damn it, David, you have to know I'm not capable of that."

"Shut up and listen," David was ready to pass sentence. "The only reason you're not in jail is because I wanted to shield my wife from the publicity of a trial."

Ray listened. He had been drinking very heavy these past few months but to commit a rape. There was no way. "How can I ever apologize?"

David pulled the stick from the computer and put it back in his pocket. "You'll start by never contacting Nina."

"But David…"

"Shut up, Ray," David snapped at him. "This is how it's going to play out."

"You can have the firm," Ray panicked. "What else do you want?"

What David really wanted was to spit in his face. "You are a piece of work. My wife is in therapy and your only concern is you. But I'm going to give you a choice."

Ray was ready to accept anything other than prison. "I'm listening."

"You can go on trial for rape," David let the reality of that sink in, "or you can plead guilty to possession of cocaine. Either way, you are going to prison."

Ray was desperate and not thinking clearly. "What can I do to change your mind? You can have the firm. I'll just walk away."

"You're going to do the right thing and plead guilty to the drug charges," David wasn't backing down, "because no matter what you choose, you're done."

Ray buried his face in his hands. Literally overnight, everything in his life had been taken away. His career. His freedom. "You know I'm going to fight this. I have to."

David expected Ray's counter and was prepared for it. "You do what you want, but if you choose to complicate this, I'll release the video. The public will turn you into a monster. And your life, or whatever is left of it, will be over."

Three months later, Ray Cooke stood in front of a judge and pled guilty to possession of cocaine with the intent to distribute. In a prepared agreement with the prosecutor, he was sentenced to five years in a federal penitentiary.

Two weeks after the court date a company called Liberty City was chosen as the successful bid. They purchased Gabriola Island.

THIRTEEN

The Year is 2019

Suzanne Lacy was alone in her living room, sitting in front of her wood burning fireplace. Even though it was a chilly day in the Yukon Territory, she couldn't remember the last time she lit a fire. And she didn't ponder it now. The dark sky and cold weather reflected her lonely mood.

It had been three years since her eleven-year old son had vanished without a trace. He was running along the Yukon River the day he simply disappeared. Abductions were rare in the north, and the first thought was he had been attacked by a bear. The search for Curtis Lacy was the largest in the history of the Yukon. Everyone was doing something to try and help the family. There was even a bounty put on the abductors head that the police were unaware of. Northern justice was different.

Starting a family and living in the north was something that appealed to both Suzanne and Tom Lacy. A year out of university, they married, and Tom took a job in the finance department with the Yukon government. Everything was going as they hoped.

While Tom settled into his new career, Suzanne worked part-time doing sample testing for mining companies in Faro and Dawson City, both remote communities north of Whitehorse. Less than two years later, Curtis was born.

Curtis and his dad loved to hang out in the garage and work on computers. It always amazed Tom how gifted his son was when it came to understanding electronics. The two would stay out in the garage and rebuild computers until Suzanne would insist it was time for bed.

When he had time, Curtis snuck out to the garage to work on a special project, a surprise for his parents. He was building a super-computer out of spare parts and started to fancy himself as a part-time hacker. He thought it would be fun to prank his dad's email account at work.

He learned a tough life lesson. His dad was having an affair with someone he worked with. The emails were graphic and reading them had devastated the young boy. He never said a word to his mom.

It took three months, but the strain of Curtis's disappearance and the blame Suzanne put on Tom finally ended their marriage. The affair came to light during the investigation and soured what was already becoming a damaged relationship. When wind of the affair circulated, the public turned on Tom and accusations he was involved with his son's disappearance grew louder.

He made the decision to return to Vancouver for his own safety.

FOURTEEN

The weather outside of John Woodlands Academic School was in direct conflict to the warmth and anticipation felt inside. A session of winter was coming to the west coast and the grounds around the schoolyard were covered in decaying greenery. The slashing rain was relentless and painful to the bare face, and people scurried like rats to get into the school and out of the weather.

Once inside, most of the fathers unzipped their rain-soaked jackets that were, in many cases, also feeling a little snug around the belly. The mothers had long since traded style for comfort. They replaced the form-fitting outfits and sky-high heels they wore in high school with attractive, but comfortable and conservative dresses and flats. Everyone lingered in the hallway outside the auditorium, waiting for someone else to be the first to enter.

Stacey Small was amongst those parents. She used a window of a nearby classroom as a makeshift mirror to check her appearance. Once she was satisfied that her hair had survived the horrendous weather, she glanced over at her husband, Robert, and pointed towards the door leading into the auditorium. That was his cue to enter, and he excused himself from the group he was chatting with.

A large Geneva clock was mounted above the stage and looked to be the same one Robert remembered when he was a gym rat at the school. It was 6:55pm and the night was about to begin.

Backstage, Miss Addison took the lead organizing students for their time on stage. She had worked at the school for ten years and was extremely well-liked by both the students and their parents. She felt responsible for the kids to look like their parents expected and had the young boys tuck in their shirts and the girls combing their hair.

A tall man with thick dark hair tapped on Miss Addison's shoulder. "Excuse me, but can you tell me where the electrical room is?"

Miss Addison scarcely looked up as she pointed the man in blue contractor coveralls in the right direction. "Around that corner. The door is marked."

She turned her attention back to the students. There were twenty that would receive awards, and the kids were getting anxious. She adjusted Joshua Small's bowtie and gave him a quick smile before she moved onto the next child.

The heavy rain continued, and the parking lot was void of any activity. Everyone was inside the school. That was until a white cargo van pulled into the lot and found a spot in a darkened corner. The driver left the engine running, but purposely turned off the headlights. He wasn't staying long.

Back in the auditorium, most of the seats were now filled and the clock indicated it was seven. Time to begin. Right on cue, the music ends, and everyone took their seats.

A man that most in the room recognized as the principal walked onto the stage to a few polite heckles. Mr. McKee had started his career as a counsellor and became the school principal in 2009. He wore a bright red, collegiate-style pullover sweater with the school logo crested on the left breast. His shoulder-length hair was sprinkled with grey and was complimented by a full mustache.

After a quick "test one, test two", the principal thanked everyone for coming, despite the nasty weather. It was a big night for these families. Following the principal's request, parents switched their phones to camera mode. They anxiously waited for their child's time in the spotlight.

"I want to welcome everyone here tonight," There was light applause. "My name is Peter McKee and I'm the principal at John Woodlands Academic School."

There was a second polite round of applause and Principal McKee continued, "Tonight, is a special night. Every year at our school, we recognize some young people with great minds. To be invited on this stage means your child has exceeded the criteria and they show great promise for the future."

Robert was already getting impatient and wondered how much longer this was going to take. He glanced over at his wife. When he saw that she was focused on the stage, he casually loosened his tie and undid the top button.

McKee continued. "John Woodlands School has a history of students going on to do great things in business and the arts. There are students being recognized tonight that will follow in those footsteps."

The crowd applauded. Every parent in the auditorium was thinking the principal was referring to their child. Stacey beamed with pride. Robert fought a yawn.

The first thirty minutes passed quickly, and the evening was on schedule when Principal McKee announced a fifteen-minute break. Most people in the crowd stood and stretched. The smokers zipped on their jackets and headed for the door to brave the elements and feed their addiction.

Stacey took advantage of the time to find a washroom, while Robert looked around the room. He wanted the night to continue so he could see Joshua get his award and then go home and catch the rest of the game on the television with a cold beer.

The man in the blue coveralls finished his work in the electrical room. No one noticed when he slipped quietly out the rear exit. With everything going on, no one thought that it was strange for a contractor to be working late on a Friday night.

"If you'd all return to your seats," McKee announced, "we will continue with our award presentations."

Joshua behaved like most eleven-year-olds. He liked video games and was starting to be curious about girls. What separated him from his peers, and even most twice his age, was his mental capabilities. He solved complicated issues that others couldn't even understand. Whether it was a mathematical algorithm or a scientific formula, there was nothing they put in front of him that challenged his intelligence. The kid was a genius.

Backstage, while waiting for everyone to take their seats, Miss Addison decided to take advantage of the few moments to stretch her legs. She walked to the rear of the staging area and noticed that the electrical room door was slightly ajar, and the light was on. She wondered if the man in the blue coveralls was still there. She gently pushed the door open, but the room was empty. Other than a half dozen electrical panels and a mop and bucket, there was not much inside the room. She turned the light off and pulled the door closed. She purposefully ignored a flashing red light on a timer clamped inside the panel board labelled A.

FIFTEEN

Everything was running smoothly backstage. Miss Addison took a sip of water and then felt an unexpected breeze against her face. She noticed that the back door was slightly ajar. The contractor must have left it open by mistake. The cool fresh air was a nice compliment to the stuffy gymnasium, so she decided not to close it. The lights in the auditorium were dimmed for a second time and the evening continued.

Stacey knew Joshua was up next. She beamed proudly. This young boy was easily the most talented student she had ever taught. On most days, he taught her.

McKee restarted the night. "For those of you who have not met this young man, you should take the time to do so. He is one of the brightest minds I've seen in my educational career." McKee paused to find Stacey and Robert in the crowd. "He is a wonderful young man and one of the most pleasant personalities to ever walk the halls of our school. Joshua Small has taken every task we've assigned him and…"

Principal McKee was interrupted mid-sentence by three sharp popping sounds coming from the ceiling. In conjunction with the sounds, there were three flashes of light. Everyone was instinctively drawn to look at the ceiling, where three ballast boxes had burst into flames.

People turned their faces to protect themselves as they were showered with splinters of glass that came from exploding light bulbs. Confusion quickly evolved into panic when parents realized that the flames from the ballast boxes were spreading across the wooden cedar beams. The building was on fire!

Pop! Pop! Pop!

More lights began to explode in a chain-reaction across the ceiling. As the bulbs burst, the auditorium faded into darkness, which magnified the flash effect from the bulbs. Smoke began to fill the room.

Panic and loud voices mixed with some hysteria was beginning to take over.

As the smoke thickened, people started to gasp for air and rush to the exits. The crowd abandoned politeness and pushed their way to safety. Robert grabbed his wife and pulled her towards the door.

"What the hell is going on?" yelled Stacey above the noise in the room. "We have to get Joshua!"

"It seems like a power surge," Robert guessed, "and we need to get out now!"

Stacey followed Robert's lead. They blended into the crowd, trying to make their way to the exit. She glanced back over her shoulder and saw how quickly the smoke and flames were spreading. She thought of Joshua, but before she could say anything, Robert forced them through the crowd and out into the hallway.

The hallway filled quickly with families that scrambled to safety. Robert pulled Stacey aside to a clear spot by the trophy case outside the administration offices. Once she filled her lungs with fresh air, Stacey screamed at Robert. "We have to get Joshua!"

Robert pulled his wife close. "You go out to the car. I'll go to the back and get Joshua."

Robert disappeared before Stacey could complain. She clasped her scarf over her mouth to avoid inhaling the smoke that was now filtering out of the auditorium and into the hallway. The fire was growing.

A teacher stationed at the front door yelled at Stacey to leave. She was the last one in the school and she had to go.

Stacey yelled back. "My son is still in here!"

"We're doing a sweep of the building and no one will be left inside. Your son will be taken to the muster point. You need to vacate the building now!"

And then it happened again. This time it was the long fluorescent tube lights in the hallway.

Pop! Pop! Pop!

The thickening smoke forced Stacey to get out of the school. She strained to see across the street to the muster station. There was no sign of Robert, or Joshua. The teacher tried to guide her away from the school with the rest of the parents, but Stacey pulled away.

She justified her resistance. "I need to find my family."

Stacey decided to ignore Robert's advice to meet at their car. That wasn't happening until she knew her son was safe. There was now thick grey smoke billowing out of shattered windows and the front entrance. The heat from the fire forced her to move further away from the building. She was beginning to panic.

And then she had an idea. Robert would have taken Joshua out a back exit. She sprinted in the rain towards the soccer field. She could see flames in every classroom now. If anyone was still inside, they had met their maker.

The first wave of emergency vehicles arrived at the school. Red and blue flashing lights reflected off the buildings. Police officers secured the grounds while firemen pulled hoses and started battling the flames.

John Woodlands school was now a massive blaze. There would

be no saving the school. By morning, it would be a pile of ashes and memories.

SIXTEEN

The police officer in charge was Sergeant Steve Smith, a twenty-three-year-veteran of the city police force. He recognized Principal McKee on the street and walked over to stand by his side. Smith shook the principal's hand. "I'm deeply sorry to see this. I know how much you've invested in this place."

"Thank you," the principal forced a defeated smile, "but it's all gone now."

The sergeant recognized that the timing wasn't great, but he still had his job to do. "Sorry, but I have to ask you a few questions."

McKee understood. "No problem. Ask away."

"What was going on tonight?"

Peter wiped the rain off his face. "It was our awards night, and then all hell broke out."

"What do you mean?"

The principal explained about the lights popping in the auditorium and how the fire spread. It all happened so quickly. He had never seen anything like it.

"Is everyone accounted for?"

"As far as I know," Peter pointed to the muster station across the street, "but they would have a better idea. I can tell you that we did a sweep before we vacated the building."

"Good to know," Smith wanted to get out of the rain. "I'll find you later to give you an update."

Stacey stopped at the soccer field to look through the rain and darkness. She shielded her eyes with her hands. It occurred to her that no one would be looking for Robert or Joshua because they didn't know they were even missing.

She felt the urge to vomit and she bent over with her hands on her knees. And then she heard some feint voices and stood up. She strained through the smoke and rain and on the other side of the field she could see a group of people huddled under some trees. She ran in their direction, yelling Joshua's name over and over. No one answered.

Then, she heard a familiar voice call her name. Her panic subsided when she recognized Robert coming up from behind. He tried to maintain his composure, but the look on his face gave Stacey the bad news. Any hope she had, vanished in an instant.

"I'm sure he's not in the school. I looked everywhere. He has to be out here."

Her body shook with fear. "What do you mean you couldn't find him? Where can he be?"

Robert could feel her body shake as he held her in a tight embrace. "I looked everywhere, and he wasn't there. I looked for him until the smoke forced me out."

Stacey pushed free of Robert. Tears mixed freely with the rain dripping down her cheeks. She tried to understand the sequence of events. Joshua was a smart kid. As soon as he recognized the danger, he would have got out of the building. "Where is he?"

Robert held up his hands. "I was told he ran out the back door."

"Who told you that? Who the hell was in charge back there?"

Before Robert could respond, the group from across the field approached them. Miss Addison led the way and stepped forward. She was soaked and shivering in her thin dress.

"I was backstage looking after the kids," she began, her teeth chattering. "Once we realized what was going on, I corralled the kids to follow me out the back door."

Stacey interrupted. "So, where is Joshua?"

Miss Addison shook her head. "I don't know. He wasn't with us when I gathered up the kids. I looked everywhere and then your husband showed up. I needed to get the rest of the kids out. I assumed he'd already left."

Stacey fought her emotions, but anger took control, "You have no idea where our son is? Do you!"

Miss Addison felt her heart pound as she faced Stacey. "I'm sorry, but I don't. I hoped I'd find him on the field, but in all the confusion I lost track of him."

"How does that happen?"

Robert realized time was wasting. "I'm going to keep searching and I suggest you two go to the front to see if he made his way there. If not, then tell the police."

Robert ran into the darkness of the trees lining the property. He was trying to minimize the tears welling up in his eyes, but he couldn't fight them. He was scared to death of what might have happened to his son. How could Miss Addison be so sure he got out? He ran further down the darkened tree line, yelling Joshua's name over and over with no response.

Stacey reached the muster point and when Joshua wasn't there, she was directed by one of the first responders to Sergeant Smith. The tall, broad-shouldered man was standing out in the rain holding a radio close to his lips.

She rushed over and grabbed his arm. "My son is missing. He might still be inside the building."

"How old is your son and what does he look like?"

Stacey gave the sergeant a description of her son.

When she was finished, Smith spoke into his radio. "We have a missing child. Aged eleven, five-foot, dark hair, and wearing black slacks and a white shirt with a red bowtie."

46

The sergeant led Stacey to his police vehicle to get out of the rain. Once in the car, he turned to face her. "To clarify, your son was backstage, under Miss Addison's supervision and she has no idea where your son got to?"

Stacey nods. "Yes, exactly."

Smith checked his watch. It was 8:25. "The alarm activated at 7:58. So, Joshua hadn't been seen for almost thirty minutes. Does he have his own cellphone? We can ping the signal if he does."

Stacey shook her head. "No, we didn't want him to have one."

"Understood."

The sergeant radioed for more personnel. He needed to initiate a perimeter search. He left the car and instructed Stacey to stay inside. He looked towards the school that was completely engulfed in flames and said a short prayer.

Within minutes, more officers were onsite. Smith quickly debriefed everyone before assigning grid areas. Once his officers went to work, he went back to check on Stacey.

With all the chaos surrounding the school, no one watched the white cargo van leave the parking lot. It slipped away with no one paying it a second thought.

When the sergeant returned to his car there was a second person in the back seat. It was Stacey's husband Robert. "I've started a perimeter search and when I get an update, I'll let you know. I need to talk to the Fire Chief."

"What's up, Steve?" Chief Lussier removed his fire helmet to wipe his brow. "I'm kind of busy."

The sergeant's expression reflected his level of concern. "We might have a missing boy. He's been gone for a while."

Chief Lussier asked the tough question, "Do you think he's still in the school? Because if he is…"

Steve didn't need him to finish his thought. "We really don't know anything other than he was in the school and hasn't been seen since the fire started. It's almost forty-five minutes."

Lussier bit his lower lip and looked upward. "Let's just pray for the best and hope he turns up."

"You guys have your work cut out for you tonight."

As the sergeant walked behind the safety perimeter, he couldn't take his eyes off the huge flames licking at the rain. Whatever started this fire it got the job done. As he got ack into his car he had no idea what to tell the parents. He couldn't imagine their grief.

SEVENTEEN

Social media buzzed with the news that John Woodlands School had burnt to the ground overnight. People uploaded pictures of the building burning and others listed memories from their time at the school. Hundreds had posted comments.

The mood dampened further when it was rumored that a young student was missing and presumed dead in the fire. Some of Joshua Small's classmates had already started a makeshift memorial of flowers and stuffed animals on the sidewalk across from their school.

The fire crews began to pack up their gear. Other than a few hot spots that were being dealt with, the fire was out. It had been a long night both physically and emotionally for the first responders. Knowing a young boy was missing made it even worse.

Fire Chief Lussier was still onsite. He sat his tired body down on a bench in front of the school. The bench was covered with damp soot, but he didn't hesitate to take a seat. Exhaustion overruled common sense. A member of his crew brought him a fresh coffee. He took a sip and stared at what remained of the building.

Sergeant Smith stood beside him. "How are you doing?"

Chief Lussier looked up at his friend. The stress of the job was evident by the darkness that circled his eyes. His face was covered with soot. "I'm too old for this shit."

The sergeant nodded. "I understand."

Lussier looked over the blackened remains. "Any update on the boy?"

Smith shook his head. "No, not yet."

"How are the parents?"

The sergeant hated this part of the job. "The dad's trying to hold it together, but the mother is a complete wreck."

"It has to be brutal, not knowing."

"I had one of my officers take them home. But something isn't adding up here."

Chief Lussier threw his coffee into a scorched garbage can. "What are you thinking?"

"Apparently, this kid is a genius and by all accounts, everyone in the staging area had lots of time to escape the fire," Smith explained, "so, where is he?"

Chief Lussier tried to stifle a yawn. "Do you think he is hiding?"

"No idea. That's the part that doesn't make sense. Hopefully, we'll know more once your crew finishes looking through the ashes."

EIGHTEEN

Things were chaotic inside and out of the Small home. Word had spread quickly about Joshua being missing and possibly a victim of the fire. Most news networks had decided to report that Joshua had perished, and it was just a formality to find the body. If the kid was alive, where was he?

Robert tried to minimize his wife's panic without revealing his own anxiety. It was eating him alive not knowing where his son was or if he was alive. Stacey was raw with emotion and lashed out at anyone who tried to comfort her. All she wanted to hear was that her son was found and safe.

"I don't need to rest." She screamed at no one in particular. "I just need my baby back."

Stacey's mother had rushed over after Robert called. The two had never gotten along, but both understood that now wasn't the time to resolve their differences. Carol had a special connection with her grandson that Robert resented. It bothered him when his son wanted to spend time with her, instead of him.

Carol put her hand on Stacey. "Joshua will be fine."

Stacey looked at her mom but couldn't say anything. The only reason they had any kind of relationship was because of Joshua. The guilt of not charging back into the school consumed her. She should have done more.

"I'm going to make some tea. I'll make you a cup. It will help you relax."

On her way by, she caught the attention of the police officer assigned to the home. The female officer followed the sixty-year old into the kitchen where she knew her way around. She pulled out the kettle and filled it with water. "Do you want some tea?"

The officer nodded. "That would be great. Thank you."

Carol wanted information. "Who is overseeing the investigation? I heard the fire might be arson."

"I can't comment on it."

"There must be something you can tell me. My daughter is dying out there."

"There's nothing so far, but when I hear something, I will pass it onto the family."

Carol stared down the officer. "I am family!"

There was an awkward silence until the kettle boiled. Carol made some tea and passed a cup to the cop. She then left the kitchen and returned to her daughter. "Joshua will be fine."

NINETEEN

Twelve hours had passed since the fire at John Woodlands, but there was still no word about Joshua Small. The bitter weather from the night before was warming. That contributed to the increased crowd that surrounded the school property. Many wiped tears as they had already concluded that the young boy endured unbearable pain in his last moments.

Incident Commander Janice Adams was prepping her team for the grid search that no one ever wanted to be part of. Recovering a body was tough, but when it was a child, the impact was going to be much harder. The team observed the devastation the fire caused, and they knew it was going to be a tough search.

Stacey Small kept checking the time on her phone. As minutes turned into hours, her fear increased. She refused any medication to help her relax. "I want to go back to the school!" She turned to the police officer. "Have they started yet?"

The officer shook her head apologetically. "I haven't heard anything. I know they fought the fire all night."

Robert was almost invisible on the end of the couch with his face buried in his hands. His bloodshot eyes were a combination of tears and the bourbon he added to his coffee. Stacey was disgusted when she realized that her husband was getting drunk, but she decided that was a fight for another day.

Carol noticed her daughter's sideways glare at Robert and squeezed her hands. "Joshua is going to be all right."

Incident Commander Adams informed her team the grid search was given the go ahead and was scheduled to begin in thirty minutes. The public and media pressure to begin the search was intense. Adams had her team huddled up. "I want you to all remember that cameras are everywhere, and long-distance listening devices are now the norm in our world. So, watch what you say because there is a grieving family out there."

TWENTY

The recovery team worked at a tedious pace. They sifted through every inch of the building and found lots of trinkets and student belongings. There were endless water bottles, or what was left of them, and scorched pencils, but they found nothing that indicated Joshua was in the building. That was good news.

Segregated away from the crowd in a police van was the Small family. Stacey's insistence on coming back had won over any objections. They were parked where they could watch the search. Robert sipped on a bottle of soda to fight his looming hangover, while Stacey watched the crowds as she cradled a cup of cold coffee.

Carol sounded impatient. "How long before we know anything?"

The officer in the driver's seat looked back over her shoulder at Carol. "It takes time. They're being careful so they don't miss anything. The fact that they're still looking means they haven't found anything yet."

"That's great news, isn't it?" Robert asked

"I agree," the officer stated cautiously, "but let them finish before we get too excited."

Robert moved behind his wife and tried to massage her shoulders, but she pushed his hands away. The tension between the two was growing and Stacey wasn't even trying to disguise her feelings anymore.

Carol saw what was going on and smiled internally. He was a useless husband and father. Her daughter made a bad decision marrying him.

Robert returned to his seat. He fought the impulse to go find another drink, but the urge was winning. With the situation surrounding his son and the anti Robert sentiment from the two women, he felt claustrophobic.

After what seemed like an eternity the Incident Commander opened the van door. Her face was darkened with soot and she grasped her water bottle like it was worth a million bucks. She faced the family.

Sergeant Smith stepped up onto a makeshift podium, flanked by the fire chief on his left and the Smalls were on the right. They had an announcement. Carol stood in the background and watched. A group of reporters clustered in the front to ask questions while hundreds of cell phone cameras faced the stage. Within seconds, the announcement would be on Facebook and other social media networks.

Smith stepped up to the microphone and read from a carefully worded statement. He knew everything he said would be scrutinized, so he was careful to only state what was currently known. "If I could have your attention…"

The crowd went silent, waiting on an update.

Smith began. "A thorough search of the school has been completed by Incident Commander Adams and her team and they are completely satisfied that Joshua Small was not in the building. No human remains were found."

Smith paused to let the rumbling in the crowd go quiet. There were shouts of happiness. Finally, a reporter in the front row asked the obvious question.

"Then where is the boy?"

The crowd fell silent, waiting for an answer. Finding no body meant even more questions. Smith stuck to his script. "At the moment, we do not know where Joshua Small is. Now that it's confirmed he was not in the school; the focus of the investigation is being handed over to police detectives."

Questions were hurled at the stage from reporters and the public.

"Did he run away?" asked one.

"Was he kidnapped?" yelled the second.

The third. "Are the parents suspects?"

Smith finished his statement. "I can't comment on any questions at this time other than to say this is now a criminal investigation."

Smith stepped back from the microphone and gestured for everyone to exit the podium. There were still questions being shouted from the reporters, but they were all ignored. The Smalls were hurried into a waiting police vehicle.

Carol decided she had enough excitement for one day and took a taxi to the waterfront. She wandered into a small café and ordered a pot of green tea and a biscuit. Out her window was a perfect view of Gabriola Island.

TWENTY-ONE

The events of the previous night at her school were extremely upsetting for Tracy Addison. She couldn't sleep knowing what Joshua's family must be going through. She hated that she contributed to their misery, but there was nothing she could do now to reverse what took place.

She climbed out of her bed and into the shower. The water that splashed against her body was the injection of energy she needed to get through the morning. After rinsing her hair, she stepped out and wrapped a towel around her body. She stood in front of the steamed mirror and cleared a circle so she could comb her hair.

Her partner entered the bathroom and gave Tracy a kiss on the cheek. "Are you feeling better?"

She pulled on her yoga pants. "Not really."

Laura sat on the toilet. "Coffee is ready. Do you want some fresh fruit and yogurt?"

"That sounds great. Just give me a minute."

Laura flushed the toilet, and after washing her hands she headed back to the kitchen.

Tracy frowned at her reflection. She was getting old. The wrinkles around her eyes reminded her the years were creeping by. Her commitment to the organization was beginning to fade. It was painful knowing she was part of a plan that separated kids from their families. Even though she still believed in the ideology, it was getting harder to function in her role as a trusted teacher. Tracy combed her hair before she headed to the kitchen.

Laura Nelsen had a coffee poured and placed a bowl of yogurt loaded with fresh fruit in front of Tracy. "So, what's the plan for today? Do you need to go to the school? Is there even a school to go to?"

Tracy appreciated the breakfast. "There's nothing to see at the school, but I might go by the Small's house to see how they're doing."

Laura reached under the table and grabbed Tracy's bare feet and started to massage them. "Or maybe you want to stay home."

"Do you think it's too soon?"

"You told me that the mother was really upset, so it might be better to give her some time."

Tracy nodded. "I have to run over to Peter McKee's place and make a few calls, but afterwards, I'm all yours."

Laura inched her fingers teasingly towards Tracy's calves. "My suggestion is we spend some time on that new bed."

Tracy loved the idea, but just not now. She needed time to process the events of last night and work through the guilt she felt. "I'll be back in an hour. Then it's just you and me."

Laura dropped Tracy's feet back to the floor to show her disappointment. She new more about Tracy's *other* life than Tracy realized. She would play along with this charade until she didn't need to anymore. "You go do what you need to. I'll clean up the kitchen."

When Tracy was certain Laura was distracted doing the dishes, she reached under the couch and grabbed a burner cellphone she had hidden there. She had one text message.

'Kid is delivered.'

She deleted the message before she switched it off and replaced it back under the couch. Tracy had forgotten her other phone in the kitchen and when it rang, she hurried to beat Laura to it. "Just ignore it."

Laura had the phone in her hand. "It's the police. Why are they calling you?"

Tracy tried to stay calm. "They're probably just calling about last night."

TWENTY-TWO

Tracy Addison steered her Honda Civic into the police parking lot and pulled into a spot close to the entrance. The call from the police was Sergeant Smith, who had some questions he'd like to ask regarding the fire.

After a quick peek in the visor mirror to check her appearance, she hurried towards the building. Even a few miles from the school the smell of the fire still lingered in the morning air.

The receptionist buzzed the steel door open and Tracy walked inside the waiting area. She stopped at the red line painted on the floor. She didn't feel nervous, but her palms were gummy. She waited to be called up and after a moment, the clerk waved her over.

She talked through a hole in a plexiglass window. "I'm Tracy Addison and I'm here to see a Sergeant Smith."

"He's expecting you. You can just take a seat."

A moment later, she stood to meet the sergeant and recognized him from outside the school last night. Smith greeted her with a tired smile and a day-old beard. "Thank you for coming so quickly, Miss Addison."

She smiled anxiously. "Anything I can do to help find Joshua."

Smith led her to a small rectangular room with a wooden table and two chairs. He pointed to a seat and Tracy took the hint and sat down. She clasped her hands and noticed the fluorescent lights, just like the ones at the school. She took a deep breath to compose herself.

Smith appeared disorganized. He had a coffee in one hand and a blue case file in the other. He took the second seat and began the interview by verifying Tracy's personal information.

"First things first, Miss. Addison," the Sergeant began. "I appreciate your co-operation by coming so quickly. We're up against the clock trying to find Joshua."

"Please call me Tracy. Miss. Addison is for the classroom."

"Ok then, Tracy," he started again, "I assume you are aware that Joshua Small's body was not recovered from the fire?"

"Yes, that's fantastic news and a great relief."

"I agree it's great news, but we still have a problem. We have a missing child, and that means someone knows where he is."

She thought about what he just said but didn't respond.

"Is it accurate to say you were the last adult to speak with Joshua?"

Tracy stared at her hands on the table. "Everything was crazy when the fire started, but I guess so."

"You said you never saw Joshua leave?" he continued, "even though there were only a few people left backstage. You said you lost track of him. Is this accurate as well?"

Tracy realized why she was at the station. This interview was more than just some questions. She was a suspect. "When the lightbulbs started exploding, there was a lot of confusion and I guess I panicked like many people. I lost track of where everybody was, including Joshua."

The long night had taken a toll on the sergeant, and even bad coffee couldn't stifle a yawn. He needed some answers and he needed them quickly. Smith pushed harder. "I need to ask some tough questions and I need honest answers."

"Okay."

Smith watched Stacey's body language. "Do you know where Joshua Small is, or who took him?"

Tracy played with a ring on her finger. "I have no idea where he is. I wish I could help you, but I don't know anything more."

Smith tossed his coffee cup into the garbage bin by the table. "Then who was the man wearing blue coveralls seen in the backstage area just before the fire?"

The question was like a sucker punch to the gut. Her expression revealed more than she intended, but she uttered nothing. She wasn't ready to answer the question.

Smith pushed her harder. "He was seen exiting the school five minutes before the fire broke out."

How did the police know about the man in blue coveralls? The security cameras were supposed to be shut down. What else did Smith know? "I, um, forgot about him."

"I'm sure you did," Smith responded, intentionally sounding skeptical. "Do you know the man in the coveralls?"

"No, I don't," she lied, "he was just some guy looking for the electrical room."

Smith feigned a message on his phone and headed to the door. He wanted Tracy to take some time to think about her answers. "Sorry, I need to take this."

Tracy sat in her chair, staring nervously ahead. She wondered about Smith's last question. How did he know about the man in the coveralls and why did he ask if she knew him?

After what seemed much longer than a few minutes, Sergeant Smith returned to his seat. He brought her a bottle of water. "You look like you could use a drink."

"Thank you."

Smith continued with his questions. "You recall the guy in the coveralls, but you didn't see him leave?"

She knew she had to take a stance. "Like I already told you, he just asked for directions to the electrical room, and then when I looked for him, he was gone."

"You didn't think it was strange that an electrician was in the building that late on a Friday night?"

"Not at the time, but now that you mention it, I guess it was."

"Can you describe him?" Smith held a pencil in hand. "Any little details might help."

"I can't tell you very much. I only saw him for a second."

He held his pencil ready. "Anything you can think of might help."

Tracy ran her fingers through her hair, pushing it back behind her ears. "He was about six-feet, dark hair, and like you already know, he was wearing blue coveralls."

Smith pushed her for more. "Was there a logo or name on the coveralls?"

Tracy shook her head. "I didn't see anything else and I'm getting the impression you think he was involved in Joshua's disappearance."

Smith didn't deny it. "I don't know. I'm just trying to develop a blueprint of how things took place last night."

"How did you know about the man?"

"Sorry, but for now I can't say." Smith stood up, indicating the interview was ending. "Thanks for coming down."

Tracy was glad it was over. "No problem. If you need anything else, you have my number."

"I appreciate that," The sergeant stood between her and the door. "Just one last question, before all interviews I do a background check on the people coming in."

Tracy stopped and looked at Smith, "And?"

"When I did one on you, I couldn't find any record of you existing prior to being hired at John Woodlands. Any reason why that would happen?"

"Really?" She tried to sound surprised. "I have no idea."

"Must be a computer glitch," Smith smiled as he waved her out the door. "Have a good day."

Once Tracy was out of the building, Smith went to his desk and made a call to the clerk in the courthouse. "Sergeant Smith here. I need a warrant to put a trace on a cell number for the next seventy-two hours."

TWENTY-THREE

It had been three days since the school fire and the Small family still had no idea where their son was. There was relief when it was determined that Joshua hadn't perished in the fire, but it created a whole new set of fears for a quiet community. A young boy was missing, and people were scared there might be a predator in their neighborhood.

The police kept the Smalls updated, but there was really nothing concrete to tell them. They were receiving tips about sightings from as far away as Seattle, but nothing came from those. As the days passed Sergeant Smith knew the odds for a happy ending decreased dramatically.

The sergeant determined Joshua Small had been targeted, but he had no idea as to why.

Robert was stretched out on his couch trying to get some sleep that he desperately needed, but every time he closed his eyes, he saw his son's face burning in the fire. The image terrified him, and it was only after a few shots of Jack Daniels that he was able to get more than five minutes of sleep.

With the help of some wine, Stacey finally succumbed to exhaustion and was sound asleep in their bedroom. It was the first time she had slept more than an hour since the night at the school.

Carol had stopped by to check on her daughter and sat in the kitchen drinking tea when there was a loud knock at the front door. At first, she was reluctant to even answer it, but when she glimpsed through the window, she recognized the man and stepped out on the porch. She pulled the door closed. She didn't want to be overheard.

"Hey," The visitor asked, "how are they doing?"

"The asshole is passed out on the couch snoring and Stacey is finally sleeping," Carol was impatient. "What are you doing here?"

"The police called Tracy in for questioning?"

Carol glared at Peter. "You came here to tell me that? You stupid fool."

The principal looked unnerved, "Why would they question her?"

Carol gave Peter an insulting shrug. "Maybe because she works at the damn school and the police are doing their job."

"You don't have to be so sarcastic," He whined. "It worries me."

"Everything is fine. Now you need to get the hell out of here. And keep your mouth shut," Carol reminded him. "They'll call you next so stick to the story."

Peter suddenly felt stupid for coming "Okay."

TWENTY-FOUR

The Cowichan Valley is ninety-five kilometers north of Victoria on Vancouver Island and for the thousands that call the area home, it's some of the most genuinely diverse landscape in the world. Over the years the mountains and valleys had transformed from being timber producing into award-winning wineries.

Cowichan Bay is where the smell of the sea lingers year-round and the harbour is busy managing fishing and recreational vessels. There are sheer rock bluffs with a narrow roadway to homes with million-dollar views.

Standing alone on the northern tip of the bluffs was a large whitewashed home that bared the wear of constant winds and long sunlit days. And because of where it was built, it was accessible only by boat or hiking on a treacherous trail.

There were three people already in the home drinking iced tea. They were waiting on a fourth before getting down to business. They saw a small water taxi heading to the dock below and knew their meeting would begin very shortly.

Bobby Marsh was a retired forestry worker who had spent his entire working life in the bush working as a rigging slinger. He was a casualty of the economy and modernization and had lost his job years earlier. Now sixty-four and living on a meagre pension, he settled in Cowichan Bay and supplemented his income by fishing and crab trapping year-round. Since he had lost his wife, he lived in a small house with his dog Shaggy, on the outer shoreline.

Before cooking supper, Bobby checked his fishing setups and

crab pots. He didn't want any surprises when he headed out in the morning. It was his nightly routine. The weather was supposed to be cold, but he didn't care. There was a late run of silver Coho returning to the river and he wanted to get his share.

When he was finished, he wandered back into his kitchen and pulled out a few crabs from his refrigerator. He tossed them into some boiling salt water. There were crab legs and a local lager on the menu for tonight. Shaggy was asleep beside his feet.

The man climbed up the stairs from the dock with ease. He wasn't even breathing hard when he reached the top. He led everyone to the kitchen, and they took a seat around the table.

"Thanks for coming," he started, as he looked at the others, "but it's stupid that we need to meet like this."

"Why such a secluded area?" Tracy Addison asked. "It has a gorgeous view, but it's a bitch getting to."

"We have our reasons," Mickey countered, "but let's stay on topic."

Tracy Addison could sense something was wrong. "I assume we're here to talk about the school. Everything went as planned."

Mickey's glare interrupted her. "That's bullshit!"

Everyone stayed quiet, waiting for Mickey to explain his frustration. He lowered his tone. "The police are investigating."

Carol sat quietly at the table, watching the reactions. "What Mickey is telling you is you were sloppy."

Mickey nodded. "Exactly."

Carol took charge. "Of course, the police are investigating. A child is missing, and their school burnt to the ground. They're doing their job. The problem is you two. The police are focused on you."

"We're not going to tell them anything," Peter McKee tried to sound convincing. "How were we sloppy?"

Mickey opened a file. "For starters they know I was in the building because someone forgot to disconnect the security coverage. And they called in Tracy because they suspect she must be involved because she went out the same door Joshua did. She was supposed to panic and leave by the front were witnesses would see her."

Carol concluded the meeting by reviewing what would be said if the police called again. Once she was convinced that they understood, they prepared to leave.

Mickey touched Tracy on the shoulder. "I have a car coming to the trail and I want you to come with me. I have a recruit I want to talk about."

Tracy reluctantly agreed. The trail was treacherous.

TWENTY-FIVE

The chilly morning winds meant venturing out onto the bay was for either the hearty or the foolish. It depended on who you asked. You had to be an experienced fisherman with a strong stomach to have the confidence to steer a smaller fishing boat in the choppy water.

On this morning, Bobby Marsh was determined to get his hooks into one of the late-running Coho and once his gear was loaded, he and Shaggy climbed onto his twenty-foot Sport Fisher and headed out.

The morning sun wasn't up yet, but Marsh headed to his lucky spot just past the bluffs. He shrunk his lanky body to get behind the protection of the windshield to minimize the effects of the cold winds. Shaggy took her familiar spot down by his feet.

When they were a mile offshore, Bobby put the motor in neutral and threw two crab pots over the side. Once the bright neon floats appeared on the surface, he piloted the boat to where he figured the fish would be biting.

Bobby pulled out his first rod and made a cast. He let the line sink to a depth of seventy-five feet and then put the rod into a holder. He grabbed his second rod and repeated the process on the starboard side, this time letting it sink to one hundred. Once everything was set, he pulled out his thermos and poured a spiked coffee into a plastic cup. He sipped on his drink as he watched the sun replace the moon.

It had been nearly an hour and still no fish. Then, when many fishermen would consider giving up, the rod on the portside showed that a fish was playing with the bait. Bobby grabbed the rod. When the timing was right, he heaved on the rod and set the hook.

Fish on!

The thrill of fighting a large salmon is something many talk about, but few can say they've really enjoyed. Bobby had experienced the thrill many times and it still got his blood moving. He set the tension on his line and let the fish run while he pulled in his second rod.

This fish was bigger than ten pounds and pulled the boat with the tide towards the rocky shores. Bobby fired up the outboard motor to compensate for the tidewaters and then turned his attention to landing this fish.

Shaggy woke up and took his spot on the bow to enjoy the excitement. He knew what was coming and he barked to encourage his owner. Then, without warning, the dog jumped off the bow and went to the stern of the boat and the tone of his bark changed. Bobby was focused on the fish and ignored his dog.

"This baby is at least fifteen pounds, Shaggy," laughed Bobby as he reeled in the line. "We're going to eat like kings tonight."

Bobby guided the salmon into his fishing net and with one strong heave he pulled it into the boat. A hard smack on the head from a wooden club and the fish was now motionless.

Shaggy ignored the fish and kept barking out into the water.

"What are you barking at?" Bobby waited for an answer that wasn't coming. "Is there a killer whale nearby?"

Shaggy continued to bark.

Bobby went to his dog's side and rubbed his neck. "What do you see? You're going to scare off the fish."

Bobby saw something bouncing in the waves. He couldn't make it out, so he grabbed his flashlight from his toolbox. He pointed the light in the direction of the object, but it was still hard to distinguish in the dark water. He grabbed an oar and reached out to pull the object closer. When he saw what he had snagged, he slumped down in his boat. "Lord, have mercy."

TWENTY-SIX

The tragic news of Tracy Addison's body being found in Cowichan Bay sent another shockwave through the community. It didn't take long for the rumours to begin that her death was somehow tied to Joshua Small's disappearance and the school fire. Many had decided that she had committed suicide to combat the guilt she felt for Joshua's disappearance.

The provincial coroner didn't agree and ruled her death an accidental drowning because of the water in her lungs. There was severe bruising all over her body, consistent with her falling down the shoreline cliffs. The theory was supported when one of her shoes was found at the base of the rocks.

Laura confirmed she went hiking with the police. Tracy had said she wanted to go alone to try and find some solace in the hills. With Joshua's disappearance and the police suspecting she might be involved; it was becoming too much for her to handle. Suicide was never discussed with the coroner or police.

The celebration of life for Tracy Addison was held a week later at St. Andrews United Church and the pews were full of grieving students, past and present. There was a screen setup on the lawn outside the church for the expected overflow.

Laura Nelsen was in the front row next to Peter McKee and other faculty members. She had never met any of Tracy's work colleagues prior to today, and there were a few bewildered glances when they realized Tracy was a lesbian. Laura enjoyed the uncomfortable looks.

The minister took his place behind his pedestal on the stage and the crowd hushed. He had thick silver hair and wore a black clergy shirt with an oversized white collar. He welcomed everyone and started with the Lord's Prayer.

Sitting in the back row trying to go unnoticed was Sergeant Smith. He wore a dark suit and tinted sunglasses that he removed once the service began. He looked like a cop and everyone around him knew he was.

He listened as people recalled their memories about their teacher and friend. It was obvious to Smith that Addison was extremely popular with everyone who knew her. The question he struggled with was why this, teacher of the year candidate, be involved with a child's abduction. Maybe his hunch was wrong.

Smith didn't support the coroner's conclusion based on theory, not medical science. Why was she hiking on private property when there were public and much safer trails in the Cowichan area?

Another oddity was why was there no family at the service? Something about this beloved teacher didn't add up. And the warrant on the phone company landed nothing. Her cellphone was never used again.

He needed to find out more about the dead teacher.

TWENTY-SEVEN

Six weeks had passed since the school fire and life in the Small's household had crumbled into decay. The media and public scrutiny were long gone and only the odd friend checked in on them now. The outside disruptions of the early days were replaced with internal anger. The finger-pointing and fighting between Robert and Stacey had escalated to a point of hatred.

Their house was a constant screaming ground, and the neighbours turned a deaf ear to the daily fights. They sympathized with what the family was dealing with, but some feared where it might lead.

"Joshua was only at that school because you insisted!" Stacey reminded him over and over. "If I didn't listen to you my son would be home safe!"

"You mean, our son!" he screamed back.

"I should have listened to my mother!"

"If you listened to your mother, I wouldn't be here," Robert reminded her. "She has always hated me."

It was now Christmas Eve and their home showed no signs of the holidays, which had once been Stacey's favourite time to create memories. There was no freshly cut pine tree decorated in their living room and Robert hadn't hung any outdoor Christmas lights or un-packed the inflatable Santa usually displayed on their front lawn. Stacey spent most of her time in her chair staring at their front door, convinced that one day Joshua would walk through it.

Robert was broken emotionally, and guilt had consumed him. He was alone in the house, even when Stacey was home and found places where he felt safe from her vicious outbursts.

He had tried going back to work, but he couldn't function under the stress. In the beginning, a shot or two of Jack Daniels helped him maintain, and now it had become a requirement to cope.

It was three o'clock on Christmas Eve and Robert stood alone in the kitchen cradling a drink. It was his third or fourth of the day and his body craved more, so he grabbed the Jack Daniels and emptied what was left into his glass. Then panic set in knowing he was out, and the stores would be closing soon for the holiday.

He grabbed his jacket and headed to the door. "I'm going to the mall."

"You shouldn't be driving. You're drunk again."

Robert ignored her as he headed out the door. "The bitch needs to mind her own business. Maybe I'll find a bar."

Stacey was too tired to fight and for the minutes he was out of their house she'd feel some relief. Her husband had become a functioning alcoholic who was in denial and she didn't have the energy to try to save him.

The weather was winter and there was a drift of snow covering the roads. It was a short drive to the liquor store, so the cold didn't concern him. Getting pulled over was another risk he was willing to take. He had driven this route a hundred times before and there were never any cops. He pulled in front of Abel's Liquor Depot and left the truck running while he ran inside.

Robert was a regular and knew the store layout well. He went directly to the Jack Daniels and grabbed two bottles. While he waited inline, he decided he needed a few of the mini-liquor bottles displayed on the counter. He grabbed four little Grand Marnier. Might as well celebrate the holidays in style.

The clerk could tell Robert was under the influence but decided not to push the point because he sympathized with what his family was coping with. He bagged the bottles and handed Robert his receipt. "You make sure you go straight home."

"I appreciate it, Abel," Robert nodded. "Merry Christmas."

It was snowing harder when Robert pulled his truck out onto the road and headed home. Once he felt safe from any cops, he grabbed the bag and pulled out one of the minis. Using his knees to steer, he opened the bottle and guzzled down the sweet liquor.

Stacey heard the phone ring but ignored it. She was curled up in her chair sipping her tea and was trying to watch some television. It had been over two hours since Robert had left for the mall, but she wasn't concerned, nor did she care.

She decided to climb into bed, and like every night, she clutched her picture of Joshua. "Merry Christmas, little man. I miss you so much. Wherever you are, I love you, and I will find you."

Stacey was nodding off when a loud knock at the door woke her. She opened her eyes and the knock repeated. "If that asshole lost his key and is drunk…"

She climbed out of bed and went to the door. She looked through the window and saw two police officers and her heart skipped a beat. She quickly unlocked it. With a big smile, she bawled and looked past the officers. "You found Joshua! It's a Christmas miracle!"

The officer shook his head. "Sorry, ma'am, but your husband has been in a terrible accident."

TWENTY-EIGHT

The early hours of Christmas morning were devastation magnified for Stacey Small. Her son was missing for over six weeks and now her husband was dead. A single-vehicle accident blamed on alcohol and speed was the cause. Robert's truck slammed into a tree after he missed a corner on a snow-covered street.

For some unknown reason, Stacey reached out to her mother. It was the first time in her adult life that she phoned her. She knew Carol wouldn't be upset that Robert was dead, but she still called.

When Carol arrived, she gave Stacey an awkward hug at the door and felt her shake uncontrollably. "Sorry to hear about the drunk? What happened"

Stacey was a babbling mess. She had been crying all morning and the reality that she was now on her own started to sink in. "He was in a car accident. He's gone."

"What happened? Was he…?"

Stacey finished her mom's sentence. "Yes, he was drunk. He had a few drinks before he left, and they found an opened bottle in the truck."

"Well at least he gave you a useful gift this year. Merry Christmas from Robert."

Stacey screamed. "Can you just let it go! I know you hated him!"

Carol said nothing else about Robert or the accident. They sat on the couch and shared a blanket to keep warm. It was still snowing outside, and the west coast was having a white Christmas.

After an hour Carol was bored and decided to make some tea and toast. She brought a mug to Stacey, but before she tried it, she leaped off the couch and ran to the bathroom. She threw up into the toilet.

Carol stayed another day. She had no where else to be on Christmas. Maybe they could reconcile some of their past. There was a long stretch of time where they never saw each other or attempted to connect. Stacey grew up with her father. When she was five Carol came home one day and announced that she didn't want to be a wife or mother anymore. She didn't like it.

And then when Joshua was almost three, Carol appeared on the doorstep. She said she had changed and wanted to meet her grandson. Stacey was skeptical, but decided Joshua needed family.

"Why are you even here?" Stacey was back on the couch. "You haven't spent the holidays with me since I was about five."

This kind of conversation was not in Carol's comfort zone. "I didn't want you to be alone, so I came to help you through this terrible time."

"You've hated Robert from the first time you met him. I haven't even seen you cry for Joshua," Whined Stacey. "Why are you here?"

"I'll admit I wasn't Robert's biggest fan, but he is the father of my grandson," Carol admitted, "and as far as Joshua, I love that boy dearly."

"I need a mother right now! Someone that wants to cry with me!" Stacey blasted. "I need a mother who pretends to care about my dead husband. And I need a mother who would die trying to get my son back!"

Carol could only nod. She didn't know how to be that person.

"You could have done so much better for yourself!" Carol argued. "You had such a promising future until you married him. I'm not going to lie. I'm glad he's dead. At least now you have a second chance."

"Who are you to judge anyone?" Stacey's anger was raw. This

conversation was a long time coming. "You married my father and then deserted us. Even when he was dying, you never came to be by his side. What kind of person does that?"

"One who has moved on," Carol told the truth. "Your father was a good man, but we were two different people. I made a decision to go out and find my life."

Stacey stormed into her bedroom and slammed the door like a grounded teenager.

When Stacey got up the next morning, Carol was eating a bowl of oatmeal while she watched the news. There was nothing about Robert's accident. The clown's death didn't even make the local news.

Stacey saw her mother's bag by the door. "When are you leaving?"

"In an hour I have a meeting to attend."

Stacey never understood what her mother did. "How is your business?"

Carol finished her breakfast, "Things are coming together."

When the taxi arrived, Stacey gave her mother a polite smile. She didn't want to fight anymore. "Thanks for coming."

Carol pursed her lips. "You're welcome."

Stacey watched the taxi drive. She finally accepted Carol was never meant to be a mother, or grand mother.

TWENTY-NINE

Even though it was the holiday season, Sergeant Smith sat in his office instead of being home with his family. The Small case had obsessed him like no other case during his career and now Tracy Addison's death intensified his commitment to solve it. He was absolutely convinced the two cases were connected.

He promised his wife he'd be home by noon so they could head to the mountains for an afternoon of skiing. She smiled at his offer but wasn't going to start packing just yet. She knew her husband was a committed cop, but this case was bordering on being obsessive.

The Tracy Addison file was officially closed which meant no more department resources would be allocated to investigate it. If Smith wanted to do further digging, it would have to be on his time. There was no way she was hiking on that dangerous trail. Someone lured her there.

He searched his notepad and found Peter McKee's phone number. He made a call, but it went to voicemail. He left a message.

"Hello Peter, this is Sergeant Smith. I have some questions regarding the fire I want to ask you. I'm hoping you can clear up some loose ends. Call me when you get this."

He hoped McKee could answer some questions about Addison's history. Smith was sure her past was somehow connected to everything that had happened.

He locked the door behind him and went home to take his family skiing.

THIRTY

Peter McKee was summoned to a meeting at the complex on Gabriola Island and he wasn't excited at the idea. The complex was a scientific research laboratory built on the island by Liberty City. It was constructed almost completely underground and used the remaining coal mine shafts in the design. Much of Gabriola remained accessible to the public by ferry and became park land. The land designated for the complex was fenced and strictly off limits. It was the headquarters for the organization.

Tracy's death was still fresh with Peter. He was convinced it was no hiking accident, but that opinion had to remain inside of him. She had just left the meeting in Cowichan with Mickey. He didn't think Mickey killed her, but something happened on that trail. He knew he had to be careful or he would be next.

When he arrived at the complex by boat he was ushered to a small laboratory by security and told to wait. While he did, he wandered around the room. He missed being a scientist. Chemical Engineering was his education and real passion, but he knew he wasn't called back to work with test tubes.

Tracy was like a sister to Peter. They were both recruited by Carol when they were only twelve. Carol found them in the child welfare system, and she chose them because of their superior intelligence. They were the beginning of the organization. When they turned twenty-one, Carol got them positions in the school system. Where better to recruit future brilliance.

Peter started as a guidance counsellor and Tracy as a teacher's aid. Within a few years he was the principal at John Woodlands and

Tracy became a full-fledged teacher. That was ten years ago.

Mickey entered the lab and gave Peter a friendly pat on the shoulder. "Thanks for coming."

Peter wasn't sure how to read Mickey's greeting. "No worries."

Mickey grabbed a juice from the cooler. "Take a seat and let's talk."

The two men knew each other. Mickey joined the organization not long after Carol established it. While Mickey was intelligent, he wasn't recruited by Carol for his brains. He had other talents that came in handy. His role expanded over time until he evolved into Carol's second in command. He believed in what the organization was striving to achieve, and he declared his complete loyalty to her. Carol was the first person to not judge him for what he was. She gave him the chance to be what he really wanted to be, a white man.

Mickey wore an expensive suit with a $500 haircut. He was extremely fit, and his

leading man smile made him a popular target for women. There was no one special in his life. There never had been. He was aware that the lifestyle he chose came with risks and could change on a dime.

Peter looked tired, dressed in a sloppy fitting sweatshirt and jeans. He had gained over thirty pounds around the waist and looked close to fifty, even though he was just thirty-eight. And he could use a haircut and moustache trim. "So, why am I here. It can't be good."

"You're right," Mickey nodded, "and I need to understand where your head is at. I need to know if you're still committed to the organization and what we stand for."

Peter rubbed his moustache. "I understand your concern and maybe it's justified. But can I ask you something before I respond?"

"Go ahead."

84

Peter took a deep breath to gather some courage. "Did you push Tracy off the cliff?"

Mickey didn't hesitate to answer. "No. We walked and talked. She said she wanted to hangout and would call for a ride. I was in a hurry to get back, so I left her, alive."

Peter wanted to believe him but knew his friend could make a problem disappear. "Is that the truth?"

"It is," Mickey sipped his juice but kept his eyes on Peter. "So, let me ask you a question. Did you intentionally forget to turn off the video surveillance in the school?"

Peter looked unsure. "I know I turned it off."

"Then what happened, because it was on?"

Peter shrugged. "The only one who knew I was doing it was…"

They said it together. "Tracy!"

Peter looked worried. "Do you think she said anything about any of us to Sergeant Smith?"

"No. Otherwise we'd have cops crawling everywhere and you'd be in a cell."

That made sense and helped Peter breathe easier. "So, what are we doing to get Smith off our asses. He doesn't believe Tracy's death was an accident."

"We need to give him a believable story. One that will satisfy his curiosity."

Peter said. "He's a smart cop. What are you thinking?"

Mickey had a plan. "It's my guess he's going to reach out to you next, and I have a story I want you to memorize."

"He left me a voicemail to call. And he did contact our human resources department to ask about her employment record and who her references were." Peter informed him. "HR had nothing."

"Perfect." Mickey grinned.

"Perfect?" Peter sputtered. "How's that perfect?"

"When you meet with him tell him Tracy was in Witness Protection," Mickey seemed pleased. "And that's why he couldn't find anything about her past."

Peter grinned brightly. He felt a sense of relief hearing Mickey had everything under control. "I love it."

THIRTY-ONE

New Year's Eve

It was a chilly night in the nation's capital and many of Ottawa's elite and famous were headed to a New Year's Eve party. The most popular and most powerful were invited to the private residence of billionaire Hugh Hutchinson. He had strong political ties and only supported causes that would increase his wealth. On the guest list and expected to attend was Prime Minister Pierre Elliot.

The Hutchinson estate was built on twelve acres of some of Ottawa's most expensive real estate along the river. The property was heavily treed and lined with ten-foot brick walls to ensure his privacy. It had everything you'd expect from a home owned by a billionaire. There were tennis courts, an Olympic sized pool, a driving range, full gym, and Hutchinson's favourite, his twenty-four-car garage. It stored a portion of his classic car collection.

His main house is a three story, forty-five thousand square foot mansion that he completely renovated when he purchased the property seven years ago. The home was full of expensive extras and epitomized his ego and wealth.

For tonight's gala his guests would be directed to a large hall he had built with food and beverage capabilities for up to three hundred guests. The costs for the evening were expected to exceed $1 million and that included two of music's biggest names making an appearance.

Security would be very tight and anyone entering the property would have to agree to a body scan and understand that absolutely no pictures would be allowed outside the actual hall. Hugh did not want his guests to end up on the cover of the Star or any trash web site.

One of the first high profiled guests to arrive was John Fisher. He was the Canadian Finance Minister who only got invited on the insistence of the prime minister. Hugh was not a fan of Fisher or how he managed the country's finances.

As Fisher's chauffeured limousine slowed at the gated entrance, photographers scrambled to try and get a sellable photo. Fisher's reputation for being in the presence of beautiful women, and his leading man smile made him a target of the paparazzi. His face on the cover sold magazines.

Hidden behind the tinted glass, the mystery woman's identity was safe. Fisher was comfortable ignoring the activity. He was used to it. "I'll never understand their interest."

The limousine stopped at the entrance. Before getting out his guest turned to him. "I appreciate you getting me through that. We're even."

He responded politely. "Will you need a ride back to the airport?"

Carol shook her head. "I'll be fine."

They both headed inside the estate and went in separate directions.

Many in attendance had made their way into the hall where the booze was free, and a blues band was the opening act. John Fisher had already found a wealthy blonde he chatted up. Carol preferred the quieter hallways, where she could go unnoticed and get done what she came to do.

As she watched the guests stroll past, she could only shake her head at some of the people Hutchinson invited. Movie actors looking to chat up producers, gay men pretending to be straight and aging professional athletes looking to transition into the business world. The best were the married couples pretending to be happy.

Wendell Presley was an Oil and Gas executive that still had his linebacker body from college. His thick shoulders and slim waist were impressive for a man now in his forties. The black man had a brash personality that complimented his big bald head and black beard. He could be an intimidating sight to those who didn't know him, and even some that did.

Carol spotted him, but before she could disappear into the lady's room, he intercepted her. "What are you doing here?"

"Celebrating the New Year like everyone else. How about you?"

He recognized that Carol was lying, but let it be. "Other than the free booze, I need some of these politicians to start supporting the west. Things are bad in the oil patch and I need to wake some of these assholes up."

Carol needed to stay on schedule. "I might be able to use you in the future. I'll reach out if I do."

Wendell knew she was blowing him off but would love to know why she was *really* at the party. He didn't want to upset her, so he never asked. "I look forward to hearing from you. Good to see you and Happy New Year."

She stepped inside the bathroom without saying another word.

THIRTY-TWO

Three thousand kilometers away on Gabriola Island, there was a team meeting on Level C inside the complex. All required personnel were inside a locked technology room. Mickey was in charge.

Tonight's assignment in Ottawa was critical for the organization and it would all stem on the success of Carol utilizing Jonny's latest creation. Jonny was fifteen-years old, and a four-year resident on the island. He was recruited for his unmatched ability to build anything electronic. The smaller and more detailed the assignment the better. He landed the nickname, *the gadget king,* from the other recruits because of the amazing gizmos he built.

He was beside Mickey chewing on a slice of pepperoni pizza while he waited for the monitors to activate. It wouldn't be long before the evening's entertainment back in Ottawa would begin. His gadget was designed to get them temporary eyes and ears throughout Hutchinson's estate. A security team had done a sweep for electronic devices before the event, but no one expected video and audio equipment to be installed during the party.

Carol learned that the prime minister was attending tonight's gala only a week ago and made it a priority to attend. She needed to get close to Pierre Elliot, without ever going near him. The prime minister was coming to celebrate but was also scheduled to attend a very exclusive meeting that wasn't on any parliamentary calendar. Carol needed to hear what was going to be discussed, but knew an invite wasn't coming anytime soon. Jonny's gadgets would do the job.

When she was alone in the bathroom, Carol reached into her purse and pulled out a small makeup kit. Hidden inside were three mechanical gadgets that looked exactly like the common house fly. She placed them on the back of the toilet and stood back. They had the ability to fly and video tape everything within twenty meters and the audio was studio quality.

Jonny went to work and activated each fly. The monitors turned on and each the view from inside the fly's eyes. Right now, a different version of Carol was on all three screens. Jonny activated the Flies and their wings began to flap. They had the capability of two hundred cycles per second, just like the one on the widow sill. Before Carol could blink, they were gone.

Prime Minister Pierre Elliot arrived without an escort and that was a headline story all by itself. He was known to share time with numerous women, but not tonight. He was surrounded by security that quickly dispersed once he was inside the estate. They were out of sight, but never far away.

He knew the layout of the home well, having been a guest of the billionaire many times in the past. They were partners on many business ventures and had a lucrative friendship.

Elliot spent the first fifteen minutes shaking hands and bestowing holiday wishes on the lineup of people eager to greet the country's leader. As previously planned, one of his advisors rescued him away from the crowd and he was taken to Hugh's study where he was the last one to arrive for their meeting.

No one saw the fly escape Elliot's pocket and take up a position where a fly wouldn't look out of place. It perched on the ceiling right above them. Inside the room was Hugh Hutchinson, John Fisher and the guest of honour, North Korean Diplomat Eon Kamahi. Pierre was greeted with a scotch as he joined the men at a table.

After some polite holiday chit chat, Pierre initiated the conversation they were all there to discuss. The fly was giving Mickey and Jonny a bird's eye view. "So, where are we at with pricing for the weapons?"

John Fisher responded. "The final purchase price will be $50 million. Half paid in advance and the balance on delivery to North Korea."

Eon Kamahi nodded. His English was excellent. "My commander is very happy with the agreement."

Pierre sipped his scotch. "Good to hear. When will we receive the deposit, Mr. Kamahi?"

When Kamahi was abroad representing the North Korean government, he came across as a brash critic of western society. That persona disappeared once he was hidden behind closed doors. He loved the lifestyle choices available in North America. "We'll send the deposit within seven days."

The men finished their drinks while discussing logistical topics and then Fisher was the first to excuse himself from the meeting. He had a beautiful blonde waiting for him back in the hall. The other men weren't far behind.

When the door opened, no one saw the fly head down the hallway. It went directly into Carol's purse that was sitting partially open on her lap. The other two returned after doing surveillance of the estate, which included following Presley. Carol was ready to go. She'll leave the celebrating to the others in attendance.

As she headed down the hall towards the door to get a taxi, she heard the commotion behind her. Pierre had returned to the party and people scrambled to meet him. It was like he was a rock star. That was about to change.

THIRTY-THREE

Sergeant Smith returned to work after two days of skiing and hot tubbing with his family at a local mountain resort. After too much comfort food and a few glasses of wine he was recharged and ready to get back to work. There was a pile of messages on his desk, but two grabbed his attention. One was from Peter McKee and the second was from a detective in Victoria. He had a missing twelve-year old named Cassie Chang.

After getting a coffee from the staff room he returned to his desk and got to work.

He called the Victoria number. "This is Sergeant Smith returning your call regarding the Chang case."

There was a sound of shuffling papers. "Thanks for calling back. I have a case that seems familiar to your Joshua Small file. I was hoping to compare notes."

Smith took a sip of his coffee before throwing the cup into the garbage. He had forgotten how bad the coffee was. "Why don't you tell me about the Chang case?"

"My girl is fourteen and she'll be graduating university this semester. Or at least she was supposed to."

Graduating?" Smith sounded skeptical. "How smart is this young lady."

"She's as smart as they come. She's done a four-year program in sciences in less than eighteen months."

"What happened to her?"

"She vanished into thin air, like your Small kid," The detective explained. "The last time anyone saw her, she was in the library studying."

"Outside her academic abilities, was there anything else special about her?"

"Funny you ask. She was working on a formula to create a vapour food that could eliminate world hunger."

"That's ambitious. Probably worth millions."

The detective corrected Smith. "You mean billions."

Smith thought for a moment. Another brilliant kid taken and it's possible that both went along willingly. "Can you send me a copy of her file and let's stay in touch."

The detective agreed and they ended their call.

THIRTY-FOUR

Carol began everyday with an early morning walk through the trails on the complex property. It was something that she enjoyed. The trails were back in the trees and impossible to see from a boat. It was important to Carol that the complex was protected from intruders.

There were sheer cliffs with sensors on the east side and the remainder of the property has eight-foot chain link fence with razor wire and security cameras every eight feet. Motion detectors were activated with a simple human touch. No one was getting inside without an invitation.

After her shower, Carol ordered some tea with fresh fruit and yogurt for breakfast. "Can I also get some pancakes with syrup and chocolate milk?"

Carol dialed Joshua. "Come to my room for breakfast. I want to talk."

Ten minutes later Joshua was sitting across from Carol. "How are you doing, gramma?"

"I'm good, and remember, you always call me Carol."

Joshua stuffed a piece of pancake into his mouth and winked.

"You're going to choke eating that fast." Carol warned him.

He nodded but kept chewing.

"So, how are you fitting in around here? Is everyone treating you okay?"

"Yup," He drank his milk. "Most of the other kids are cool. I really like Curtis."

"Yes, Curtis Lacy. He has a wild side, so be careful around him."

He stuffed another piece of pancake in his mouth. "Yes, ma'am."

"Does anyone suspect we're related?"

He shook his head. "I've never mentioned it."

"Good."

Joshua swallowed his food. "When do I get to see my mom and dad? I miss them."

Joshua didn't know anything about his dad's accident and Carol had no intention of telling him. She needed to keep him focused on a big project and nothing was getting in the way. Not even a dead dad. "They're travelling in Europe right now, but we can discuss a reunion when they return."

"That will be great." Joshua wiped his hands. "I have to go."

"One last thing. I have someone I want you to meet."

"Who is it?"

Carol looked satisfied. "Her name is Cassie Chang."

THIRTY-FIVE

Curtis Lacy wore khaki shorts with a t-shirt, and his ball cap was reversed on top of his wavy blonde hair. That was his attire pretty much everyday. A typical fourteen-year old when it came to fashion. What separated him from nearly every other teen on the planet was his computer skills.

He was a fledging bedroom hacker when he discovered that his dad was having an affair at work. It devastated the then eleven-year old. He was already on Carol's radar and when the email scandal broke, Mickey moved in to recruit him.

Curtis was furious at his parents for ruining his life and he agreed to come to the complex to get even with them. Over time his anger towards his mom disappeared when he finally realized that she was a victim too.

When his feelings for his mom turned to guilt for abandoning her, Curtis took a massive risk by hacking into her computer. He knew he could never contact her, but he at least wanted to see how she was doing. If he got caught, he was ready to accept the punishment.

He watched her cry on the third anniversary of him leaving and it hurt. It really hurt.

Curtis had evolved into one of the best hackers on the planet and his role was to raise capital by stealing money from offshore banks. He targeted cartel and organized crime syndicates because they would never contact the police when they were robbed. They had their own internal collections and Curtis knew he had a bounty on his head. It never worried him because he was never getting caught. He had an exit strategy. So far, he had raised over $1 Billion, but it was never enough. Carol always needed more, but never told him why.

Curtis eyed up his salmon rod in the corner. He was ready to take a break and he loved to fish. It was what he did with his dad. He brushed off the idea. Maybe he'd go later.

He accessed his mom's computer. There were times when it was hard on him to see what web sites she visited. The shopping and travel sites were okay, but on a few occasions, she had visited a dating site. She was thinking about a new boyfriend. That was weird to see for Curtis.

He checked her email account. He never read any until today. There was one from a bank that got his attention.

Dear Mrs. Lacy

The Citizens Bank of Canada understands the hardship you and your family have endured over the past three years. Unfortunately, we must make you aware that your account is now overdrawn by $75,232.44.

We will need you to make payment arrangements to address this outstanding balance within thirty days or we'll have no choice but to foreclose on your mortgage. Please feel free to contact us to talk through your payment options.

Again, we are deeply sorry.

Ted Boyden
Branch Manager

Curtis was sick to his stomach and angry. He knew his mother was in trouble because of him. Without worrying about any consequences, he transferred money into her account. Her troubles were taken care of.

THIRTY-SIX

The recruits were gathered in the board room cracking jokes and just being kids until Carol entered. Then the mood got serious and the laughter died. Inside the complex, Carol insisted that their energies were focused on completing assignments. That was there purpose.

She had a guest that no one recognized. The young Asian girl smiled nervously. She took a seat beside Carol. "I want to introduce our newest recruit. This is Cassie Chang."

Everyone smiled and said hello. Jonny snuck an extra glance.

Carol continued. "Cassie joined the organization because she agrees with our platform. She is working on something special and being here in the complex will give her the resources to complete it."

Curtis bit his lower lip. He was thinking. This girl must be working on something amazing if Carol is doing the introduction. Most recruits get the quick handshake and then sent off to work. "Are we allowed to ask what she is working on?"

Cassie was born and raised in Victoria by her immigrant parents from mainland China. She spoke four languages and finished public school at age ten. Carol had already given her the okay to discuss her project. "When I had time from my university studies, I worked on a solution for world hunger."

Jonny was searching for a reason to speak to her. He was attracted to her cute smile. "Did you say you were in university?"

"Yes, fourth year," She replied proudly. "I will graduate in a few months."

Jonny frowned. "Wow, that's impressive. I didn't even finish high school."

Curtis had a question. "So, how will this vapour food work?"

Cassie's face lit up. Her passion for the project was obvious. "When it's completed, we will be able to set up feeding locations where people go into a secure area and simply breathe. The particles they inhale will contain everything a human requires to survive."

Now he knew why Carol was there. What she just described will be worth billions. "You'll be rich. How close are you to finishing?"

Cassie scowled at him. "It's not about making money. I want to help people."

It's always about the money. Curtis pushed his chair back and held up his hands in defeat. "I'm sorry. I never meant to make you angry."

Carol ended the meeting. "Everyone back to work. We have a tight schedule."

Jonny timed his exit to match Cassie. He wanted to introduce himself. She infatuated him.

Curtis left the meeting and headed back to his workstation. He was trying to figure out how Cassie and her vapour food fit into the bigger picture. For now, he'd just keep an eye on her and listen and learn.

THIRTY-SEVEN

Ray Cooke paced in his cell like a caged animal wearing black and white prison issued coveralls. His five-year sentence was coming to an end. The calendar on the wall was his reminder that the days behind bars were almost over. There wasn't a day that passed that he didn't think about who framed him with the rape charge.

He spent as much time as he was allowed in the prison library. He discovered he enjoyed reading fiction, but there wasn't a night before lights out that he didn't chastise himself for succumbing to David's ultimatum. The cocaine wasn't his, and over time he had convinced himself he never attacked Nina.

He replayed the video over and over and a key piece of evidence that he never investigated was the car. It looked like his BMW, but was it? And there was no DNA evidence recovered from Nina to support the sexual assault charge. The worst part for Ray was he looked at David's family as an extension of his own, and they had turned on him.

Today was the day most prisoners had circled on their calendar and Ray was no different. It was his turn to go in front of the parole board and if everything went as he planned, he would soon be a free man.

With his legal background, Ray understood the system and how to work it in his favour. Once he was comfortable with the prison routine, he had volunteered for any work detail or study group that would take him. He spent hours helping other inmates with their legal woes and it wasn't long before he was a valued resource within the prison population. He did it all to make a resume for the parole board.

Ray was escorted by a guard to a small simple room where his future for the next few years would be decided. There was a portrait of Queen Elizabeth on the far wall and that was it for wall decor. When he was inside, his handcuffs were removed, and told to take a seat at a small steel table that was bolted to the floor.

Directly in front of Ray was a larger table with three empty chairs. Ray glanced back and saw the prison chaplain sitting in a visitor seat, clenching his bible like he always did. He flashed Ray a supportive smile. There was no sign of Tiffany, and that disappointed him.

A moment later a balding man in his fifties entered through a side door wearing an outdated business jacket and dark slacks. He was followed by two conservatively dressed women who both wore a lot of dark colors. It made Ray remember his days in university. They all could pass for professors.

The man seemed to be in charge, and he began. "So, Mr. Cooke. I'm Doctor Zolob and I'm chairing your bail hearing."

Ray smiled graciously. He had rehearsed this moment many times. "Nice to meet you."

"It's this committee's duty to determine if you've been rehabilitated and are ready to re-enter society," His eyes were fixed on Ray. "I've reviewed your file and I will tell you that I am rarely impressed by an inmate's accomplishments while they're doing their sentence."

Ray kept a straight face. His idea seemed to work. "Thank you."

"I've read the warden's reports and I have to say the way you provided services to others is very commendable," Zolob sipped his water. "You've completed all of the mandatory drug counselling ordered by the court, so I'll finish by saying I am glad to see you made the effort."

"I tried to turn a negative in my life to a positive."

The woman to the doctor's left took her turn. She wasn't going to be a fan as much as her colleague. "Mr. Cooke, my name is Jeanne Webster. Regarding your offer to help other inmates with legal advice, your file says you did it once a week. Is this correct?"

"It was actually twice."

She pretended to glance at her paperwork. "I'm sorry, you are right. Can I ask why you did this?"

Ray did as he rehearsed. He delayed his response and appeared to be thinking. "I never thought about the why. I guess I did it to pass the time and to help others because I could. Most of the inmates I met lacked any real education, so I decided to help those who wanted it. I felt good and I was helping myself as well."

"What do you mean, helping yourself?" questioned Webster. "Did you think it would help impress this panel?"

Ray was careful. "What I mean is I'm a fifty-two-year old privileged white male who lost sight of how good my life was, and I ended up in here. It was a shock to the system and once I got through the self pity process, I decided to use my education as a tool to help others, and yes, myself."

"Do you still admit your guilt to your charges of possession of cocaine?"

Ray was blindsided by her question. He had already pled guilty in court, so her asking made him suspicious. After a short hesitation he replied. "I admitted in court to possessing the cocaine with intent and I've done my time accordingly. I hope that answers your question?"

She nodded and looked at the third member of the panel.

The second woman pushed her hair out of her eyes and leaned forward. Ray decided she could use a trip to the salon. It was like she was challenging Ray to a staring contest. "If you're granted parole by this panel, what do you plan to do?"

This time Ray deviated from the script. "I'm not sure. My law career is over so maybe I'll continue what I started here."

She interrupted him. "And what's that?"

"Helping others," Ray stated easily. "But otherwise, I have no real plans."

She pushed harder. "You're obviously a very intelligent man, so you must have some idea what you want to do when you're released."

Ray glanced behind him for effect. "I was hoping my wife would be here, but as you can see it's only the preacher and me, so I guess that's what I'll do first. I'll call my wife and see if she answers."

"Well, good luck with that." She was finished.

Before they all stood, Dr. Zolob ended the meeting with a standard statement. "We will review your file one last time and you will have our decision within a week."

They left the room the way they entered.

THIRTY-EIGHT

Sergeant Smith took a side trip on his way to a meeting with Peter McKee, who agreed to get together in an hour. Smith was going to stop by Stacey Small's home and update her on Joshua's case, even though there wasn't much to report. Most of his case was built on speculation and the truth was, the case was getting cold. He hoped McKee could shed some new light on his theories.

Stacey was pleased to see the sergeant. Visitors had stopped dropping by to offer condolences or care packages of food and flowers. It was just her alone in her home.

"Come in. Do you want a coffee or some water?"

He declined both. "I wanted to offer my condolences for Robert. I can't imagine how you deal with everything."

"It seems like I've been crying forever," She seemed apologetic. "The men in my life have had a tough go."

He wanted to console her with a hug but resisted. He had been the bearer of news like this so many times in his career. It never got easy.

She looked at Smith. "So, anything to tell me about Joshua?"

"To be truthful there is not much to go on," Smith knew he was disappointing her, and it bothered him. "I still believe Joshua is out there and he was taken to serve a purpose."

"What does that mean?"

Smith debated on what to tell her and decided she deserved some hope. "There was another abduction in Victoria."

"Oh my god!" Stacey shrieked. "Who?"

"The reason I'm bringing it up is because of the similarities to

Joshua's case. She's a girl around his age that was taken from her university."

"University? I thought you said she was Joshua's age?"

"A year older but graduating university this spring," Smith confirmed. "Like Joshua, they're both brilliant and young."

He never bothered to mention that both cases indicated the kids were involved in their own abductions. That bit of news would be devastating. "We're looking into possible connections and if anything materializes, I'll let you know."

"Do you still believe Joshua's case is linked to Miss. Addison's death?"

"It might just be my paranoid police mentality, but I don't think her death was an accident."

"You're convinced she was pushed, aren't you?" Stacey paused. "You think she was involved in Joshua's abduction and someone shut her up."

"That's a big assumption. I do believe someone in the school was involved. Was it her, or did she see something she shouldn't have? That, I don't know."

Stacey thought of the possibilities. "If Addison was murdered, that would mean Joshua is alive."

Smith checked his watch. He had to go. "I'll keep you updated on anything new if it comes up."

Stacey suddenly had a reason to smile. "That would be great."

THIRTY-NINE

They agreed to meet in a downtown coffee shop with an outdoor patio. They could talk and have some privacy. Smith suggested they meet outside the police station. He wanted to keep Peter relaxed.

Peter arrived first and fidgeted with his phone. He had gone over Mickey's story a hundred times. He was ready. He wasn't comfortable lying to the police, but the thought of going to prison scared him even more.

Sergeant Smith sat down. He unzipped his jacket and threw it over the arm of the chair beside him. "Thanks for meeting with me."

"No problem," Peter put his phone away. "Can I get you a coffee?"

"A real one would be a nice change from the crap at the station."

Peter returned a few minutes later and handed Smith his double, double. "I know you're busy, so how can I help?"

Smith pulled the lid off and let the steam escape. "I have some questions about the school fire and Miss Addison. I want to put both files to bed, but there are some loose ends that have me bothered."

Peter pursed his lips, pretending to be confused. "I thought I heard Tracy's death was ruled an accident."

"It was, but I still have a few questions to clear up in my own mind and I think Miss. Addison deserves a thorough investigation."

"Fair enough."

"Were you the person who hired, Miss. Addison?"

"I was apart of the interviewing process, but Human Resources would have made the final decision."

"That would normally make sense, but they have no file on her," Smith sipped his coffee and watch Peter's reaction. "I'm wondering how she got paid."

Peter realized Smith had done some investigating. He was prepared. "I have no idea. That's another question for HR."

"You worked together for almost ten years, so did she ever mention family, or say where she grew up?" Smith asked. "I didn't see any relatives at the funeral."

Peter was surprised to hear Smith attended the Celebration of Life. "We never talked about it."

Smith pushed. He needed answers. "Are you sure? That's a long time to share a lunchroom, attend Christmas parties and just hang out to never once discuss family. I'm having a hard time believing you never talked about anything besides work."

Peter decided this was the perfect time to activate Mickey's strategy. He pasted a serious expression on his face and made eye contact with the taller sergeant. "I was never supposed to reveal this, but since she's gone, I guess it doesn't matter anymore."

Smith raised his eyebrows. "What doesn't matter?"

Peter tried to appear consoling. "Like you said, Tracy and I became friends over the years and on the odd occasion, we would go for drinks. One day, she seemed terribly upset and when I pushed to find out what was wrong, she finally told me. It was hard for her to open up."

Smith sipped his coffee and listened. "About what?"

"When she was in college, she witnessed her parents being murdered." Peter watched Smith's reaction. "She saw the killers, so when she testified in court the two men were sentenced to life. They were part of the mob, or something like that."

Smith scratched his head. "Why would the mob kill her parents?"

"She said her dad owed them money, I guess." Peter was told not to give too many details that the cop could check up on. "She never said too much, and I didn't push the subject."

Smith pretended to be stunned but didn't believe a single word. Peter's story was rehearsed. Nothing he said could be checked up on. The case files would be locked. "I appreciate you sharing that with me."

Peter felt confident Smith believed him. "Tracy swore me to secrecy. I hope you understand."

Smith pushed on. "The day she went hiking. Were you aware she was going to Cowichan Bay?"

Peter was there the day Tracy died. They were at the same meeting. But did the cop know that? "No. Why would I?"

Smith shrugged. "I know this is a tough question. But do you think Tracy fell off the cliff, or was she pushed to her death. What's your gut feeling?"

Peter knew the truth. "Your question seems to hint I was involved. I'm telling you, that you are way off base. The coroner's report ruled her death as a tragic accident, so why don't you just accept that?"

"Because Joshua Small is still missing."

Peter settled into his seat. "Any update on that, or am I still a suspect?"

"Everyone is still a suspect until they get cleared," Smith explained. "Is there anything you can tell me? Anything you've remembered since our last conversation?

"Unfortunately, no. I told you everything I remembered that night. Has anything new come up?"

Smith sensed McKee's resistance. He lied. "We were able to recover some video coverage from across the street."

Peter felt a twitch in his stomach. "Really?"

It was obvious the principal didn't expect that, and Smith tightened the screw. "It's at the lab being enhanced. We should have it back within a week."

McKee's voice tailed off. "If it helps find Joshua, that will be great."

He knew he had hit a nerve. Like Addison, he was sure McKee knew more than he was saying. The question was still, who were they protecting. "We're hoping that'll be the case."

Peter tried to stay calm. "Can you tell me what you saw on the video?"

"I can't say anything," Smith told him, "but it gives us a view of the gym exit."

Peter remembered that he had stood in the doorway. "Okay."

Smith decided to throw McKee another bomb. "And we got the fire inspector's report."

"And what did it say?"

"We know the fire was arson," He revealed, "and it was started by the man in the blue coveralls."

Peter felt the walls closing in. "But you have no proof of that."

"I'm confident that when the video is enhanced, I'm going to find you by the back door. When I saw you at the school, you were wearing a red pullover. Someone on the video was wearing red."

Peter had heard enough. "If I knew you were going to accuse me of something this serious, I would never have met you without a lawyer."

Smith raised his voice, just a little. "Do you need a lawyer, Peter?"

Peter stood up and pulled on his jacket. "I think it's time I go."

Smith stopped him. "You need to understand that I'm going to find out what happened that night. If I find out you're involved, I will charge you with kidnapping and arson. You will spend a long time behind bars."

"I had nothing to do with Joshua's disappearance. He was a great kid and I'm sick he's missing," Peter blasted. "As for the fire, my response is still the same. You're way off base."

Smith challenged Peter. "Are we?"

FORTY

When Carol first started to visualize the concept of an organization, she was twenty-eight years old and lived with her husband and a young baby in a small apartment. She felt trapped in a boring marriage and her only connection to the outside world was watching the evening news after Stacey fell asleep.

It was the 1980s and wars were being fought around the world. Oil and other natural resources were in high demand and greed directed many governments. She became obsessed with a television station that covered the news twenty-four hours a day. Violence and corruption were taking over the planet. It was the only channel she watched.

And then one day she rolled up her loose change and went to the store and bought a binder with paper. The concept of the organization was born. Her mind was like an episode of Star Trek and her ideas were decades ahead of reality.

Six months later she was so enthralled in her idea that she walked out on her family. She never told them why, other than to tell her husband that their marriage was over. It was years later before she shared her idea with anyone. It was with a homeless boy who painted her deck for food. His name was Mickey.

Strutting into the office ten minutes late, Curtis had his usual cocky grin and reversed ballcap. "Hey, Carol. What's happening?"

Carol usually ignored Curtis's cocky outbursts, but not on this day. "Sit down and drop the beach boy attitude!"

His grin vanished, and he took a seat as ordered. "Why are you so grumpy?"

Carol bit her lip. "You are the only person that gets away with talking to me like you do."

"That's because I make you so much money."

She slapped a bank statement down in front of him. "Speaking of money, can you explain this transfer without my approval?"

Curtis didn't need to look at the statement and pushed it back. His cockiness had deserted him. "I was going to tell you, but I haven't had time."

"Don't you ever lie to me!" Carol snapped, "and don't ever take me for a fool. You're too smart for that."

"I'm sorry I didn't tell you."

"That's not good enough!"

Curtis fidgeted in his seat. "I needed the money."

Carol corrected him. "You mean, your mother needed the money!"

He knew he was caught. "Yes, she did."

"You stupid boy. By doing this you have left our accounts exposed to regulators. You're too smart not to know that."

Curtis didn't regret helping his mom, but knew Carol was right. "I guess you also know I've been accessing her email account?"

Carol looked disappointed. "Another mistake."

"That's how I keep my shit together in this place," he conceded. "I need to know she's okay."

Carol needed him to focus on his next assignments. "This disobedience has to stop."

Curtis took a deep breath and looked apologetic.

"I understand you want to look after your mother, but I can't let you do anything that will expose us. Don't take it upon yourself to be the man in her life because your father screwed up."

Curtis resented the shot at his father. "I don't blame myself for my dad, but that doesn't make it any easier to see her in trouble."

Carol shredded the bank statement. "You made a selfish decision. You risked exposing us and I can't allow that."

"Look, I said I'm sorry."

Carol liked Curtis, but she couldn't ignore what he did. "You broke some serious rules, and you will be punished."

This was the first time Curtis had been caught crossing the line and the usually confident teenager slumped back in his chair. "What does that mean?"

"Take the money out of her account." Carol ordered.

Curtis resisted, "Like hell I will! My mom isn't losing her house!"

Carol glared. "What do you suggest I do?"

Curtis tried to justify his mistake. "I've raised over a billion and I'll keep doing it. Just leave my mom alone."

Carol needed a guarantee. "Stop with the self-pity speech. If I let your mother keep it, I need you to promise me that you'll never do anything this stupid again."

Curtis was relieved by Carol's compromise. "I promise."

Carol had another project, "Things are ramping up and I need you at the top of your game."

"Absolutely," Curtis had his smile back, happy that was behind him. "What do you need me to do?"

"The finance minister has set up an offshore account for the North Koreans to send their deposit for the weapons."

"Our government doing business with that fat communist pig is bullshit!" Curtis scowled. "I'll find the account and drain it."

"It's going to be $25 million and I want it all."

"I'll get on it today," Curtis assured her. "It might take some time to get through the firewalls, but I'll get it done."

Carol pulled out another file and brushed him away. "I have

things I need to get to, so get to work."

Curtis headed to the door, "Thanks for helping my mom."

Carol never bothered to looked up.

FORTY-ONE

Sergeant Smith called Detective Murphy and asked him to drop by his office to review the evidence in the Small and Addison cases. Smith was hoping a fresh set of eyes from the narcotics detective would help. Smith was getting pressure from the top floor and decisions on priority cases had to be made. The Addison death was already ruled an accident and the Joshua Small file grew colder by the day.

The detective walked into the office with a week-old beard and sloppy hair. He was on another case. "Hey, buddy. What's going on?"

Smith's frustration was written all over his face. He shook Murphy's hand. "Did you review the cases I sent?"

Murphy nodded. "It's going to be hard to prove they're connected. We would need a confession, and it sounds like no one will talk to us."

"Addison didn't fall. She was tripped," Smith sounded convinced. "There are countless hiking trails around Cowichan. Why would she pick one on private property? It makes no sense."

"I think your best option is to push McKee even harder."

"That's probably true, but I don't have any funds for surveillance, and he'll lawyer up if I call him back in," Smith flipped through his notebook, looking for a name. "There is one person I've missed who might want to know the truth.

"And who is that?"

"Her name is Laura Nelsen, and she was Tracy's partner. I remember her from the funeral, and she seemed sincerely upset."

FORTY-TWO

Suzanne Lacy was stretched out on her couch, wrapped in a grey woollen afghan trying to use her morning soap opera as a distraction from real life. Even Victor Newman couldn't take her mind off her troubles. She had hardly slept over the weekend after she received the message from the bank. It was devastating.

She had no idea how she was going to fix it. There was no one she felt she could call for help, and that included her ex-husband. And even though she had no solution she decided she wasn't going to stress over it. It was just another page out of her life, a life that was terrible for the past three years.

The house no longer felt like home and since her family was gone, it had become an object she could learn to live without. Maybe it was time to focus on a new direction and this could be a fresh start. There wasn't much left for her to lose.

When her phone rang, it startled her. She wasn't expecting any calls and she thought about ignoring it. After the fourth ring she picked it up, "Hello?"

An unfamiliar male voice was on the call. "Is this Suzanne Lacy?"

"Yes," she responded softly. "Who is this?"

"I'm Ted Boyden and I'm calling from the Citizen Bank."

Suzanne sunk into her chair and wrapped the afghan tighter, preparing to hear more bad news. "What can I do for you?"

The banker's tone was surprisingly upbeat. "Actually, there's nothing you need to do."

Suzanne was confused. "I got your letter, and I spent all weekend trying to find a solution. But I can't."

Now Boyden was the confused one. "Are you aware that your overdraft was paid in full?"

Suzanne nearly dropped her phone as she sat up. "Are you sure you have the correct Suzanne Lacy?"

"Yes, I'm sure."

Suzanne was a mix of shock and confusion. "Who would do that?"

There was a short pause in the conversation while Boyden shuffled through some paperwork. He came back on the line. "All I can tell you is that it was transferred from a private account. There is no name attached to the transfer."

"Oh my god," Suzanne started to cry, and for the first time in a long time, they were tears of happiness. "Why did someone do this for me?"

"Seems like you have a guardian angel, Ms. Lacy," laughed Boyden. "I'll let you go and if you ever need anything from our bank, I'm here for you."

Suzanne tossed her phone onto the couch and wiped a tear as she looked out at Grey Mountain. "A guardian angel, my ass. I know you were involved in this somehow, Curtis."

FORTY-THREE

Security around Confederation Park in Ottawa was tight, but not obvious. A black sedan pulled into the parking spot beside a green SUV. There was a third vehicle, a rental car that was about one hundred yards away on a side street that no one took a second look at.

The finance minister climbed into the backseat of the green SUV. "Sorry I'm late."

The other man was obviously irritated. "Leave earlier if you have to, but don't keep me waiting."

John Fisher was immune to Hugh Hutchinson's self-serving rants. He had heard it all before. "Unlike you, I have people I need to report to, and can't just disappear when you call."

"Let's get this mess with the North Korean money figured out." Fisher began. "We've had a breach of security."

"That's the best you got?" Hugh growled. "How does $25 million go missing from an account that isn't supposed to even exist?"

Fisher scrambled for an answer. "I have my best forensic auditor looking into it. She's confident they'll trace it."

Hutchinson took a heavy breath, emphasizing his frustration. "How are you explaining the money to the auditor? And what are you doing if she finds it? Will you have the thief arrested for stealing the corrupt money? What we need to know is how anyone knew about the account in the first place. You are such an idiot."

Fisher absorbed the insult.

"What if the thief knows what the money was for? What's your story if they go public?"

"We'll find the money." Fisher insisted, but his fears were etched on his face.

"You better find it and do it soon."

Fisher understood Hutchinson was a friend of the prime minister, but he had taken enough. "Like I said, I have my best person looking into it."

Hutchinson scoffed. "Whoever took the money made your security systems look like a joke."

Fisher didn't want to debate, "When we find something, I'll let you know."

Hutchinson didn't let up. "How are you going to explain to Pierre that our money was stolen, and he might face treason charges. Any ideas on that?"

"Pierre doesn't need to know anything at this point. Until we get this figured out, there is no reason to worry him."

"If your auditor doesn't fix this in the next few days, I'll personally update Pierre."

"You stay out of it," Fisher had heard enough and reached for the door. "We'll find the money and when we do, we'll deal with who took it. In the meantime, I suggest you remember who I am."

Hugh laughed at Fisher's attempt at bravado. "You have forty-eight hours to solve this."

"We're done talking," Fisher snapped. "I don't need to listen to your threats."

"You better take me seriously," Hugh threatened, "and remember that your boss works for me!"

Fisher started to get out of the car, but before he exited, he turned to Hutchinson and took a parting shot. "You really are a piece of shit, you know that."

"Get the fuck out of my car." growled the billionaire.

With all the anger and insults inside the car, neither of them noticed a fly perched on the steering wheel. It recorded everything. When Fisher exited, the fly flew back to the rental car and climbed into Mickey's pocket.

Two hours later, Mickey and his little companion were on a flight back to Gabriola Island. He couldn't get the smirk off his face. He had a video of the finance minister and the country's richest man implementing the prime minister in a federal crime. It was a good day.

FORTY-FOUR

Detective Murphy tapped on the screen door and waited for an answer. Sergeant Smith stood beside him. After a brief phone introduction, Laura Nelsen agreed to meet at her condo. She was concerned about Tracy's death being ignored and agreed with Smith's theory that it wasn't an accident. She wanted to hear his thoughts.

She was wearing an oversized Woodland's school sweatshirt and some tight-fitted ripped jeans. "Which one of you is Sergeant Smith?"

The sergeant stepped forward. "I'm Smith and this is Detective Murphy."

They went inside where Laura led them to her small living room. The furnishings were clustered, and nothing matched. It was the result of two people moving in together and each having some of their own furniture.

"Do you boys want some water?" Laura offered.

"Yes please," Murphy wanted a moment to look around without being obvious. "Water would be great."

Murphy ambled around the room looking for anything that might tell them something about Tracy's past. Other than a few pictures of her hiking, there was nothing. No diploma or family photos on display. It felt strange to him.

Laura returned and handed out the water glasses. She looked at Smith. "Your call has me curious to hear what you think about Tracy."

Smith thanked her for the water. "Why's that?"

"I had wondered why the police never contacted me to discuss Tracy's death," Her disappointment was obvious. "I've heard nothing."

"I'm sorry about that," Sergeant Smith placed his glass on a coffee table. "I'm investigating the Joshua Small abduction and I believe the two cases are somehow connected."

"Tracy mentioned you were working the case. How can I help?"

"I'm hoping you might shed some light on her past."

Laura sighed. "I'm not sure what else I can tell you. I know her death was ruled an accident and I've chosen to accept that. But I agree with you."

Murphy jumped in. "Do you think her death could be a murder?"

Laura shrugged. "Murder is a big jump, but maybe. She was a good hiker and I have no reason to believe she decided to hike on that trail on her own. It makes no sense."

Smith took a sip of water. "I know an average defense attorney would destroy my theory in a courthouse. But I'm having a hard time believing that her school burns to the ground, her favourite student is abducted, and she falls down a cliff is all just a coincidence."

Murphy nodded. "That girl had a string of bad luck."

"And you don't think it was suicide?" Laura asked.

"I'm not sure," Smith admitted, "but I'm trying to find a young boy that someone went to great lengths to take."

"How do you think I can help?"

"I'm hoping you can tell us about her past."

"Ask away, but it's complicated"

"Let's start with her family," Smith pulled out his notepad. "What can you tell us about her parents?"

"What about them?"

While Smith questioned Laura, Murphy kept his eyes on Laura. Even under her baggy sweatshirt he could tell she had a smoking body. Too bad she was a lesbian.

Smith started. "We can find anything out about her prior to her time at John Woodlands. No work history, no education, nothing. What can you tell us about that?

Laura ran her fingers through her hair. She was thinking about where to begin. "I can explain some of it. It's quite the story."

"Take your time," Smith remembered McKee's version. "We want to hear everything."

Laura took a drink to rinse her dry mouth. "She told me about her past because it wasn't long after she moved in, she started having bad nightmares. She shrugged them off at first, but they were intense."

"Did she tell you what they were about?"

"She tried to brush them off as bad dreams. But, when they continued night after night, I became a nag and she finally came clean."

Laura took a second to compose herself. This was hard for her. "One morning, after a really bad episode, I convinced her to talk to someone. I think she finally opened up just to get me off her back."

Murphy wrote notes. "What caused them?"

"When she told me, I understood why she was so reluctant to talk. When she was in university, she decided to surprise her parents at Christmas by coming home a few days early. She also wanted to tell her strong catholic parents that she was a lesbian. Not an easy discussion."

"No, it wouldn't be," Smith had been raised catholic. "Where did she go to school?"

"Somewhere in the mid-west," Laura told him. "She never mentioned her school. She wasn't allowed to."

"What do you mean, she wasn't allowed?"

"Let me finish and you'll understand?"

"Sorry," Smith apologized.

"She was worried about how her parents would react to having a gay daughter. She knew they needed to know, and she headed home from school a day early."

"I imagine her parents didn't take it very well." Murphy chirped.

"They never found out."

"What happened?" asked Smith.

"When she arrived at the family farmhouse, there was a car in the driveway that she didn't recognize. She didn't want to block them in, so she parked behind the barn. When she entered through the back door, she expected her mom to be in the kitchen baking Christmas goodies."

"But she wasn't?" Murphy guessed.

"No," Laura hesitated, "but she heard noises come from her parent's bedroom upstairs. She thought they might be fooling around, and she felt embarrassed. She decided to wait in the kitchen."

Smith raised his hand to interrupt her. "You have no idea where she was?"

"None. She never told me where and I never asked."

Smith remembered McKee's answer to the same question. "Take your time."

"Tracy said she heard her dad arguing with someone about money. And then there was a scream from the bedroom, and she recognized her mother's voice. She knew that they were in trouble."

"What year was this?" asked Murphy.

"It would be around 2005," Laura determined. "Tracy had run into the garage to get her dad's rifle, but it was missing. And then she heard more screams and finally four or five gunshots. Everything went silent. She snuck back inside the home and heard two men joke about her mom while she hid in the closet."

McKee's story and Laura's version were remarkably similar.

Too similar, Smith thought. "So, her parents were murdered?"

Laura grabbed some tissue. "Yes."

Murphy sighed. "That must have been awful for her knowing the people who killed your parents were only steps away."

Laura continued. "She saw the men through a crack in the closet door. One was covered in blood and the other was grinning like he didn't have a care in the world. Little did they know."

Smith frowned, thinking about what Addison witnessed, "She saw them?"

"She did," Laura confirmed, "and she kept it together enough to get the license plate of the car as they drove away. She was a strong person."

"Why would they kill her parents?" Smith questioned Laura.

"When it went to trial, it came out that her dad borrowed money from some bad men and these guys were sent to collect. Things got out of hand," Laura wiped a tear. "When Tracy finally got the nerve to go upstairs, she found her dad on the floor with half of his head blown off. Her mother was spread-eagled on the bed. They raped her and forced her dad to watch."

Smith let everything sink in.

"Anyway, Tracy testified at the trial and both men got life sentences. They were mob-connected, so Tracy had to vanish."

Smith thought about McKee. He appeared to be telling the truth, but there was one piece that concerned Smith. Why did Tracy tell two different people her story? A big part of the witness protection program was secrecy. "This explains why we couldn't find any record of her."

Laura agreed. "Exactly."

Smith figured he had enough, and he didn't want to overstay their visit. "Did Tracy have any other friends or family?"

She had to think about it. "The only person she ever mentioned regularly was Peter McKee. They'd meet for coffee the odd time. That was about it."

"Is there anything that would make you believe that Tracy could be involved in Joshua Small's abduction?"

Laura's face cringed with anger. "How can you even think that? She was a complete mess because of what happened at the school. She adored that boy."

"Sorry, but we're just searching for answers and following where the evidence leads us."

Laura didn't apologize for defending Tracy and her guard was up. "I know that you're doing your job, but you're looking in the wrong direction. Tracy loved that kid, and she was always talking about how smart he was. It actually drove me crazy."

"We've taken up a lot of your time," Smith stood up. "If there is anything else you can think of, we'd appreciate a call."

Laura walked the officers to the door. "Please keep me posted."

Once inside their vehicle, Murphy looked over at Smith. "What did you think?"

"That was well-rehearsed." Smith announced.

"That means you think that the principal and Laura might be in on this."

"Maybe." Smith drove away.

FORTY-FIVE

It was seven-thirty and the cafeteria in the complex was full of people eating breakfast before heading to their workstations. Joshua was one of them. Cassie sat across the table and nibbled on a piece of dry toast. She watched impatiently while he gulped down his chocolate milk and licked syrup off his fingers. It was obvious that she was annoyed that he kept her waiting.

"Are you almost done?" Cassie urged. "I have something to show you."

"Give me a minute. Let me clean my hands."

Cassie finally had enough stalling and grabbed Joshua's arm. She yanked him out of his seat. "I don't have a minute."

He stuffed the last piece of bacon in his mouth and reluctantly followed her to the laboratory. He had to be at his own workstation in thirty-minutes, so he didn't have much time. They passed through a security check point and Cassie scanned them into her laboratory.

"Why am I here?" Joshua asked.

Cassie pulled on her lab coat and pointed to her microscope. "Because I'm told you're the smartest kid here, so I want your opinion."

Joshua took the compliment in stride. Being around girls made him uneasy. He stepped up to the microscope. "What am I looking at?"

Cassie couldn't contain her excitement anymore. "I've done it!"

"Done what?" Joshua focused the microscope. "What am I looking at?"

Cassie bubbled with excitement. "My vapor food is finished. It's ready to be tested. We will eliminate world hunger!"

Joshua looked in the microscope. "All I see are tiny dots. They're all different colors."

"Each of those dots is equivalent to a full-sized meal. They contain enough nutrients to provide a human what they require to survive for a day."

The enormity of what Cassie accomplished began to sink in. "This is huge. You're going to be Oprah rich."

Cassie pretended to frown. "Why do boys only think of money? I did this because of stories my grandparents told me. Thousands of people starved to death because they couldn't find or afford food."

Joshua was sorry for his Oprah reference. "I'm really sorry to hear that."

"It's okay." Cassie forgave him. "I asked you here because I need a favour."

"What's that?"

She handed him a spreadsheet. "I'm trying to figure out the best way to distribute the vapor. You must remember that some countries will resist my invention. They use weakness to control their people."

Joshua looked at the paper. "You should talk to Jonny. He invents some really cool stuff and I'm betting he'd love to take on this project."

Cassie loved the idea. "Can we meet after work today? Maybe at the park. Will you ask Jonny to come?"

"Why don't you ask him yourself?"

She smiled shyly. "I just thought you might see him."

Joshua sensed Shirley liked Jonny. It was weird. "I'll see if he can come."

"Let's meet at the park at five."

Joshua left Shirley's lab and hurried to get to his workstation.

He ran around the corner and nearly smacked into Mickey. He looked apologetic. "Sorry."

Mickey grinned. "I see you're in a hurry, so I'll be quick. Do you want to come fishing with me tonight?"

"Seriously. Id love to, but I've never fished before."

"No worries. I think you'll figure it out. Let's meet on the cliffs at five-thirty."

Joshua remembered his commitment to Cassie. "Can I make it six?"

"Sure. Maybe you'll get your first fish tonight."

"That would be awesome," Joshua was excited. "See you."

Mickey watched him race down the hallway. He had some news to share with him.

FORTY-SIX

Outside it was a cold and damp British Columbia morning and Ray sat alone in the prison cafeteria choking down another breakfast. After five years, it still puzzled him how the kitchen could screw up something as simple as scrambled eggs and hash browns. How hard was it to cook an egg?

He leafed through a Janine Fulla self help book that he checked out of the prison library. He chose that book for a specific reason. It would verify to the parole board that he was still working to improve himself. He would continue to kiss their asses until he was released.

He flipped a page when out of the corner of his eye he saw a guard coming towards him. Ray closed his book and looked up. "Hello sir."

"Get up Cooke," The guard ordered. "You're wanted in the warden's office, so let's go."

Ray packed up his tray. "Do you know why?"

The guard was impatient. "Does it look like I know? The warden doesn't like to wait, so let's go."

A few minutes later he stood outside Warden Currie's office. His hands and feet in shackles. Brad Currie was a thirty-year veteran of the provincial penitentiary system. He was average height with a thick upper body and big hands. He was nearing retirement, but he still enjoyed the power he was bestowed inside his cement walls.

When they entered the warden's office the warden instructed the guard to remove the shackles and leave them. He offered Ray a seat. "Would you like coffee? A good cup and not the piss in the cafeteria."

Ray rubbed his wrists. "I'd love a good cup of coffee, sir. Thank you."

The warden handed him a mug and Ray gripped it like he'd never let it go. It had been a long time since he had such a simple pleasure. The smell was overwhelming, and he took a moment to enjoy it.

The warden looked comfortable behind his desk. "I'm guessing you've figured out why I called you?"

Ray was anxious. "I'm hoping you've got some great news."

The warden nodded. "I do. Your parole has come through."

Ray was thrilled. He was finally going home. "Thank you, sir."

"Don't get too excited yet," Warned Currie. "There are a few conditions tied to your release that we need to discuss."

The idea that he was getting out started to sink in. He'd do almost anything to be free again. "What are they?"

The warden looked at his computer. "I've read your file and you're obviously a very smart man."

Ray rolled his eyes. "Apparently not smart enough. I ended up in here."

"As long as you agree to the conditions, you will be released." the warden told him.

Those words were magical. "Can I ask what the conditions are?"

The warden shifted in his seat. "The first few are fairly standard. No drugs, no alcohol, check in with your parole officer. Keep your nose clean. The standard stuff."

Ray tried to contain his excitement. "Is there anything else?"

"Yes, there is," The warden hit a buzzer under his desk and the door behind Ray opened. It was the same door that he entered. A large man with shoulder-length hair and a big beard entered. "I assume you remember Detective Murphy?"

Ray nearly choked on his coffee. It was the same Detective

Murphy who busted him for cocaine. "Yeah, I do."

"It's been a while, Cooke," Murphy walked over and took a seat beside Ray. "How have you been keeping?"

Ray despised the narcotics detective for what he had done to him. He kept his anger in check. "Why are you here?"

Murphy smirked. "I'm the last condition of your parole."

FORTY-SEVEN

The prime minister entered Hutchinson's estate after his security team gave it the all-clear. He pulled off his coat and hung it over the back of a wooden chair. Pierre Elliot was now in his mid-sixties and was famous for his magnetic personality that could still dominate any room he entered. He had never married and had no children. That was a conscious life decision.

Elliot's meeting was with a man he had known for years. They both had massive personalities, and that caused them to clash on more than one occasion. The difference between them was that one had billions and the other was a civil servant with major power. They chose different paths and had varying opinions, but both had enjoyed success.

Hugh Hutchinson closed the door behind him. They were the only two inside the office. He threw his jacket over Pierre's and headed to a liquor cabinet. "Do you want a drink?"

"Pour me a double of your good scotch," it was more of an order than a request, "and get me a good Cuban cigar to go with it."

Hutchinson chirped sarcastically. "You're the prime minister and you need to come to my home to get a good scotch and cigar? What's with that?"

Pierre chuckled. "You have a bigger budget."

The billionaire poured two healthy shots from a bottle of private stock he had distilled in the Highlands of Scotland. He had a vested interest in the distillery. "Here you go, Mr. Prime Minister."

"Thank you." Elliot tasted the scotch and let the flavour unfold. "Tell me, what the hell is going on with North Korea?"

Hutchinson wasn't sure himself. "All I can say is you might want to shake things up in your Cabinet. You can start by replacing your fool of a finance minister."

Elliot had heard about their meeting and was prepared. "It's not that easy and we both know why. Remember, he's apart of the deal and it could be damaging if we suddenly push him out. He's one of only four that know about our agreement with the North Koreans and it's imperative that it stays that way."

"I don't need to be reminded of what's at stake," Hugh sipped his drink, "but Fisher is a weak link that could sink this deal. He lost $25 million and that exposes us on many levels."

"I agree, Fisher could be a problem, but leave him to me," The prime minister wanted to enjoy his cigar. "The real question is how did the person who stole our money even know about it?"

Hugh agreed. "My point exactly. There's something we're not in control of."

"We've taken numerous precautions and the circle is small," Pierre puffed his cigar until the embers glowed. "There has to be a mole amongst us and that's a serious issue."

Hugh nodded.

Pierre faced his friend. "Can I trust you?"

Hugh slammed his fist down on the table. "Are you fucking serious?"

Pierre didn't even blink at Hugh's outburst. He'd seen it before. "The stakes are high, so I don't know who to trust. But I do know you'd screw your own mother if the price was right."

Hugh laughed. "You're right. I would. But I will tell you this only once, I am not the thief."

The prime minister believed him. "Let's chat about your New Year's Eve party."

"What about it?"

"I heard that Carol attended."

"She came with John Fisher," Hugh shook his head. "There's another example of his terrible decision-making."

"Did they leave together?"

"She took a taxi to the airport, and she left alone."

Pierre paused to think. "Why was she at your party? She doesn't do the social scene and why with Fisher of all people?"

"I have no idea," Hugh replied.

"Let's walk through the events of that night," Pierre finished his drink and tapped his glass on the wooden table, indicating he wanted another. "She arrived with Fisher to the biggest party of the year and leaves without even celebrating the New Year. She had no reason to be at your party. But she was there?"

"I have no idea what the wacky bitch is up to and I don't have time to care," Hugh topped up their drinks. "I never saw her and why does it matter?"

Pierre disagreed. "Maybe she's the mole."

"That's crazy. How?"

"Even if Fisher were stupid enough to tell her anything, only a super genius could hack through the security to steal it. Anyone with that kind of talent would be on the government's radar."

"True enough," Pierre wasn't convinced. "What next?"

"If I find anything, I will let you know."

"We have a few more things to discuss before I pick up my date."

"You have a date?" Hugh couldn't hold his laughter. "Who would want to date an old fuck like you?"

"Is there a question in there," Pierre wasn't amused, "because the answer is a gorgeous blonde who likes money more than my looks."

Hugh grabbed the bottle of scotch and continued to snicker. "I do have a serious question, Pierre."

"Ask away and I'll decide if I can answer it."

"Why are we dealing with the North Koreans?" Hugh had wanted to ask this numerous times in the past. "I understand the numbers, but if this goes sideways, you're going down in history as one of the most corrupt world leaders of this generation."

"I'll never be connected to it." Pierre replied confidently.

FORTY-EIGHT

It was just after five when Joshua arrived at the park entrance. It had been a long day and all he really wanted to do was meet up with Mickey and fish. He stood at the gate holding a rod in one hand and his tackle box in the other. He couldn't see Cassie or Jonny. Maybe they were running late.

The green space was a dozen acres and was comparable in design to any provincial park. There were wooden picnic tables with firepits spaced out along the winding trails. And a freshwater swimming hole with a high diving board was a popular spot with the younger recruits. A wall of towering fir trees provided protection from the ocean travellers.

Joshua started through the trails and found Cassie at a picnic table. Her eyes were glued to her iPad. He took a seat. "Been here long?"

"Ten minutes," She looked up, "so where's Jonny?"

"He said he'd be here"

"I was hoping he could help me," She sounded disappointed. "I wanted to discuss designs for a new gadget."

Joshua glanced at his fishing rod. "Then why am I here?"

"You were supposed to bring Jonny." she admitted. "Sorry."

To Joshua's relief, Jonny appeared. He wore cut-off jeans and a sleeveless t-shirt. "I'm going swimming after we're done."

Joshua slid over to make space for Jonny. "I don't have a lot of time, so let's get at it."

For the next thirty minutes the three geniuses discussed ways to get the vapor dispersed in crowds. They discussed wind, height, and volume, but never came up with a solution. There problem was they had no idea where Carol would use it first.

Joshua paid close attention to the time. He didn't want to be late. "I'm off to meet, Mickey."

Jonny stood up. "Let's finish this later. I'm going swimming." He looked nervously at Cassie. "Do you want to join me? We can get a pepperoni pizza when we're done."

Cassie pushed her long black hair out of her eyes and revealed a smile that left no doubt what her answer was.

FORTY-NINE

Joshua hurried down to the waterfront to join up with Mickey, who was already casting his line into the water. As Joshua got closer, he saw a big fishtail sticking out of a five-gallon bucket. Mickey had landed a big one.

This was Joshua's first-time to fish. His dad wasn't a fisherman, so they never went. He paid close attention to Mickey, watching him cast his lure into the waves. The thought of catching a fish thrilled Joshua, but the idea he might screw up made him nervous.

Curtis talked about how he and his dad used to fish in the Yukon. Joshua could never contribute father and son stories like that. It had already been four months since that rainy night when Mickey hurried him out the back door of the auditorium. It seemed a lot longer. His last image of his parents was their frightened look when the bulbs began to explode.

Mickey stood on a large rock watching the tip of his rod. He was dressed for the misty conditions with a raincoat and big rubber boots. When he saw Joshua, he reeled in his line. "The fish are biting, so let's get you in the water."

He taught Joshua how to setup his rod. The kid was a quick learner. When he was ready, Mickey walked him over to some rocks that were half-submerged in the saltwater. "You keep an eye on the tide and make sure you always have a way back to the beach."

Joshua looked uneasy at the rocks, but he wasn't going to complain. He trusted Mickey. "Yes, sir."

"Get up there," Mickey ordered, "and here's your rod."

After a quick lesson in casting, Mickey returned to his own spot.

The two fished and traded barbs for the next two hours and Joshua had the time of his life. He never once thought about anything other than his next cast.

And then his line whipped off his reel. He had a fish on. After getting over the surprise, he remembered what Mickey taught him and kept the line tense. He started reeling. When it was all done his first fish was an eight-pound Coho. It was a highlight of his young life.

When the sun began to set, Mickey decided it was time to call it a night.

"One more cast?" begged Joshua. "Please?"

"Okay, only one more," Mickey chuckled. "You still have to clean your catch."

Joshua's eyes bulged. "Clean?"

"You're not a real fisherman until you stink of fish. Grab your knife from the tackle box."

On the hike back, Mickey stopped on the trail and put his gear up against a fallen log. Joshua did the same. Both admired the half-moon rising from the ocean. There were sailboats enjoying the beautiful evening and the air was peaceful.

Twenty-five years ago, this was the spot where Mickey's life changed forever. It was where he fought and killed a Golden Eagle gang member. Years later Mickey learned that the police had ruled Frank's death an accident. His friends told the police he was goofing around and tripped over the side.

Mickey left Gabriola that night and stowed away on a freighter the next morning headed for Asian ports with a cargo of west coast lumber. After a day of hiding under a tarp, he needed to relieve himself and was caught sneaking out of the bathroom.

He was hauled into the captain's quarters where he was given a choice. The grey-haired man was wakened from his sleep and wasn't in a forgiving mood. He put Mickey on latrine duty, warning the kid. "We usually throw stowaways overboard, so those toilets better be clean boy. If you're still on board tomorrow, you'll get one meal a day."

The bathrooms stunk, but Mickey figured out the smell wasn't as repulsive if he stuffed his nostrils with toilet paper soaked with liquid soap. The Filipino sailors would pick on him and intentionally forget to flush to make his job even more repulsive. It never bothered Mickey.

Whenever he was alone in the bathrooms, he used the mirrors to shadowbox, and he got skilled using a mop handle as a kali stick. He never lost his passion for the martial arts and he worked on his techniques whenever he had the chance.

Joshua looked up to Mickey like most kids admire a professional athlete. He idolized this man. "Where did you learn to fish, Mickey? Did your dad teach you?"

Mickey didn't mask his hatred for his father. "My dad never taught me anything."

"Oh." Joshua said apologetically.

"He was an asshole. I taught myself how to fish over the side of a ship."

Joshua was full of questions. "Really?"

"I got caught stowing away on a freighter when I was fourteen."

"Why were you hiding?"

"That's a different story for another time," Mickey shrugged. "I had to catch fish if I wanted to eat anything healthy."

"Did you always catch fish?"

"Nope and on those days, I only got a piece of bread and a cup of warm water to live on," Mickey smiled, remembering those days clearly. "I once went two days without eating anything other than a stale bread."

"Seriously?"

"It's like anything in life," Mickey picked up his fishing gear. "If you want something bad enough, you have to be willing to fight for it."

"Did you fight?"

Mickey pointed to the scar tissue above both eyes. "I got this learning how to take a punch."

Joshua tried not to gawk at the scars. "What did you do on the ship?"

"When I wasn't cleaning toilets, I was part of the entertainment. They had contests to entertain the crew."

Joshua was entranced by Mickey's story. "What kind of contests?"

Mickey stopped them on the trail. "Are you sure you're old enough? It's pretty graphic."

Joshua bubbled with excitement. "Yes. I'm old enough."

Mickey took a seat on another log and Joshua sat beside him. "The ship's captain would put up twenty-dollars for the winner of a bare-knuckle fight."

"Did you enter?"

"I didn't really have a choice," explained Mickey. "As a stowaway, I was considered a criminal in the minds of the sailors. I had to fight. They wanted to see the Indian get a shit-kicking. They didn't care that I was only fourteen."

Joshua could hardly sit still. "Who'd you fight?"

"A big South American sailor they called Boulder," Mickey remembered the fighter and the fear he had felt. "He got his nickname because of his big head. He was undefeated and was a vicious fighter."

"Did you fight him?" Joshua didn't want to hear about Mickey losing. "Did he hurt you?"

Mickey could remember the smell of diesel and the loud cheers in the background. None were for the underdog. "He definitely tried, and he came close. I remembered what I learned from my mentor."

"Is that Bruce Lee?" The story fascinated Joshua. "Was he really tough?"

Mickey patted Joshua on the head. "We'll have to watch one of his movies one day."

"Cool," Joshua beamed. "I'd love that."

"Anyway, Boulder and I climbed into this roped off box they used as a ring."

"Was there a referee?"

"Not exactly," Mickey remembered how scared he felt, knowing everyone on the ship wanted Boulder to kick his ass. "If you were knocked down or tried to escape, the sailors pushed you back inside. You couldn't run or quit. It was fight until someone couldn't fight anymore."

"Wow," Joshua wasn't aware things like this even happened. "That must have been crazy to see."

Mickey laughed. "Try being in the ring."

"What happened next?"

"I had to out-think him because I wasn't going to win a slugfest," Mickey recalled. "I knew the big man would tire quickly if I kept him moving. I stayed away and let him chase me until he dropped his guard."

"Did he hit you?"

"Yes, but I was lucky because they were just glancing blows. After deking back and forth, I found my range and when his hands got heavy, I started hitting him at will."

"What does heavy hands mean?"

"Tired arms," Mickey explained. "He dropped his guard and I peppered him with jabs. I remember the crowd going silent when they realized their champ was about to go down."

"You knocked him down?" Joshua was excited. "How hard did you hit him?"

"After a strong uppercut that knocked him backwards, I finished the fight with a side-kick to the head. He was out cold before he hit the deck face first."

Joshua cheered. "Did you really knock him out?"

Mickey smiled. "We need to get these fish on some ice."

When Joshua got back to his room, he googled Bruce Lee. The man was just like Mickey.

FIFTY

The realism that he served five miserable years behind prison walls was made harder knowing that he was innocent. Someone had set him up and they planned it perfectly. He decided over time that the person responsible for him being in prison was someone he knew. That made it even harder to accept. The one question he needed answered was, why?

Revenge was a common topic at mealtime, and Ray wasn't immune to it. He was about to walk out the front gate a free man. He was leaving with a much better understanding of how precious life is. Someone took five years of his, and he was determined to return the favour.

Ray sat on the edge of his cot for the last time. He was wearing the same clothes when he checked in. They fit loosely. He had dropped almost ten pounds eating prison food. He had celebrated his fiftieth birthday doing a crossword puzzle instead of drinking fine champagne and having sex with his much younger wife.

His legal career was flushed down the toilet and his old circle of friends he had before he pled guilty were long gone. He didn't care. Fuck them. The one question that he needed an answer for was if his wife would even take him back. He hadn't seen or spoke to her since his day in court.

Ray was escorted to the front gate and the first thing he did on the outside was take a deep cleansing breath. He let his lungs enjoy the fresh air. It was free, just like he was. He had a small bag filled with his things that he dumped into the first garbage can he passed. He wanted nothing that would remind him of the past five years. It was over.

Ray found Detective Murphy sitting in an older van with the windows sealed. It looked and smelt like an undercover vehicle. One of the conditions for his parole was to help Murphy with an assignment. That was all he was told. "Thanks for the ride."

"Get in before you get wet." Murphy barked.

This was not how Ray envisioned his first hours of freedom. He was stuck in a smelly van with the man who put him in prison. He rolled down his window and stared up at the cloud covered sky. "Ready when you are."

After driving for nearly ten minutes, Murphy finally broke the uneasy silence. "We're meeting with Sergeant Smith."

"Who's Sergeant Smith?" Ray had a request. "Before we do, can we stop and get something to eat? I skipped breakfast."

Murphy grunted. "We'll find a drive-thru."

When Murphy pulled into the police station, Ray felt uneasy. He had some bad memories from this building. "I'm not sure how I can help you guys."

"The sergeant thinks you can, "Murphy barked, "so, let's go."

The men said nothing else until they were inside Smith's office. Murphy pointed to a chair. "Want a coffee?"

Ray nodded but refused to sit. He was done taking orders from authority. He looked around the office. There wasn't much to it. A small wooden desk with a filing cabinet. Didn't the police know about e-files?

Murphy returned and handed Ray a cup of steaming black coffee. He watched Ray's face and waited for his reaction. The detective remembered Ray's comments about prison food and the station coffee was terrible. It was a rookie prank.

Ray took a sip and looked for a garbage can to spit it out. "That crap is pathetic."

Murphy laughed. "Welcome home."

Sergeant Smith entered his office and gave Ray a firm handshake. "Thanks for coming. I'm sorry about the coffee."

Ray glanced at the detective, who still had a smirk on his face. "I didn't have much of a choice."

Murphy disagreed. "You always have a choice, like when you chose to plead guilty."

Ray knew exactly what Murphy was reminding him of. "You're such an asshole."

Smith stepped between them. "I apologize for pulling you in here. I'm sure you have a long list of places you'd rather be."

Ray didn't disagree.

"I'm investigating the kidnapping of an eleven-year old boy and the possible murder of his teacher," Smith jumped right into why he wanted Ray there. "And I don't have much time."

"A murder?"

"That's what I believe," continued Smith, "and that's why you're here. Did the detective tell you what I need you to do?"

"Not a word," Ray answered, "but you've got my attention.

FIFTY-ONE

It had been a week since Peter reported back to Mickey regarding his meeting with Sergeant Smith. Mickey did some of his own investigating and discovered the sergeant had lied to Peter about the video. It had been a ruse to see what Peter might reveal under pressure. The question was: what did he say?

Peter was called back to the complex for a second meeting. This time it was with both Carol and Mickey, which indicated something serious was going on. Peter sat in the office and tried to remain calm, but it was impossible.

He stood up, hoping it would ease the butterflies in his stomach. It didn't, so he finally decided to grab a water. It didn't help either. He couldn't stop himself from wondering why he was called back. Tracy was never far from his thoughts.

Mickey entered with Carol.

Peter noticed that they both seemed relaxed. It was a good sign. Mickey grabbed a juice and then they settled around the table. He could sense Peter was nervous and got things going. "Thanks for coming. I know it's inconvenient, but I have some great news."

Peter seemed surprised. "What's that?"

"There's no video," Mickey assured him. "The sergeant lied to you."

"Why would he lie?"

"That's what they do," Carol explained. "To see what you might tell them. Did you say anything, Peter?"

"Just what I was told to say."

"That's good to hear," Mickey sounded reassured. "Carol and I both think it would be a good idea to get you out of here for awhile. At least until things settle down."

Peter was curious. "Away where?"

Carol said. "To New York. We have an assignment that's perfect for your skillset and it'll give you some time out of the spotlight."

"I agree that all of this shit has me freaked out," Peter admitted. "I'm not wired for this kind of stress."

Mickey nodded in agreement. "And that's why the assignment in New York will be perfect. We need a chemical engineer and you're the best."

Peter knew the decision was already made for him. "When do I leave?"

Carol slid him an envelope. "Tomorrow morning."

Peter walked with them until they got to the doorway. "Thanks for the assignment. I won't let you down."

Carol smiled. "I know you won't. You'll be contacted when you arrive."

Peter exited the complex and boarded a boat waiting to take him back to Nanaimo.

Carol walked with Mickey. "Is everything in place for Peter?"

"Yes, ma'am," He assured her. "Everything is good to go."

FIFTY-TWO

John Fisher took an aisle seat on their Q series Bombardier private jet. The sleek aircraft could carry up to fourteen passengers, but today there were only four. They were returning from a weekend of fun in the desert.

The pilot was waiting for permission to take off from Sky Harbor International airport in Phoenix. Everything with the aircraft was ready. Besides the crew, Fisher was joined by three generous party supporters. They were returning to Ottawa after three days of golfing and too many pitchers of cold beer.

When the finance minister made the choice to escape the pressures in Ottawa, he knew it would come with a barrage of criticism. And he knew where the criticism would come from, but he didn't care. Travelling on a private jet and staying in a five-star resort was a perk of the job that he enjoyed taking advantage of.

The captain announced they had received clearance and would be taking off in a few minutes. He instructed his passengers to take their seats and buckle in. Everyone did as they were instructed, and John closed his eyes. His cellphone rang. He recognized the number and reluctantly answered. "Hello."

"John, it's Hugh Hutchinson."

Couldn't this asshole wait until he was back in his office on Monday. He knew the reason for the call but asked anyway. "What can I do for you, Mr. Hutchinson?"

Hutchinson was more blunt than usual. "Pierre and I want an update on the $25 million. Anything to report?"

"We're still working on it." Fisher wasn't in the mood for an interrogation. He wanted to nap. "Like I've already told you, when I get an update, I will tell the prime minister."

Hutchinson pushed Fisher. "There is a real concern about your focus and how seriously you're taking this."

Fisher turned away from his guests and kept his tone civil. "I'm taking it very seriously and I don't need you calling me to tell me my job."

"I hear you're in Phoenix golfing with some buddies," Hutchinson already knew the answer. "Is that true?"

Fisher was ready to end the call. "I don't report to you and I strongly suggest you back off. Like I said, when I have an update, I will tell the prime minister personally."

Hugh yelled into his phone. "You've had four days to solve this, but instead you went golfing! You're an incompetent fool!"

Fisher fought back. "It was my decision and I'll stand by it, with or without your approval."

"It was a stupid decision," Hutchinson scowled sarcastically. "You have a safe flight, and we'll see you back in Ottawa."

Fisher sat in his seat while the plane took off. He was still angry when they levelled out at twenty thousand feet. The flight attendant brought him a drink and snacks. Thirty minutes into their flight home the plane hit some rough turbulence over Colorado and the captain turned on the seatbelt light. And then, without any warning, the plane stalled and fell out of the sky.

Everyone onboard died upon impact.

FIFTY-THREE

For the next hour, Ray was brought up to speed on current affairs around the city. A lot had taken place while he was away, and it upset him to hear about the fire at John Woodlands. He attended the school with David in the early eighties.

Smith handed Ray two photographs.

"Who are these kids?"

"The young girl is Cassie Chang. She was last seen in her university dorm a month ago."

"Any idea where she went?" Ray knew it was a stupid question before he finished asking it. "I mean..."

Smith held up his hand. "No idea. Like the kid in the second picture, she simply vanished. My theory is both kids participated in their disappearance."

Ray didn't agree. "That's a stretch. There would have to be something very enticing to lure them away. You said they were both highly intelligent?"

"They're little Einstein's," Smith took the photos from Ray. "The Chang kid could be worth billions if her food formula works out."

"Do you think that's why she was taken?"

Smith glanced over at Murphy. "We both do."

"And the boy?" Ray asked. "Is he going to be worth billions?"

Murphy shrugged. "Probably."

"There's been a lot going on since I left," Ray decided. "So, let's talk about what you need me to do."

Smith continued. "There is one big piece we haven't mentioned yet."

"And what is that?"

Murphy handed him another photo. "Her name is Laura Nelsen."

Ray gazed at the photo. She was gorgeous. "How does she fit into all of this?"

"She was Tracy Addison's girlfriend. They lived together, and we think she knows more than she's telling us."

Ray took a second look at her photo. This beautiful girl was gay? Too bad. "Why do you think she's holding back? Could she be involved in all of this?"

"We met a few days ago to see if she could help us."

"Was she able to?"

"She had all the right answers," Murphy said, "and she had a great story that covered everything we asked."

"You don't sound convinced?"

Smith responded to Ray. "What we don't understand is why everyone is working so hard to keep us from finding out what really happened that night."

Ray still didn't see how he fit in. "How can a disbarred lawyer fresh out of prison help you?"

The big Irish detective grinned. "We want you to roleplay for us."

Ray was completely confused now.

"We want you to become Tracy Addison's long-lost piece of shit older brother," Smith told him. "You show up at Laura's door and claim to be Tracy's brother and you're here to collect her life insurance money."

"Does she even have a brother?"

Smith answered. "We have no idea and if we're right, Laura won't know either."

"Why wouldn't Tracy tell her about me?"

"Because you are a world class asshole that she hated." Murphy was enjoying himself.

Smith studied Ray. "Are you in?"

"Do I have a choice?"

Smith thought about his answer. "No."

"What if Laura doesn't buy the story?"

"You get the hell out. If we're reading this right, these people aren't scared to kill you."

Ray sighed. "Nice to know."

FIFTY-FOUR

The tragic plane crash with Canada's Finance Minister on board was a front-page story across the country. John Fisher's death was mourned on Parliament Hill by all three parties. The National Transportation and Safety Board was heading the investigation, with the RCMP keeping close tabs on their findings.

Carol read about the crash while lying in bed. She recalled her time with Fisher and how easy it was to get him to reveal a secret. The man loved gorgeous women more than money and power.

Fisher spent an hour in Carol's hotel room with a beautiful associate that Carol introduced as a friend. When they were done in the bedroom, the finance minister had revealed much more to Carol than she expected on the ride to Hugh's party.

He confirmed his involvement in a weapons deal with the North Koreans and explained in detail how the money was going to be handled. The video from the Fly verified everything he said and incriminating against those who were involved. Did someone find out he had loose lips?

"That plane crash was no accident." Carol muttered to herself, as she adjusted her pillow. "Somebody wanted him dead."

She slept with a clear conscience that night.

FIFTY-FIVE

Getting the assignment to take the $25 million from the finance minister's offshore account excited Curtis. He didn't usually know the people he robbed, but this time the name was familiar to him. Taking the money from an account that was used to hide a North Korean transaction gave him some gratification. He didn't know what the money was for, but he knew by the effort to hide it that it had to be dirty.

A week after he emptied the account, he read a news article. It was about a plane crash in Colorado. One of the victims was John Fisher. Curtis couldn't help but wonder if his robbery motivated the crash.

Jonny walked in and startled Curtis. "What are you up to?" Curtis shut his laptop. "You need to knock, dude."

Jonny didn't apologize. The gadget genius wore baggy sweats and his scattered hair looked like he just got out of bed. "Do you have five minutes?"

Curtis yawned. "I could use a break. What's up?"

Jonny helped himself to a soda out of Curtis's fridge. "Do you ever wonder what we're doing here?"

"Everyday. Why the question?"

Jonny opened his soda and slurped in the foam fizzing out of the bottle. "It's great that I get to work on cool gadgets, but I'm curious about the end game."

Curtis looked disinterested. He already had an end game that he wasn't ready to discuss with anybody. "If you came here for answers, I can't help you dude."

Jonny scratched his head. "I wonder if Carol or Mickey even have one?"

"There is definitely an end game," Rebutted Curtis. "They didn't build this place or risk life in prison for kidnapping without a serious plan. There is something big going on and I think it's getting close."

"Do you think she'll ever tell us?"

"Why would you want to know?" Curtis asked. "We were brought here to create or execute. Look at what you do and then look at me. How is that connected?"

Jonny waited for an answer.

Curtis continued. "I don't have the answers and I'm not expecting Carol to stroll in here one day and invite me for tea."

Jonny sipped his soda. "That makes sense, I guess."

"But things seem to be changing." Curtis suggested.

"What do you mean?"

"The Chang girl. She's the first person they've brought on board that already had a project. Her vapor food. That tells me things are coming together."

"So, how are gadgets, money and vapor food connected?"

Curtis threw his arms up. "I have no idea."

"Me neither."

FIFTY-SIX

All the recruits and key staff received an email notification from Carol. She summoned them all to the board room for an important introduction. No details were attached to the message. Just be there at ten.

Curtis ran into Joshua on the way. "Any idea what's up?"

Joshua rolled his eyes. "No idea, but it must be important if my…." He caught himself. "…if Carol is calling us together."

Curtis shot Joshua a sideways glance. He said nothing, but the staggered comment caught his attention. They entered the board room. There was a long table with a dozen chairs circled around it. A side table had some refreshments, and they both grabbed a cookie.

Cassie sat alone at the table and looked like she felt out of place. She was still trying to fit in. It didn't take long for Jonny to plunk himself down on the seat beside her. He had a crush on the new girl.

Joshua wanted to leave them alone, but Curtis had the opposite reaction. "Let's join the lovebirds."

He reluctantly followed Curtis and the four sat side by side. He caught Cassie's attention and they exchanged polite smiles. Joshua hadn't said anything to anyone about his meeting with her. He knew that Carol would never allow Cassie to make an announcement that her vapor food was completed. It would simply be another ticked box on the list and Cassie would be assigned a new project.

Mickey showed up and went straight to the refreshment table and grabbed a bran muffin. He locked eyes with Joshua and gave him a thumbs up. They were both thinking about their night of fishing and Mickey's stories.

Mickey wasn't sure why he felt so comfortable around Joshua. The stories he told the twelve-year old were something he had never shared with anyone. All he knew was that for the first time in his life he trusted someone. It was weird that it was a kid.

It was now ten o'clock and Carol strolled into the room. The conversations all stopped, and everyone took a seat. Her gaze had away of making you feel guilty of a crime you didn't commit. She took her usual seat at the head of the table and before saying a word she took a second to do a quick head count. Everyone was there. "I don't have a lot of time, but I thought I should make this announcement personally."

Joshua glanced at Shirley, wondering if.

"Okay, let's get at it," She began. "Because of the growing demand on my time, and Mickey's, I decided I need to bring someone on board to keep you all focused on your assignments and their deadlines."

She let that sink in. Curtis didn't like it.

"No questions. Good," Carol continued. "As you all know, things are getting busy and there is still a lot that has to be done. The man I'm bringing in has an engineering background and you will now keep him updated and run everything through him. I'll only get involved if necessary."

The room was quiet. Everyone was hanging on her every word. Even though these recruits were brilliant minds, they were used to structure and consistency in their lives. This was a major change for most of them and the anxiety it created showed on their faces.

Cassie held up her hand. "Can I ask a question?"

Carol nodded, giving her the okay.

"Is this new person going to be able to take control of our projects if they choose to?"

Carol licked her bottom lip. "Why do you ask?"

"When I was in university no one cared what I did with my spare time until my concept started to become reality. Then the school wanted to take over," Cassie took a second, "and that is why I chose to come here. You promised me control till the end."

Carol realized she had an audience and was on the spot. She didn't like the position Cassie put her in. Her tone was sharp. "We'll do what is best for the organization. No one is an individual here."

Joshua couldn't look at Cassie, but he felt her disappointment.

"Okay, like I said, my time is limited," Carol looked at the open doorway and in stepped the biggest and blackest man Joshua had ever seen. "I'd like to introduce Wendell Presley."

Jonny twitched nervously. "I know that guy from somewhere."

No one heard him. They were all wondering how this man was going to interrupt their lives.

FIFTY-SEVEN

Suzanne Lacy was filled with a young person's energy when she realized her money troubles were behind her. For a brief time, she enjoyed the positive experience. She knew in her heart of hearts that Curtis was behind the mysterious deposit. That meant he must be alive and watching her.

She battled with her moral obligation to update Tom. The ex husband had a right to know that his son might be alive, but she had no obligation to mention the money. She had to come up with a believable lie.

Tom stood in the kitchen of his rented condo. The alcohol was winning. He looked ten years older than he was. Hitting the pub scene every night after work and living on fast foods was his life at this point. He had no reason to stop. In his diluted mind, he was the reason Curtis was dead.

He leaned up against the counter to stop the shakes while he poured his morning coffee. When his phone rang, he recognized the Yukon number and wanted to ignore it. It was his ex-wife, and he wasn't in the mood for another rant about his infidelity. It wasn't long after his return to Vancouver that his new girlfriend left when he chose to enjoy whiskey more than he enjoyed her.

He splashed some water on his face. "Hey, Suzanne." He grabbed his coffee and headed to the patio to have a smoke. "To what do I owe the pleasure?"

Suzanne regretted the call already. "Look, I know you're busy with what's her name, so I'll keep this brief."

Tom ignored the obvious shot at his ex-girlfriend and decided not to give Suzanne the satisfaction of an update. It would only give her another reason to badger him. "What can I do for you? It must be important if you're calling me."

Suzanne could tell Tom was hungover but chose to ignore it. She had decided he had a right to know everything. "I have some news I need you to listen to before asking questions. Can you do that?"

Tom took a long drag from his cigarette and let the smoke escape through his nose. "I'm listening?"

Suzanne struggled to get the courage she needed to admit her mistake. "I got myself into some financial trouble."

Tom didn't even blink. "How much?"

"Seventy-five thousand, give or take," She waited for the beratement, but it never came. "I spent it hiring people to look for Curtis."

"Are you calling for money? I have a little, but nothing like the amount you're talking about."

"No, I don't need your money. That's why I'm calling," She thought about her decision. "Someone paid off my debt in full and I think it was Curtis."

Tom wasn't sure how to respond. "Are you serious? Why would you think that?"

"I just have a hunch he was involved."

FIFTY-EIGHT

Suzanne could smell the whiskey over the phone and was worried about Tom after she hung up. Their son would be horrified to see how far his father had fallen since he went missing. She had a hunch that the bimbo he slept with was no longer in his life. For that, she had no pity.

She needed some fresh air and decided to take her new puppy for a walk. She was tired of being alone in the house and found herself a new companion in the shape of an energetic Siberian husky she named Rupert. She grabbed her jacket and gloves before hooking Rupert up to his leash. The temperature was minus ten and her dog was anxious to get outside. Rupert loved this kind of weather.

When they were in the backyard, the puppy pulled towards a snow filled trail on the east side of her property. It headed along the Yukon river and was the same trail Curtis took on that fateful day. This would be her first walk on it since the search ended.

The trail joined up with a main walkway along the river and Suzanne pulled her toque down to protect her ears from the nasty winds. There was no one else in sight and she was leery against going too far. With the wind drifted snow and icy patches, the trail was dangerous, but Rupert wanted to explore.

After what was fifteen minutes, but seemed much longer, she decided it was time to turn around. Rupert pulled and she tightened her grip. They started back up the trail. "Let's go home boy."

Without any warning, Rupert caught the scent of something, and the puppy pulled harder. The sudden jerk caused Suzanne to lose her footing and fall to her knees. The pain from hitting a rock caused her to let go of the leash and Rupert ran off into the woods.

After the pain subsided, Suzanne picked herself up and turned her attention to the dog. "Get back here, you little bugger."

The puppy wanted to play and used his freedom to run and explore with no real purpose. Suzanne followed him into the trees and stepped carefully. "Rupert, get back here."

The more she coaxed the puppy, the further Rupert ran into the trees. Suzanne could see that her dog had no intention of coming, so she followed him deeper. She finally caught up to him sniffing at something that had his full attention. "You stay there, you silly puppy."

Rupert made no attempt to escape. The dog was preoccupied with clawing at something buried in the snow. She thought he had found an animal carcass and wanted to get him away before he ate it. When she got closer, she realized it was a green garbage bag partially frozen in the snow. "Leave the that alone."

She grabbed the leash while the dog was distracted. When she got closer, she saw a black ballcap with a large orange 'U' embossed on it sticking out of a hole that Rupert made. She ignored the bag and focused on getting back to the trail. "Let's head home."

An hour later Suzanne was enjoying a hot chocolate when it hit her. She grabbed her phone and started flipping through old photos. There it was. Curtis playing catch with his father, wearing the same cap.

FIFTY-NINE

A hostess at the Sword and Barrel restaurant greeted Ray and led him to the corner booth that he had requested over the phone. It offered some privacy. Tiffany and Ray had shared this table on many special occasions and the restaurant held a lot of great memories for them. It was also where he was headed on that forgettable night.

After he was seated, he requested two menus and a black coffee. He remembered all the key points Smith told him to emphasize. The sergeant needed answers to determine the direction of the case. They were counting on him to get them.

Ray second guessed his decision to even get involved. What if he screwed up? And then he recognized Laura Nelson in the lobby from her picture. She was simply stunning, and she was headed in his direction. This gorgeous lady is a lesbian? What a waste.

As she stepped closer, Ray tried not to stare. It was hard not to. Her form fitting woolen sweater barely reached her belly button. It was obvious she was also braless. This was going to be an interesting lunch.

He stood and held out his hand, but she ignored it. "You must be Laura Nelsen. Thanks for meeting with me."

Laura took a seat and Ray did the same.

After a moment of awkwardness, Ray started slowly. "I hope you like this place. The food is good here."

"I'm sure it is." Laura sized him up. His jacket was expensive, but he could probably dump the Simon Cowell open shirt look. "So, why are we here. You were very mysterious on the phone."

Ray couldn't stop staring at her. She was as beautiful as his wife.

"To be truthful it's a little embarrassing."

They were interrupted by their server. "Can I get you anything from the bar?"

Laura requested a coffee and decided to order lunch. If the conversation got boring or uncomfortable, she could exit early. She requested the grilled chicken salad and Ray asked for a medium rare steak sandwich.

Once the server left them, they exchanged some pleasant conversation. They talked about the weather, work, and where they grew up. Neither had a problem lying to the other when answering questions.

Ray decided to turn it up a notch to gauge her response. "I appreciate you meeting on such short notice. I imagine you're busy."

"I'm not that busy and your voicemail was confusing," Laura's tone was defensive. "You mentioned Tracy and something about an insurance policy. That got my attention."

Ray remembered Sergeant Smith's first key point. "I was hoping you could help me with Tracy's life insurance. Things like the policy payout amount and who she listed as her beneficiary?"

Laura's fake smile disappeared. Who was this jerk across from her? He seemed a little old to be a brother. She decided to do her own investigating. "Why are you here? Are you a private dick working for someone?"

"I'm not an investigator and I'm sorry if I came on too strong," Ray backed off. "I know you lived with Tracy, but I'll bet she never mentioned me."

"I'll pass on making the bet," Laura scowled and already regretted her decision to come. "and what do you want? I don't have time to play games."

His strategy was paying off. She was upset. "When I heard Tracy died, I decided I should probably come and pay my respects and help out."

Laura controlled her anger that was building. "Help with what, exactly?"

"Whatever needs to get done, I guess."

"First, look me in the face and not at my tits," her tone was ripe, "and second, how are you connected to my Tracy?"

Ray lifted his head and dropped a huge surprise. "I'm her older brother."

Laura's face went blank, but her tone grew louder. "Are you serious? Why are you here now?"

"I can tell that Tracy never told you about me. I'm sorry to just show up and drop this bombshell on you. My sister and I weren't close."

"No shit," Laura didn't believe him. "Why are you really here?"

"We haven't spoken for over ten years."

Laura detested the man across from her. "Why haven't you talked to your sister in so long?"

Ray hesitated for effect. "When I was younger, I made some bad decisions and I turned into quite the asshole. Tracy resented my lifestyle."

"What was so bad that you couldn't speak to your sister?" Laura wanted to know. "She was an amazing spirit. You must have done something really awful to upset her so much that she never mentioned you."

"Did she ever talk about our parents?"

"She told me the entire story. How they died. That your mom was raped. Everything."

"I'll bet it wasn't the *whole* story." Ray challenged.

"What does that mean?" Scowled Laura. "If your sister would trust me with something as personal and painful as your parents' murder, why do you think she left you out of the story?"

Ray lowered his head for effect. "Because it was my fault they got killed."

There was a silence while Laura processed what he just told her. "What the hell does that mean?

Ray took a deep breath. He was a natural at this acting stuff. "I'll start by telling you that I never got along with my parents. There were times that I genuinely believed I hated them."

"That's too bad." Her voice dripped with sarcasm.

"Our dad owned an appliance store and he believed that I'd take over one day," Ray sounded unenthused. "Selling microwaves and dishwashers to lonely housewives wasn't the future I dreamt about."

"Were you too good for that?" The sarcasm continued.

Ray scratched the back of his neck and grinned half-heartedly. "Maybe I thought so back then. Instead of becoming the sales guy in cheap shirts and dirty ties, I decided I wanted to wear flip-flops on a beach, so I headed to Mexico."

The waitress arrived with their lunch, so they took a moment to get their food organized. She asked if they needed anything else.

Laura wanted something stronger than coffee. "What the hell, bring me a double vodka soda with a squeeze of lime?"

Ray stuck to coffee.

Laura picked at her salad. The short interruption had given her a few moments to process what Ray had told her so far. She watched him cut his steak and take his first bite. He chewed his meat like he didn't have a worry in the world. What was this guy up to?

Once her drink arrived, their conversation continued. Laura took a sip of vodka and looked at Ray. "The whole time you were in Mexico, did you ever reach out to your family?"

"Never," He took another mouthful of steak. "When I left, I knew I'd never talk to my parents again. I wasn't sure about Tracy."

"How'd you know that?"

"They were really pissed when I chose the beach over the family," Ray explained. "I was an embarrassment to them. I wasn't good in school and I developed what you might call a chemical dependency."

"Cocaine?" guessed Laura.

"Yeah, that too," nodded Ray. "I was into everything back in the day."

"What about Tracy? Did you ever talk to her again?"

Ray looked up from his plate. "Why do I feel like I'm being interrogated?"

"Because you are," Laura pushed her lunch to the side. "You show up here pretending that you want to help. Your sister died weeks ago and you're asking about life insurance. What's there not to believe?"

Ray pretended to understand her point. "I get it."

"By your own admission, you're a selfish prick," Tracy chewed aggressively on a carrot stick, "so I'm trying to figure out why we're sitting here pretending to enjoy our lunch?"

"I told you," Ray pushed the charade, "all I wanted to know if there is anything I can do to help."

"You've never answered my question. Did you ever talk with Tracy again?"

Ray nodded. "There was one last time, and it didn't go well. It was when I came back before our parents died."

"You came back from Mexico? Why?"

Ray chewed on a fry. "It doesn't matter."

"Yes, it does," She disagreed. "A piece of shit like you would have a plan."

Laura was a spark plug. He liked it. "I was running from some bad people that I owed money. They threatened to cut off my balls if I didn't pay them."

170

Laura was steering the conversation and she enjoyed it. "So, you went home with your tail between your legs?"

He looked down at the coffee cup. "When I was back, we accidentally ran into each other."

"You came back to the family you abandoned and you're telling me you accidentally ran into your sister," Laura hated the person across from her. "Were you out for a stroll? Or was it planned by you?"

Ray took a deep breath and paused. "It was in my dad's store after it closed. She was cleaning up and I was there to borrow some money."

"Now I get it," Laura was disgusted. "She caught you robbing your parents' store. How did that turn out?"

"It was the last time we talked, so how do you think it went? I needed money, so I borrowed some from my dad's safe and that made Tracy angry. It was none of her business."

Laura finished her vodka. "You really are a world-class asshole."

Ray was convinced Laura believed him. "There's more."

"What else can you add to this pathetic story?" She was enjoying his lie. "I'm listening."

"The money I took was for payroll and bills," Ray continued. "Tracy forgot to deposit it. That's why there was so much in the safe and she had to tell our dad that she messed up."

"You're blaming her?" Laura tried to maintain her control. "You pathetic piece of shit."

"I needed the money to pay off my dealer," Ray tried to justify the decision. "My dad scrambled and borrowed money to pay his staff. That's when he got into debt to the men who…"

She cut him off. "You mean the guys who raped your mother and murdered your parents?"

"Yes."

171

"You really are a pathetic piece of shit," The conversation got animated and the tables around them started to stare. "You're the reason your sister lost her family."

He stuck to the script and asked a key question. "Did she ever tell you the name of the store?"

"No, and I can't listen to your crap anymore," Laura looked for the waitress. She wished she had another drink. "How could anyone do what you've done, and then have the audacity to come here now?"

Ray lowered his voice. "It was the addiction. I never meant for my parents to get murdered."

"Did you attend their funeral?"

"No," he admitted. "I just need one thing from you."

Laura stood up. "And what's that?"

Ray braced for her response. "Since I'm Tracy's only living relative, I was hoping you could help me collect her life insurance. I need the paperwork."

Laura grabbed her glass and threw it at Ray. The glass only missed his forehead by inches. "Are you for real? I wouldn't help you if you were dying on the street."

Lunch was over.

On her way out she winked at Mickey, who was enjoying a healthy piece of lasagna a few tables over.

SIXTY

There were over twenty countries from the western world represented at the finance minister's funeral. It was held in his hometown of Montreal. John Fisher's death was a shock to everyone who knew him. Even his harshest critics paid respectful tributes to the man.

The funeral was held at the historic St. James Church and the overflow crowds lining the property were estimated in the thousands. Many were there to offer their sincere condolences, while some were only there to get a glimpse of the celebrities or political powers that would be in attendance.

Hugh Hutchinson arrived just minutes before the service was to begin and was ushered to a pew a few rows from the front. Arriving seconds later, was the prime minister with a much younger attractive blonde attached to his arm. The cameras snapped pictures and the race was on to find out the mystery woman's name.

John Fisher had been a popular political figure in Montreal, and many credited it to the fact he never stayed in one position too long. He spent three years as a city councillor and was elected mayor of Montreal for one term, before being convinced by Pierre Elliot to try his hand at federal politics.

The funeral began on time and everyone in the church sat quietly while the Archbishop gave his eulogy about John Fisher the man, as though they were the best of friends. He exaggerated the antidotes he was given by Fisher's family and friends and at every opportunity, he preached about the virtues of the church.

Prime Minister Elliot followed the Archbishop's sermon and

pulled out a short speech prepared by his staff. He had glanced at it on the ride over. "I want to begin by saying how sad I am that I've lost a great colleague, but more importantly, a better friend. John and I have known each other for thirty years, and we've accomplished a lot as friends and members of the government. So, today I'm finding it awfully hard to say goodbye."

"Good friend, my ass." Hutchinson muttered under his breath.

Elliot scanned the crowd and smiled at some of the recognizable faces sitting in the front pews. He gave his escort a quick smile and then stopped to look at Fisher's mother. "I remember when John left a successful accounting firm to join the political world. It was his goal to rebuild a financial landscape that desperately needed his help. That's how John Fisher should be remembered. He was a dedicated public servant who worked hard on our behalf."

"He was a useless twit." Hutchinson muttered.

SIXTY-ONE

Prime Minister Elliot and his lady friend were escorted out of the church by two large RCMP officers. Elliot ignored the questions shouted at him from the media. His friend did her best to hide her identity behind a colorful scarf. She held it in place until they were safely inside their vehicle and the tinted glass. They both burst into laughter, knowing the stir she caused. Pierre liked to mess with the media.

There was a private reception being hosted by the Liberal Party at the Governor Hotel Place Dupuis on Rue Saint-Hubert. It was a gathering to remember Fisher and give political powers the opportunity to speak freely without the scrutiny of the press or public.

When the prime minister arrived, he wandered easily amongst the guests and engaged in small talk. His date had her arm interlocked with Pierre. After a few minutes he was reminded that a U.S. senator had attended on behalf of the president and wanted a quick word.

"Hello, Senator Lopez," Pierre shook the man's hand. "I appreciate you taking the time to attend today."

"It was important to come," The senator responded respectfully. "I'm sorry about your friend. It sounds like you two were close."

"We were," Pierre thought about the missing $25 million. "I'm looking forward to meeting your new president. He seems like quite the character."

Lopez rolled his eyes to show is distain. "He's a self-centred son of a bitch."

Elliot smiled. "So, I've heard."

175

"He told me to tell you he'll think about Canada Day. He said you will have to serve maritime lobster if he comes."

"You can tell that Republican President that I will personally boil it." Laughed Elliot. "He'll only get the best."

Lopez had a flight to catch. "I should give the family my condolences before I head out."

The two men shook hands again and Pierre left to greet more guests. Once they were out of earshot, Pierre looked at his date and mumbled quietly. "The new president is an asshole. He sent a democratic senator to make a statement."

Hugh Hutchinson saw Elliot approaching and excused himself from the couple he was talking to. He turned to greet the prime minister. "Hello, sir."

"Hugh, I'd like you to meet Cherie Beliveau. Cherie, this is my good friend, Hugh Hutchinson."

They knew each other from a party a few months back, but both chose not to reveal that to Pierre. "It's nice to meet you."

"You as well." Cherie responded politely.

Hutchinson was surprised the prime minister was careless enough to be seen in public with a professional escort, especially at a funeral. Beliveau was a very well compensated companion, whose beauty and special skills kept her in high demand with the rich and powerful.

Hugh tapped Pierre on the shoulder. "Can I talk to you in private for a moment?"

Cherie got the hint. "You boys go discuss your business. I'm going to find the ladies' room."

The prime minister followed Hugh to a quiet corner where they were guaranteed privacy by the circle of security surrounding them. "The North Koreans are upstairs, and they have questions."

Pierre wasn't concerned. "Tell them to relax. Nothing has

changed because of Tucker. Things will go as planned."

"Anything new to tell me about Fisher's crash?" Hugh wondered. "Have they figured out what happened yet?"

"You sound a little nervous," Pierre countered, "and I heard you two had an unpleasant phone call only minutes before the crash."

Hugh decided to drop the topic. "I'll head upstairs and talk to our communist friends. You get back to Ms. Beliveau."

"That sounds like a good idea," Pierre was giddy, knowing what was instore for him. "I plan on getting out of here and spending some time with Cherie. Maybe you can drop by the house later tonight with an update."

Cherie caught the prime minister's attention with a sexy wink. After spending a few moments with Fisher's family, they snuck off to a room on the tenth floor.

Hugh went through a quick security check before he could get on the elevator. The billionaire then disembarked on the twelfth floor and was surprised by the military presence. He counted six heavily armed soldiers in the hallway, each holding semi automatic weapons. He walked straight ahead and said nothing.

When Hugh was allowed into the suite, Eon Kamahi was no where to be seen. The room was empty, but the door to the attached bedroom was slightly open and he could hear female giggles. When Kamahi appeared, he closed the door behind him, and the giggling went silent.

Eon greeted Hugh with a traditional bow. "Can I pour you a drink, Mr. Hutchinson?"

"I'd love a scotch," Hugh scanned the liquor on the table, "and please call me Hugh."

The North Korean diplomat wore a loose-fitting white shirt and some traditional wide legged pants. "I think I'll have the same."

Hugh took his drink and glanced in the direction of the bedroom. "I can see you're pressed for time, so let's get our business done."

Eon nodded in agreement.

Hugh sipped his drink. It was cheap scotch. "I've got the prime minister's assurances that even with Fisher's accident everything will stay on schedule."

"That's good to hear," Eon nodded, "but my commander in chief wants to renegotiate the price."

"Why should we renegotiate the price? That won't happen, so let's move on."

Kamahi lit a cigarette. "I think you need to understand the circumstances. They've changed and I'm sure your prime minister will agree."

Hugh had no idea what Kamahi referred to, so he treaded softly. "Why do you think Pierre will renegotiate and what is your number?"

"Five million," Eon responded without hesitation as cigarette smoke floated to the ceiling. "And we will not make the final payment of $20 million until we receive the weapons. We know about your deposit being stolen. That has us worried about your incompetence."

Fuck John Fisher. Even in death he haunted Hugh. "It was a simple banking error."

"We don't believe your lie so don't insult me."

Hugh had wondered more than once if the North Koreans were somehow involved with the plane crash. There was no evidence that pointed that way, but it was a strange coincidence it took place a few days after the money was stolen. He decided this wasn't the time or place to debate the North Korean guilt. Not with six guards standing outside in the hallway. "Let's discuss the $5 million. Why would

Pierre even consider doing that. If nothing else, I'm curious."

"I expected you to be curious," Eon opened his laptop and faced it so Hugh could see what was on the screen. "I think what we are about to witness will convince your prime minister to agree."

Hugh sipped on his drink and looked on with interest.

"Now watch," Kamahi ordered. "You will see why we're suggesting a discounted price."

The twenty-four-inch computer turned into a video screen that had live feeds downloading from a remote camera setup. They were focused on a king-sized bed. "Where is this?"

Eon sucked on his cigarette. "It's on the tenth floor. Two floors below us."

A skinny man hopped around the bed. He wore a skimpy red tutu. Hugh stared at the screen. "Is that who I think it is?"

Eon had a confident smirk on his face. "It is your prime minister."

Hugh's eyes were glued to the screen. "What the hell is he doing?"

A person wearing a full teddy bear outfit appeared and seemed to chase Elliot with something in her hand. The prime minister jumped onto the bed on his stomach and lifted his rear, exposing his naked butt. "I think it's obvious. He likes to take the boy toy usually used by women. He's a kinky man."

Hugh watched the bear climb onto the bed behind Pierre and unzipped the outfit and let it drop to her waist. "I should have guessed. It's Cherie. What is Pierre doing?"

"Losing five million." Laughed the North Korean. "Elliot will love to see this."

Hugh gulped down the scotch and didn't wait for an invite for a second. He helped himself. "Turn that off. Where did you get this?"

The North Korean butted his cigarette. "It's happening on the tenth floor as we speak. It's a live performance."

179

Hugh started to chuckle when he thought about what Pierre's reaction will be. "I'll tell him tonight, but your price is way to high. Knowing him he'll give you the middle finger."

"As long as it's not used."

Eon laughed hysterically at his own joke and Hugh had to join in. This could be a profitable agreement after all.

SIXTY-TWO

Tiffany agreed to allow Ray to stay in their home, but he was relegated to the guest room. He didn't put up any resistance. He was happy to have a place to stay and understood that the process to reconcile would take some time. There were boundaries that she insisted on and one of those was having no sex. That was going to be hard for a guy who just spent five years with some ugly men.

Ray found some obvious signs that his wife had entertained some male guests while he was away. That was something he was going to have to accept and get used to. He never asked how many, or if it was going to continue. The possible answer scared him. He decided the domestic beer in the fridge could stay, but the used toothbrush was tossed into the garbage.

It was a week since his release, and Ray had made no effort to reach out to David. He was waiting for the right time. He needed some concrete evidence to support his theory and he hoped to have that soon. He headed down the stairs and ran into Tiffany in the kitchen. "Good morning."

She looked up and smiled. "Are you going to be home for dinner? I was hoping we could have an honest conversation on where certain things stand between us."

Her question made his stomach feel uneasy. "I definitely have the time and I like the idea of having an honest conversation. We need that."

"Okay, dinner it is," She refilled her coffee. "You need to understand that a lot has changed while you were away. I want certain things to remain the same."

Ray admired her beauty. She hadn't aged a minute while he was gone. "Does that include continuing to see your boyfriend?"

"Maybe," she responded, "but he's not really a boyfriend, but more of a boy toy. Remember, I wasn't in prison and wasn't going to be punished too."

Ray tried to laugh off his wife's honesty. "I understand that you had needs and I will need to accept that. But we still need a real conversation about where things are between us."

Tiffany didn't want this conversation now. She wanted to tell him that she spent many nights alone wondering about their future. Walking away from the marriage would have been an easy escape, but something wouldn't let her do that. "What are your plans now that you're out?"

Ray decided his undercover gig with Smith and Murphy was not something he wanted to reveal. Hopefully, it was over now. "I spent a lot of time in the prison library. I realized that I enjoy helping others. I discovered I was good at it."

"Good for you," Tiffany sounded impressed, "but you still haven't answered my question."

Ray wasn't sure what to say. He had no job prospects yet. "I want to focus on us. I have a lot to make up for."

Tiffany decided her morning plans could wait. She stood and gently grabbed Ray's hand. "Let's sit on the couch and talk. You can tell me about prison life."

Ray took her hand and before long they were cuddled on the couch. Her smell made him excited. It had been so long. He shared prison stories and the drastic changes he adapted to. He recalled the awful food. They laughed together and it felt good.

Tiffany changed the mood with one question. "Did you do it?"

"Did I do what?" Ray was disappointed she asked but understood why. "I'm innocent."

"Then why did you plead guilty?" She gazed into his eyes. "I need to know."

Ray bit his lip. "To protect a close friend."

"Must be a hell of a friend for you to serve five years. You gave up everything you had, including me," She reminded him. "I hope you'll trust me enough one day to tell me the whole story."

Ray smelled her hair that was so close. He craved her body. "I hope to tell you everything very soon. But, for now, I just want to take my wife to bed."

Tiffany didn't resist as her husband pulled her anxiously into their bedroom, where they were both naked in seconds. The love making was aggressive and passionate and ten minutes later they were both exhausted.

She cradled Ray in her arms and stared up at the ceiling. She was in deep thought. Hopefully, you can tell me your whole story one day soon, because I also have a story for you. But I need to know I can trust you first.

SIXTY-THREE

Curtis had been at his computer for almost four hours without a break until now. He was starving and needed to use the bathroom. Carol had ramped up his workload and she expected results. He had two new assignments. The first was to track down the new account that Hutchinson would be setting up for the final deposit from the North Koreans. Carol was certain they would not be re-using the account Fisher setup.

The second assignment was to raise another $10 million for operations. She gave Curtis a list of targets to research and he had until the end of the day. He had taken in just over $4 million, so there was still some work to do.

After a trip to the bathroom, hunger had won over work. He decided a trip to the cafeteria was in order. Chicken strips with fries was on the menu. When he walked back into his work area, he was outraged to see the new guy at his computer. "What are you doing?"

He ignored Curtis's outburst. "Are you almost done?"

Curtis wasn't sure what to do. He wasn't going to physically remove Wendell Presley. The man had monster arms. "Done what?"

"Raising the ten million."

"Why would I tell you?"

Wendell sensed the kid's distaste for him, and the feeling was becoming mutual. He was prewarned that this one had some self-image issues. "You do realize that you report to me now?"

Curtis mustered some resistance. "If that makes you feel important."

Presley stepped away from the computer and made a point of turning it off. "Cut the crap kid. I hear you have a knack at finding money and I know you need to find ten million by the end of the day. So, how's it going? It's a simple question."

"Four million so far."

Wendell rubbed his chin. "How much are you skimming?"

Curtis said nothing, but his eyes deepened.

The question hit a nerve and Wendell saw that. "I don't care how smart you think you are, or how much money you steal. You remember that you answer to me. Do you understand?"

Curtis was only concerned with how much this guy might know. "I only report to Mickey or Carol." He said defiantly. "Now I need to go."

Wendell clenched his fist. "If I ask you a question, you'll answer me."

Out of nowhere, Mickey appeared at the door. "This conversation is over."

Wendell turned to see Mickey. "This doesn't concern you."

Mickey never took his eyes off the much bigger man. "It's time for you to go."

Wendell didn't like Mickey challenging him in front of the kid. "What are you going to do?"

"Are we going there, Presley." Mickey rolled up his sleeves. "You can decide how you leave."

Wendell made a calculated decision. He knew this wasn't over. "I'll leave the kid with you, but I won't be taking shit from a twelve-year old."

"I'm thirteen, you asshole!" Curtis yelled at him.

Wendell left.

Curtis turned to Mickey. "Can I ask a favour?"

"What's that?"

Curtis faked a one-two punch combination to Mickey's mid-section. "Can you teach me how to fight?"

"Why would a young man with your potential want to learn how to fight?"

"I want the respect you get." Curtis revealed. "I saw the fear in Presley's face."

"You don't get respect through fear," explained Mickey. "You get it through self confidence and the way you treat others. When I was your age, I had to fight. I was an Indian kid in a white man world. I had to defend myself. My dad was never around."

"My dad was an asshole too," Curtis remembered somberly. "He really hurt my mom."

"Your dad made a mistake," Mickey knew about the affair and drinking. "Don't let it define how you remember him. You're going to make your own mistakes and you'll understand that forgiving is a cure for happiness."

"Okay. But will you still teach me?"

SIXTY-FOUR

Tiffany slept peacefully when Ray emerged from the shower and got dressed. Since their reconciliation they had spent much of the last two days in the bed making love. It was now Friday morning and Ray had an early morning meeting with Sergeant Smith. He gave her a loving kiss on the cheek without waking her and headed downstairs to grab a quick breakfast.

On his way out, he saw a note on the table. It was from Tiffany:

'Forgot to mention that I will be away for a few days. Pre-planned. Glad you're home. Love Tiff.'

On his drive to the police station, Ray made a quick detour to grab three fresh coffees. There was no way he would drink what they brewed at the station. He hurried inside, holding the tray.

"Good morning, gentlemen," Ray placed the coffee on Steve's desk and grabbed his. "I decided to treat you to a big boy coffee."

Murphy grabbed a cup and pulled off the plastic lid. "How do you think things went with Laura Nelsen?"

Ray had developed a theory. "Laura loved Tracy and she is very protective of her. But I do agree that she knows more than she's letting on."

Smith leaned back in his chair. He wasn't so sure. "Maybe, maybe not. Our goal was to see if she had any knowledge of Tracy's past. For that, we scored a zero."

Ray disagreed with the sergeant. "I think Laura believes what Tracy told her."

Smith sampled his coffee. "How does that connect anything?"

"We all believe that Tracy was connected to the kid's abduction," the other two nodded, "and judging by Laura's aggressive display she wasn't the submissive in their relationship. If Tracy was involved, then so was Laura. All we have to do is keep tabs on her and she'll lead us to something."

The cops looked at each other.

Ray saw that they had a concern. "What's up?"

"Laura Nelsen disappeared," Smith revealed. "We had an officer go by her place this morning and she was gone."

Ray was shocked by the news. "Why would she run? Maybe she's with a friend?"

"In our line of work, we meet all kinds, but mostly accomplished liars," Smith told Ray, "and I think Tracy and Laura are just that."

Ray couldn't disagree. "Are you sure she's gone?"

"Her apartment didn't have much, but anything of value was taken," he answered, "and all her personal belongings were gone."

Murphy removed any doubt. "We did a background check on Nelsen, and like her girlfriend, she only started existing ten years ago."

Smith tested the coffee. "Cops don't believe in coincidences."

"Why did she put on such an act," Ray rubbed his chin, "if she knew my story was a pile of shit?"

"Probably to see how far you'd go," shrugged Murphy, "or to deflect suspicion away from her."

"I hope I didn't do anything to compromise your investigation."

"You were more help than you know." Smith patted him on the shoulder. "It supports my theory that Tracy didn't fall. It also strengthens my belief that Joshua Small is still alive."

"Well that's good, I guess." Ray concluded.

Smith looked at Ray. In their short time together, he had grown to like the man, but something didn't fit with him either. "I need to ask you a question, so I understand you better."

"Ask away."

"You pled guilty," Smith reminded him. "Why?"

It was becoming a popular question and Ray stole a glance of Murphy, who was looking right at him. "I trusted a friend."

"Not much of a friend," countered Smith.

"I learned that the hard way," Ray nodded, without seeming upset. "Now I'm off to a car rental place."

SIXTY-FIVE

Suzanne Lacy had slept little that night. She tossed and turned and constantly checked the time on her bedside clock. The sun rose at 7:12 and by the time it was bright enough to safely walk the trails, she was wired on three cups of coffee and was dressed for the morning chill. She gathered the tools she needed from the garage and once Rupert was on his leash, they were on their way.

Suzanne debated calling the police but decided against it. There was still a chance that the discarded clothing was some garbage from a reckless hiker. If it turned out to be Curtis's clothes, she'd call the police and then update Tom.

The walk was a brisk twenty minutes before Suzanne found the spot she was looking for. She put an old piece of carpet on the frozen ground to kneel on to protect her knees. She then began chipping away at the ice and frozen dirt. Just like an archeologist, she staked the area around her dig and slowly scraped away, one spoonful at a time. The frozen ground made it a slow process, but after almost an hour she got the bag free.

Suzanne held it against her body and took slow deliberate breaths. The chilled air particles hurt her lungs, but the excitement of what she might be holding made her heart pound. When she finally stood up and had everything safely packed, she headed home to examine what she found. Her walk was brisk, with Rupert in tow.

She put the frozen bag in the sink to thaw. She thought it would melt faster if she looked at it. Her adrenalin pumped when the bag was thawed enough to start extracting its contents. The first thing she removed was the ballcap with the large 'U'. She was convinced it was Curtis's cap, but held her emotions in check until she pulled out the next item. It was a pair of jeans. She unfolded them on the table and examined them closely. She recognized the label and size. She was certain they belonged to her son. She still resisted any celebration.

Then she checked the pockets and found a folded piece of paper. She read the message. It was an email from Tom's computer at work.

Oh my god! Curtis knew that his dad had a girlfriend.

SIXTY-SIX

Peter McKee was thrilled to be sent to New York on a new assignment. He was being allowed to work in a laboratory as a chemical engineer. It will be his first time back in a real lab in over ten years. He understood the danger of the assignment and the risks that were attached, but he quickly agreed to be involved when Carol and Mickey offered him the chance.

Mickey had explained that he would be going to a location in Manhattan to pick up a package containing two extremely sensitive chemical compounds. When mixed properly, they became a deadly air borne chemical. If he were captured by the police, he was on his own and would most likely be charged as a terrorist and face life in prison. Knowing all of that, Peter was still eager to accept the assignment.

The trip to New York was exactly what he needed to feel involved again. It was a relief to put the John Woodland's fire and everything connected to it in the rear-view mirror. He was returning to his passion in the lab.

Peter was twelve and the organization was in its infancy when Carol took him in. Carol was now living on her own, but the development of her organization had started to take shape. She needed a brilliant mind and Peter was that. He was the reason Carol started to focus on young people as recruits. They had no emotional baggage. They just wanted to be accepted.

The thing that amazed Peter was how Carol kept her organization and everything it was doing under the radar from the government for so long. Very few people even knew that she existed, and she liked it that way.

The landing at Kennedy International airport was almost perfect. Peter retrieved his luggage and jumped into a cab. Forty minutes later he was at his home for the next few weeks; The Trump International Hotel.

He checked in and once he was settled, he threw on some sweatpants and sneakers. A short jog around Central Park would be a great way to begin his stay. He'd decide on some dinner when he returned.

When he returned there was a white envelope on the floor. He had been contacted. Feeling a little paranoia, he closed the curtains and took the envelope into the bathroom before opening it.

It was old school. A typed note had a time, address and who to ask for. He tore the paper into a bunch of little pieces and flushed it down the toilet. He was set.

Peter jumped in the shower before heading out for some Chinese.

SIXTY-SEVEN

Back on Gabriola, Wendell Presley had moved on from his confrontation with Mickey. He decided on a different approach for his next meeting. Armed with a large hot pepperoni pizza and a few cans of soda, he knocked on Jonny's door.

"Enter!" Jonny yelled from inside.

Wendell walked into Jonny's work area and slid the pizza box on a table that was covered in papers. He tossed him a can of soda. "I heard you love pepperoni."

"You heard right," Jonny grabbed a slice and pushed the box back. "What can I do for you?"

"Since I'm the new guy I thought I'd come by and say hello. I reviewed your files and you've done some amazing stuff. You're an impressive young man."

Jonny had his guard up. He got a heads up from Curtis, so he was prepared for a visit. He took a second bite. "Thanks. I love doing this stuff."

Wendell piled on the compliments. "Your toys have unlimited capabilities."

Jonny stopped him before he carried on. "They're not toys we'll sell to rich kids. I prefer the term gadgets. It's cooler."

Wendell stroked his beard. "Fair enough. What are you working on now? I'm told it's a complicated and key piece to the operation."

"It's another insect."

"Seriously?" Wendell glanced at some paperwork on the desk. "I wasn't aware of that. What insect are you working on now?"

Jonny cracked open a soda. "It will be a dragonfly."

"Really?" Wendell sounded impressed. "Why a dragonfly?"

Jonny was busy and grew bored with the questions. He didn't trust the man and knew he had no real interest in what he was working on. He was fishing for something else. "That's a Mickey question."

Wendell held his tone. He tried another approach. "I need to review your drawings. Where are they?"

Jonny closed the pizza box. "That's not happening without Mickey approving it?"

Wendell's temper was ready to explode. "What is with you kids?"

Jonny remained calm. "First, bringing me a pizza doesn't make us friends. And you're not one of us. I have no idea why Carol thought we needed someone like you."

Wendell took a step back. "What do you mean, I'm not one of you?"

"We're geniuses and your just muscle," Jonny pointed out. "We can buy more muscle, so if I were you, I'd be careful."

SIXTY-EIGHT

Peter climbed out of bed earlier than planned. He decided a walk before breakfast would be a good way to clear his mind and get ready for the day. It was going to be stressful. He pulled on a dark ballcap and sunglasses to shield his face from the CCTV cameras on every street corner. He knew he had to be cautious. He had no idea who might be watching.

His pickup was scheduled for 10am and if everything went as planned, he'd be back in the hotel by four. He was alone in New York and the success of the assignment rested on his shoulders. Peter was excited to do the job and that surprised him. He was not used to being a risk taker.

He was clear on the penalty if he was caught with the chemicals. He would be arrested and charged under the Homeland Security Act and would be labelled a domestic terrorist. If convicted, he would serve the rest of is life in a maximum-security prison in Colorado. He would be roommates with Dzhokhar Tsarnaev, the Boston marathon bomber. He should have been scared, but he wasn't.

After some breakfast at the hotel, he was off to the Café Brazil. He tried to blend in with the crowds of tourist walking along Central Park. He kept his head down and increased the pace as he turned onto 61st Avenue. The café was a block away.

Standing outside the green and gold painted building, Peter took one last deep breath to calm himself. He checked up and down the sidewalk before he entered the café and was greeted by the smell of strong dark coffee. He sat in a booth and grabbed a menu, even though he had no intention of eating.

A young waitress approached his table. Peter could help but admire her perfect olive skin and friendly smile. "Can I help you, senor?"

"I'd like a black coffee to go."

"Are you Peter?" she whispered with a Spanish accent.

Peter nodded as he looked at her name tag pinned to her chest to confirm she was who she was supposed to be. "And you are Gabriella."

"Gabi is good," she told him. "I will get what you came for."

Peter's eyes followed her into the back and then he looked around the small cafe. It wasn't busy and no one seemed to care that he was there. He tried to relax.

Gabi was only gone for a few minutes before she returned with a coffee in a to-go cup. She passed it to Peter. "Your coffee is extremely hot, so be careful. Adios."

Peter stood on the curb outside the cafe, and as thousands do every day in New York, he waved down a yellow taxi. He placed the cup gingerly beside him while he buckled in. Once he was done, he held the cup while the driver steered back into traffic.

"Where to mister?"

Peter handed the driver an address and after he read it, the driver looked in the rear-view mirror at Peter. "Are you sure this is the correct address, mister?"

"Yes. Why?"

The driver glanced back in the mirror. "This is a dangerous neighborhood. You're awful white to be going there. Just saying."

Peter looked at the cup and knew what he was holding. "That's where I need to go, so please hurry."

Thirty minutes later the driver pulled up to what was left of a curb. Chunks of cement had been removed and used as weapons

197

during a recent demonstration. Peter looked out at the neighborhood, and other than a few kids bouncing a basketball on the street, he saw no one.

"Here you go. Twenty-six dollars before danger pay."

Peter paid the driver forty and got out without waiting for the change. He was focused on one thing. Holding the cup steady. The contents inside that cup if mixed prematurely could wipe out everyone within miles if the winds blew in the right direction.

He glanced at the address on the card and walked over to what was an old laundromat. The machines were long gone but the weather-beaten sign still hung above the door. The two-story wooden structure was crammed between two other old buildings that were boarded up tight to keep the vagrants out.

Peter was having a hard time believing this was the right place. Before going inside, he confirmed the address one last time by comparing the number he had with the address screwed on the doorframe. They matched.

He was relieved, but not surprised to find the door unlocked and he felt safer when he was off the street and away from the eyes he knew were watching. A white man was not a common site in this neighborhood.

There was a single lightbulb burning in a hallway and at the end was another door. He walked towards it. Every step caused the dry wood to crunch under his feet and he moved quickly, worried he might fall through. He still wasn't convinced he was in the right place. And then he saw a small Chinese lady wrapped in a dirty blanket perched behind a counter.

"Hey, mister," she said with a strong Asian accent, "are you McKeen?"

He didn't bother to correct her. "Yes."

She pointed to another door at the end of the room. "You go in there. It's open."

He nodded his thanks and walked through the door and it was like something magical transpired on the other side. He had entered in to a small, well lit laboratory that would have everything he needed to do his work. It was shiny and spotless. He carefully placed the cup inside a glass enclosure before pulling on a white lab coat and some safety goggles.

For the next three hours, Peter followed the steps in the formulas to the letter. He constantly dabbed the sweat from his forehead. The cause was the intense lighting and stress. Now he was nervous.

When he was finished, he had produced enough of the deadly gas to fill a small one-ounce vial. It was enough in the right circumstances to kill thousands. He packed everything up except the vial. It was stored in a special container and would be picked up by someone Peter would never meet.

On his ride back to the hotel Peter finally asked the obvious question. What did Carol have planned for the deadly gas?

He remembered Tracy.

SIXTY-NINE

Ray had finished his meeting with Smith and Murphy and drove through morning rush hour traffic with no concern for the time. It was an advantage of being an unemployed lawyer. He had his Porsche out of storage and was taking it for a ride. This time he respected the speed limit, and checked the trunk before he left his house.

He was headed to Status Luxury Machines. He hoped that they kept rental records for at least six years. If they didn't, any chance of proving his innocence just got much harder.

When he pulled into Status, he found a parking spot and took a second to admire a black Ferrari displayed on the lot. The old Ray would take it for a spin. The new one went inside.

The only person in the showroom was a tall blonde woman with a red lip stick smile, squeezed into a tight blue dress that was meant for someone twenty pounds lighter. She was on the phone behind the counter, so Ray just wandered around and admired the vehicles. It took five years to get here, so another few minutes wouldn't matter.

She finished her call and smiled cheerfully. "Which car gets you excited?"

Ray approached the counter. He tried not to stare at her ample chest. "I'm not here to rent a vehicle. I have a situation that I'm hoping you could help me with."

She could smell men with money and Ray's haircut and leather shoes were an indicator that he had some. She pushed her hair to the side, believing it made her look younger. "How can I help you with your situation?"

"How about I start by introducing myself," His smile kept her attention. "I'm Ray Cooke."

"I'm Sabrina."

"Just like the teenage witch." joked Ray.

Sabrina giggled. "Yes, but I'm not a teenager."

Ray gave her hand a gentle shake. "I'm hoping you can help me out with a little problem."

"I'd love to take that Ferrari for a spin?"

Ray smiled. "So, would I, but it just can't be today."

Sabrina didn't hide her disappointment. "If you're not here to rent a machine, then what can I do for you?"

Ray needed to keep her on his side. "Maybe we can go for a drive tonight? But I do need a favour."

Hearing that Ray changed his mind, her smile brightened. "What do you need?"

"Actually, its for my mother."

"Your mother?" Sabrina was confused. "How can I help your mom?"

"She rented a car a few years back, but she can't remember what model it was."

Sabrina was still confused. "Why would she want to know that now?"

"Like I said, I need a favour." Ray winked.

"Favours can be expensive," Smiled Sabrina. "What does your mom need?"

Ray placed a hundred-dollar bill in Sabrina's hand. "I need to know if your records go back over five years?"

Sabrina shoved the money into her bra. "They can?"

Ray remembered the car he drove back then. The same one that was in David's driveway in the video. "Did you have a 2012 black BMW in your rental fleet?"

Sabrina played with her mouse. "Yes, we carried two makes back then. Which one is she looking for?"

"It was a 3 Series."

Sabrina was still maneuvering her mouse, "What were the dates?"

If his hunch was correct, he was about to find out who set him up. He tried to control his excitement. "She thinks it was on May 24th or 25th. It was black and the year was 2013."

"Damn it, Ray, that's over five years ago. You're going to owe me dinner," Sabrina found the screen she was searching for. "What is your mother's name?"

Ray just threw a name at her. "Diane Jones."

"Sorry, no one with that name rented a car on those dates," She wanted to please him. "Could it have been rented under a different person?"

"That's possible. Do you have a list of people who rented a car like that on those days?"

"Dinner's going to include wine," teased Sabrina, "and this isn't for your mother, is it?"

Ray felt comfortable that Sabrina would help him. "Okay, I'm busted. I'm trying to get a friend out of prison."

"The poor man," She pretended to care. "What's he in for?"

"They framed him for drug possession."

Sabrina printed off a copy of the rental agreement. "I hope this helps. I'll see you at six."

He held the paper in his hand. He had no intention of going out for dinner, but he'd send Sabrina a dozen roses as a thank you with an apology note. He hurried back to his Porsche. Before he drove away, he unfolded the rental agreement and saw the name.

"Unbelievable!"

SEVENTY

The Curtis Lacy abduction story was back in the headlines after three years, thanks to Rupert, the Siberian husky. The puppy had found what search teams couldn't and the story was a major play on news and social media networks across the country and around the world.

Suzanne knew she had to give her ex-husband a heads up before he heard about it in a drunken stupor. It was almost four o'clock, so he'd still be at work and probably sober. She called his cell phone and after a few rings he finally answered. He was still in his office. "Hello, Suzanne. Twice in one week. Something's up."

She stood in her bedroom holding the note. "There's something we need to talk about."

Her tone worried him. "Is it about Curtis?"

"Yes."

He assumed the worse. "Just say it."

She clenched the paper. "I was out walking on the trails behind the house with Rupert."

"Hold on," He interrupted, sounding almost jealous. "Whose Rupert?"

"He's my new puppy."

Tom chuckled. "You have a puppy named Rupert?"

"I do," she wanted to stay on topic, "and when we were out walking on the trail, he found a garbage bag frozen in the snow."

"What was in it?"

Suzanne was worried about his reaction. She knew the news could destroy his fragile state. "It was a bag of Curtis's clothes. It was what he wore the day he left."

Tom tried to catch up. "You're telling me that you were out walking with your puppy and the dog sniffed out a bag of clothes that have been there for three years? How do you know they're his?"

"There was a sheet of paper in the pocket of the pants."

"Damn it, Suzanne," Tom realized his son might be alive, "what was on the paper?"

"It's an email you sent to your girlfriend," She felt guilty telling him. "Curtis found it and it's very graphic. That might be why he left."

Tom fell back into his office chair and rubbed his eyes. He wanted to scream. "I'm so sorry. It's my fault he's gone."

Suzanne reacted differently. "If that's true, then it means our son is alive and we need to find him."

"I'll admit I was having my doubts, but I'm starting to believe you might be right." Tom told her. "You've had a busy week."

She suddenly felt alone. "I guess so."

"You really think Curtis had something to do with paying off your debt?"

She felt a tear on her cheek and wiped it away. "Who else would help me like that?"

"That's a lot of money," Tom couldn't dismiss the note in Curtis's pocket. The consequences of one stupid email had cost him a relationship with his son and ended his marriage. "I'm really sorry you found that note."

Suzanne sighed. "Look on the bright side. It proves our son is alive."

"I guess it does," Tom remembered his friends were waiting for him at the bar. This news was a great reason to have a few drinks. "Look, I have to go, but thanks for calling. Keep me updated."

"One last thing, Tom."

"What's that?"

"Fuck you!"

When the six o'clock news opened with the Curtis Lacy story, there was one person who watched the report with great interest. It was Stacey Small. Once the segment was finished, she headed to her computer and found out everything she could about the case. She was incredulous at the similarities. It was like they were brothers. Both were eleven when abducted and both were geniuses.

And both could be involved with their own abductions.

Her next step was to reach out. She decided to introduce herself. Stacey dialed the number, and the phone was answered immediately. "Hello, I'm looking for Suzanne Lacy."

"You found her," Suzanne didn't recognize the voice. "Who is this?"

Stacey apologized for the unexpected call and after a quick introduction, it wasn't long before they talked like best friends. They had a lot to cover. They compared stories about failed marriages, thoughts of suicide, and the unbearable pain of not knowing. And then Suzanne explained about her bank experience.

"So, someone just paid off your debt," Stacey was intrigued, but wasn't sure how it connected to her son, "and you think Curtis had something to do with it?"

"He's a whizz with hacking computers and I think he accessed my account somehow and found out I was poor."

"Where would he get the money?"

"Maybe from the people who took him." Suzanne guessed.

After another hour, the women ended the call with the promise they'd stay in touch. They were both relieved and excited to have someone to talk to who understood their anguish.

After she tossed her phone on the sofa, Stacey stared out her living room window and rubbed her growing belly. "We're going to find your big brother."

SEVENTY-ONE

After a short thirty-minute flight back from Montreal, Hugh Hutchinson had his chauffeured sedan take him to 24 Sussex Drive. It was the home of the prime minister and he was not looking forward to the conversation that they needed to have. Seeing Pierre in a red tutu spread-eagled on the bed was an image that he couldn't erase. It was going to be an interesting, but an unavoidable talk.

After the usual security pat down, he was escorted inside. He was a regular visitor to the house and got a welcoming smile from a member of Pierre's staff, who led him to the library.

"The prime minister will join you shortly. Have a nice evening."

It had been a long day that began at the Fisher funeral. And it was coming to an end with a discussion about the prime minister's sexual indiscretions. Squeezed in the middle was his meeting with Eon Kamahi, who wanted to extort them for $5 million. Not a normal day in the life of a billionaire.

While he waited, he wondered about Pierre's choices at times. Bringing a paid escort to such a public event was not a smart decision, but that was Pierre. He'd worry about the headlines in the morning.

The prime minister waltzed in looking like he didn't have a worry in the world. He headed over to a well-stocked bar and poured two scotches before acknowledging Hugh was even in the room.

"Thanks for coming by," Pierre handed him a glass. "How was your meeting with the North Koreans? Anything we need to be concerned with?"

"That's why I'm here. It's been a tough day."

Pierre laughed. "How tough can it be when you're a billionaire?"

Hugh didn't want to debate the advantages of being rich. "The North Koreans want to change the terms of our agreement."

Pierre took a seat in a chair across from Hugh. "What does that look like?"

"They want you to drop the price by $5 million."

Pierre didn't take the request seriously. "What makes them think I'll agree to that?"

Hugh sipped the drink. "They have a video?"

Pierre didn't seem concerned. "A video of what?"

Hugh had rehearsed what he'd say to Pierre, but there was no easy way to tell him. "When I was with Eon Kamahi, he showed me a live feed from another room in the hotel."

Pierre knew what Hugh was going to say next. "And?"

"It is a video of you and Ms. Beliveau having some X rated fun."

Pierre thought back on his time with her and a thin smirk appeared. "So, the nasty little communist thinks he can blackmail me?"

Hugh nodded.

"I hope you told them to go fuck themselves! If they think they can extort me, they're crazy."

Hugh let the reality of the situation sink in. "You should think about what this could do to you. I'm not suggesting you cave to their demands, but this is an election year and what's on the video would destroy you."

What Hugh said did make sense. "What do you suggest?"

"Think big picture and drop the price."

"It pisses me off that those fucking communist bastards think they can do this to me," Pierre thought for a moment. "You go back to your North Korean buddy and tell him he can take the video and put it on *Entertainment Tonight*. There is no way I'm adjusting the agreement."

"It's a gutsy call, but I like it."

Pierre started to chuckle. "They thought my ass getting stuffed by a beautiful woman was worth $5 million. I guess I should take that as a compliment."

"I'm glad you see some humor in it," Hugh was only thinking of his piece of the $50 million, "and I assume you want me to get the video."

"Absolutely. No video, no weapons."

"As long as you remember this is an election year. It's not a coincidence that they're doing this now."

Pierre stood firm. "You tell them if I don't have the only copy within forty-eight hours, the arms deal is done. I'll keep their deposits."

Hugh didn't remind him the deposit of $25 million was still missing and probably long gone. He didn't agree with the strategy, but in the end, it was his political career he was playing Russian roulette with. "You do know that Cherie was involved, don't you?"

Pierre sipped his scotch. "I do."

SEVENTY-TWO

Peter paid the taxi and stood on the sidewalk outside Trump Plaza. Before going inside, he took a moment to catch his breath and look around. He almost expected the FBI to rush up and arrest him. When that didn't happen, he took a deep breath to settle his heart rate before heading in.

He walked through the lobby towards the elevators.

"Hey, Peter!" A voice he recognized from the lounge got his attention. "Over here."

Peter turned to the sound of his name. His heart was pounding again. "Wow! What a great surprise!"

She ran over and gave him a tight hug around the shoulders. "I really missed you."

Peter's surprise was obvious. "What are you doing in New York, Tiffany?"

"I decided to come visit," she giggled, "and so I jumped on a plane."

"I'm glad you did," Peter had questions he decided against asking. "This is a great surprise."

Her goofy grin and bright smile said she had been in the lounge for awhile. "Join me for a drink and then we can go to your room if that's okay. I could use a hot shower and a relaxing back rub. It was a long flight."

Peter hadn't expected his girlfriend to fly across the country. Her offer of a hot shower and a massage was all he needed to hear. "I'd love to have a drink with you."

Since Ray's release, they continued to see each other discreetly and Peter hoped her trip to New York was a positive sign. Tiffany was his first real girlfriend and he pinched himself knowing that someone so beautiful would be with him. "Let's have one to celebrate New York and then I'll give you that massage."

One drink led to a second and the conversation turned to ideas about dinner. "Let's go get cleaned up before we head out on the town."

Peter agreed. "Do you still want a massage?"

"Absolutely," Tiffany teased her lips on a cube of ice. "I want a massage before and after dinner. Are you up for that?"

Peter paid the tab and they headed upstairs. She snuck into the bathroom and it wasn't long before she emerged wearing only a hotel bathrobe. "Get undressed."

Twenty minutes later, Peter was exhausted and fell back onto a pillow. He stared at the ceiling as his chest heaved with each breath. "What did I ever do to deserve you?"

Tiffany wrapped her naked body under a bedsheet. "I could ask you the same question, but I'm starving. Let's go have dinner."

Peter's insecurity appeared. "How's your husband making out?"

Tiffany pulled herself off the bed and walked naked to the minibar. She helped herself to a red wine. "Boy, can you ever kill a mood."

"Look, I'm sorry, but…"

"But nothing," she interrupted firmly, "and to answer your next question, yes he knows I'm sleeping with another man, and no he doesn't know it's you."

"I'm sorry, but I needed to know."

Tiffany returned to the bed. "There was some domestic beer in our fridge, which was a dead giveaway. And he almost used your toothbrush."

Peter grinned. "How does this effect us?"

"It doesn't," Tiffany assured him. "We both knew he would get out of prison, but I'm still here."

Peter felt stupid asking the question. "I'm sorry."

"Ray had his share of fuck buddies before he went inside and I'm sure he will again," Tiffany showed no animosity. "The decision is yours. Do you want to run and hide, or step up and take control?"

Peter wasn't prepared for an ultimatum. "I love our time together. I'm just worried it's going to end."

"Everything ends," Tiffany put her arms around Peter's neck, "so let's take advantage of this great room. I've always wanted to have sex against the window in a tall building. Are you interested in voyeurism?"

He followed her to the window, naked as a jaybird. "You are one crazy lady."

SEVENTY-THREE

In a larger and better-equipped laboratory across the continent, Cassie had prepared for her presentation to Wendell Presley. She had read and re read her notes countless times. In her mind, she was ready.

She had been made aware of Presley's intense manner and that added to the pressure. Her vapor food was ready for field testing, but she still needed his approval for funding.

Minutes before Presley was supposed to arrive, she got a message that the meeting had been rescheduled in his office. She had twenty minutes to get there and it unsettled her. She rushed to pack everything up and headed down the hall.

When she arrived at his office, she found him behind his desk looking bored and he wasn't prepared to do any testing. The room was a mess and Cassie started having serious doubts. She had to feign a coughing sound just to get his attention.

"Sit down." His tone was rough.

She did as she was told. "Is there somewhere you want me to set up?"

Presley shook his head. "No need."

She was surprised by his total lack of interest that she was even there. "Is something wrong?"

"Just the opposite," He finally sat up. "Everything I've read and seen is great."

She didn't feel confident. "What is my next step? Can we start field testing?"

He grabbed a cigar from a humidor and sniffed it under his nose.

"There is no next step. Go celebrate."

"What do you mean, there's no next step?"

Wendell huffed impatiently. "You finished what you were brought here for, so you're done. Go do what teenage girls do."

Cassie started to shake. "This is so wrong."

Presley shrugged as he stuck his cigar in his mouth. "If you think so then deal with it. But get out of my office and leave your stuff here."

"You can't do this! I'm telling Mickey!"

"You're dismissed," Presley pointed to the door. "You do what you want but get out of my office."

Cassie wouldn't let herself cry. "You're such an asshole!"

"That seems to be the consensus around here," He pulled out his lighter and lit the tip of his cigar. "Now get out. I'm busy."

SEVENTY-FOUR

After a second energetic round of lovemaking against the 40th floor window, both were ready for something to eat. Peter suggested room service, but Tiffany quickly rejected that idea.

"We're in the greatest city in the world and I want to see it," Tiffany countered. "Let's walk in the park and find a nice restaurant. Preferably some Italian."

Since they had met in a local pub three months earlier, Peter's social skills had improved immensely. He still couldn't believe someone with Tiffany's beauty and intelligence was attracted to him. Maybe it was true; women loved men for their brains. That first night, they spent hours exchanging stories at the bar until she finally invited him back to her place.

"Any ideas where to have dinner?" Peter slipped on a sports jacket and checked his appearance in the hall mirror, while Tiffany fixed her makeup in the bathroom. "I'm starving."

She did an inventory of her purse and joined Peter in the room. "I did a search while I was waiting and there's a nice Italian restaurant about six blocks away on 57th Street."

After an enjoyable stroll through Central Park, the two lovebirds headed over to find their restaurant. The Manhattan skyline was mesmerizing. Off in the distance was the Empire State Building on 34th Avenue.

"I'm happy I came to meet you," Tiffany took Peter's hand. "What a great city with an amazing guy."

Tiffany's smile and a fifty-dollar tip got the manager to find them a seat on the patio where they could enjoy the pleasant evening.

215

They ordered a bottle of Finger Lakes Riesling from a local winery to get started. She fancied herself as a fledgling wine connoisseur and had read good reviews about the wine on her flight.

Peter forgot about his assignment. "Thank you for making the effort to find me."

The waiter served the wine and took their dinner orders. Tiffany chose a seafood linguini while Peter decided on the meat lasagna. After toasting their company, they sat and enjoyed the New York evening.

Peter finally leaned forward and mustered up the courage he had never found previously. "I'm in love with you and I'm ready to fight for you."

"I know you are." Tiffany picked up her wine. "Let's toast to that."

After enjoying a delicious dinner, they walked back to the hotel and Tiffany suggested they have a nightcap in the lounge before heading upstairs. "Let's end the night with some brandy heated in a snifter."

It wasn't hard to persuade Peter. "That sounds great."

The lounge was filled with business suits enjoying the benefit of corporate cards and everyone was listening to some energetic southern blues that played in the background. Tiffany smiled when she noticed all the young twenty-something girls clinging to their bosses, hoping they'd make that life-changing connection.

The waitress returned with their drinks. "Are we putting these on your boyfriend's room?"

Peter liked the sound of, 'your boyfriend.' "Why not?"

They raised their glasses and toasted to a great evening. And then they enjoyed the music and talked about plans for tomorrow. Peter's work was complete, so he had all day to enjoy her company.

Tiffany finally suggested they call it a night. They walked hand

and hand to the elevator and rode it to the 40th floor. Peter changed into sweatpants and a t-shirt and pulled a bottle of water from the mini fridge. "Wow, what a great day. Thank you."

"You're welcome." Tiffany grabbed a couple mini scotches from the bar. "Why don't we enjoy one last drink and talk about our plans for tomorrow? We can sit and admire the view while we talk."

"That sounds great."

She poured the scotch over ice. Peter was preoccupied and never noticed when she reached into her purse. Tiffany took a seat on the couch. "Come join me, so we can talk."

Peter took a seat and sipped the scotch. "Cheers."

"Back at you," They touched glasses. "I just want you to know I think the world of you."

He sensed bad news was coming. "But what?"

Tiffany smiled like she had no concern in the world. "I do need to tell you something."

Peter took another drink, sensing something bad was coming. "And what's that?"

Tiffany took his free hand. "I need you to understand that I never wanted to hurt you."

"Hurt me how?"

"I really do love you, but I have a job to do."

Peter knew that something was wrong with him. He thought of Tracey as he gasped for air and his body stiffened. He couldn't move. When he realized what was happening, his expression saddened. He knew he had been poisoned.

Tiffany stood up and watched Peter begin to convulse. There was no stopping the poison now. His eyes rolled back in his head. He wasn't in any pain and only had a few moments left. His glass slipped from his fingers and he collapsed face-first onto the floor. Death was imminent.

"The organization couldn't let you live after making the chemical compound. You became a liability."

Peter couldn't respond.

She wasn't sure if he understood her. "I'll always remember you, but I really do love Ray. And you knew this was coming when you doubted the organization. Tracy was the same."

Tiffany caught the red eye flight back to Vancouver and it was the next morning before she was back home and crawled into her own bed.

Ray opened his eyes. "How was your trip?"

"Exhausting."

He had to ask. "Were you with him?"

She yawned. "I was, and it's over."

She couldn't see his smile.

"Good night."

SEVENTY-FIVE

The Federal Coalition Party has been the official opposition to the majority Liberal government for the past eight years. Having a majority government meant the Federal Coalition were only sideline players, with no real influence on the day to day government decisions. They hadn't been considered a serious threat to get elected in almost twelve years. And Pierre and his Liberal party liked it that way.

The Federal Coalition Convention was scheduled for May in Vancouver and everyone associated with the party knew they had to shake things up. They needed a dynamic new leader with a platform that would get the voter's attention.

Other than Mickey, no one else in the organization knew of Joshua's relationship with Carol and she wanted it to stay that way. Her grandson could never garner special attention. If anything, he had to work harder.

Mickey knew the relationship between the two was headed towards some awkward times. Carol didn't put family first and Joshua had no idea his dad was dead. He thought his parents were travelling in Europe. That was why Mickey kept a close eye on him. Even though his intelligence ahead of nearly every adult on the planet, he was still a young boy in many ways. Mickey understood having a dysfunctional family.

Carol checked her watch before she entered the boardroom. She put on a stern face and went directly to her seat. "Are we ready?"

Everyone could sense Carol was in a volatile mood and the room was full of young recruits scared to breath. Other than Curtis, the rest stared at the table or fidgeted with their hands.

"I'm told that you've all had you first encounter with Mr. Presley and based on his report I have a room full of snot nosed kids!" Carol glared at everyone around the table. She made eye contact with Curtis. He had seen he act before and he wasn't as scared as the others. "How did your meeting go, Curtis?"

He looked around the table and there was no support coming his way. He shifted in his seat to face Carol. "He just walked in without warning and accused me of being a thief."

"Are you?"

"Am I what?"

"Stealing?"

He paused briefly. He thought about the money he sent his mother. "No. I like living too much to be that stupid."

Carol had made her point. There were rules to follow and everyone in her complex needed to remember that. She purposely chose Curtis because he was viewed as a leader by the recruits.

She continued. "There is a Federal Coalition leadership convention coming up in about a month."

Cassie was relieved that Carol didn't choose to use her as an example. "Can I ask why we're interested in a political convention? Politicians are what's wrong with this country."

Carol didn't disagree. "Many are and we're going to change that."

The heads around the table looked towards Carol. She had gotten their attention.

She continued. "We will be making an impact at that convention. The days of complaining and standing idly by are over. The organization is getting into the government business."

Curtis put up his hand like a kid in school. "I like what I'm hearing, but what exactly does that mean?"

Carol ignored Curtis. She turned to face her grandson. "What do the numbers look like, Joshua?"

Joshua opened a spreadsheet on his tablet. "I did an analytical study for each registered member who can cast a vote…"

Carol interrupted him. "There are over twenty-five hundred registered members."

"There are twenty-four hundred and eleven to be exact," He respectfully corrected her. "To get the report you wanted I needed to know that."

Carol nodded. "Go on."

Joshua didn't need to look at his notes. His photographic memory made recalling numbers second nature. "I created a profile for each member to determine who they are and how they vote. I then put the information through an algorithm and came up with an interesting summary."

"And that tells us what?" Carol asked.

"There are nine people that control ninety percent of the vote. These nine run the Federal Coalition. Get them onside and you control the party."

"And do you have a list of those nine names?"

"I've already emailed them to you," Joshua felt good, knowing his work was thorough. "Everything you should need is in the email."

Mickey stood in the back of the room. He was grinning. Well done Joshua. This was a huge piece of information.

When the meeting was over Mickey followed Carol back to her office. He closed the door and turned on the kettle to make her some tea.

Carol sat at her desk. "Any word from New York?"

Peter grabbed a tea bag and put it in the pot. "Yes, the vial was picked up and is on route to Ottawa."

"And what about Peter?"

"He was found dead in his hotel room." Mickey stated easily. "He suffered a massive heart attack as you suggested."

SEVENTY-SIX

Ray was relieved that Tiffany was home from her trip and back in his life. He had no idea where she had been, or who she was with. She said it was over and he wanted to believe her. He knew whatever it was, had to end.

He watched her sleep and wondered who his wife really was. She wasn't the sweet innocent girl he knew when they married. Something had changed while he was away. His curiosity was finally getting the better of him and he touched her bare shoulder. "I know what you told me, but I need to hear it again."

Tiffany wasn't ready to wake up and struggled to turn under her blankets. She didn't have the energy to have a conversation. "I meant what I said."

"It's over, Ray." She yawned. "I told him you're back in my life. Now I really do need some sleep."

"Just out of curiosity, where were you last night?"

Her eyes were already closed. "In New York City, having dinner."

Ray fell back into his pillow. "New York City? I love you, but I have no idea who you are."

Tiffany was sound asleep.

Ray slipped out of bed and into the shower. He had an early breakfast meeting he didn't want to be late for. It was time to start taking his life back. He pulled into a Denny's restaurant and found an empty table in the back. The waitress followed him with a silver pot. "Can I get two menus? And please fill the second cup. My friend loves his coffee."

David didn't look excited when he entered the restaurant and spotted Ray. It had been five years and he didn't know what to expect from his ex-partner. He knew this get-together was inevitable, so doing it in a very public restaurant at seven in the morning seemed as safe as anywhere.

Ray stood and the two shook hands. It wasn't a greeting full of enthusiasm, but neither expected that. They took their seats.

"Hello, David. Thank you for coming."

David tried to keep things light. "You look good. Prison was good for you."

Ray laughed. "And you look older."

David instinctively grabbed his coffee and took a sip. "I can't believe it's been five years."

"Don't remind me." Ray kept the tone upbeat.

"No problem."

"I wasn't sure if you'd come. We have a lot to catch up on. The last time we saw each other, it didn't go well," Ray reminded him, "but I'm glad you're here now."

When Ray reached out to set up the meeting, David was reluctant because he couldn't think of any reason they needed to talk. The truth was he feared Ray. Prison changes people. Ray was insistent and David finally agreed.

"Look, Ray. I'm not real comfortable being here so let's get to why you called me."

"Fair enough," Ray nodded. "I just did five years in prison for a crime we both know I didn't commit."

David strongly disagreed. "You confessed to the drug charges to avoid a messy rape trial and a much longer sentence. This is old news. You raped my wife."

"Are you sure?" Ray countered, sounding confident.

David's hatred for Ray resurfaced. "I'm not interested in hearing some bullshit story full of excuses five years later."

"I understand your anger. If it were my wife, I'd probably be in jail for murder," Ray had waited a long time to confront his accuser. "I want to talk about the video."

"What about it?"

"The only thing on that video that links me to the attack on Nina is the car. Do you agree with that?"

He wasn't ready to agree to anything. "Maybe."

Ray continued with his prepared questions. His courtroom experience was coming in handy. "If I was as drunk as your video showed, I did a great job avoiding the cameras."

David wasn't interested in rehashing the evidence. "You knew where the cameras were."

"You two set me up. I never touched her, and I can't figure out why she said I did."

The waitress inadvertently interrupted what had quickly become a tense conversation. "Are you boys ready to order?"

Ray smiled at her. "I'll have some blueberry pancakes with crispy bacon. And a glass of good orange juice. What about you David?"

He wasn't planning to stay much longer. "Just more coffee."

David waited until the waitress had left. "You're saying I staged my wife's rape? Did I hear that correctly?"

"I know someone did. The only person to benefit from me going to jail is you," Ray pointed out. "You got the firm."

David bit his lower lip to control his anger. "I never set you up for rape, but I did…"

"Did what?"

David stopped. He knew he had said too much already. "I had nothing to do with what you saw on the video. But, when I saw it, I did want you dead. Nina is still suffering the effects of the attack."

225

"I don't think she is," Countered Ray, knowing it was a touchy stance. "Let's talk about the car in the video."

"What about your car? It's in the video, so how do you explain that?"

"It's actually easy to explain," Ray reached into his pocket and pulled out the rental agreement he got from Sabrina. He handed it to David. "Look at the type of car that was rented the day Nina was attacked. And look who rented it."

David stared at the signature. "This is bullshit."

"No, David, it's not." Ray countered confidently. "Nina rented the car in your driveway. My question is why?"

David examined the rental agreement. He looked at it, hoping the names would magically change, because if it were real, he had made a huge mistake. "Why would Nina stage her own rape?"

"I can't answer that yet," Ray sensed David was becoming a believer, "but I'm going to find out. I need to know why."

David was on the defensive. "She had no reason."

"Even you have to admit your wife was behind this now," Ray finished his coffee and craved more. "If you didn't know anything about the rape setup, then you were involved with the cocaine. I think you really believe your wife was attacked and you wanted to protect her. That means she is involved with all of this."

David slapped the rental agreement on the table. "You're accusing the victim. That's pathetic."

"Am I?" Ray knew he was getting to David. He was a lawyer and he had to follow the evidence. "I'm *the victim*. I'm the innocent one who went to jail."

David needed answers. He rose from the table, feeling stressed. "I'm not interested in hearing any more shit."

Ray pointed to David's chair. "Sit down! There's more. You'll listen to what I have to say or I'm going to the police. Do you want

Nina to get involved in that?"

David looked around the restaurant and realized people were watching. "Say what you came here to say and then we're done."

"I lost five years of my life because of your wife. You need to fix that," Ray knew exactly what he wanted. "Your wife ruined my life and I want payback."

"Or what, Ray?"

"Do you really believe I attacked your wife?"

"Why should I think otherwise?" David looked at the rental papers. "Those don't prove anything."

"Talk to Nina," countered Ray, "because she has the answers."

David left as Ray's breakfast arrived. Neither man saw the man sitting at the counter watching them argue. Mickey was spreading some peanut butter on his toast when David stormed out.

SEVENTY-SEVEN

After Hugh Hutchinson left the prime minister's residence, he had his driver take him home. He was relieved that Pierre didn't go crazy when he heard Kamahi's demands. Hugh never doubted that a wave of retaliation would come from Pierre. He was simply happy that it wasn't tonight.

The day had been long, and at times, complicated, and Hutchinson needed a hot shower and a cold drink. He wanted some time to workout a solution for the North Korean deal that would benefit Hutchinson Enterprises. Solving the money issue was not going to be as easy as Pierre expected. Eon Kamahi still had the video, so the North Koreans had the better poker hand.

After a quick shower, he threw on some cargo pants and a t-shirt. He was glad to be out of his suit. It was a snug fit. He stepped on the scale and saw that he had gained another pound.

At this critical juncture Hugh had no intention to replace the finance minister in the North Korean deal. Fisher's death meant more work, but it also gave him control of the finances. That was a good thing.

Pierre seemed to have checked out of his political career. He had done a long shift and was more focused on living out his sexual fantasies than running the country. That made the video even more valuable. Hugh planned on keeping a copy. It could be a great insurance policy or get out of jail card.

Hugh entered his study and nearly screamed when he saw Carol sitting behind his desk. He was sure his heart skipped a beat.

"Hello Hugh. We need to talk."

He was not happy she was in his house. "How did you get in here? I'll have security throw you off my property."

Carol scoffed at his bellowing. "How do you think I got in here. There are things more valuable than money."

"What the hell does that mean?" Hugh decided on water instead of scotch. He thought about the extra pound. "And why are you here? I haven't seen you since you hijacked your way into my party."

"Like I said before, I think we should talk."

Hugh shooed her out of his chair. "What do you need to talk about that made you break into my home?"

"Let's begin with our prime minister. I hear he likes to play dress-up."

"I don't know about that," Hugh defended Pierre, "but he can be an interesting person at times."

"Are you going to continue to throw your public and financial support behind his political career?"

"Why not?" Hugh shrugged. "It's been profitable."

"Is Hutchinson Enterprises guaranteed more contracts to maintain your status quo?"

Hugh didn't answer. He was curious to hear how much she knew about their partnership. "What do you want?"

"I know you lost a key piece of your network when Fisher died," Carol watched his reaction. There was none. "Who's stepping up to finish the North Korean deal?"

Hugh was careful. Where did she get her information from? She had to have someone on the inside. "What do you know about the North Koreans?"

"Enough," Carol pretended to be disinterested in that topic. "You're right. I did come here with a purpose and I'm hoping you'll consider an offer."

"And what is that?"

"We both know Elliot is becoming a useless troll and needs to be replaced."

Hugh was interested to hear more. "I don't disagree that Pierre is getting tired, but who are you thinking could run against the Liberals and win?"

"I have the perfect person," Carol boasted, "and the perfect plan. I can guarantee a win."

"That's pretty confident, even for you," Hugh sipped his water. "Did you figure out how to manipulate the voting machines?"

"No, that's something that happens in the United States," She corrected him. "I can control the voters."

Hugh decided he wanted a scotch. "Okay, you have my attention."

SEVENTY-EIGHT

Joshua was committed to work on the boxing techniques Mickey had taught him. He pounded the heavy bag, waiting for his next sparring session in the ring. His sweat soaked t-shirt clung to his back and his thin shoulder muscles ached as he pushed himself through another set.

The thought of working out in a gym as part of his daily routine was something Joshua had never considered prior to his life at the complex. Outside of the occasional walk in the park, his parents didn't engage in a physical lifestyle. Working out was the first time he felt he was apart of something. He included hanging out with the guys.

Another regular in the gym was Curtis, who favoured working out with the weights for body strength. He watched from afar when Joshua started to show up and work out with in the boxing ring Mickey. Curtis felt a twinge of jealousy.

"How's the boxing coming?" Curtis tugged on a towel draped around his neck. You look like you're figuring it out."

"I'm getting better, but my hands hurt."

Curtis flashed his big smile. "You'll get used to it. It takes time. I've been coming almost everyday for two years."

Joshua was impressed with Curtis's muscular arms. "Maybe you can teach me about weights some day? If you have time?"

Curtis liked the idea of hanging out with the younger boy. Something about him was different. "We'll start you on technique."

Mickey joined them. "Hey, Curtis, how's the weight training? Do you still want to climb in the ring?"

He imitated a series of bodybuilding poses. "I'm working it and yes, please."

Mickey laughed at the comedic routine. "If you're finished trying to impress the girls, let's go for a run."

They raced through the maze of trails. Mickey was in great shape and led the entire way. Curtis gave it an effort and Joshua pulled up the rear. He was disappointed and promised to be better next time.

"You got lucky, old man," Curtis was bent over, gasping to fill his aching lungs. "Next time, you're mine."

They wandered over and enjoyed the cool breeze while they watched the Queen of Burnaby ferry head out on it's two-hour sailing to Vancouver. Mickey pulled up his t-shirt and wiped the sweat on his face. "Curtis, I need a few minutes with Joshua."

Curtis knew that was a signal for him to leave and tapped Joshua on the shoulder. "We'll start weight training tomorrow."

Mickey stood over Joshua. "How's it going for you here? Judging by today, you seem to be fitting in."

Joshua watched the ferry disappear around the island. "I'm good. I don't think about home as much as I used to."

"That's good," Mickey took a seat on a log. "We need to talk."

"What's up, Mickey?"

"You've been reassigned."

"What does that mean?"

"You're being transferred to Level C," Mickey revealed, "where the important work happens."

Joshua had heard rumors about Level C but had never met anyone assigned there. "Can I still go to the gym?"

Mickey knew the gym was important to him. He also understood the minimal interaction allowed for anyone working on that level. "I'm sure I can work something out for you."

"That's great. I love going to the gym and Curtis is going to teach me how to lift weights."

"I see you're fitting in with the older boys, but you have to remember why you're here. We have some big projects with serious deadlines. They can't be ignored."

"I understand." Joshua didn't want to disappoint Mickey. "What will I be working on?"

"Remember, you tell no one." Mickey emphasized. "It's with human animatronics. You'll be building a person."

SEVENTY-NINE

David couldn't get home fast enough after meeting with Ray. There was a lot running through his mind. He had time to calm down and think about what Ray had showed him. If the rental agreement were real, it would give Ray a great defence in court. It created serious reasonable doubt.

Ray's case wasn't going to court, but David knew he had to make things right if it was true. He found his wife in the kitchen eating a slice of toast. David hadn't let himself be persuaded just yet. He was anxious to hear Nina's side of the story. It had to be good because if Ray was right, he was sent to prison on a lie. A lie that was perpetrated by his wife.

He poured a coffee. "Do you have five minutes to talk?"

Nina finished her toast. "Do I have to ask how things went with Ray?"

"That's going to depend on you."

Nina's carefree attitude disappeared. "I don't like the sound of that. What did he say?"

"He still denies he ever raped you."

Nina huffed in disgust. "He's been saying that for five years. He went to prison on drug charges, so either way, he's a felon."

"I need to know the truth, Nina," David knew he had to ask. "Did Ray really rape you or was it a setup?"

Nina glared at her husband. "You've been through the entire process with me."

"Yes, I have," David thought about showing the rental agreement. "He feels he's found some evidence that proves his innocence."

"There's no evidence for him to find," Nina didn't sound certain, "and if there was something, we'd know about it by now."

David decided it was time to push for the truth. "Ray showed me something. It has me thinking that everything isn't as I was told."

Nina looked at her husband and saw the guilt in his eyes. "He went to jail on drug charges, but he's still going on about my assault. Why would he do that?"

"Maybe he believes in his innocence and he needs to come to peace with it."

"Or maybe you're trying to clear your own conscious?" Nina countered defensively. "Since you seem to want a *'come to Jesus'* moment, let's have one."

"You know that I set Ray up on the cocaine charge so you could avoid a stressful and public trial," David reminded her, "but I've always believed you were attacked by him."

"And now you don't?"

David threw up his hands. "I want to believe you, but I need you to explain something Ray brought up this morning."

Nina wasn't ready to admit to anything. "And that is?"

"He had a copy of a car rental agreement."

Nina shrugged. "So?"

"Did you ever rent a car like Ray's?" David studied his wife's reaction. "In fact, did you rent it the same day you were attacked?"

"I've never rented a car like Ray's, but I know who did," Nina knew it was time. It was over. "I think we should grab some wine. It's time to tell you the whole story."

David checked his watch. "It's only eight-thirty in the morning."

Nina led him by the hand to the couch in the living room and they sat on opposite ends. She filled her glass. David rejected her offer to pour one for him. She sipped the wine and took a big breath to get her head straight. This was going to be hard. "Ray never attacked me. It was part of a bigger plan to protect you."

"How can faking a sexual assault and ruining a man's life be part of any plan you're involved with? And how the hell does it protect me?"

Nina slowly rocked her head. "If I didn't agree to go along with it, they were going to kill Ray."

David needed more answers. "Who was going to kill him?"

"The person who drove the car."

EIGHTY

Ray felt confident he had made an impression with David. He knew his ex-partner would want answers and confront Nina. The next piece of the puzzle was to find out who was in the hoodie. When he found out who they were it would be over.

He felt good about how things were coming together as he left the restaurant and headed to the police station. The receptionist expected him and buzzed him through the security door with a pleasant smile. He went straight to Sergeant Smith's office.

Murphy was already there and tossed Ray a bottle of water. "The coffee has hit a new low, so I'm suggesting you stick to this."

Ray thanked him and followed the detective into a conference room. There were three faces he didn't recognize at the table. Smith was the fourth. Everyone in the room was a parent of a missing child. It was heart wrenching to see, but he had no idea how Smith thought he could help.

Smith turned on a laptop and activated the Zoom screen. "This is Suzanne Lacy, who lives in Whitehorse. Her son, Curtis, has been in the news again after Suzanne and her dog made an amazing discovery. Thanks for joining us."

Suzanne waved nervously. "Thank you for inviting me and a big thank you for getting this organized."

"I'm hoping by having a group conversation someone will say something that will jar a memory. We could all use a little luck."

Stacey glanced at Ray. "How do you fit into this?"

Ray looked at the sergeant. "I'm not really sure, but they seem to think I might be able to help, so here I am."

Gloria Chang was the first to speak. She was a small Chinese woman that had her grey hair hidden under a scarf. She wore a pair of big round prescription eyeglasses that were too big for her face. Behind the glasses were tired eyes.

When she talked about Cassie, her voice squeaked, and she beamed with pride. She didn't understand how her daughter got so smart but was happy to talk about Cassie's dream of solving world hunger.

Stacey Small agreed to go next and rubbed her growing belly. She was almost five months pregnant. She talked about the school fire like it was yesterday and the panic she felt watching the school burn to the ground without knowing where her son was. It was an emotionally charged story.

There wasn't a dry eye in the room, including Ray.

She explained her relief when Joshua's body wasn't found in the ashes and how she plunged back into panic when she understood the alternative. She mentioned the strain on her marriage and a tear formed when she talked about Robert's death on Christmas Eve. Like everyone in the room, she believed her son was alive and she wondered out loud if Joshua knew about his dad's death.

It was Suzanne's turn, and everyone faced the computer and listened. They had all seen her story on the news, and she was somewhat of a celebrity. She described her son as an outgoing and energy-filled boy who loved the outdoors. "He always wore a stupid baseball cap and loves his chicken strips and fries."

Suzanne finished by pulling Rupert up onto her lap so everyone could say hello. It was a much-needed happy moment.

Stacey got Suzanne's attention, "Are you okay talking about your bank story?"

Suzanne nodded. "When my husband left, I put everything into finding my son. I hired private investigators and even a psychic, who told me Curtis was living up in the mountains. So, I chartered a helicopter to look. I feel kind of foolish because before I knew it, I was overdrawn seventy-five thousand dollars."

"Oh my gosh," Gloria Chang gushed. "My husband would kill me if I spent that much money."

Ray paid attention.

"Please go on, Suzanne," coaxed Stacey. "Tell them the rest."

Suzanne held up her bank statement to the computer camera. "I know I was careless with my finances, but it gave me hope."

"What happened?" asked Smith.

A rare smile appeared on Suzanne's face. "I got a call from the bank manager to tell me my balance was paid off in full."

Smith wanted to be sure he heard her right. "You're telling us that someone deposited seventy-five thousand into your account?"

Her face beamed. "Yes."

Stacey asked a question. "And you're sure that Curtis had something to do with this. Is that how you still feel?"

"My son was a genius with hacking into computers and so he could easily do it," Suzanne explained. "I know he's watching me."

Detective Murphy leaned towards the monitor. "Did you ask the bank to do a trace on the deposit?"

"They only knew it was from an off-shore account," Suzanne sounded disappointed. "I did get an email from the bank manager a few days later telling me that it might have been from a company called Liberty City, but he wasn't sure. I googled them and it was a dead end."

Ray leaped up. "I've heard of them."

Everyone looked at him.

Murphy asked. "How?"

"I was involved with the Gabriola Island land purchase until I went to prison," Ray blurted before thinking. "Liberty City was the winning bid."

Stacey shot Ray a bewildered look. "You were in prison?"

Smith interrupted the meeting. What Ray just divulged needed to be discussed outside of this audience, so he recommended a fifteen-minute break. Everyone agreed and side conversations started as soon as they left the room.

Smith closed his office door behind him. Detective Murphy had taken a detour to the washroom. "What can you tell me about Liberty City?"

Ray thought back. "It was very clear from the beginning they wanted to win."

"What does that mean?"

"It started the night I was brought in for a DUI," Ray began, "and I had a cellmate named Bjorn. He told me that if I chose Liberty City as the winning bid all of my problems, including the new drug charges, would go away."

"So, why didn't you?"

"I wanted to, but when I contacted the jail, they had no record of anyone named Bjorn ever being there."

Smith listened with an open mind. "You know what you're accusing the department of?"

"I do now. If there is no record of Bjorn, then he had to be a plant by someone within the police."

"You seem sure."

"The one thing I'm sure of is the cocaine wasn't mine."

"If you were innocent then why did you plead guilty?" asked Smith. "Innocent men fight for their freedom."

"That's a story for another time." replied Ray.

Detective Murphy joined them, and Ray went silent.

EIGHTY-ONE

After an early morning jog through the trails behind her house, Tiffany took a hot shower and dressed in a pink off-shoulder blouse with a form-fitting knee-length powder blue skirt. She had a lunch date with a friend, and it had been a year since they last saw each other. She was looking forward to some wine and good conversation.

When she arrived at the Bistro Café, she found her friend on the patio talking up the waiter while she sipped her drink. The hostess took Tiffany to the table and the two women embraced affectionately.

Tiffany ordered a glass of wine and took the seat across from her friend. "Dam it girl. You look hot."

"Thanks, Tiff," Laura beamed, "and I love your outfit. You still have your smoking' body."

"I'm getting older, so I have to work much harder."

Laura Nelsen's new longer hairstyle complimented her high cheekbones. The butch hairstyle as a lesbian and the wardrobe that went with it were gone. "How are you? Are you still married to the mystery man?"

"My life is good, but still too busy," Tiffany laughed as her wine arrived, "and married life is a journey, but I've made it to six years."

Laura toasted her glass. "Here's to married life and hopefully one day I'll get to experience it."

"You're still too wild to get married." Tiffany reminded her.

"When do I get to meet your guy? It's like you're hiding him from me."

"Hopefully one day, but we should keep our friendship away

from our personal lives." Tiffany suggested.

"I understand, but it would be nice to live like normal people, even if only for a day or two," She admired her friend's perfect skin. "And you haven't aged a bit in the years we've known each other."

"Believe me, I'm getting older. I'm simply better at hiding it."

Before the women continued with their barrage of compliments, the waiter appeared and took their order. They decided to share a craft of red wine and each chose the house salad with a strawberry vinaigrette dressing. Laura added some chicken. She wanted the protein to offset the alcohol she planned to drink.

"I understand you just returned from New York." Laura sipped her wine. "How was that?"

"I did." The thought of Peter being dead made her sad. "He was a nice man."

"I don't care about the assignment. It's just a payday." Laura shrugged with disinterest. "Did you do any shopping while you were there?"

"You're unbelievable. A man dies and you want to talk shopping," chortled Tiffany. "I had no time to shop. After the assignment, I was on a red eye back to normal life. What about you? I heard about Tracy's death."

Laura sipped her wine. She stared past Tiffany and said nothing.

Tiffany knew about their relationship. "It had to be difficult."

Laura showed no emotion. "Are you asking me if it was hard to push her off the cliff?"

Tiffany nodded.

"Yes and no," Laura glanced around to make sure their conversation stayed private. "It was tough pretending to love a lesbian for two years. But that's our job, isn't it?"

"What was she like?" Tiffany twirled her wine in her glass. "What was it like being a fake lesbian?"

Laura burst out in laughter. "A fake lesbian? I'm not sure it was fake."

"What was she like?"

Laura remembered back. "The stress of her role with the organization was taking its toll and she was seriously considering going to the police. Carol decided it was time to end it. When Tracy saw me, the look in her eyes told me she knew. She was expecting it and put up no resistance."

There was no sympathy for the victims. There couldn't be. "I poisoned Peter. I watched him choke on his own vomit while his body shut down. Not pleasant."

Their salads arrived and the waitress filled their glasses with more wine before she left them to enjoy their lunch.

"What's next for you?" Laura asked.

Tiffany picked a cherry tomato from her salad and put it between her lips. "I'm not sure. I've had no contact from the organization yet, so I'm using the time to get to know my husband again."

"What does that mean? Are you guys having problems? Was he screwing around? I'll kill him if you want. No charge."

"Relax," Tiffany laughed at her friend's warped humour. "He just got out of prison. Did five years for a drug charge."

"Seriously?" Laura sipped her wine. "You're not as domesticated as you like to let on. Is he a bad ass?"

"Actually, he was set up," Tiffany told her. "He's a corporate lawyer, albeit an unemployed one."

"You married a fucking lawyer?" Laura loved how this conversation was playing out. "You said he was set up. Do you know who did it? Maybe we should kill them."

"I do know." she responded sheepishly.

"Well, don't just sit there," pushed Laura, "did you whack them?"

Tiffany laughed quietly. "I didn't whack anyone."

"Why not?" Laura looked puzzled.

Tiffany put her glass on the table. "It's me."

Laura blurted out a laugh. "You set up your own husband? What for?"

"The organization viewed him as a threat," Tiffany shook her head, thinking back. "The stupid thing was he pled guilty to drug charges. I set him up for rape."

Laura hung on every word. "Now I'm confused. You set your own husband up on a rape charge. He must have really made you angry."

"He did," she recalled. "I was angry that he deceived me. And I'll admit, I had anger management issues."

"Does he know?" Laura knew the answer from Tiffany's expression. "What if he finds out?"

"He won't," she responded confidently. "If he plays detective, everything leads back to his ex-partner's wife. I used the dumb bitch's credit card to rent a car."

"What an intriguing life you live," Laura enjoyed taunting her friend. "You really are a vindictive piece of work. Remind me never to cross you."

"Let's move onto something more cheerful," Tiffany knew they had both said too much. "Tell me about what you're doing next."

"I'm going to a political convention. My target is an influential man in the world of politics."

"You'll be good in that role," Tiffany bit a slice of cucumber. "Do you have any plans after Vancouver?"

Laura pushed her salad to the side. "Hopefully, an exotic trip somewhere."

Tiffany lowered her voice. "I might try other things."

Laura was amused. "You're not exactly in a business where you give notice. If they decide you're staying, you *know* you're staying."

"I understand the consequences, but it has begun to eat at me. I have nightmares."

"Look at you," Laura didn't expect this, "an assassin with a conscious is not a good combination."

Tiffany gulped down her wine and refilled her glass. "Let's talk happy shit."

Laura agreed. "Let me tell you a funny story about Tracy."

"I hope it's not about her falling down a cliff."

"I got a call from some asshole pretending to be Tracy's estranged brother."

Tiffany interrupted her. "How'd you know he was lying?"

"Because I lived with Tracy for two years. I knew everything about her. She never mentioned a brother."

Tiffany nibbled at her salad. "Why did you meet with him?"

"Simple curiosity, and I was bored," responded Laura. "The cops were still investigating her death as a possible murder. They were thinking McKee was involved. I was sent to find out what they knew."

"What did this guy want?"

"He claimed he was after her life insurance money," her look indicated her despise for the guy, "but I knew none existed."

"Do you think he was a cop?"

"I don't think so, but he was definitely working for someone," she retorted, "and I think he was trying to catch me in a lie."

Tiffany was curious. "What did he look like?"

Laura recalled his handsome features. "He was about fifty but looked younger and was in good shape. Dark hair and a thin moustache that didn't suit him."

"Did this guy have a name?" Tiffany asked. "Maybe he's investigating all of us?"

"He did."

"And that was?"

Laura took a sip of wine. "He said his name was Ray Cooke. Probably another lie."

Tiffany nearly choked on her salad. She grabbed her napkin and held it to her mouth.

"Did I say something funny?

Tiffany wiped her lips, feeling embarrassed. "Tell me more about this Cooke guy."

"Not a lot to tell. Like I said, he was handsome and had a solid body. I considered inviting him back to my place," Laura sounded serious. "You have to remember I was a lesbian for two years, so I'm ready for a man in my life."

They couldn't be talking about *her* Ray Cooke, but the description fit. Why would he be asking about Tracy? "Are you going to meet with him again?"

"He definitely isn't a second chance kind of guy."

They finished lunch and Tiffany remembered an appointment she had to be at. It was with her husband. They needed to talk.

"Let's stay in touch," suggested Laura, as they walked out of the restaurant, "and next time you can bring your husband along."

Not a chance. "I'll ask him."

EIGHTY-TWO

Carol was agitated when she returned to the complex after her quick back and forth from Ottawa. Stormy weather had delayed her departure and it was now after mid night. The first thing she did was message Mickey.

He was waiting for her and had the kettle boiling when she walked in. "Sorry it was such a long day for you."

She threw her purse on her desk. "How is everything here?"

"Good," The kettle steamed, "and I talked with Joshua. He's excited to be working in the new department."

"If anyone can get us over the finish line, that boy can," Carol took her tea. "His parents definitely didn't give him his intelligence."

"Not many people on the planet have that kid's brain," He changed the topic. "How was your meeting with Hutchinson?"

"You were right," Carol tested the tea. "As soon as I dangled a big enough carrot, he grabbed it."

"So, he's on board for the campaign?"

Carol looked satisfied. "And much more."

"What did you promise him for his support?"

"It doesn't matter. It's a check he'll never get to cash."

Mickey checked the time. He had an early morning. "What does Hutchinson think about deserting Pierre?"

"He doesn't care and never did. For Hutchinson, Elliot was just the key to the vault full of taxpayer's money. They're both criminals that need to go."

"So, we'll just let the billionaire think he's in control and getting richer?"

"Exactly. He thrives on power and wealth and we'll give him both."

Mickey was impressed with the idea. "And when he thinks he has it all we'll take it away."

Carol pulled off her shoes and sat on the couch. "I hear Presley is still a problem."

"The recruits don't like him if that's what your asking."

"Send him to Washington DC to pick up the p."

"Okay," Mickey yawned, which was an indication the meeting was over. "One last thing. When do we announce our candidate for the Federal Coalition?"

"Good night, Mickey." Carol answered. "I'm going to bed."

EIGHTY-THREE

"I'm in no mood to play twenty questions," David screamed at his wife. "I want to know who drove the car."

For the first time in their marriage, Nina was fearful of her husband and what he might do. He was full of rage. There was so much more going on in their lives that David didn't know about, and now Ray was back. If Cooke insisted on playing detective, it could be very disruptive, and he might need to be dealt with. "You need to lower your voice."

"And you need to put the wine down," He countered back. "It's becoming a habit you're losing control of."

Nina reluctantly put her glass on the table. "Get our jackets. It's time to clear this up."

"What is there to clear up?"

"You're asking the wrong question," Nina grabbed her coat out of the closet. "It's not about who was driving the car. It's about why. Get your jacket and let's go."

The winds off the mountains were cool enough to zip up their coats. The mood was like the weather and nothing was said at first. They just walked, each waiting for the other to start.

David got things going. "Who was driving?"

"First things first, you have to believe me when I tell you I did not rent the car."

Davey pulled the rental agreement out. "Your signature is on the bottom."

"I didn't rent it." She insisted.

"Your credit card receipt disagrees," David pushed. "Are you telling me someone used your credit card to rent a car. Then they drove back to our house and pretended to rape you? That's a big stretch."

"Sort of."

David stopped on the trail and put his hands on her shoulders. "Tell me what the hell you're involved with. How did your name get on that contract?"

She let out a deep sigh. "I was told to give the driver my card. When I knew the plan, I wanted nothing to do with it."

"But you did, and Ray went to jail for five damn years," David was disgusted with his wife. "How do you make that up to him?"

"Ray was never supposed to go to prison," She pleaded, "it was only going to be used as leverage. But then you came to my rescue and the police were involved. You were my Prince Charming, but it screwed up everything."

David threw his arms up. "Who wanted to have leverage on Ray and why are you involved with people like this?"

"I can't tell you."

David was angry. "I sent my best friend to prison for a crime he didn't commit because I thought I was protecting you. The real victim here is Ray. And now you're protecting some dangerous people."

Nina tried to lighten the mood but failed. "Kind of ironic, isn't it?"

"Is there a plan for Ray to get his life back?"

"No idea," She replied flatly. "My role was to play the victim and that's it."

David eyes were razors. "You still haven't answered the question. Who rented the car?"

Nina finally gave in. "Ray's wife."

EIGHTY-FOUR

Hugh Hutchinson laid in bed thinking about the new opportunity Carol had offered Hutchinson Enterprises. It was a great offer, but his problem was he didn't trust her. She might tell him she's not into the money, but he knew she loved control more than any of them.

On the other hand, Hugh was concerned about the prime minister's current state of mind. There was a video out there with a dildo stuck in his butt and he didn't seem to care. He was playing a dangerous game of Russian roulette with the North Koreans.

If the video ever got leaked his political legacy would be re-written as a late-night talk show punchline. Hugh didn't want to be associated or be responsible for being the prime minister's alibi. The fallout would be crazy and there would be plenty of it. Maybe it was time for a change of allegiance. He decided he wanted to know more about the Federal Coalition and their mystery leader.

He owed Eon Kamahi a call, so he dialed the over seas number.

Eon's mastery of the English language reflected his American university education. "Mr. Hutchinson. How are you?"

"I'm good but we should get to business."

"I was expecting your call," Eon was anxious for good news. "What did your prime minister decide?"

Hugh remembered Pierre's exact words but didn't repeat them. "With a few conditions we have a deal."

Eon was curious. "What are the conditions? Remember we have the video."

Fuck the video. I'm not on it. "The first condition is the discount is only three million and the second is you'll allow Hutchinson Enterprises to use your engineering facilities to develop some oil extracting equipment."

Eon snickered. "You don't want to upset the environmentalist in your country I see?"

"It didn't take you long to put it together," Hugh's voice dripped with sarcasm. "And about the video. I get it, and I'm talking about you removing it from the cloud or anywhere else you might have it saved. I want the only copy."

There was a pause on the other end. Eon confided with someone else. He finally came back on the line. "So, the deal is we still keep the five million and we charge you a small percentage for our factories. You can have the tape. No one wants to watch an old man with a stick up his ass wearing a tutu."

Even Hugh had to laugh. "Done."

Hugh hung up and decided to celebrate with a Cuban and a brandy. He would call Pierre with the good news in the morning. Pierre would be happy to hear the video was deleted, and he'd have to accept that the discount rose to $7 million. It was the cost of being stupid.

EIGHTY-FIVE

It had been a month since his release and Ray tried to stay upbeat as he worked to re-establish a new life. He wasn't sure if he'd ever practice law again. His relationship with his wife was a pleasant surprise and less complicated than he had imagined. Tiffany seemed ready to put their past behind them and that's what he needed to do.

He just had one last thing to do to close the book. The person in the hoodie had to pay.

He was running late for another meeting with the cops. His relationship with Detective Murphy was forced at best. If it weren't for Sergeant Smith and the missing kids, he'd give Murphy the middle finger and move on. He had met his bail obligations, but his moral compass to help find those kids kept him involved.

He pulled into the coffee shop, and two middle aged women sitting outside enjoying their lattes stopped what they were doing to admire the sexy sports car, and the good-looking driver. Ray pushed his sunglasses onto his forehead. "Morning ladies."

He grabbed a black coffee and a muffin from the counter and joined Smith and Murphy. Smith greeted him with a nod and Murphy just grunted. Ray ignored it. "What's on the agenda this morning. I have to be somewhere in an hour."

Murphy scowled. Something bothered him. "We'll be done when we say we're done."

Cooke shot Smith a look and gave him a hidden wink that Murphy never saw.

Ray sipped on his coffee. "Is there anything new about Liberty City."

Smith's expression didn't look encouraging. "I had forensics do some digging and whoever put the money in Suzanne's account covered their tracks. They didn't find anything to trace it back to it's origin."

"Not surprised," Ray bit his muffin. "If it is the same company, they would have strong legal representation."

Murphy wanted more coffee. "Is there anything else you can remember? You were rattled when you heard their name."

"More like surprised," Ray rebutted. "It's a name I haven't heard or thought about in years."

"What do you remember about their bid?" Smith asked. "Was there anything that stood out?"

Ray had lied when he said he hadn't thought about Liberty City. He thought about them every night when he was locked away. He was convinced they were involved with his incarceration. "I remember they were the last to submit their bid just under the wire. And everything from price to their land usage application was perfect. They were going to incorporate the old mind shafts into their design to minimize soil disruption. It was perfect."

Smith scratched an itch on his chin. "What are they doing over there?"

Ray chewed on his muffin. "I think they were into environmental sciences and technology. Very advanced stuff. The building was designed to be self sustained. They generate their own power and could live there year-round. It was designed like the space station."

"Too bad you got busted," Murphy teased, "or maybe you'd know."

The comment touched a nerve. "Maybe if your jail did a better job, you'd have a record of Bjorn being in my cell. He was definitely there and connected to them."

"Or maybe you were so drunk you dreamt him up." Murphy shot

back.

Smith could see this meeting was about to end. "I'll look into Bjorn and see what I can find out."

Murphy stood up. "I got the Bjorn thing. I'll check."

"No, you won't." Ray muttered as he stuffed the rest of his muffin in his mouth.

EIGHTY-SIX

Curtis was almost an hour into his own workout when Joshua finally made an appearance in the gym. The young boy was running late and looked embarrassed when Curtis told him to hurry up. The clock was ticking.

Dressed in some over sized blue shorts and a t-shirt that amplified how skinny his arms were, he stepped nervously towards Curtis. "Sorry for being late."

Curtis wiped the sweat off his face. "Let's get you at it, and remember, no pain no gain."

For the next hour, Joshua followed Curtis from station to station and learned about the world of weight training. By the time they were finished, Joshua could barely lift his arms. He was relieved that the workout was over, but he felt exhilarated.

Joshua asked. "What's next?"

"I usually hit the Juice Bar for a protein shake," Curtis tossed his gloves and towel into his gym bag. "I like chocolate."

Joshua wanted to fit in. "How do they taste?"

"You'll like it," Curtis ordered two and a few minutes later they were ready. "Let's take them outside."

They ended up in the flower garden. It was usually a place where people hung out after work. Tonight, there was no one. It had a view of the water and the trees were a nesting area for a lot of west coast birds. They sat at opposite ends of a bench made from washed driftwood.

Joshua enjoyed the shake. "Thanks for the work out."

"No worries."

Joshua watched a Red-breasted Sapsucker balance skillfully on a branch only a few feet away. It had a bug of some kind hanging from its beak. "Did you know that ninety different birds live on this island?"

"I do now," Curtis made no effort to mask his sarcasm. "Who knows stuff like that?"

"I guess I do," Joshua felt self-conscious. "I read a book about the island last night."

Curtis stirred his shake. "When do you find time?"

"It was only two hundred pages," Joshua told him. "It was no big deal. It took an hour or so to read."

"An hour?" Curtis chuckled. "You're a machine, buddy."

"Can I ask you a question?"

"Shoot."

"Do you ever think about your family and getting out of here?"

Curtis shot Joshua a suspicious look. "This place is like Alcatraz. You don't get to just leave."

"So, do you ever think about it?" Joshua repeated.

The thought crossed Curtis's mind all the time, but he was curious why Joshua suddenly asked. "The price of coming here to escape your family and work on really cool stuff was your one-hundred percent commitment to the organization. You don't get to leave."

Joshua finished his shake. "I know that. I just had a bad dream last night about my mom. I miss her."

"Your only eleven, dude," Curtis consoled him, "You're allowed to miss her."

"I'm actually twelve," Joshua corrected him. "Today's my birthday."

"Well, happy birthday," Curtis patted him on the shoulder. "You're a part of something special here. Not many get chosen and you're the smartest kid I've ever met."

Joshua shook his head. "That's not why I'm here."

Curtis tossed his cup into the garbage. "What are you talking about?"

"I'm here because of my grandmother," Just saying it brought relief to his face. "She brought me here."

"Who the hell is your grandmother?"

Joshua paused to be sure he was ready to say it. He was. "Carol."

Curtis was stunned. "Holy shit, how did you keep that a secret this long?"

"It was easy," he said. "I never thought about it."

"She might be your grandmother, but that's not why you're here."

Joshua remembered what he told Mickey. He hated that he broke a promise. "You can't say anything. I'll get in big trouble."

Curtis was already thinking about ways he could use this information to his advantage. "Your secret is safe with me."

"Good," Joshua looked past Curtis into the garden. "Can I trust you with one more thing?"

"Sure." Curtis said. "What is it?"

"Turn around."

"Oh my god," Curtis looked like he saw a ghost. "Who is that?"

EIGHTY-SEVEN

Carol had reviewed all the reports before she summoned Wendell Presley to her office. He had completely disrupted the comfort zones that the recruits had created for themselves. There wasn't a single person that said a complimentary thing about her latest addition to the organization.

There were accusations that he physically intimidated some recruits, accused others of being thieves, or was just a downright rude and disruptive person. They all feared him.

Carol couldn't stop her smile. That went exactly as planned. Many of the recruits had become complacent and a dose of the big black man's attitude was all they needed to get refocused. And she wasn't the bad guy this time.

Wendell had served his purpose at the complex and now she had a new assignment for him. His bigger than life personality made him the perfect fit. He'd hate the job but that didn't concern Carol.

Presley entered Carol's office with his usual swagger. He wore his dark black shirt with tight jeans and black cowboy boots. All that was missing was the horse. He plunked himself down on the couch and put his feet on the coffee table. "What's going on? Your message sounded urgent."

"Get your damn boots off my furniture," Carol glared at him. Compared to his massive size, she looked like a small child beside him. "Show some respect."

He did as he was told and sat up in his chair. "Why am I here?"

"Because you've done a pathetic job with the recruits," Carol dug in her heels. "You think intimidating kids is how you get results.

259

You're ridiculous."

Wendell waited until she was finished before countering her points. He also took the extra time to scan the room to see if Mickey was lurking nearby. "These kids are all smart mouthed assholes who need a good smack with my belt."

Carol shook her head in disgust. She was a good actor. "You were definitely the wrong choice. All you did was disrupt everything and put us behind schedule."

Wendell didn't expect this. "What are you planning? If you're firing me, I still want the money you guaranteed me."

"Just relax you fool," Carol slid a large manila envelope to him. "There's a new job assignment and some cash in there. I'm taking you away from the recruits and sending you on a trip."

Wendell resisted. "Do I have a choice?"

Carol's glare was his answer. "There is an airline ticket with travel instructions in there."

"When do I leave?"

"Your flight is in four hours," Carol informed him. "There is a boat charter waiting to pick you up and get you to the airport. So, I suggest you get packed"

EIGHTY-EIGHT

The entrance to the law firm had changed from when he had been a partner. Gone was the shiny glass doorway with bright lighting and brass trim. It was now replaced with modern steel and an ocean blue theme. The kick to his groin was the name now embossed in twelve-inch letters above the door.

THE MAGILL LAW FIRM

Cooke was long removed and forgotten.

He tried not to glance in the direction of the boardroom as he walked to the reception area. It was where his career as a lawyer had abruptly ended. It was also the same place he was accused of rape.

As he approached the receptionist, he noticed Nina's immediate influence with the staff. Gone was the cute young bubbly receptionist who chatted with the clients and openly flirted with the rich ones. She had been replaced by a stern older woman who wore a dark grey business suit that didn't compliment her rounded form. She looked up from under some thick eyeglasses when Ray approached. "Can I help you?"

"I'm Ray Cooke," he stated quietly, thinking she'd recognize the name. She didn't, "and I'm here to see David Magill."

"Take a seat," She sounded robotic, having probably said those exact words a thousand times before. "I will tell Mr. Magill you have arrived."

Ray poured a coffee at a self-help station. Gourmet coffee was a nice treat. The firm must be doing well. Ray had barely gotten comfortable when David hurried over to him. "Let's go to my office."

'*You mean my office,*' was what Ray wanted to say. "I'm coming."

There was noticeable tension between the two and neither was sure where to begin. It had been a few days since their breakfast and there was still much to discuss. They both knew the past had to be reconciled.

Ray's usual confidence was in reserve mode, but he played the first card. "Have you come up with a solution?"

David's expression revealed nothing. He wasn't prepared to accept the blame Ray hoped for. He was comfortable in his new lifestyle and ready to defend it. "Before I *'make things right'* as you referred to it, you need to know the whole story."

"What do you mean by: *the whole story?*" Ray questioned. "I think I already do. You and your wife set me up."

David shook his head. It indicated there was more. Much more. "You only know a small portion of the story. We both agree that you deserve to know everything, but I want to qualify that what you are about to hear I only found out after our meeting. I did talk to Nina."

Ray was surprised that David had talked to her. He could only imagine how that conversation must have gone. *'Hey honey, did you fake getting raped?'* "What did she tell you? Did she admit setting me up?"

"Yes, she did."

Ray exhaled. Redemption was close, knowing his name was finally cleared. Someone besides himself now knew the truth. "What did she tell you?"

"It's an astonishing story that was hard to believe. You need to hear it from Nina."

As if on cue, Nina entered the office and took the seat beside David. Ray wasn't sure how he felt at that moment. The reason he went to prison was sitting only a few feet away.

EIGHTY-NINE

"Hello, Ray. It's nice to see you again," Nina showed no signs of remorse. "It's been a long time."

Ray clenched his hands. "It's been over five years. Why are you here?"

"Because David asked me, and because it's time you heard the truth."

Ray wanted to pounce. "I'm waiting, so start talking."

Nina put her hand on her husband's, to indicate to Ray she was speaking on behalf of them both. She had David's full support. "I'll start by reaffirming what David told you. He knew nothing about this."

"Just start talking."

Sensing Ray's resentment, she eased into the story. "Fair enough."

David butted in. "Ray, you need to relax, because we all want the truth to come out."

Nina moved closer to Ray to remove any doubt that he intimidated her. "I'm sorry for what happened. I'm aware nothing I tell you will get you those five years back."

Ray thought about the nights he was locked away. He already had a verdict. There was nothing she could say that would justify what she had done.

Nina continued. "We both agree that you deserve to know the truth, and ultimately, it's up to you to determine what you choose to believe."

He glared at David. "Tell her to get on with it!"

David agreed.

Nina reached into her bag and pulled out a large envelope. She placed it on the corner of the desk. "Her plan started a few months before the night of the incident."

"Is that what we're calling it now," Ray scowled, "the night of the incident?"

Nina ignored Ray's sarcasm and continued. "She was covered in cuts and bruises when she came to my house. She had been beaten badly."

Ray interrupted. "Who are you talking about?"

Nina looked at David. "Your wife. It was Tiffany."

"You're joking," He looked at David. "Tell me this is a joke."

David just shook his head.

"Who did this to my wife?" Ray's voice grew frantic, "and why would she go to you and not me?"

Nina squeezed David's hand. "She told me you did it."

It was like the oxygen was sucked from the room. The office went silent for a moment while Ray dealt with Nina's explosive remark. "You are crazy! I've never touched my wife."

Nina knew that accusing Ray of being a wife beater would devastate him and she was braced for an angry outburst. But instead of screaming and losing control, Ray leaned back and stared at the ceiling.

"She told me you were really drunk and wouldn't remember it."

Ray wouldn't have guessed this in a million years and was in shock. "She actually said I beat her?"

Nina dropped another bomb. "She said it happened more than once."

Ray stood up and paced the office. He finally turned to David. He was desperate. "Why are you lying?"

David pursed his lips. "How well do you really know Tiffany?"

Ray snapped. "What kind of question is that?"

David stood his ground. "An important one. Sit back down, Ray. Listen to what Nina has to tell you."

"I know this is hard to hear, but you want the truth," Nina gave Ray a moment to gather his thoughts. "I helped clean up the cuts and bruises. They were real and I wanted to call the police, but she threatened to leave if I did."

"Why didn't she call if I'm such a monster?"

"She didn't think the police would believe her since you were a big shot lawyer." Nina explained. "In the end, I listened to her and it was a huge mistake."

Ray turned to David. "You've known me for almost my entire life, and you took her word without even talking to me. You threw me to the curb."

"David didn't know!" Nina reminded him. "This isn't easy, so sit there and listen. There's more."

"No one in this room is having fun," interjected David, "so listen."

"This better be good."

Nina went on. "After the first episode, Tiffany agreed to stay in touch. I convinced her that if you ever touched her again, we would call the police. It was our terrible secret."

David squeezed his wife's hand. "Just tell him the rest."

"A month later, Tiffany called and said you did it again and this time you threatened to kill her. Your anger had accelerated," Nina looked at Ray. His eyes were blank. "Tiffany never came over this time, so I never saw any cuts or bruises. But I had no reason to disbelieve her. I insisted we call the police."

"Did you?" Ray questioned.

"You know we didn't," responded Nina. "She said she had a better way to deal with you."

265

"You need to believe I never laid a finger on her," Ray thought of his beautiful wife a sleep in their bed this morning. "What did she mean by that?"

"We believe you."

"If I understand this, you're saying it was Tiffany who wanted me sent to prison."

Nina held up her hands. "Exactly."

"I don't believe that," Ray challenged. "She loves me. She's my wife."

"Let me finish. A couple of weeks later, Tiffany came over for coffee. She needed my help and that started with her borrowing my credit card."

"Why would she need your card? She has her own."

"She said that you monitored her spending and that was one of the reasons you beat her," Nina's answer was plausible. "I felt sorry for her and lent her mine."

"Let me guess. She rented a car."

"Yes, she did."

Ray saw the envelope on David's desk. "What's in that?"

Nina pulled out some photographs. She handed them to Ray. "Evidence."

Ray felt sick to his stomach when he saw Tiffany's beaten face. "She said I did this?"

"Yes."

Ray only had one last question. "And who was driving the car?"

They both answered in unison. "Tiffany."

NINETY

Wendell Presley mounted his first horse when he was only six. It wasn't a rare sight to see him sporting a cast to mend a broken bone in his early teens. His adopted father pushed him harder than his own boys. Being a young black man in the cattle industry, he was told he would have to work harder than the white cowboys if he wanted to succeed. That was just the way it was.

All the hard work paid off and was displayed on the fireplace mantel. Shiny belt buckles that Wendell won on the rodeo circuit were proudly displayed, but he was never allowed to wear one.

His father was an old boy rancher who worked hard during the week and enjoyed whiskey on the weekend. When he drank, he had a cruel side and could be vicious to the boys, especially Wendell. More than once the old man used the boy as a punching bag to take out his frustrations.

Wendell didn't shed a tear when after too much whiskey his dad climbed into a live-stock pen and got careless. A two-thousand-pound bull named Festus gored him in the ribs and tossed him out of the pen like a doll. Vince Presley was pronounced dead on the way to the hospital.

Presley was an hour into his seven-hour flight to Washington and was already bored. He sipped on his second vodka tonic and was still upset that Carol sent him to Washington DC to be a lousy courier. Hadn't these people heard of FedEx?

He was aware even before they took off in Vancouver that the woman sitting beside him was a knockout. A sexy haircut with long toned legs that stretched out from her short skirt had his attention. Her intimidating beauty kept him at bay until the vodka kicked in. She wasn't wearing a ring, which was a great start. "Where are you heading?"

She looked up from a copy of Vogue. "The U.S. capital."

"Me, too. Business."

"I'm going to the Smithsonian," she giggled, "because I've always been a little geeky and I enjoy museums."

"Really?" He couldn't stop staring at her legs. "Anyone calling you geeky needs a smack up the side the head."

She put her magazine in the rack on the seat in front of her. "Aren't you cute, coming to my defence."

Wendell wasn't expecting her to be so receptive. Women were usually cautious in his presence. "You said you're going to a museum?"

"The Smithsonian. It's a fascinating place," She sipped her wine. "I have a few errands to run, but otherwise I'm going to be a tourist and see the sites.

He puffed out his chest, "My organization has some meetings in Washington I need to attend."

"You don't sound too excited about it?"

He shrugged, looking for pity. "The trip came up suddenly. Last-minute thing and I hate surprises."

She pretended to feel sorry for the big man. "That's too bad."

Wendell was fascinated. He needed to find out more about her. "Is the Smithsonian the only reason you're going?"

"I have a little business as well, and then I'm going to enjoy the sites," She smiled invitingly. "I want to see some museums and possibly the White House. The usual stuff tourists do."

Wendell was captivated by her sheer beauty and took a chance. "Are you meeting anyone there? I'm sorry to be blunt, but I'm curious why someone as beautiful as you would be flying solo."

"I am solo. And thank you. You'll make me blush."

"I have a meeting tomorrow with some government official and then, like you, I'm free for the rest of my trip. I might take in a hockey game."

"You like hockey?"

At every chance he glanced at her firm body. "I like the physicality of the game."

She was aware of his stares. "Do you like Ovechkin?"

Wendell was impressed. "A beautiful woman that likes hockey and knows the players. Can't get any better than that."

The stewardess walked by and Wendell called her over. "Can I get another vodka and a glass of wine for the lady, please?"

When the stewardess left, he extended his hand. "I'm being rude. My name is Wendell Presley."

She accepted his hand and shook it softly, letting their fingers slowly slip apart. "Nice to meet you, Wendell Presley. My name is Laura Nelsen."

NINETY-ONE

Sergeant Smith decided it was time to take a chance and either move forward with the Small case or put it onto the cold case pile. That was a last resort. It was five months since the school fire and while he had some strong suspicions, he had nothing to take to a prosecutor. The two people that he was convinced were involved, were both now dead.

Smith hung up the phone. He had made an informal booking with the shore patrol. It was an impromptu ride over to Gabriola Island. He stuck his head into Murphy's office. "Are you up for a hike?"

"Anything to avoid paperwork," Murphy nodded. "Where are we going?"

"Gabriola Island," Smith told him. "It's time to check out what's going on over there."

Thirty minutes later their faces were soaked with sea mist as the platoon boat bounced over the waves. The weather was warm with no breeze, a perfect day to go for a hike.

Smith had the captain do a pass where the complex was built to see what was visible from the water. There was literally nothing. You could sail past a hundred times and never know anything was built there. The architects did a great job keeping the location private.

Smith knew it was a stretch that there was any connection between his case and the complex. His curiosity was based on the Lacy deposit and Ray Cooke's memory of Liberty City. He had investigated there ever being a Bjorn in the cell the night Ray was in custody. There was no record of a Bjorn prisoner ever being in the jail. Smith was getting to know Cooke and the man didn't seem to be a liar. Making up a prisoner made no sense. What was the upside?

Smith moved up beside the captain. "Can you unload us over by those rocks? There's a trail that leads inland."

They thanked the captain for the ride and once they got their land legs back, Smith led them to a trail opening. After a tough trek on a rough over-grown trail they found the main route used by weekend hikers.

Smith stopped Murphy. "Do you know anything about this place?"

Murphy took a gulp of water while he looked around. "Should I?"

The sergeant wandered over to the edge and peered down at the rocks below. "I was a rookie when it happened."

"What happened?"

"There was a famous fight here," Smith remembered the night like it was yesterday. "Three gang members came over here to raid a marijuana grow-op run by some hippies living on the island."

"Sorry, I've never heard the story."

"They were intercepted by some skinny native kid."

Sweat was pouring off Murphy and he enjoyed the break. "What happened? Did he get his ass kicked?"

"The kid was fourteen if I remember right. He was walking the trails when the gang members showed up unannounced."

Murphy took another gulp of water. "You're telling me a fourteen-year old kid tried to stop three gang members from stealing some pot."

"That's what I'm telling you. They were members of the old Golden Eagles gang."

"Those guys I've heard of. They were a tough crew back in the day."

"Most are either dead or doing long prison terms," Smith informed him. "You're right. They were a violent crew."

"I'm scared to ask how bad the kid got beat."

Smith's big grin indicated Murphy was way off. "That's not how it played out. One gang member died falling off this cliff and the other two were so savagely beaten they needed medical attention."

Murphy stepped to look over the edge. "And you believe this story?"

"I was in charge of securing the area," recalled Smith, "and the two remaining members both told the same story. It was clearly a case of self-defence."

"What happened to the kid?"

"They said is name was Mickey. He disappeared that night and was never seen again. He's probably a thousand miles from here."

"That's a great campfire story," Murphy started down the trail and Smith followed. "What exactly are we looking for?"

"No idea," conceded Smith, "but keep walking and keep your eyes and ears open."

NINETY-TWO

Jonny pranced around his workstation with his hands raised like a prizefighter after a victory. There was no one else in his lab to celebrate with, but he didn't care. He continued to prance and talk to himself. "This is my best gadget yet. I need to let Mickey know it's finished."

He was disappointed when Mickey didn't pickup his phone. He wanted to celebrate, so he called Cassie next. "Hey, what are you doing right now?"

"Talking to you," She giggled, "and you sound excited. What's up?"

"I was thinking about hanging out by the pool. Do you want to join me?"

"Is this a date?"

He never had a date before, and his stomach started to churn. "I just want to hang out. Are you in?"

"Sure," She sounded disappointed. "I can be there in fifteen."

"Perfect," Jonny admired his steel blue dragonfly. "I'll see you there. I have a surprise."

The three-inch gadget looked exactly like a dragonfly and had all the abilities of a real one. It could reach speeds of thirty miles an hour, stop in mid-flight, and even fly backwards. The U.S. military had instilled much of what a dragonfly can do into the stealth bomber design.

Jonny knew the risk of taking his gadget for a test flight without Mickey's okay. He wanted to impress Cassie. He grabbed a pizza on his way out.

NINETY-THREE

After working their way through a maze of trails with no real strategy, Smith and Murphy stopped to catch their breath and figure out where they were. The tall trees and steep inclines made it tough. They found refuge under a shady tree and out of the direct sun.

Smith stood tall and took deep breaths. "I need to get back in the gym. I can't believe how out of shape I am."

Murphy was just as bad. "What the hell are we looking for?"

"I'm not sure," Smith admitted, "but these guys have paid a ton of money to stay under the radar. I'm curious why."

Murphy saw it first. "Is that a fence?"

Smith turned and it took a second to see what Murphy saw. "That's a strange place for a fence."

Murphy clawed his way through some thick brush and up a steep incline. "Come check this out."

Smith followed him up. "That's a serious fence."

The ten-foot chain link was topped with razor cable and there were security cameras perched on top of each pole.

"These people don't want any surprise visitors," Murphy perched on a boulder. "Those cameras are filming us now. They must be motion activated."

"The question is, who are 'these people'?

Murphy looked up into the camera. Whoever was filming would have a great shot of his face. "What's the plan?"

Smith checked the time. He knew the ferry ran on the hour, so they had forty minutes. "There's not much we can do without a warrant, so let's catch our breath and head back to the ferry."

Murphy was about to stand up when a noise caught his attention. "What's that?"

Smith looked up. "It's just a dragonfly."

"Do they usually hover like that?"

Smith had no interest in the bug. "I guess so. I know they're good flyers, but that's the extent of what I know."

Murphy couldn't stop looking at it. It hung effortlessly in the air. "I think it just blinked at me."

Smith laughed. "I think you got too much sun. Let's start heading back."

Murphy took a half-hearted swat at it, but the dragonfly never moved.

"Did you hear that?" Smith leaned against the chain link fence. "Shush."

Murphy pushed his ear against the fence. "It sounded something like, *I can't wait to show, Joshua.*"

"Are you sure?" Smith's heart rate jumped. "Is that what you heard?"

Murphy shook his head. "I can't be sure, but can you smell that?"

Smith sniffed the air. "It's a pepperoni pizza."

NINETY-FOUR

Joshua wasn't scheduled back at his workstation for a few hours, so his plan was to stay in his room and play his video game and eat potato chips. Do what most twelve -years old do. When there was a bang on the door, his first reaction was to ignore it. He wasn't expecting anyone.

The door burst open and Curtis waltzed in wearing his usual reversed ballcap and bright smile. He was in a great mood. "Hey, little buddy. We need to talk."

Joshua tried to ignore Curtis, but it was impossible. Joshua put his controller down. He had been expecting him. "You know I can't talk about it."

Curtis ignored him. "What the hell are you working on? What I saw last night was amazing."

Joshua regretted the prank in the garden. He wished he could take it all back, but it was too late, and Curtis wasn't going to just overlook what he saw. "I need you to forget about it."

"Screw that," Curtis scoffed, "you can't pull that off and just expect me to forget it."

"Have you told anybody?"

"No, I'd never get you in trouble," Curtis assured him. "I just want to know what it was. It was like a robot, but so much better."

"Have you heard of animatronics?"

Curtis shrugged. "Isn't that what they use in movies to make dinosaurs look real?"

"That's old school," Joshua sipped his water. "I'm working on creating a human clone. The perfect being."

"What I saw in the garden looked awful close to being perfect to me."

Joshua struggled to keep a straight face. "You got it all wrong."

Curtis was confused. "What did I get wrong?"

"It was me in the garden," Joshua laughed. "You taught an animatronic being how to weight train."

NINETY-FIVE

Stacey hated to admit it, but she was getting used to being alone in the house. There were times when she thought about Robert and missed him, but the hatred and screaming at the end was gladly forgotten. She had been so engrossed in Joshua's abduction she couldn't remember if she even shed a tear for her husband.

Joshua was a different story. She still had flashes of guilt for not protecting him better. In the beginning, she blamed Robert because it was easy. And then as time passed, she came to understand that neither was at fault. The blame belonged on the people that took her son.

It was almost a mile to the teahouse, and when she felt up to a walk, she treated herself to a chai tea and something chocolate. Tonight, it was going to be a fudge brownie. She wanted to have a little celebration. Joshua was going to have a baby sister.

The baby would be Robert's legacy. She wondered if Christmas Eve would have been different if he knew he was going to be a dad again. His death was ruled an accident, but she often wondered if he just needed to end the pain.

When she walked, her thoughts were always on Joshua. She wondered where he might be and what he was up to. Was he getting taller, was he brushing his teeth and eating properly? Simple, but important thoughts.

The barista gave her a welcome smile. "What's your treat today?"

"The fudge brownie please," Stacey ordered, "and my usual chai tea."

They would bring her order over, so she found a table.

"Do you mind if I join you?"

Stacey was pleasantly surprised. "How did you know I would be here?"

Smith grinned. "Your neighbor. The nosy one. Plus, I'm a cop."

"I'd love the company."

When her order arrived, Sergeant Smith asked for a black coffee. Then he turned to Stacey. "So, how are you feeling?"

She patted her belly. "We're both good. I found out I'm having a girl."

He was genuinely happy for her. She needed something positive in her life. "I'm glad I found you."

"Where's your partner?"

"Detective Murphy is taking some personal time. I'm not sure what he's up to," responded Smith, "but I do want to talk to you."

Stacey perked up. "Do you have some good news about Joshua?"

"I'm not sure, but I need to tell you that Principal McKee is dead. He was found in a hotel room in New York."

"New York?" Stacey was shocked. "What happened?"

"An apparent heart attack."

She sensed his doubt. "And what do you think?"

"Another untimely and coincidental death of someone close to your son. It's getting contagious."

Stacey lost her appetite and pushed the brownie to the side. "So, what's next?"

Smith pushed his mug back and forth on the table. He was apprehensive. "I went to Gabriola Island with Murphy this week."

"Did you find anything?"

"Murphy thought a dragonfly was spying on us. It did hang around for a long time. It freaked him out."

Stacey rubbed her belly. "Why is a dragonfly important?"

He sipped his coffee. "Because of what happened next."

"What was that?

"I want to tell you that neither of us is certain on what we might have heard. So, I don't want you freaking out in your condition."

Stacey was anxious. "Talk to me, Steve. What's going on?"

"We heard some voices."

She leaned forward as much as her belly would let her. "Whose voices? What did they sound like?"

"They sounded like kids," He was getting her hopes up. Not the best idea. "There was a boy and a girl. They were both laughing."

"They must have said something for you to come here and tell me."

Smith reached for her hand. He held it tight. "They said, '*Wait till we show Joshua*'."

"Oh my god!" Stacey gasped. "Is it my Joshua?"

"We have no idea." He let go of her hand. "That's all we heard."

Stacey was suddenly a mixture of excitement and uncertainty. "I appreciate you coming here to tell me this. I know it's a long shot, but it's something."

Smith continued. "Murphy thinks the dragonfly was an expensive toy and the kids were controlling it. He's sure they were spying on us."

That was the most encouraging news Stacey had heard since this terrible ordeal had begun. "We need to find those kids."

NINETY-SIX

For the remainder of their flight, Laura pretended to enjoy Wendell's chauvinist attitude. She even encouraged him with more vodka. It was a test and during the last few hours, when the drinks really kicked in, that she got the results. He had failed miserably. The booze loosened his lips and he complained freely about the organization. He told her anything she asked. Mickey made the right decision.

Wendell couldn't believe his luck. Getting seated next to this gorgeous woman who was single and liked to drink was perfect. As the vodkas added up, his eyes wandered freely over her body. He didn't even try to hide his intentions.

Their flight landed at Reagan National airport just after one in the morning and even though it was late, Wendell pestered her to join him for a drink at his hotel. Laura gratefully declined. Seven hours sitting beside this asshole was enough. "I have an early morning, but maybe we could meet for drinks at four."

Wendell wasn't happy with her rejection, but knowing they'd get together again was an acceptable compromise. He wanted another chance to get up her skirt. Those legs were delicious.

They disembarked the plane together and Wendell was obviously drunk, while Laura showed no signs of being impaired. That was because she wasn't. The stewardess had been prewarned, and she served Laura grape juice the entire flight and charged the big spender for an expensive merlot.

They stood side by side at the luggage carousel and without any warning, he wrapped his arm around her waist. He held her tight and whispered drunken ideas into her ear. "Come to my hotel and you can save the cost of a room."

If your hand touches my ass, I'll break your fingers. "That's sounds like a great idea, but I have an early morning. We can talk about saving money over dinner."

When their luggage arrived, Laura helped Wendell remove his hand from her waist before grabbing her bag. He stumbled grabbing his, and they headed to the airport exit to catch separate taxis

Laura climbed in the first one, maneuvering her way out of a good night kiss. "Here's my number. Call me tomorrow."

Her taxi pulled away. Her trap was set.

"Where to ma'am?" The driver asked.

"The Hilton downtown. And drive quickly."

Presley threw his bag in the trunk of the next taxi and stumbled into the back seat. "I'm staying at the Hilton downtown. But stop at a liquor store on the way."

NINETY-SEVEN

Hugh Hutchinson was escorted to the prime minister's office. Security knew Elliot was expecting his friend, so they allowed him to wait by himself. The billionaire felt no shame helping himself to Pierre's brandy. He slumped into a comfortable chair and let out a deep breath. His workload had escalated over the past months and he began to show the tell-tale signs of getting older.

The modest office was mostly hardwood panels with photos of past prime ministers. Harper, Chretien, and Trudeau were three of the many past leaders displayed in simple black wooden frames. Hugh had been in the office numerous times, but never took a moment to understand the history that surrounded him. Most days it didn't matter to him.

He chuckled when he looked at Pierre's portrait. Dressed in a suit, his expression was serious and every hair he had left was in place. A different image than the man on the video.

Pierre entered and caught Hugh snickering. "What's so funny?"

"I'm thinking about the future," He lied easily. "Nothing serious."

Pierre pointed to the glass in Hugh's hand. "I see you made yourself at home."

"With the money I've thrown your way, I think I paid for that bottle,"

"Fair enough."

Hugh sipped on his brandy. "Anything new on Parliament Hill that I would care about?"

Pierre tossed his jacket on the chair. "The west wants a pipeline, and the east is focused on the climate crisis. Same stuff, different day."

Hugh raised his glass. "You sound like you should join me."

"Cheer me up and give me some good news about the North Koreans," Pierre poured a brandy. "Did you get the video taken care of?"

Hugh remembered the adjusted deal with Eon. Pierre would never know the truth. "Yes, we have the video, but they raised the discount to $7 million. Not the best deal, but your image is safe and that's important."

Pierre only cared about the video. "Did you destroy it?"

Hugh pulled a memory stick from his pocket. "This is the only copy," he passed it to the prime minister, "unless Beliveau has one."

"I'll add this to my collection," Elliot ignored the Beliveau reference. "I like to watch them."

Hugh didn't know how to respond. "I bet you do. One day, you're going to push the envelope too far."

"If you can't enjoy yourself, then why live at all?"

Hugh refilled their glasses. "Any update on President Tucker's visit?"

Pierre's face soured. "Why did you bring up that asshole?"

"Just curious on how you plan on handling him."

NINETY-EIGHT

Laura was booked at the Hilton Hotel in Washington, and even though it was two in the morning when she finally checked in, she still requested an early wakeup call. A run along the Potomac River would be a great way to start her visit in Washington. It would also clear the jet lag and give her some time to figure out the logistics of her assignment.

Her flight with Presley turned out as expected. Just add alcohol and he became an asshole. His reaction to her legs in the short skirt was exactly as she expected. By the fourth drink he revealed organization secrets without much urging. He was a huge liability that had to go.

After her morning jog, she took a long hot shower and got ready for her day. She had noticed a nice sidewalk café attached to the hotel. She decided that's where she'd have breakfast and setup surveillance. It was only eight-thirty, so Presley was still inside the hotel.

Laura took a seat at a small table in the café. She chose one in the corner that was partially obscured by a large fern. With a quick seat adjustment, she had a clear sightline to the hotel entrance.

Her server arrived. "Can I get you something to drink?"

Laura lowered her sunglasses. "Some coffee would be great. And can I get some yogurt with fresh fruit."

"Absolutely," The waitress nodded. "Is there anything else?"

"Actually yes," Laura appeared confused. "My boss is staying here, and I'm supposed to meet him in thirty minutes. But I can't remember his room number. He's in a meeting and is going to kill me if I interrupt him again."

"I'm not supposed to give out room numbers but let me see what I can find out. What's his name?"

"Wendell Presley and thank you very much."

Wendell struggled to get out of bed. Stopping at the liquor store to get a bottle of Jim Beam turned out to be a bad decision. What was left in the bottle was on its side on the table.

He climbed into the shower and stood in the same spot for almost five minutes, thinking it would wash away the hangover. It wasn't until he was drying off that he thought about the woman on the plane. He couldn't remember her name or most of their conversation, but he remembered her long legs.

He ordered a pot of coffee and toast from room service. While he waited, he checked his phone for messages. The instructions in the envelope said he'd get a text with further information. There was nothing yet.

While Laura finished her coffee, she got a text from Mickey. He explained that Wendell's meeting was delayed by an hour and she had time to go buy some shoes. He supplied the store address and a salesclerk. Laura paid her bill and had the concierge call her a taxi.

She entered the boutique and made her way through the store, stopping a few times to look at shoes. When she got to the counter there was a small Dominican woman putting sale tags on a stack of boxes.

Laura waited until she had her attention. "Is Camila in?"

"I'm Camila. Who are you?"

"Laura."

"You stay still," It was an order and Laura did as she was told. Camila disappeared behind a curtain. She wasn't gone long and when she returned, she looked nervous. She handed Laura a bag that had a shoe box inside. "Your shoes are ready. Now go."

Laura noticed the bag was heavier than normal shoes. She nodded and headed out to her taxi.

NINETY-NINE

The Federal Coalition Leadership Convention was in Vancouver in less than a week and the country's response to the event was lukewarm at best. Based on history the public just wasn't excited by what the party offered. It was the same thing from the previous three elections, just recycled.

The media sent junior reporters to cover the event. The Federal Coalition needed to shake up the country to have any chance of upsetting Prime Minister Pierre Elliot and his Liberal party. If it were a Vegas bet, the oddsmakers would be offering one hundred to one.

Carol was in a foul mood when she checked into the Pan Pacific Hotel and Convention Centre. She had just left a meeting with the mayor of Vancouver and it didn't go as anticipated. At their meeting, Mayor Richard Anderton announced that he was putting his support behind Tyler Browning to be the next leader of the Federal Coalition. The mayor explained to her that they played minor professional hockey together and he couldn't turn his back on an old teammate.

When the mayor made the announcement there were a couple of dozen reporters and close friends in attendance. Carol sat in the back and watched for an opportunity. It sat in the front row. Anderton's wife had a fake smile pasted on her face. She was in attendance supporting her husband for the media, but her mind was miles away. Carol knew the look of an unsatisfied wife.

When Carol was alone in her suite, she sent out a few messages. One was to Curtis and another to Mickey. The mayor needed to learn a lesson about commitment. He had made one to the organization and changed it at the last minute. He made a bad choice changing his mind to support a man who could shoot a puck.

Once she was done sending messages, Carol studied the floor plan of the giant suite she rented for the week. The floor to wall windows offered spectacular views of the mountain vistas to the north and the busy waterfront. The amenities were not why Carol set up shop in the expensive suite. She needed a space to host a meeting away from the options the hotel offered. Privacy would be critical.

The organization would have a strong, but discreet presence at the hotel during the convention. Mickey had thirty rooms booked with two being designated command centers for his own security team. There was a third specially equipped room for their guest of honour.

This convention had been on Carol's radar for many years. It was the trigger point that would activate her plan to move forward. The years of planning and sacrifice was now ready to pay dividends. Anyone that got in the way would be removed, and that included Mayor Anderton.

The Federal Coalition Convention was going to be front page news.

ONE HUNDRED

When the text message that Wendell was waiting for finally arrived, he was relieved to see he was given an extra hour. He had sobered up enough to realize he was acting like an idiot. If he wanted to have any chance to re-establish himself within the organization, he knew he needed to pull himself together. These were not people you disappointed.

The message gave him basic instructions. It did not lay out what he was in Washington to retrieve. That would come later. He used the extra time to rehydrate his big body and organize a plan. He had a car ready to chauffeur him.

As the fog cleared between his ears, he started to piece together his time on the flight. He found Laura's number in his pocket and recalled the luscious lady with fabulous legs. He would call her once he knew how his day was going to play out. Wendell had an idea how he wanted it to end.

Thirty minutes later he received a second message. It was a location. When he googled the address, he discovered it was a military operations building a few blocks from the Pentagon. Why was he going there? How was the military involved with the organization?

An hour later his driver pulled up to a gated building with a large American flag waving proudly off a guard house. When the vehicle stopped, an armed Military Police officer approached. Wendell rolled down his window. "I'm Wendell Presley and I'm here for a meeting on the tenth floor."

Wendell expected a request for identification, or other papers that he realized he didn't have. But he was never asked. The MP went back inside, while a second guard circled the vehicle using a mirror to look for explosives.

The driver was instructed where to park and a few moments later Wendell was showing his ID to a guard at the building entrance. They had him place his hand on a scanner and when the light turned green, he was allowed inside the lobby.

A female officer, who looked tougher than most men he knew, greeted him with a gruff hello and led him to the elevator. It only took a few seconds to ascend to the tenth floor. His escort said nothing until they exited into the hallway. It was a simple, "Follow me."

"Where am I going?"

She never looked back. "I'm taking you to your meeting."

When they arrived at the office, there was a brass name plate screwed to the door.

'Commander Joan Wakefield'

She knocked once, like it was a password. Without waiting for a response, she opened the door and pointed him inside. Once he was in the office, she was gone.

The commander stood stoically behind her desk. She had worked hard to earn her stripes. Wakefield was an attractive woman in a simple way. Now pushing her mid-fifties, she kept herself in shape and her limited make up was wisely applied. "Have a seat, Mr. Presley. How was your flight?"

"Nothing special."

Wakefield tested Presley. "I heard they had to carry you off the plane."

"Are you following me?"

"Not following you, but I'm making sure you're worthy of our trust."

Wendell treaded carefully. "Why am I even here? Information

on my end is slow."

"You're taking some very important information back to where you came."

Wendell wondered. "With all the means of communicating today, why couldn't you just courier whatever it is? Or maybe by email?"

The commander wasn't interested in Presley's opinion. "You'll just do what I instruct you to do."

Another power-hungry woman. Must be a friend of Carol's. "So, what are my instructions?"

Commander Wakefield had dealt with a lot of self-serving men in her military career and she knew she didn't trust the man in front of her. He wasn't ex-military and had no respect for her rank.

She checked her account before he arrived. Her payment to co-operate was deposited. "When you leave the building, you'll be given a small package by the MP you met on your way in. You know who to give it to."

"Must be something important."

"If you lose it don't go home," She told him flatly. "It's pretty simple. I suggest you stay sober and don't screw it up."

"I think I can handle it." He stifled his sarcasm.

"I have another message for you."

"What's that?"

Wakefield leaned forward and talked deliberately. "You were followed to Washington."

Wendell wasn't sure he believed her. "Who followed me?"

"Remember the lady beside you on the plane. She's here to kill you."

ONE HUNDRED & 1

Cindy Austin was an ambitious young beat reporter finally getting her chance in front of the camera. After struggling for two years writing dead end articles for a community newspaper, she caught a break and got a job in the big city doing on location television reports. The twenty-four-year old perky blonde with a big smile and curvy body recognized that her female assets helped get her the position. She was okay with that. Her dream was to make it big as a television reporter and she was willing to cross the line and do what it took to make it big.

Her latest assignment was the same as the half dozen other reporters covering the Federal Coalition convention. Everyone knew that Tyler Browning was going to be the new leader, so her job was to find a controversial storyline that would grab her viewers attention.

Cindy was still new to the city and her network of reliable sources was minimal at best. She had no contacts on the inside of the Federal Coalition party so it was going to be near impossible to find that story that would create interest. She was scheduled to broadcast her first live update from the Pan Pacific hotel in thirty minutes. She was going to need a miracle to separate herself from the other reporters.

Cindy got her cameraman's attention. "I'm going to the ladies' room to check my hair."

The cameraman smirked. "Your hair looks great."

She gave him an annoyed glare. "That's girl's code for I'm going to pee, dumbass."

She used her limited time to check her appearance and think

about what her broadcast would look like. She needed something and quickly. Her blonde hair had enough chemicals in it to keep it in place in a windstorm and her smile was camera perfect. After a quick brassiere adjustment, she stepped inside a stall.

Before Cindy headed back, she took one last glance in the mirror. She didn't see the woman standing between her and the door until she nearly walked into her. The woman was twice Cindy's size. Dressed in a sleeveless jean jacket and biker boots, she was an intimidating figure.

"Excuse me," Cindy tried to step around the woman but was blocked. "I said excuse me. I need to go."

The woman put her hand out. "Are you Cindy Austin?"

Austin looked at the woman but didn't recognize her. "Who are you? I'll scream if you touch me."

"Relax," The woman pushed her stringy hair out of her eyes and smiled. She was missing a front tooth. "I'm not here to hurt you. I'm here to give you something."

Cindy determined that leaving wasn't an option.

"Are you Cindy Austin?" the big woman repeated, "the lady on the news?"

Austin nodded and relaxed a little when she realized this woman wasn't there to harm her. "What do you have?"

The woman pulled out an envelope. "Read it before you leave and do what it tells you to do."

Cindy took the envelope and looked curiously at it. "Who is it from?"

The woman headed to the door. "Just do what it tells you."

"Why would I do that?"

The woman grinned. "You want to be a star, don't you?"

Cindy was in no rush to follow her out. She knew she only had a few minutes before going on the air. She opened the letter.

Are you a gambler, Ms. Austin?
If you are, then do as I ask in this note
For your first news segment, I want you to announce that
an unknown candidate will be stepping forward to run for the
Leadership of the Federal Coalition party.
You will have his name for your next update.
If you agree to do this, then give us a thumbs up when you
leave the washroom. You won't see us, but we'll see you.
You'll be a star in the morning!

Cindy read the note over and over. Was the note a joke or was this really the chance she was hoping for? Should she get approval from the network anchorman Dane Wilson? If it were a hoax, she'd be on the next bus back to Smallville.

She stepped outside the bathroom and looked around the lobby. The big woman was gone. She thought for a moment and realized she had nothing to lose. What the hell. She put up her thumb.

The fly on the wall above Cindy recorded everything.

ONE HUNDRED & 2

Six o'clock approached and card-carrying members of the Federal Coalition party began to fill the convention center. Tonight, was the first of two nights to celebrate a new beginning and elect a strong leader. That was the hope, but the room and the people tat filled it were lacking enthusiasm. Things needed to change if their party was going to upset Pierre Elliot and his Liberals out east.

Bruce Springsteen's music blared through the deejay system and the drinks were poured freely. Everything pointed to a Tyler Browning victory. For the optimistic, he was the man to lead them to a federal victory, but for much of the country he was just another pretty face with no government leadership experience. The polls showed that Canadians were cautiously optimistic.

The Pan Pacific was a buzz of activity when the first broadcasts were about to be aired. There was a row of media networks stationed along the lobby wall. Reporters scrambled to get prepared for their sixty seconds.

Television camera lights were turned on, and last-minute details were attended to. Most reporters took the easy route and found a party member to interview. They had the standard safe questions. 'Was Tyler Browning going to be your next leader?'

The booth on the end was from CKNTV. Cindy stood to the side with a distracted expression. It caught her cameraman's attention. "Are you okay? You look like you're going to puke?"

She wasn't sure.

ONE HUNDRED & 3

Up in the suite Carol was perched on the end of her bed, waiting to watch the six o'clock news. This was a big risk, but she was sure Cindy Austin would make the wise choice. Austin was chosen because she was new. A seasoned reporter would never take the chance on their career.

Hotel staff were in the main area of her suite putting the final touches on a theatre setup. There was a large screen with ten seats and a designated media setup. Everything was ready for the big announcement and the introduction of the next leader of the Federal Coalition. His name was not Skyler Browning.

The organization had invited the heavyweights in the Federal Coalition to attend. They were the names on Joshua's list. These were the people who controlled the party's direction and thought their identities were protected. They were all invited on the promise of a corporation wanting to make a substantial donation. Mayor Anderton would be in attendance and Carol looked forward to his expression when he learned he was about to change his vote. His old boy's club was ending.

Down in the lobby, standing unnoticed, was a well-dressed man in a black pinstripe suit and bright blue tie. He stepped up to the registration table. "How do I become a member?"

The female volunteer looked up. "You just fill in these forms."

He took the clipboard and started writing.

The cheery volunteer was wearing a red dress with matching lips. Being a volunteer was her social life and this convention was a big night. "I just need some identification."

"No problem," He pulled out his driver's license. "What next?"

She took back the clipboard. "Everything looks great, Mr. Cooke. And if you're not doing anything later, here's my number."

Ray wasn't sure if she was serious. "If I can't find my wife, you just never know."

Mickey entered the suite wearing a blue blazer with grey slacks. He looked handsome. Everything was setup. The special guests would be coming in thirty minutes.

"Is everyone confirmed?"

Carol smiled. "Nobody turned down your invitation. But I'm expecting trouble from the mayor. Did your men find out anything on his wife we can use to influence him?"

Mickey chuckled. "Oh yeah. That's one interesting family. I think you can count on his support."

"Good."

Mickey changed topics. "We might have a problem with Sergeant Smith. He was outside the fence line yesterday at the complex. He's getting closer and I'm not sure how."

"Was Murphy with him?"

"He was."

"Get an update from him." Carol suggested. "Now let's watch the news."

ONE HUNDRED & 4

Back down in the lobby the cameraman gave Cindy a signal they were going live in thirty seconds. She was still unsure about her decision and was never this nervous before a broadcast. She glanced at the booth beside her. The reporter for a local radio station was interviewing a past president of the Federal Coalition. Her mind was made up.

The cameraman gave her the ten-second signal and Cindy pushed her hair nervously away from her eyes. She checked the microphone to see that it was on and gave him the thumbs up. He counted down from five with his fingers and she was live on the air.

Dane Wilson was the veteran anchor at CKNTV and a trusted news source for almost twenty years. As popular as he was with the viewers, he was hated by the young female reporters that he loved to bully into tears. Cindy was stronger than the other girls, who often just gave up and quit. She wasn't quitting. She wanted his job.

She watched the monitor for her cue. Dane was on the air giving the viewers a quick summary of what they could expect over the next hour. And them it was her turn to shine.

Wilson and his phoney smile were on the monitor. "And now we're going to join Cindy Austin, who is live at the Pan Pacific hotel covering the Federal Coalition's leadership convention. How's it going Cindy? Is there anyone going to take a run at Tyler Browning for the leadership?"

Cindy smiled into the camera and appeared calm. It was now or never. "Good evening Dane. Things are beginning to get serious down here. They're expecting a crowd of over twenty-five hundred members to show up. It should be a great party."

The screen cut back to Dane. "Is it still a one-man race with Taylor Browning or is anyone stepping up to challenge the former hockey player?"

The moment of truth arrived. "Actually, Dane, I have it on good authority that Tylor Browning will face a strong competitor and there's talk he might even be defeated."

Wilson did a good job hiding his anger at Austin. Didn't this bitch know surprises on live TV were suicide. He flashed a fake smile. "Wow, this is quite the surprise. Can you tell us the name of this mystery person and why the late announcement?"

This was her moment to become a star. "Actually, I can't. I have no idea who this person is, but I'm relying on my source to supply the name before our next update."

Dane was rattled. "How do you know this person even exists?"

Cindy winked at the cameraman who had a big smirk on his face. "I trust my source and sometimes you just have to believe in people, just like you'll have to trust that I'll have a name in an hour."

You'll be lucky to be employed in an hour was Dane's first thought. "Okay, we look forward to your next update. It sounds like it's going to be quite the night down at the Pan Pacific hotel."

When the network cut for a commercial, Dane ripped out his earpiece and tossed it away. He glared at his producer. "What the hell was that?"

The producer held her hands up. "I have no idea, but if it comes through, she'll be an instant star."

Dane huffed off to his dressing room. He needed some self pity time.

Back in the lobby, the cameraman switched the lighting off and moved beside his reporter to talk quietly. "What was that?"

"Probably suicide," Cindy vibrated, "but let's hope not."

He pulled out his phone and handed it to Cindy. "Your Twitter and Instagram accounts are on fire."

Cindy saw the giant from the washroom standing a few feet away. "I did as you asked. What now?"

"Go to the executive suite," she locked eyes with the cameraman, "and take him."

"But...?"

The woman interrupted her. "You need to go now."

ONE HUNDRED & 5

Inside the suite, waiters were serving drinks and handing out finger foods on little white napkins. Everyone on the list had arrived and there was a noticeable level of uncertainty amongst them. Carol only wanted invited guests when the introduction was announced so the wait staff did one last round and left the suite.

No one knew the real reason they were in the room, but their curiosity garnered their interest. Whoever was their host obviously had money and influence. The suite with this view had to cost at least ten thousand a night.

The mayor had showed up reluctantly and looked like he could be a problem. He had a persuasive voice in the party and Carol wanted no surprises. Mickey had assured her he was ready if the mayor got out of control.

Richard Anderton scowled in the back row with his wife.

Hiding out in the bedroom, Mickey reviewed his notes one last time. He was ready, and so was the guest of honour. Mickey gave the signal, and everyone took a seat. He nodded to his guest that it was time. They walked side by side to the front of the crowd.

Cindy Austin was setup in the small media area beside the stage. The camera scanned the room full of familiar faces. She leaned on her cameraman. "What's going on?"

He shrugged. "I think this is where you become a star."

Mickey stepped up to the microphone. Things were now in motion and there was no turning back. Everyone was looking at the handsome man, wondering who he was. "I want to thank everyone for coming. I know it's a busy night, so I'll get right to why you're all here. I'd like to introduce the man beside me that you'll all be supporting to become the next leader of the Federal Coalition party."

Cindy's heart skipped a beat. "Bingo!"

ONE HUNDRED & 6

The prime minister was entertaining a new female friend in his bedroom when he excused himself to make a call. He had seen the news clip from the convention. He called Hutchinson. "Where are you?"

"I just arrived in Richmond. I'm at the airport."

Pierre was curious, "Are you going to the Federal Coalition convention?"

"That's the plan. Why?"

"I just watched some blonde reporter announced there was a new candidate putting his name forward. Any ideas on who it might be? I hate surprises."

Hugh's luggage was delivered to his car and they started towards downtown Vancouver. "No idea, but I'm sure we'll find out."

"What about the reporter?" Pierre wanted more. "What do you know about Cindy Austin?"

"Only that she's new and aggressive," Hugh had no idea who Cindy Austin was. "I need to get ready."

"Find out," ordered the prime minister, "we need to get on top of this."

"Anything else?" Hutchinson hated it when Pierre treated him like an employee. "I have a busy night."

"Just get some damn answers."

ONE HUNDRED & 7

Wendell returned to the Hilton and was in such a hurry to get to his room he bypassed the elevator and sprinted up the six floors of stairs. When he arrived at his door, exhaustion had replaced adrenalin and it was all he could do to gasp in enough air to fill his burning lungs. Sweat poured down his cheeks.

On the drive back, he couldn't ignore what Commander Wakefield had told him about Laura. How could this beautiful woman be a contract killer and who put the price on his head? It wouldn't be the organization. He had their package and whatever was on it was extremely valuable to someone.

He moved his big body inside. There was no sign anyone other than housekeeping had been there. The bed was done, and his dirty glasses had been replaced with new ones in paper wraps. And the Jim Beam bottle was upright.

He laughed anxiously when he realized he was safe. He reached into his pocket and pulled out the paper that Laura gave him with her number. Did she really come to Washington to kill him or was Wakefield full of shit?

There were quiet whispers that Mickey had a team of killers on his payroll, but nothing was ever proven. Was Laura sitting beside him on the plane a setup? Carol did book his ticket, so maybe.

He came up with a solution while he took a shower. He headed down to hotel security with a fifty stuffed in is pocket. Time to do a little detective work. He created an believable story. "And so, before I file a complaint, I want to be sure some one entered my room and I'm hoping you could check your security tape."

The man at the desk was ex city police and he was glad he had something to do. Doing security at a hotel was not like being a cop. Most days all he did was give directions to the bathroom. "You said you were on the sixth floor?"

"Yes. I was gone from 10am till now."

"Let's see what we find."

"I appreciate it." Wendell glanced around the lobby. "I can't believe how forgetful we get as age sets in."

The guard laughed in agreement.

After watching the tape, they learned that only one person entered the room. It was an older woman from housekeeping.

"That's Stella Jefferson. She has been here for years and we've never got a complaint about her."

Wendell tossed the fifty bucks on the counter. He was satisfied. "Appreciate your time. Buy yourself a beer after work."

A few blocks south of the Hilton Hotel there was the Jamieson Pub, that was once the Irish hot spot in Washington. The old timers still rave about the Irish stew and the music. And some of the best Celtic bands in the country played on its stage.

That was thirty years ago, and its glory days were long gone. The only thing Irish is a dusty half bottle of Bushmills Irish Whiskey that was full of dead fruit flies. Now it was just an old rundown building waiting for someone to buy it and tear it down.

A woman wearing an old woollen sweater and worn runners swung the door open and headed straight to the bar. "Can I get a beer, Cecil?"

Cecil had been the afternoon bartender at the pub for over twenty years and the large black man was anything but Irish. "You're here early today. You get canned Stella?"

Stella cracked a smile, exposing her cigarette-stained teeth.

"Pour me a shot of bourbon. I'm celebrating today."

Cecil grabbed the Jim Bean and poured a healthy shot. "What are you celebrating? It isn't your birthday."

She giggled like a young schoolgirl. "Some rich, white bitch wanted to surprise her husband, so she paid me five hundred bucks to lend her my uniform for an hour. If she wants to play a kinky slut and pay me a week wages, I'm good with that."

Cecil leaned up against the bar. "You're telling me some lady gave you five Benjamin Franklins to take an hour off so she can roll with her old man. I'm calling bull shit!"

"I can't make this shit up," She downed the bourbon like a pro. "I think she was really checking up on her old man if you ask me. He must be swinging with someone else."

"Maybe," Cecil was trying to solve the mystery. "Crazy people out there."

"Get me another shot and pour yourself one," She decided. "I'm celebrating."

ONE HUNDRED & 8

The most excited person in the suite was Cindy Austin when she realized there really was a mystery candidate. Dane would lose his cookies when he found out the newbie scored the story of the week. And it was her story. Cindy was already developing a script in her head for her next broadcast.

Carol stood in the shadows of the bedroom and watched everything unfold. This night was a long time in the making, and she felt no guilt for ruining some lives. These people all deserved what they would get. They had used the party and whatever leverage it had for their personal gain. And now it was about to collapse.

Mickey got everyone's attention. "You were all brought here tonight because I have an announcement that effects you all. The Federal Coalition will be electing a new leader tonight and it will not be Skyler Browning. It will be the man to my left, Mr. David Magill."

The reception to the announcement was silence. Everyone that was invited was literally stunned. They all had objections but waited for someone else to start. Finally, a member of the executive stood and requested to speak. "Who are you to tell us how we manage our party. And who is this man, David Magill?"

Mickey responded. "I won't be getting into a debate tonight, but your questions are fair and expected ones. To answer your first, it's not your party anymore. You will all be resigning your positions at the AGM tomorrow morning. We have people who will replace you. The second question is easy. You chose a man who couldn't even succeed at hockey and thought he gave you a legitimate shot at running the country. It was a terrible choice and that's why we've told Browning he's out. In four months, David Magill will be the next prime minister. You used your position within this party to benefit personally and those days are over."

Mayor Anderton stood up so abruptly that he knocked over his chair. He was furious. "Who the hell are you to think we'll just bow to your demands? And I resent you insinuating that we took advantage of our positions!"

Mickey picked up the remote and hit play. On the screen a bank statement appeared. There was a balance of over $2 million. The account owner's name wasn't visible, yet. Mickey looked at an older man cowering in the second row. "Do you want me to scroll down?

The man's dress pants turned dark in the crotch. He was so scared he peed on himself. "Please don't."

The mayor gathered his thoughts. He wasn't ready to concede control just yet. "If our treasurer is a thief then he should pay, but that doesn't mean I'm jumping on your band wagon."

Mickey looked directly into the man's eyes. "Are you sure, mayor?"

Everyone turned and looked at Anderton. The camera was rolling. He had committed and he knew it. He was all in. "Yes."

Mickey hit play and knew the mayor had no idea the video existed. He was about to torpedo his career, or his wife was. Everyone had their eyes glued to the screen, anxious to see what was coming.

The video started with his wife drinking wine by their pool. There were two teenage boys taking turns on the diving board between swigs of what looked like Jack Daniels. Mrs. Anderton, whose back was to the camera, stood up and headed to the pool. There was no doubt she was topless.

"Turn it off. You have his support!" Yelled Mrs. Anderton. "You bastard!"

The video continued. Mickey looked at the mayor. "Do we?"

He glared at his wife before giving in. "Yes. Now shut it off."

The screen went white, but everybody in the room knew what was on the video next. There was no more opposition.

Mickey gave David the floor. "I'd like you all to meet David Magill. The man who will be elected tonight as the new leader of the Federal Coalition."

Everyone stood up and reluctantly they all clapped.

Carol closed the bedroom door. She had an important meeting to prepare for. Cindy Austin was already on the elevator.

ONE HUNDRED & 9

Wendell returned confident that only the housekeeper was in his room while he was out. If Wakefield's intel were correct about Laura wanting to kill him, it only made sense she would try to do it somewhere private. The hotel room was the logical answer.

She wouldn't try to do it in a public place like a restaurant, or at the Smithsonian museum where there would be lots of potential witnesses.

With the distraction that Wakefield's information caused, he nearly forgot about the package he picked up. It was only the size of a Rubik's cube. He pulled it out of his pocket and stuffed it into the room safe. He never noticed the small camera mounted on the ceiling that recorded the combination.

Curiosity killed the cat, or in this case Wendell. He sent Laura a text message. He invited her out for dinner and drinks. The possible risk was worth the reward of getting Laura in his bed. The adventure excited him.

Laura responded. She suggested burgers after a trip to the Smithsonian. He liked the museum idea. The security would be tight and there was no way she could get a concealed weapon through the detectors.

'What hotel are you staying at? I can come by at 4.'
'The Marriot Marquis. I will meet you in the lobby.'
'See you soon.'

Laura needed to get to the Marriot Hotel before Wendell arrived. It was just after three. She was two floors above him in the same hotel wondering what to wear. It had to be something practical, but still easy on his eyes. On her way to the closet, she stepped over a brown housekeeping uniform that she paid five hundred dollars for. It was worth every penny.

She decided on a purple V neck sweater with tight jeans that were complimented by flat bottom shoes. After applying some makeup, she headed down the stairwell. She still had twenty minutes before Wendell would arrive at the Marriot.

Wendell pulled on a two-toned brown sports jacket that went well with his Wrangler blue jeans and a light dress shirt. With the cowboy boots, he was a true reflection of his prairie upbringing. He glanced at his watch and it was time to go.

Before leaving the hotel, he stopped by the concierge desk. "I'm in room 613 and I need you to deliver me a bottle of Jim Beam and a couple bottles of Merlot."

"Yes sir." The concierge punched in the order. "Anything else?"

"Yes, a box of condoms. Have them put under the pillow."

Laura sat in the lobby of the Marriot pretending to read a magazine when Presley arrived. She saw the big man sauntering her way and tossed the magazine on the table. He was hard to miss with the big cowboy hat and bright smile.

"Don't you look great. I love those boots."

They greeted with a friendly hug and after some chit chat, they headed out to get a taxi. Ten minutes later they stood on the sidewalk outside the Smithsonian and admired the historical building that was constructed around 1855. She loved the Gothic and Roman influenced architecture.

Wendell was relieved when Laura didn't set off any alarms when they entered the museum. That meant she wasn't packing a pistol. They spent over two hours looking at displays. There was so much history to be seen. They took selfies in front of the Wright Brother's

1903 Flyer and Wendell got excited when he saw the Apollo 13 capsule exhibit.

They both agreed it was time for a burger and headed outside. The restaurant Laura recommended was only a few blocks away, so they chose to walk. Once seated inside they ordered a pitcher of beer and two of their infamous cheese mushroom burgers with fries.

Laura sat back in her chair. Her face was glowing. "That place was amazing. I can't believe how much of a history geek I am. Thank you for coming."

"I'm glad I did," he smiled, "and maybe after dinner we can head back to my hotel."

"I like the sound of that," Laura teased him. "What are we going to do back at your hotel?"

"I was hoping we could sit in the lounge and have a drink. We could get to know each other."

Laura twirled her hair between her fingers. "Do we have to have that drink in the lounge?"

Wendell's face lit up. "Absolutely not."

ONE HUNDRED & 10

After her coffee with Sergeant Smith, Stacey went home and tried to get some sleep. It was impossible with all the thoughts she now had running through her head. What if those kids were talking about her Joshua? The idea that her son might only be a few miles away was driving her crazy.

She thought about Suzanne Lacy. Look at the break she got after three years. Maybe it was her turn. When the seven o'clock ferry left the dock to Gabriola, she was on it.

She found the trail Smith had described and started up the incline. It was going to be harder than she imagined, and she was excited to see the trail level out after about ten minutes. She was exhausted. After another thirty minutes she spotted the large boulder Smith had described. It was where him and Murphy spotted the fence.

She found a place to sit and pulled out her water bottle. She could see pieces of the fence through the trees. She rubbed her belly. "We're almost there, baby. We're going to find your brother."

Louis was about to have his lunch when he got interrupted by a radio call. He was a courier. "There is a box here that needs to clear security and it's marked urgent. I need you back here now."

He glanced at his hot lunch.

Joshua was at the next table and overheard the message. "I can do the delivery if you want."

The guard picked up his sandwich and took a bite. "That would be awesome. I'll radio Petra that you're coming."

When Joshua arrived too pickup the package, he was directed

to Petra's desk. The blonde Scandinavian girl pushed a small box at him. "Thanks for doing this. It's for Cassie Chang."

Joshua was captivated by all the activity in the room. "Do you like working here?"

Before Petra could respond, there was a red alert on her screen. "Not again."

Joshua tried to sneak a peek. "What's going on?

"I'm not sure," Petra worked her mouse and the camera on the fence pole zoomed in. "We have a woman shaking the fence. It's the same area we had two men at the other day."

"Can I look?"

Petra mumbled. "Look at this nut job. She's pregnant."

Joshua couldn't stop his reaction. He nearly yelled at the lady.

Petra saw his expression. "Do you know her?"

His mom was pregnant. "I don't think you need to alert security."

Petra knew procedure. "They'll just make sure she's okay and tell her to move on."

He wondered where his dad was. Didn't his grandmother tell him his parents were in Europe? "Please leave her alone. She'll go away."

ONE HUNDRED & 11

Ray wandered inside the crowded convention center without any real purpose. He didn't know anyone and hadn't found a group of people that he was comfortable to join. Ray hadn't drunk alcohol since that faithful night, but the bar looked more inviting every time he did a walk by.

He was only at the convention to find Tiffany. Nina had dropped a hint that she might be over here for an assignment. He wasn't clear on what that meant. So far there was no sign of Tiffany. He wasn't sure how he'd react if she were there with another man.

He was still in denial that his wife was behind him going to prison. It meant she had a deep dark side and that worried him. What was she really capable of? He sipped his coke and moved away from the bar.

And then the activity in the convention changed. It was like a breeze blew through the hall and everyone lowered their voice. Ray watched as a small group of people entered the convention through a side door. It was obvious by the attention they garnered that they were important people. What stood out was their scowls. These people were not happy. Ray recognized the last two to come through the door. It was the mayor of Vancouver and his wife.

Something was going on. He had thought about leaving, but he decided to stick around and find out what had all those people upset. Ray's phone vibrated. It was Nina. Maybe she knew.

Mickey loosened his tie and sat on the end of the couch staring out the window. Carol joined him. They were alone in the suite. "I think that went well."

Carol cracked a rare smile. "I loved the look on the mayor's face. Next time he'll know better."

"I'm going to head downstairs to check on things," Mickey stood up, "and I hear Tiffany's husband is in the building."

"Are you expecting trouble?"

"No, but I want to keep him in sight."

Carol wandered over to the window. She watched the lights flicker on Grouse Mountain. "After the AGM tomorrow, we'll have full control of the Federal Coalition. Magill will be the next prime minister."

"It'll happen," Mickey assured her as he headed to the door. "and that's only the beginning. In time, the organization will control everything."

Carol stopped Mickey. "Any update from Washington?"

"The package was picked up," Mickey told her, "and Presley will be taken care of tonight."

Ray stepped out in the lobby where it was quieter. "What is it, Nina?"

"Where are you?"

"At the convention. You told me I might find Tiffany over here."

Nina noticed Ray never mentioned David, so the announcement was still coming. "I never said Tiffany was at the convention."

Ray was having a hard time hearing her. "Why did you call?"

"It's about David."

Before Nina could finish, Ray and the rest of the stragglers out in the lobby were ushered back into the convention hall by party volunteers. A big announcement was coming.

The hall was packed, but the energy from the membership in the room was noticeably different. Something was going on and it caught Ray's attention. He found a spot against the wall in the back. He watched people around him, but the loud music made it impossible to overhear anyone. His curiosity finally took control.

He tapped the shoulder of a man beside him. "Can you tell me what's going on. It seems like an unexpected announcement is coming."

The man had a big FC button pinned too his shirt. "Someone has entered the leadership race and there is a rumour Tyler Browning has dropped out. There will be an update in a few minutes."

Ray thanked him and leaned back up against the wall and sipped his coke. Since there was no sign of Tiffany, he decided that once the announcement was over, he'd catch a flight back to Nanaimo. "Why would anyone with half a brain get into politics?"

The night was about to begin, and the lights in the room were dimmed. A tall man with a neatly trimmed goatee and a head of salt and pepper hair walked out onto the stage and took his place behind the microphone. Some stage lighting was turned on to emphasize his presence.

The emcee began. "Good evening everyone! Welcome to the Pan Pacific Hotel and home for the Federal Coalition Leadership Conference. My name is Ben Markland, but my friends call me Bean."

Everyone in the crowd knew Bean and cheered. The room was energized again.

"I will be your host for as long as it takes to elect the new leader of the Federal Coalition. Before we begin, I have an announcement," Bean knew he was about to create an uproar. "There has been an addition and a subtraction to the candidates list."

Ray faced the stage. "Skyler Browning has pulled out of the race and a new name will be added. His name is David Magill."

Ray's coke shattered on the floor.

ONE HUNDRED & 12

Joshua left the security area with the package, fighting back tears, which took some effort. Seeing his mom being pregnant and pulling on the fence in a panicked state was hard for him to watch.

Joshua went to the gym. "When you finish admiring yourself in the mirror, I need to talk to you."

"Hey buddy. Are you the real Joshua, or the other one?"

Joshua didn't react. "I need you to do me a favour."

"And I need you to do me one too."

"I was in the security office today getting a package and there was a breach at the fence. A lady."

Curtis didn't seem interested. "That happens a lot."

"I saw the lady's face."

Curtis shrugged. "So? She was probably lost."

"She was pregnant," Joshua explained, "and she was by herself."

"Why do you care so much about some lady?"

"I need you to help me find her."

"Again, Why?"

"Because she was here looking for me."

Curtis threw up his arms, "One last time. Why, and how do you know that?"

"Because she was my mom!"

ONE HUNDRED & 13

Suzanne Lacy stepped inside her mudroom and pulled off her boots. She had just finished an enjoyable walk along the Yukon River with Rupert. Spring had arrived in the north and the river that was used by goal miners over a hundred years ago was going through its annual breakup. The big river took no mercy. Chunks of ice the size of a bus floating with the current would destroy anything in its path. This was a celebrated time of year in the Yukon.

Suzanne tossed her jacket on the coat rack and turned on the kettle. Her phone buzzed and she saw the number. "What a nice surprise. How are you and the baby doing?"

Stacey liked to rub her belly. It helped her relax and feel safe. "I'm doing well considering how fat I'm getting."

"If you're getting bigger that means the baby is healthy," Suzanne reminded her. "Anything new with the investigation?"

"Maybe. That's why I called."

Suzanne made some tea and found a comfortable spot on the couch. She had a hunch their call might be long. "That sounds intriguing. What's up?"

"I ran into Sergeant Smith this week."

"You ran into each other? How coincidental," Suzanne laughed. "What did he have to say?"

"He told me that he went on a hike on Gabriola Island with Detective Murphy. They found the fence and said they heard some voices."

"Voices? Why is that different?"

"The sergeant said they sounded like kids. One of them said

320

something like '*they couldn't wait to tell Joshua*'."

"Did he think they were talking about your Joshua?" Suzanne pushed Rupert away from licking her feet. "Are the kids being held against their will?"

"The sergeant said the voices seemed happy, so I'm not sure."

Suzanne watched Rupert give up on her feet and settle on a piece of rug in the corner of the kitchen. "What are you thinking because I sense you have a plan."

"It might sound far fetched, but whoever took Joshua was willing to burn down a school to get him. And the Chang girl simply disappeared from her dorm with not one camera filming her. I'm convinced that the kids helped with their own abductions. The people that took them are up to something and my guess is they needed our boys."

Suzanne tested her tea. "It's hard to argue with your logic. Finding the bag with Curtis's stuff supports it. Now we have to figure out who wanted them."

"I went hiking on Gabriola yesterday," Stacey revealed, expecting to be chastised. "and did some exploring."

"Are you telling me you went over to the island in your condition?"

"Yes," She admitted. "I got to the complex. I know our boys are in there."

"What if something happened to you?"

"I know you're right, but I'm going back," Stacey told her. "I'm going to set up a camp and stake it out."

"Are you crazy? You can't be doing that by yourself in your condition."

She knew Suzanne was right. "The reason I called was to invite you down to visit. You can be my camping buddy."

Suzanne thought for a moment. "Are you sure?"

"We'll bring wire cutters. I'm going to find out what's on the other side of that fence."

"What if we get caught?"

Stacey smiled. "I want to get caught. What are they going to do to a pregnant woman?"

"I have no idea, but I'll enjoy finding out," Suzanne chuckled. "I'll book a flight tonight. I'm looking forward to meeting you in person."

ONE HUNDRED & 14

Cindy Austin's cameraman scrambled to find a good location in the lobby to get set up. They were on the air in five minutes and her brain was still processing what she witnessed. She sensed big things coming her way, but instead of being excited she was worried. So much could still go wrong.

The cameraman waved. "We're ready to go."

She gave him a thumbs up.

He had to ask. "What did we just see up there?"

Cindy never mentioned the woman in the bathroom. "For some reason, we've been chosen to get their message to the people, and I'm all in."

"Cool. Two minutes."

Cindy applied some gloss on her lips. "I want to see the look on Dane's face when I break this story."

The cameraman pointed to his headset. "Speaking of the asshole, Dane is calling. Are you ready?"

Cindy gave him a confident grin. "Put him through."

Dane got right to the point. "How did you scoop a story like this?"

Cindy rolled her eyes at his abrasive tone. "I guess I just got lucky."

Dane Wilson was Cindy's boss who was the typical male chauvinist who wasn't above using his celebrity to gain favours. "The senior management wants me to confirm you're coming through with a breaking storyline. Are you coming through? Because if you are, they want to go national."

"National?" Cindy knew this was a huge opportunity. "I have everything on video to support my story. The new candidate is a man named David Magill."

"What do you know about him?"

Cindy hadn't considered that question. "He seems to be the chosen one. I'll tell you more on my broadcast"

"Don't mess it up," Dane warned.

The real story was the other man upstairs in the suite. "I have to get ready."

"How did you get access to a story like this?" Dane finally asked. "No other station mentioned anything about a new candidate. Who's your contact?"

Cindy wished Dane could see her happy smile. "I don't have time to get into the details, but I can tell you this segment will be huge."

Wilson interrupted. "Are you sure you want to cover this story? You could pass it on to a professional like me."

Fuck you, Dane. "I think I can handle a national broadcast," her voice ripe with spite, "and if I need any help, I'll ask."

"Relax, we'll call back, so be ready. And don't blow it."

She wanted to spit on him. "I won't."

"I sure hope this Magill guy wins," chuckled the anchor scornfully, "otherwise you're going to look like an ass."

Cindy rolled her eyes. "I appreciate your support."

Back in Ottawa, Cindy Austin had a curious new fan. The prime minister had sent his friend home in a taxi. He was done with her and now he wanted to watch the news. He wanted to hear Cindy Austin's next update. He was intrigued by this new sexy blonde.

The camera zoomed in on Cindy Austin. Her bright

smile and energy were contagious, and the camera loved her. Since her first broadcast, she had gained some fans who surrounded her. They had to be coaxed to be quiet. "I can confirm that David Magill is the new candidate and has a big lead after the first ballot, and everything is pointing to him winning the leadership before the end of the night."

Dane appeared. "What can you tell us about Skyler Browning? What happened with the pre-convention favourite?"

"I can tell you he's not even in the building. I'm told he had a sudden change of heart and decided he wasn't cut out for politics."

Dane continued, "And what do we know about Mr. Magill? Anything the people need to know?"

Cindy brightened her smile. "He's a breath of fresh air. It's early, but there are rumours that he is going to shake up the country. The Liberal party will need to be ready for a battle. This man seems like the person that Canadians will support and get behind. The next four months leading to the federal election will be interesting."

Dane wrapped it up. "Thank you for that report. Great job and we'll have more on our eleven o'clock broadcast!"

Hugh Hutchinson was at the Pan Pacific Hotel inside Carol's suite. They had a special meeting scheduled. Hugh had a gorgeous blonde that was half his age hanging onto his arm. She was dressed to party with a low-cut red cocktail dress and knee-high leather boots. Her dangling diamond earrings were a gift from the billionaire. She seemed a little drunk.

"Introduce me." She insisted.

"Carol, I'd like you to meet Tiffany Cooke. We met a few weeks ago in Ottawa."

Carol held out her hand to greet the stunning woman. "It's nice to meet you, Tiffany. How did Hugh ever get so lucky?"

ONE HUNDRED & 15

As soon as they were off the air, Cindy's phone buzzed. It was Dane and she

didn't want to answer. She was enjoying her new-found celebrity and knew he would ruin her moment. "Hello, Dane."

He didn't disappoint. He was his usual disrespectful jerk. "I want to know how you got this story. Did you promise Magill something?"

Cindy thought about hanging up. She knew people were watching her, so she faked a smile. She held her phone close and talked softly. "Not everyone is a dirtbag like you."

Dane hated her insolence. If she weren't so popular, he'd fire her now. Her time would come. "You need to remember who I am. Your big moment will be a memory in a few days, so you need to be careful. I'm a star in this industry and you're just another pretty face that will come and go."

In Cindy's mind, Dane Wilson was just an insecure old man with too much plastic surgery. He was right about her time in the spotlight. She needed to follow this up with something bigger. And then, as if scripted, David Magill stood in front of her. He waited politely while she finished her call.

When she realized Magill was there, she interrupted Dane. "I have to go."

David held out his hand to greet her. "I just wanted to come over and thank you for believing in us and taking the chance you did."

Cindy was awestruck. He was so handsome. "Not a problem, Mr. Magill. I think I'm becoming a fan."

"Please, call me David," He pulled out his card and gave it to her. "I wanted to talk to you about doing a one on one interview with me to launch my campaign platform. A thirty-minute special. Does that interest you?"

Cindy could hardly contain herself. She wanted to leap into his arms and kiss him. She was already thinking about the outfit she'd wear. "I would enjoy talking to you about it."

"Great." David grinned. "I'll give you a call to set it up."

Cindy beamed. "I'll wait for your call."

ONE HUNDRED & 16

Wendell reached for Laura's hand as they walked along the Potomac River. When she didn't resist his advance, it was another reason to think Wakefield was wrong. The mood was comfortable, and they took a seat on a bench and watched some kids playing with a remote-controlled boat.

"I know a kid that could make a killer one of those," Wendell remembered Jonny's dragonfly. "He can make anything."

"Those burgers weren't a disappointment, but now I have to work off the calories."

Wendell wanted to make a suggestion but decided to keep his mouth shut. "This walk will be good for us."

It was beginning to get dark and he suggested they head back to the Hilton for that drink. Laura didn't object. Along the way a street vendor selling hats was closing for the night. She was his last customer and bought a straw hat. It was something out of a hillbilly commercial.

Wendell didn't hide his objection and laughed. "Why that one?"

"It makes me feel silly," she looked at herself in front of a mirror, "but I really like it."

Wendell offered to pay to make up for his poor humour, but Laura declined. She grabbed his hand and they headed to his hotel. "Are we still skipping the lounge?"

Wendell squeezed her hand. "Absolutely. I have some wine waiting for us."

Laura gave him a sideways glance. "Were you expecting me to come to your room?"

He raised his big black eyebrows. "A guy can always hope."

Laura leaned into his shoulder. "Let's hurry. I love wine."

When they entered the lobby, Laura pulled her hat down to block any good view of her face from the cameras. It was a move Wendell noticed. Suddenly he had some doubts again.

"Let's go upstairs." She pulled him towards the elevator.

Wendell didn't resist. He stood behind her with his hands on her shoulders while they rose to the sixth floor. He knew he could remove any fear by simply snapping her neck. It was something that he did consider, but he still wasn't convinced she was an assassin. Pulling on her hat wasn't an indication of guilt. "I hope the wine is chilled."

Laura twirled around in his arms and before he realized it, she was passionately kissing him. "I've had a great time with you, Mr. Presley."

The doubts disappeared and the smile was back. If he was going to die, being in bed with this gorgeous woman was a great way to go. "I'm glad you have."

Once inside his room, Laura tossed the hat onto a chair and fluffed out her hair with her fingers. "That thing made my head itchy."

"Why are you taking it off?" he asked jokingly. "I was just starting to like it."

Laura huffed at Wendell's comment. "Can you put on some light jazz?"

He chose Diana Krall.

"Great choice. She's a Nanaimo girl."

Wendell grabbed the wine and poured two glasses. He also uncorked the Jim Beam and poured some shots. He handed her one of each. "To a great day."

Laura put the bourbon on the table. "Thank you, but I'll stick to wine. I don't want to pass out."

Wendell shot the Jim Beam and slid the empty glass back by the bottle. "I won't let you fall asleep on me."

They fell back on the couch and for the next thirty minutes they told each other stories about themselves. Wendell relived his life on the ranch and Laura made up a fantasy about growing up on the prairies.

The first bottle of wine was finished, and Wendell had slipped in a few more shots of bourbon. He was getting drunk and loud. "I think it's time to party. Why don't you get naked while I take a piss?"

So much for the gentle soul at the museum. Laura wanted to keep the mood friendly. "Do you think you're getting lucky tonight?"

"We both know I'm getting lucky," He slurred aggressively. "I'll be right back."

Laura waited till the door closed before going to the room safe. She pulled down the camera and took the box. Once they were inside her purse, she poured Wendell another double Jim Beam.

When he returned, she handed him his drink. She headed into the bathroom. "It's my turn to freshen up. Why don't you get into the bed and get ready? I'll join you in a minute."

Wendell grabbed the bottle. "You go get ready. I'll be waiting."

"I bet you will," She was amazed how quickly the alcohol had changed his personality. He would be a violent drunk so she would need to be careful. "I'll be right back."

Laura was contracted to kill Presley. Mickey had decided he was a loose cannon and too risky to keep around. Judging by his personality when he got drunk it was a good decision. It was time to get to work.

She took a seat on the toilet and opened her purse and pulled out a nail file. She carefully inserted the sharpened end into the side of the toilet paper holder. It was easier this time. Earlier in the day, it had taken some careful carving to get the unit out of the wall without leaving a mess.

Laura pulled the metal roller out of the wall and reached into the hole and retrieved her pistol she put there this morning. She replaced the holder and flushed the toilet for effect. She headed for the door and paused to check her gun. She took a few breaths to relax. She was about to kill a man.

There was a loud bang on the hall door. Who the hell was that? She could hear a muffled voice yelling. She couldn't risk being seen, so she locked the bathroom door. She only wanted to deal with one dead body. The banging continued.

Presley was naked on the bed and the interruption made him angry. "Who the fuck is it?" When no one answered, but the banging continued, he pulled on his pants and went to the door. "This better be fucking important!"

Wendell pulled open the door and before he could react, he was pushed violently backwards. His drunken state didn't help his balance. He fell back over the bed and landed on his back. The intruder took advantage of Presley's vulnerable state and pounced on top of him. This man was as big as Presley and his hand gripped Presley's neck, while the other held a pistol aimed between his eyes. "Where is she?"

Wendell's reaction was to fight back until he saw the gun inches from his face. "Who?"

The intruder kept the gun aimed on Wendell. "Don't fuck with me. One last time, where is she?"

Wendell looked for an opening, but this guy knew what he was doing. The intruder had put his knee against Wendell's crotch and used his leverage to hold him in place. "Who are you looking for?"

The man pushed the barrel of his pistol into Wendell's mouth. "You stick to that story and you'll die right here."

Wendell saw Laura in the corner of his eye with a pistol pointed at the stranger. It happened quickly. Before the intruder could react, there was a single bullet wound between his eyes, and he was dead.

Wendell struggled out from under the intruder. The dead man's blood had dripped on his face. His wondered if that bullet was supposed to be for him. He was happy to be alive but wondered for how long. "What just happened?"

Laura kept her gun trained on Wendell. "That man was sent to kill both of us."

Wendell grabbed a towel and wiped the blood splatter from his face. He looked at the dead body. "How do you know that?"

"Because I know him," she replied, "and we need to talk. We're both screwed."

He sat on the side of the bed and grabbed the bottle of bourbon. He didn't need a glass. "What do you mean, we're both fucked? Where did you get a gun?"

"In your bathroom," Laura shrugged, "and yes I was."

He chuckled at how easy she made it sound, "Are you still going to? Who wants me dead?"

Laura kept her distance. She wasn't sure what her next step was, but she knew he was a powerful man that she didn't want to fight. "I can't answer that."

He took a swig and wiped his lips with the back of his hand. His immediate mission was to get as drunk as he could. "What are you going to do?"

She shrugged again, "I need to think of something."

Wendell looked at the body. "Who is that on the floor?"

"He's a cop. His name is Ken Murphy."

ONE HUNDRED & 17

Tiffany refreshed Hugh's drink and then walked him out onto the patio off Carol's suite. She fed him a bacon wrapped scallop and playfully wiped some sauce from his chin. They both giggled.

Tiffany was there to keep the billionaire happy and distracted when it was required. She was not allowed to sleep with him. Men like Hutchinson lose interest once they get what they want from a woman and Tiffany needed him looking straight ahead. She leaned over the railing. "What a wonderful view."

Hugh agreed. "The best part of my view is that you're in it."

Tiffany blushed. "That was so kind."

"I don't mean to be a bad date, but I have some business with Carol," he looked apologetic, "so I'm hoping I could have an hour with her and then I have a surprise for you."

Tiffany was happy to have some free time. Mickey had given her a heads up that Ray was downstairs. She was curious to hear how her husband ended up at a political convention. Was it a coincidence, or did someone point him in this direction? "I'll go back to my room. You have a good meeting and I'll find you back here in a couple hours."

Hugh gave her a polite kiss, but his hand did grab her firm ass. She backed away. "You focus on your meeting. I'll see you later."

Yes, you will. "Be good."

Before Hugh headed back inside, a large electronic billboard down on the corner caught his attention. The script was in large red and white letters, just like the Canadian flag.

VOTE CANADIAN - VOTE MAGILL

He went back inside and now it was only him and Carol. It was time to talk business. He put his drink down and replaced it with a bottle of water. Carol waited at the table.

"Nice looking girl. Where did you meet her?"

Hugh shook his head. "I'm not even sure. She just showed up in my life."

Mickey's girls were the best. "Well let's get down to work."

Hugh sipped the water. "I'm impressed, Carol. I had my doubts you could pull this off. But I was wrong. I hear your guy is killing it downstairs."

Carol nodded. "I know compliments don't come easy. So, thank you"

He took a seat and looked at a contract waiting for him to review. "Let's see if Hutchinson Enterprises and your organization can work together and make some history."

"Don't forget the money." Carol reminded him.

ONE HUNDRED & 18

After reviewing the contract, Hugh requested only a few minor changes. The terms were as they discussed in Ottawa at Hugh's estate. He was ready to sign off on it and get to work.

Hutchinson Enterprises had agreed to put its full support behind David Magill and the Federal Coalition party. This agreement was just as big as the Magill announcement. To get Hutchinson Enterprise's support away from the Liberal party was going to be a headline story. It gave instant credibility to the Federal Coalition.

And it would give Prime Minister Elliot a major headache.

In return for his support, Hutchinson Enterprises would be guaranteed a minimum of $1 billion in government contracts for every year David was in office. It was a thirty percent increase from what he received from the Liberals.

There business was almost completed. Carol had one more thing. "Now that we're partners, I need a favour."

Hugh gave her a sideways glance. "And that is?"

"I'll let David tell you. It's not a biggie."

ONE HUNDRED & 19

After a two-hour flight from Whitehorse, Suzanne hopped onto a ferry sailing to Nanaimo. Stacey was going to pick her up on the other side. It was a beautiful day on the water, so Suzanne decided to spend the entire trip on the promenade deck enjoying a James Patterson novel.

They were still a half hour away from docking when Suzanne was interrupted by some noisy sea lions barking off the port side. She put her book down to look. She saw about a dozen of them roll in the water and up on the beach. She looked at an older man sitting beside her. "Excuse me, but what's that island called?"

"That's Gabriola."

So it is. She walked over to the railing and wished she had some binoculars to get a better look. Other than rock bluffs and tall pine trees, there wasn't much to see from the ferry. She wished that Curtis would run out of the bushes and wave at her.

When Suzanne walked into the passenger area, Stacey Small wasn't hard to spot with her pregnant belly. They went straight to each other and embraced tightly. Both started to cry.

"Welcome to Nanaimo," Stacey held Suzanne's hand and led her outside. "You picked a beautiful day to come."

They loaded into Stacey's minivan. It was old, needed a tune up and had a strong smell of mint from the air freshener tree hanging from the mirror. Suzanne cracked open her window to clear the smell.

"Let's get you to my place. We can talk about our camping

adventure over some lunch. You must be hungry."

"That sounds great," Suzanne looked at Stacey's belly. "How is the baby doing?"

"She kicks like a soccer player."

Suzanne had thought about their adventure. "Are you sure you're up for a camping trip? It could be tough."

Stacey kept her eyes on the road. "I'm going, and I'll be fine. You can look after me."

For the remainder of their drive they exchanged stories about their boys. They laughed and cried, and both enjoyed being able to talk to someone who really understood the emotional toll a missing child can have on a parent.

When they got to Stacey's house, Suzanne got settled in the guest room that she assumed was Joshua's bedroom. It was strange to look at his computer. The scattered papers on the desk was an indication that Stacey had touched nothing. She understood. Curtis's room hadn't been touched either.

Suzanne asked. "What's the plan for tomorrow?"

Stacey didn't have one. "We'll catch the first ferry. I've already packed some food and water. We can share my tent."

"You're organized. I like it," Suzanne grinned. "Do you still think the boys might be over there?"

"I have to. Having hope helps keep me sane," Stacey chewed on the end of a carrot stick. "Does your husband know you're here?"

Suzanne shook her head. "You mean ex-husband, and the answer is no. If we find anything, I'll call him, but for now it's between us. Does the sergeant know about our adventure?"

Stacey didn't hesitate. "Nope."

"What if we find something?"

"If I told him he'd try and talk us out of it," Stacey explained, "and I think he regrets that he told me about the voices."

"You mentioned something about a dragonfly. He said it was spying on them."

Stacey chuckled. "I think the heat got to Detective Murphy. I'm sure they not building toys over there."

Suzanne helped herself to a sandwich. "True enough."

ONE HUNDRED & 20

Since her encounter with Wendell in his office, Cassie had kept a low profile. She was embarrassed and angry by how she was treated. She tried to hide it from the other recruits. Cassie had left what was a comfortable lifestyle because of a promise from Carol. She would have access to everything she needed to finish her vapor food and have final say on how it was utilized. Now it seemed that she lied to her.

An escort came to her lab. He had a message. He explained to Cassie that Mickey was off sight but wanted to talk in an hour. She would be taken to a communications room where they would talk. She didn't even know the room existed. There seemed to be a lot going on inside the complex that she wasn't aware of.

The hour had passed, and Cassie was now inside a cubicle. She was alone in the room and wore some headphones and a mic. She sipped on a bottle of iced tea to offset her dry mouth and anxiety. What did Mickey want to talk about?

She didn't know Mickey very well, but the boys always raved about him. They insisted he was fair, and Joshua liked to point out how tough the man was. She thought he was handsome.

Her Dell monitor came alive and an icon appeared in the middle of the screen. She clicked on it and there was Mickey, with a friendly smile. She could see he was in a hotel room.

Mickey began. "Hey Cassie. Good morning and thank you for taking the time to talk with me."

She instantly liked his friendly tone. The boys were right. "No worries, sir."

"Please, call me Mickey."

Cassie felt relaxed. "I will, thank you."

"I thought it was time that you and I talk about what happened with Wendell, but I'd like to get to know you better. Is that okay?"

She nodded.

"I heard about your grandparents struggle to get into Canada. It sounds like you were very close to them."

Cassie pursed her lips. "I loved my grandparents. They had a hard life."

"So, you've dedicated your brilliance to help future generations, so they don't suffer like your grandparents did. That's amazing to me."

"Thank you," Her eyes filled with sadness. "My grandparents were everything to me and they told me stories before bedtime. They wanted their journey known. They had family and friends that died in the fields from malnutrition. When they came to Canada they worked hard and sent what they could back home to family. It was a struggle being Chinese in a new country."

"I understand what it's like to be a minority, and my ancestors are from Canada."

Cassie looked puzzled. "Are you Indigenous?"

Mickey smiled. "Didn't you know I was an Indian?"

"I guess I don't care."

Mickey beamed. "Aren't you a breath of fresh air. I was born on a reserve but ran away when I was young. I wanted to be like the others. But do you know what I found out?"

Cassie was intrigued. "What?"

"I found out they were just as unhappy as I was."

"How did you deal with racism?"

He held up his fists. "With these in the beginning, but I was fooling myself thinking they would change after a beating. It got worse. So that's when I decided to join them."

"What does that mean?"

"I cut my hair short, I dressed like them and I even read their books," He admitted. "I sold my heritage for acceptance. Big mistake. That's why I'm so impressed with what you're doing."

She blushed again. "Thank you."

Mickey held up a file folder. It was Cassie's presentation that Wendell took from her. "This is why I wanted to talk to you. What Presley did is not acceptable, and I'm sorry."

Cassie was relieved to see Mickey had it.

"As you probably heard, he's gone, and I want to let you know your field testing has been approved. We're going to start in a week."

Cassie fought to contain her elation. "Thank you, Mickey."

"There's more. Because of the controlled environment and secrecy that we require, we can't do the testing in Canada."

"Where then?"

"North Korea. There are millions of people going hungry there."

"How are we going to get into North Korea?"

"We have a friend who will help. He just signed a contract with us, and he does work there."

"I already know how to speak Korean."

Mickey wasn't surprised. "Of course, you do."

ONE HUNDRED & 21

Prime Minister Elliot was alone in his office squeezing a near empty water bottle. He contemplated something stronger to escape the troubles he knew were coming. His free time was rare and for a short moment he enjoyed the solitude from staff and the ambitious assholes that were after his job.

His closet lifestyle was no longer a secret and he knew at anytime it could become a frontpage story. The humiliation and damage to the Liberal party credibility would be

unimaginable. The calls for his resignation would be immediate.

And yet he wasn't worried about it. The thought should scare the hell out of him, but it didn't. He had wondered if maybe his time was up, and that he should step away from politics. He loved the power and the access to women the job offered.

He was concerned that he had put all his faith in Hutchinson to clean up his mess with the North Koreans. That was dangerous. Hutchinson told him it was taken care of, but Pierre knew differently.

And now for the first time in a long time the Federal Coalition seemed like they might have a legitimate leader. But who is David Magill? So far not much was known about the former lawyer.

Elliot waited for the president to take his call. He had been on hold for twenty minutes. Pierre was not a fan of the new president. Daniel Tucker was a narcissistic man who didn't worry about how he was portrayed in the media. He was a fan of Sinatra and he did things his way.

Daniel Tucker, once the Governor of Colorado, was the twentieth

Republican elected as the president. Early in his first term he made some decisions that had both parties stand up and pay attention. He campaigned on the platform he was going to create a strong economy and put Americans back to work. He didn't care who he upset or stepped on.

The prime minister's personal secretary handed Elliot a private phone. "He's ready for you now, sir."

He waited until she closed the door before he answered. "Good afternoon, Mr. President."

"Hello, Elliot," the President bellowed, "sorry to keep you waiting, but I had some important things I needed to deal with before I could fit you in."

Pierre bit his lip. He wasn't used to being the belittled one. "We're both busy, so let's get to the reason I called."

Tucker interrupted him. "I know why you called, and I need a few things before I can commit to being there on July 1."

Pierre knew this was going to be controversial. "I'm thinking this isn't about your lobster."

Tucker snickered. "Lopez told me you're getting me a big one. That's great, but it's not the lobster I'm thinking about."

"What is it?"

"I want to be able to put some of our navy vessels in Nanoose Inlet," Tucker revealed. "It's on Vancouver Island."

Pierre knew where Nanoose Bay was. "For how long?"

"For as long as North Korea is governed by a nut job. I want our navy to take control of the entire base for as long as we deem necessary. It's been closed for years so what's the issue?"

Pierre knew Tucker was a bully when negotiating. "I can't see that happening on many levels."

The president's quick fuse ignited. "Make it happen! We need to neutralize any advantages the North Koreans might have in the

Pacific."

Pierre thought about his own relationship with the North Koreans. "Let me talk to my inner team."

"Remind your inner team who your biggest trade partner is." Tucker's threat was obvious.

"As prime minister I only have so much authority."

Tucker tightened the screws. "From what I'm hearing, your days as prime minister might be numbered."

Pierre fumed. "My political future is fine."

The president smirked. He knew he had gotten under Elliot's skin. "One last thing. I hear you have a friend who likes to role-play. Make sure she's available for my visit."

ONE HUNDRED & 22

Cindy had one more remote broadcast for the eleven o'clock news. The party inside the convention was in full swing and the crowd had doubled since the evening began. The lineup to become a member of the Federal Coalition was suddenly active and the volunteers struggled to get through it.

Cindy found her tired cameraman looking stressed. "Are you ready?"

"Where the hell did you go? You're on in five."

"I went outside to get some fresh air," she hated lying to him, "and I had to make a call."

The cameraman knew that Dane had called Cindy's phone twice. Her phone was in the bag on the floor beside him. He knew something big was going on. He had been a cameraman for a long time, and he had never seen a reporter get the breaks Cindy was getting. Her phone buzzed again.

The cameraman shot her a look. "Out making a personal call, my ass."

Cindy grabbed the phone. "Hello?"

Dane was angry. "Where the hell have you been?"

"I was in the bathroom," She shot the cameraman a look. "What do you want?"

Dane resented her new-found confidence. "What's your update?"

"I have another surprise, but you'll have to wait." She teased him.

"Bullshit! I need to know what it is now!"

Cindy mocked his anger. She could only imagine the mood back at the station. "All right if you insist. Mr. Magill has offered to do a one on one thirty-minute interview to launch his campaign with me being the host. Isn't that wonderful?"

Dane was already thinking about how he could hijack the interview. "Are you sleeping with this asshole."

"Be very careful what you say, Dane," she warned him. "Maybe he actually thinks I'm a good reporter."

Dane backed down. He couldn't afford another sexual harassment lawsuit. "Real reporters work for years to get a shot like this."

Real reporters? "I guess I just got lucky."

"Once you're finished, you need to come back to the station," Dane ordered. "I need to talk to you…"

She interrupted her soon to be ex-boss. "After I'm done, I've been invited out for drinks. I'll see you next week."

ONE HUNDRED & 23

Tiffany had changed into something more conservative before heading down to the convention. The David Magill announcement had been broadcasted and Tiffany walked into a wild celebration. Alcohol flowed and the dance floor was full. It was party central. Somewhere in the crowd was her husband.

It was time to have an open conversation with her husband, who was on the verge of becoming an unwanted distraction. If he caused a scene with David, it wouldn't go well for him.

She thought about her complicated relationship with Ray over the last six years. It was problematic. Ray believed their introduction on the patio at the country club had been a beautiful coincidence that was meant to happen. The truth was, he was a target and she was tasked with the assignment.

Tiffany's beauty and sophistication captivated Ray. Within days he was madly in love with her. When her assignment was over and he went to prison, she was supposed to file for a divorce, but she never did. She was supposed to kill him, but she couldn't. She was in love with him.

Tiffany kept a low profile as she worked her way through the crowd. She needed to find Ray before he found her. She was relieved when she saw him headed to the men's washroom. She grabbed his shoulder. "Where are you going?"

He was surprised to see her. "Where did you come from?"

She put her finger to her lips. "Come with me. I have a surprise for you."

Ray pulled back. "What are you doing here?"

"I want you to come with me," she responded softly, taking his hands. "I have something for you."

He wanted to be upset with her but couldn't. "Where are we going?"

"To my room."

"Why?"

"We need to fuck this marriage back into shape," she whispered in his ear. "and I only have thirty minutes, so let's go."

Ray stepped on the elevator. "Why only thirty minutes?"

"Because I'm on a date," she told him truthfully, "and he's upstairs doing some business."

Ray never asked another question until he laid sexually exhausted on top of the bedsheets. The door wasn't even closed before Tiffany pushed Ray back onto the bed and removed his pants. They made energetic love and once they were both exhausted, she climbed off the bed and grabbed two waters from the mini fridge.

Tiffany tossed him one. "It's time to clear up a few things."

Ray leaned up against the headboard. "Where do we start?"

Tiffany sat on the corner of the bed wearing only her long blonde hair that rolled onto her shoulders. She was never shy about her body and counted on it as one of her most effective weapons. "I'll begin by telling you I'm sorry about sending you to prison."

"Okay. That answers my first question."

"Do you remember Liberty City?"

Ray sighed. "Why does everything seem to lead back to that company?"

"It's a company the organization I work for uses for acquisitions and a few other projects. The shareholders are all dead, so board meetings are short."

Ray smiled but was confused. "Why all the secrecy around it?"

Tiffany started to get dressed. "What I'm about to tell you could get us both killed."

"Then don't tell me?" Ray looked concerned. "I want to know everything about you, but not if it puts you in danger."

"It's complicated and involves a lot of people and the number grows bigger daily. And they are powerful people."

"How does David fit into this?"

"He became the chosen one just before we met," she explained, "and he will become the next prime minister."

"How can you be so sure?"

"Because Carol wants it."

Ray shook his head in disbelief. "You're telling me that one lady is behind all of this?"

"She is enormously powerful and there's much that I don't know and never will. We all have our roles," Tiffany touched up her lip gloss. "One thing to be aware of is she is revengeful as hell if you cross her. She was the one that put out the contract on you."

Ray paused to think. "Why didn't you kill me?"

"I talked her into letting me destroy your reputation instead. She knew I fell in love."

He loved hearing her say it out loud. "So, I married an assassin."

"I guess so," she shrugged, "and do you have a problem with that?"

"Strangely enough I don't," He had no feelings either way. "So, my ex partner is going to become the next prime minister. I'll believe it when I see it."

"Don't bet against him." She warned. "This has been planned for years and now it's time."

"What's the end game?"

"I can't tell you because I don't know," Tiffany checked the time. "I have to get to my date."

Ray sighed. "My buddy is going to be the prime minister and my wife's going on a date."

"You sound jealous."

"I'm frustrated," He corrected her. "I'm an unemployable lawyer and David's about to become the next prime minister. It seems like he got the better deal."

"No one's coming to your pity party, so grow up," Tiffany pretended to sound annoyed, "and I wouldn't be bad-mouthing Carol."

"Who's the date with?" Ray tried to sound disinterested. "Some politician?"

"A billionaire."

"Seriously?" The surprises kept coming. "Who?"

"Hugh Hutchinson."

Ray was aware of who Hutchinson was. "How'd that happen?"

Tiffany didn't answer his question. "Why don't you take a shower and be horny when I get back."

ONE HUNDRED & 24

Laura Nelsen was back in her own room at the Hilton and she was in a foul mood. Her assignment to kill Presley went completely sideways when Detective Murphy barged in carrying a gun. How did the detective know where she was, and why was he sent?

And now Wendell Presley was missing. He had volunteered to help dispose of Murphy's body and she took him up on his offer. Everything was fine until they loaded the body into a van Laura had lined up. While she was checking a message Wendell sped off, leaving her in the parking garage. How was she going to explain this to Mickey?

Detective Ken Murphy was a fifteen-year veteran of the police force and a part-time contractor for the organization. Murphy liked to play the ponies and his tab got out of control. The organization cleaned up is debt in exchange for services. His latest assignment was to stay close to Sergeant Smith. Keep his eyes and ears open and keep Mickey posted if Smith found something significant.

Laura wanted to stay in Washington and find Presley, but that could take days or even weeks. She knew he'd eventually surface and when he did, she'd finish the job. For now, it was time to head to the airport. On her way out the door she tossed the straw hat angrily into the garbage. "What a waste of twenty bucks."

Eight hours later Laura knocked on Mickey's room at the Pan Pacific. She was exhausted after a cross continent flight. When he opened the door, Mickey let her in and shut the door. She stepped to the middle of the room, uncertain of the reception she'd receive.

Mickey looked relaxed, "I hear Washington was a shit show?"

Laura shrugged, "How do you know that?"

"Because you're standing inside my room instead of sleeping in your own bed," Mickey surmised, "and because I haven't heard from Murphy."

"So, you knew Murphy was there?"

"I sent him."

"Didn't you think I could get the job done?"

He shook his head. "I got a tip that Wendell was on to you. He knew you were there to kill him. That's why I sent Murphy. To cover your back."

Laura felt foolish.

"Is Murphy dead?"

"I shot him between the eyes before I realized who it was."

"And Presley?"

"Somewhere in Washington and alive," She left out how he got away. "I'll find him."

"Look, I need to head downstairs. Why don't you crash here? We can talk later."

Laura eyed the big bed. "Maybe I will."

ONE HUNDRED & 25

Joshua was in his lab working on the final pieces to complete his animatronic being. The months of work had begun to pay dividends. The pressure was immense for anyone, especially a twelve-year old. Genius or otherwise.

One last algorithm to develop DNA integration and the animatronics would be a perfect human duplication. They would breathe and bleed and integrate perfectly with society. What the young genius didn't know was the purpose behind them.

He took a break to order a sandwich delivered to the lab. He was distracted still by the image of his mum pulling on the fence. There was no audio. but it was obvious that she was yelling at something or someone.

How did she find out about the complex? Did she know he was inside? And what about her being pregnant? And where was his dad? Lots of questions with no answers. Maybe it was time to talk to his grandmother. There were times he regretted his decision to leave with her.

His face soured when he recalled the nights that he hid under the blankets to try and block out the screaming between his mom and dad. It terrified him to hear the threats of divorce, or that his dad was drunk again. He thought it was his fault and that's why he agreed to leave.

He was eating his sandwich when his phone buzzed. "What's up?"

"How's life down in the dungeon?" Curtis sounded hyper. "I haven't seen you in the gym for a while."

"I've been busy."

"Come tonight. We need to talk," Curtis pressured him. "It's serious crap."

Joshua decided he could use a break and agreed. "I can be there around six. I need to work on my legs."

Curtis laughed. "You need to work on your entire skinny ass body. See you at six."

Joshua arrived at the gym at six like he said. Before he left his lab, he had solved the final piece to the puzzle. It was an amazing relief, and he was so excited. His animatronic being was built to perfection. When he contacted Carol to give her the good news, the only thing she told him was to keep his mouth shut.

Curtis was excited to see Joshua and waved him over. He was wearing his standard khaki shorts and a sweaty t-shirt. He gave Joshua a high five. "Glad to see you made it. Let's get to work."

After hitting the circuit for thirty minutes, Curtis sensed Joshua's mind wasn't on the weights. "What's going on with you? You're going to get hurt if you don't focus."

Joshua sat on the workout bench. "Sorry, I just have a lot going on."

"How are your robots? Are you done yet?"

Joshua remembered Carol's stern warning. "I can't talk about them."

"I bet you're close, and that's why you're distracted. Is Carol on your ass to finish?"

Joshua wanted to tell him. "I just ignore her."

Curtis put his arm around Joshua and guided him away from the weights to where no one could overhear him. "I need a favour."

"What do you need?"

Curtis whispered. "I need access to Level C."

You need top level clearance to access Level C. It was where the secret projects were worked on. Curtis didn't have it, but Joshua did.

"Why do you want to get down there?"

Curtis kept his voice low. "I need you to trust me."

"Getting you by security will be impossible."

Curtis didn't agree. "I have a plan for that."

Joshua wasn't convinced. "If I do this, I need a favour back."

Curtis's face lit up. "Anything. What is it?"

"I need you to get a message to my mom. I know you have access to an outside server," Joshua said, "so, do we have a deal?"

A fist pump said they did.

ONE HUNDRED & 26

The morning sun flickered through the blinds onto Suzanne's face when she woke, and the smell of bacon encouraged her to get out of bed. She knew she didn't have a lot of time, so she dressed and packed up her things for the camping trip.

When she walked into the kitchen, Stacey gave her a plate with scrambled eggs and bacon. "I hope you like cheese. I figured we'd need the extra carbs."

"Thank you. This looks great," Suzanne shoved a piece of bacon into her mouth. "You sure are cheerful this morning."

She rubbed her belly. "We're both excited to have you here. It's going to be a great day. How do you feel?"

"I'm not sure if I'm excited or scared."

They finished breakfast and they had to hurry if they wanted to catch the first sailing. When she loaded their gear into the van, Suzanne noticed a metal tool sticking out of her pack. "What's that for?"

"The fence," Stacey smirked. "We're cutting our way in."

Suzanne chuckled. "I just brought a camera."

Stacey looked at her phone. "Damn."

"What is it?"

"I have a message from Sergeant Smith," She tossed the phone between the seats. "I'll listen to it on the ferry. Let's go!"

They found some seats on the upper level of the ferry. Both sat quietly and thought about the day ahead and what might take place. They were excited to be doing something but were apprehensive of the unknown. What was going on inside the complex? Were their boys there? Their adventure was underway.

While Suzanne was absorbed with all the activity on the water, Stacey reached for the phone. There was a second message from the sergeant. What did he want? She was scared to hear what he might have said. It might be bad news. She slipped her phone back into her pocket.

Suzanne watched Stacey ignore her messages.

When they got off the ferry, they hitched a ride to the trail entrance. Stacey garnered a few stares being pregnant and carrying a backpack. Suzanne decided that someone had to be the sensible one and insisted on taking breaks every ten minutes. Stacey didn't resist the idea.

"On our next break why don't you check Smith's message," Suzanne suggested with a little sarcasm. "Ignoring it won't make it go away. It could be important."

"It's messages," Stacey corrected her. "Once we get to the campsite I will."

The backpacks slowed their progress, but after almost an hour Stacey was relieved to see the graffiti rock. "Our campsite is up ahead."

Suzanne's body was drenched in sweat. "Thank god."

"After we get setup, there's a freshwater spring that we can soak our feet in."

Suzanne loved that idea. "Do you know how to setup the tent?"

Stacey scoffed. "That's why I invited you. You live in the Yukon."

"Just because I live in the north doesn't mean I like to camp."

What should have taken twenty-minutes was almost an hour of frustration. They laughed at their incompetence. When they finally got their camp setup, they headed to the spring and stripped down to their underwear and slid into the water. It was a priceless feeling.

Suzanne said. "When we get back to camp you will listen to your messages, and I'll scout the fenced area. There is no need for you to climb the steep hill."

Stacey didn't resist her idea. "You said you brought a camera. Maybe you can take some pictures."

The dip in the water restored their energy and once they returned to their camp site, they were all business. While Suzanne organized her camera gear, Stacey listened to her messages from Smith. Her expression sunk.

"What did he say." Suzanne was ready to go. "You look worried."

"He said if I was thinking of coming over here I shouldn't. He said it was a bad idea."

"A little late now," Suzanne countered. "Did he say why?"

"Detective Murphy is dead."

ONE HUNDRED & 27

David Magill laid in his bed at the Pan Pacific Hotel and stared up at the ceiling. It had been a spectacular night. Everything that Carol had planned happened exactly as she said it would. It was amazing to be a part of. He was now the new leader of the Federal Coalition. It had begun to sink in the he would be the next prime minister of Canada.

David checked the time on his phone. He was hungry and knew Carol had a busy day scheduled for him. He decided to order some room service so he could eat in private. He learned last night how quickly life changed when you become a public figure. One lady was so determined to meet him that she shoved her panties in her pocket with a room key. He politely declined her offer, but now understood why he needed a security detail.

His phone vibrated on the bedside table. The chime was assigned to Nina. "Good morning. How are you?"

Nina sounded happy. "Congratulations on the big win. I was glued to the news."

"I'm not sure I'm the one who deserves the congratulations," David pointed out. "There were a lot of people working on my behalf."

"Speaking of that, who was the perky blonde reporter? Did you know about her?"

David sensed some jealousy. "Her name is Cindy Austin, and I met her last night like the rest of the country. Finding a fresh face was part of the strategy. You sound concerned."

"I'm not concerned," She lied, "but she does seem young."

"Like I said, it was a Carol decision," David sounded annoyed. "Anything else?"

Nina knew to move on. "What are you doing today?"

"There's the AGM to elect a new board of directors. And then I have more meetings with strategists and public relations. It will be a long day."

Nina did feel some jealousy. She had done so much for the organization. "I wish I could be there with you."

"You'll be with me soon enough," There was a knock on his door. "My breakfast just arrived. Can I call you back tonight?"

"Yes, and I'm sorry about the reporter thing."

"Don't worry about it," He assured her. "Now I have to go."

On his way to the door he stuck his head into the bathroom and spoke loud enough to be heard over the water. "I hope you like pancakes?"

Cindy stuck her head out from behind the shower curtain. "I love them, and can I have my panties back?"

ONE HUNDRED & 28

Suzanne was blindsided by the news. "What happened to Detective Murphy?"

"Smith never left any details," Stacey glared at the fence. "He's another person connected to Joshua's case that has died. What's going on in there?"

Suzanne tossed her pack over her shoulder and headed up the hill. "Hopefully, I can find out."

Stacey watched her scale the hill using roots and embedded rocks as grips. When she reached the top, Suzanne scanned her surroundings before clawing through the bushes to the opening beside the fence. She was prewarned about the security cameras and kept her head down.

While she caught her breath, she pulled out her camera. There wasn't much to photograph. The bushes on the other side of the fence were thick. And there were no voices.

She decided to scale the edge and move along the fence to try and find a photo opp. There were none. Before long she stood precariously on the edge of a cliff. A hundred feet below her were barnacle covered rocks and certain death if she fell.

The views were amazing, so Suzanne decided to get some photos. The blue water with strips of white were enticing and Suzanne snapped away. For a moment she let herself forget why they were there.

Stacey had followed on the trail below. "Anything exciting?"

Snap. Snap. Snap. "Just majestic views."

Stacey pointed out towards the water. "Look at that boat coming this way."

Suzanne found it in her zoom lens. "It's more like a yacht. Might be a charter wanting to get a closer view of the sea lions. There's no where for it to dock around here so the captain better be careful."

Stacey got animated. "That boat is still coming this way. Are you sure there isn't a dock?"

Suzanne lowered her camera. The yacht was only a hundred yards offshore. It didn't steer away from the island. It came right at them. "I hope the captain knows what he's doing. If he hits the rocks, he's in trouble."

The captain still made no effort to avert its course. The women were concerned for its safety. And without warning a metal structure stretched out from behind some rocks. It was an instant dock. Suzanne fired up her camera. "Unbelievable."

"What's going on?" Stacey didn't move any closer to the edge to improve her vantage point. "What can you see?"

"A dock just materialized," Her camera was focused and ready. "I'll try to get pictures of the crew and passengers."

Stacey could only wait, and it drove her crazy. She took a seat on a stump. It wasn't comfortable, but for the moment it would work. She was beginning to recognize that coming over in her condition probably wasn't smart.

Suzanne snapped pictures until the yacht unloaded its passengers and headed backout into open water. She watched the dock retract before heading down. The two headed back to camp. Suzanne suggested that Stacey have some lunch while she downloaded the photos onto her iPad. "How are you feeling?"

"If it's okay I think I should head home. This was a stupid idea for me to think I could do this."

"That is a brilliant decision," nodded Suzanne. "How about we have some lunch, then pack up?"

"Can I look at the photos why we eat?"

Suzanne handed her the iPad. "There were three passengers that got off."

Stacey took the tablet and started to scroll through the pictures. She got to the first man and had no idea who he was. Then the second man, it was the same things. And then she got to the third person. A woman. She stared intently at her picture. "Oh my god!"

Suzanne thought Stacey was going into labor. "What?"

Stacey pointed at the screen. "This woman."

Suzanne leaned across the picnic table. "Do you know her?"

Stacey took a painful breath. "She's my mother."

ONE HUNDRED & 29

When the charter pulled up to the retractable dock, a reflection of light from the cliffs temporarily blinded Carol. Mickey hurried her off the boat and inside the complex. Her schedule at the convention was exhausting, and after a quick stop in her office, her plan was for an afternoon nap.

Mickey turned on the kettle to make some tea. "That was a good week. What's next?"

Carol took a seat behind her desk and switched on her computer. "The interview with Cindy Austin is vital to get our message out. Magill has to be perfect."

"We've been prepping him for years." Mickey reminded her.

"I don't care. It's for real now and he needs to be perfect."

He ignored her little outburst. He was used to them. "He'll be ready."

"Send someone onto the cliffs behind the dock. There was something up there that deflected the sun into my eyes. Make sure it wasn't a camera."

Mickey left Carol's office and headed down the hallway towards the cafeteria. The plan was to grab a sandwich and then find Joshua. He had some questions about his assignment. Halfway to the cafeteria his radio buzzed. "Did you solve the reflection on the cliff?"

A security staff answered. "I think so. We found two women on the property. And one has a camera."

Mickey stopped. "How did they get around the fence?"

"Chain cutters. They cut their way through."

Mickey determined. "Where are they now?"

"We brought them to the detention room."

Mickey was upset to hear they were in the complex. The stakes were raised. "You know what this means?"

"Yes, sir. But they wouldn't leave," the guard explained, "and one asked for Carol by name. She is very pregnant."

"How does she know her?"

"She says she's her daughter."

Mickey knew this was trouble. "What's her name?"

The guard checked his notes. "Stacey Small."

Mickey hadn't seen Stacey since the night of the school fire. "And the other one?"

"Suzanne Lacy."

Curtis's mother was here too. Dam! "I'll be right there."

ONE HUNDRED & 30

Other than the mandatory security required at the Sussex Street property and a skeleton staff, the prime minister was having a quiet evening at home. He wore loose-fitting pants and a blue pullover while he sat in the kitchen reading the Ottawa Citizen. He had made himself a ham and cheese sandwich.

It was one depressing headline after another. There was nothing that the Liberal party did that received any positive coverage. The country was in disarray over climate change and fossil fuels. The divide in the country was getting deeper. Everyone blamed him. He felt his leadership was being challenged unfairly and it angered him.

He flipped through the pages and came to a full-page advertisement that grabbed his attention. It was a photo of David Magill. It ran with a headline in big red letters with a Canadian flag embossed in the background: *Meet Your Next Prime Minister.*

He dialled Hugh Hutchinson, but it went straight to voicemail.

Hugh Hutchinson was across town in a very upscale Italian café with Tiffany Cooke. They were seated at a table with a window view of a flower garden. There were a dozen fresh cut yellow roses in a crystal vase that were on display beside them. A bottle of Dom Perignon was iced in a wooden pail. It was obvious that Mr. Hutchinson was out to impress his date.

They had skipped out of the convention, and on Hugh's suggestion, took his private jet to Ottawa for dinner at his favourite restaurant. Their main course of seafood linguini was the best Tiffany had ever tasted. Now they waited on a large piece of chocolate swirl cheesecake to share.

Hugh thought he was on a date with a successful fashion model out of New York that had his full attention. Tiffany was on another assignment. Nobody would die tonight unless Hutchinson did something real stupid. After they landed in Ottawa, she excused herself to use the lady's room. While she sat on the toilet, she sent Ray a text that her plans had changed, and she was going to be late.

Hugh's phone vibrated and he glanced at the number on the display. It was the prime minister, and he chose to ignore it. The woman seated across from him was worth any wrath Pierre might send his way. He topped up their champagne and signalled the waiter to bring another bottle.

Hugh's face glowed. It was from all the wine and having such a gorgeous woman sit across from him. It turned into a great day. "Once we finish dessert, I'm hoping I take you back to my estate for a nightcap?"

He expected a yes.

Tiffany leaned forward just enough to give the billionaire a glimpse of what he hoped to see. Her black vest fell away from her breast. He made no attempt to look away. "I'd love too."

The lovebirds enjoyed their cheesecake and giggled over who would get the last mouthful. Tiffany was prepared for a night at his estate but had no intention of sleeping with the man buying dinner. The little pill in her pocket guaranteed it.

Hugh raised his glass. "Let's have an after-dinner coffee and then we can head to my place."

Tiffany agreed. Another drink would make the pill's job easier. "That sounds wonderful, but will you still be able to perform with so much to drink?"

Hugh called over the waiter. "Bring us two French coffees."

Tiffany went to work. "I think it's great you're joining David

Magill, but aren't you still working with Pierre Elliot?"

"If I put my media machine behind Magill, he'll get elected. That's how Elliot got in."

"Wow," Tiffany feigned to be impressed. "You're amazing."

"And when he gets elected, I'll control the party," He boasted. "Carol thinks she'll be in charge, but I'll push the old lady to the side when I'm ready."

Bingo. It was what she needed to know.

The French coffees arrived. It was her turn to raise her glass. "I'm looking forward to spending the night. I bet you have an amazing bed."

Hugh engaged Tiffany's compliment. He puffed out his chest and reached for her hand. "We can walk along the river and relax in the Jacuzzi."

Tiffany noticed the two tall men in deep blue suits enter the restaurant and stand in the foyer. This wasn't good. The men glanced around and then headed in their direction. She reached into her purse and unclipped the safety on her pistol.

Hugh had no idea what was going on until the two men stood by their table. He recognized them immediately. "You got to be kidding me. What does Pierre want now?"

"Sorry to show up unannounced Mr. Hutchinson, but we need you to come with us," The agent glanced at Tiffany. "Sorry, ma'am."

She looked disappointed and closed her purse.

"What does he want," Hugh complained, "that couldn't wait until tomorrow?"

"You know we don't know that sir," was the rehearsed response by the senior officer. "But we need you to come now."

Hugh's disappointment was written on his face. "I'm sorry, my love, but duty apparently calls."

"I'm really disappointed," she lied convincingly, "but we can finish our plans another night. Can you have the jet ready when I get back to the airport?"

"Yes."

"I hope you enjoy your visit with the prime minister," She smiled like she meant it. "Call me in the morning."

Hugh took one last glance at her before he headed out. He hated Pierre at that exact moment. "Whatever Pierre wants, it better be fucking important."

On the drive to the airport, Tiffany realized she was excited to be headed home. She missed Ray.

ONE HUNDRED & 31

Mickey stood outside the detention room and looked through the one-way glass at the two women. He recognized both, but they wouldn't know him. How the hell did they find this place? Sergeant Smith was getting too close. Seeing them here wasn't something he was ready for. His options were limited.

He took a breath to compose himself and stepped inside. "Hello ladies. I understand you decided to sneak onto our property. Can I ask you why?"

Stacey's frown showed she was in some discomfort. "I want to see my mother."

"Before we get too excited, can I get you anything? I don't want you to feel uncomfortable."

His kindness caught them off guard. "Can we get some water?"

"Sure. Is there anything else you need?"

Neither answered.

He gestured at Stacey's belly as he passed them water. "Why is someone in your condition climbing through fences?"

Stacey was defiant. "Who cares about the fence. Where's my mother?"

Suzanne recognized him as one of the men she photographed. "What's your name?"

"My name doesn't matter. I'm told you're Suzanne Lacy and your grumpy friend here is Stacey Small. Why don't you tell me why you're really here?"

Stacey wasn't going to be silent. "Cut the bullshit. I want to see my mother. I know she's here!"

Mickey turned to Stacey. "How are you so sure?"

Stacey tried to lean forward, but her belly stopped her. "We have pictures!"

Suzanne gently squeezed Stacey's hand. "You need to relax for the baby's sake," She turned to Mickey. "I took some pictures of you getting off a boat."

"Can I see them?"

"My camera is in my bag over in the corner," Suzanne pointed. "I'll show you them."

Mickey retrieved the bag and handed it to Suzanne.

Stacey jumped back in. "You never said who you are or what you do here."

"We're a research facility," was his rehearsed answer, "and I am in charge."

"Do you have a name?"

Maybe knowing his name would ease her stress. "It's Mickey."

"Does my mom work for you, Mickey?"

He wasn't sure how he was going to explain Carol's presence. He turned to Suzanne. "Can I look at the photos?"

Suzanne handed him the tablet. He went through each picture and studied them closely. He remembered Carol complaining about a reflection on the rocks. It was the camera lens. "You took these from the cliffs?"

"Yes."

He looked at the photos and wasn't happy to see his face. He deleted them one at a time. "Sorry, but I can't let you keep these."

Suzanne wasn't surprised. She never mentioned that she emailed a set to her home computer in the Yukon. "That's fine."

He faced Stacey. "How well do you know your mother?"

"We're not exactly close. Last time we talked I was told she sold real estate, but I know that's a lie. Everything about our relationship is based on a lie."

"If you dislike her so much why did you go through the trouble to try and find her? Whatever you have to say must be important."

Stacey scowled. "I don't care about my mother. We're here to find our sons."

Suzanne jumped in. "Are they here, Mickey?"

ONE HUNDRED & 32

Steve Smith tried to enjoy a rare day off from being a police officer, but relaxing wasn't a skill he had mastered yet. He had thrown on some old sweatpants with patches on both knees and a t-shirt that Helen wouldn't let him wear outside the house. It was at least twenty years old.

He was sitting in the kitchen drinking his second cup of coffee while he struggled doing a crossword. This was as relaxed as Helen had seen him since the Joshua Small case fell in his lap. For some unknown reason, this particular case had consumed him. He couldn't separate himself from it.

She was used to life as a cop's wife, but over the past few months she witnessed subtle changes in his lifestyle. His face showed signs of ageing and his once powerful upper body had begun to sag.

"Do you want some more coffee, honey," and without waiting for his answer, she grabbed the pot and refilled their mugs, "or anything else to eat?"

Steve looked up from his crossword and gave her a thankful smile. "The coffee is fine."

Helen watched him over the brim of her mug. "Can we talk?"

He never looked up from his puzzle. "What's up?"

"Please put the magazine down," It was a demand, not a question. "We need to talk about how your job is taking a toll on your health. The stress is killing you."

He tossed the puzzle book on the table. "I'm just a little tired from all the extra work that they've given me. It'll slow down."

Helen didn't agree. "You've always had a heavy workload, but the Small case has taken over your life. You're only one person."

Steve sipped his coffee. "I'm fine. It's not a big deal."

"Damn it, Steve," His denial upset her. "You wake up in the middle of the night with bad dreams and you're still investigating the Addison case even though the coroner ruled it an accident. And now your partner is found murdered. That's a lot for you to process. You should be getting help."

"I deal with it. It's no busier now than it has always been."

And then she revealed his little secret that she found snooping through his things. "But you've never hid a vodka bottle in your desk before. You're drinking to cope and you need to stop before it gets out of control."

The guilt flooded through him, knowing he disappointed her. For the first time in his life, he was the one that needed help. He didn't know how to ask. "I'm sorry you found it."

Her tone softened and her love for her husband was obvious. "You have to stop before it takes control. I'm not blaming you, but we need to talk."

He was surprised how much relief he felt, knowing that she knew. "What are you thinking about because I know you already have a plan?"

Helen smiled at her husband and for the first time, he looked vulnerable. "We've been married for over twenty-five years and raised two great boys, but now it's our turn again. You need to slow down, or you'll never live long enough to be a grandpa."

"A grandpa," Steve realized how much living he still had to do. "Wow, we are getting old. What am I going to do when I'm not a cop anymore?"

"You'll start by sleeping better," she laughed. "So, what do you want to do?"

Steve had never thought about life after being a cop. "I do want to finish the Small case and yes, maybe it has become personal. When I see the pain in his mom's eyes, I can't let it go."

"And that's why you're such a great police officer and an even better person, but now it's my time."

He knew she was right.

"I love you," She pursed her lips. "You're everything to me."

"I know you do, and I love you too." Steve grabbed his wife and gave her a tight hug. "Why don't we grab our coffee and go to the computer room?"

She gave him a quizzical look. "We don't have a computer room."

"Okay, the bedroom," He smiled cheekily. "We can research European vacations and see where it heads."

ONE HUNDRED & 33

Carol was still on her computer when Mickey returned. She looked up and was surprised to see him. "What are you doing back here?"

"We need to talk."

"I don't like the sound of that," Carol stopped what she was doing. "Is everything okay?"

Mickey grabbed a juice from the cooler. "Two women cut through the fence and they demanded to see you."

"See me?" She walked out from behind her desk. "Has the complex been compromised?"

Mickey shrugged. "I'm not sure yet. But we need to talk about the women. They're in detention."

"You put them in detention?" Carol was furious. "You know what that means. They can't leave here alive."

Mickey stepped in. "They're looking for their kids?"

"Who the hell are their kids?"

"Curtis and Joshua."

Carol jumped up and pushed her chair away. "Are you kidding me? Stacey is here?"

"And she brought her new friend," Mickey responded. "The reflection you saw on the cliff was their camera. That's how they know you're here."

"Did they tell you what led them to that cliff?"

"Not yet, but your daughter is demanding to see you."

"Who cares what Stacey wants." Carol huffed. "I'll decide what she does next."

"One last thing."

"What is it?"

"You're going to be a grand mother again," he grinned, "and very soon."

The news didn't phase her. "You know they can't leave. Stacey will run straight to the police."

"We need to think this through. We can't just kill them," Mickey challenged. "She's your family."

She stared coldly at him. "If that's what I decide then that's what you'll do. No one will interfere with the organization. Not even my stupid daughter."

"They didn't come here looking for you. They think their boys are here."

"That still doesn't change anything," Carol fumed with anger, "and why would they think that?"

"Sergeant Smith is my guess. Remember, him and Murphy were here last week, and Murphy got killed before I could debrief him."

"That cop might be next," She growled. "He's getting too close."

"What do you want me to do with the women?"

Carol grabbed her purse. "I'm going for a nap. After I get some sleep, I'll tell you my decision."

ONE HUNDRED & 34

Sitting alone in the back seat of a government vehicle on his way to the prime minister's residence was not how Hugh Hutchinson had envisioned his night playing out. Instead of drinking more wine and enjoying a romantic hot tub with a beautiful friend, he felt a little concerned over the array of topics that might have Pierre wanting to meet this late at night. There was no way the prime minister could already know about his agreement with Carol.

After using a bathroom, Hugh was directed to the library where he was surprised to find Pierre wearing a jacket and ball cap. "What's going on?"

"Keep your coat on. I feel like a walk along the river. I thought we could talk and get some exercise at the same time."

Hugh actually liked the idea. It would help clear his head of the champagne and get Pierre on neutral ground. He knew the prime minister didn't summons him to be his walking buddy. There was something more going on.

They walked down a well-lit stone path to the river. Two security staff kept their distance but were never too far away. When they stood on the riverbank, they both felt the chill from the water and tightened their jackets. They sat on a wooden bench and stared out at the water.

Pierre began. "I use to come down here and fish. I loved the solitude, but I hated it when I got skunked. I'd yell at the fish, reminding them who I was. They didn't care about me. It was about self survival."

Hugh listened. He knew there was a message in there.

"I hear your date was gorgeous beyond description."

"She was definitely hot," Hugh yearned. "What's so important it couldn't wait until morning?"

"I need to talk to someone I can trust."

Hugh was relieved to hear he only wanted an ear to complain to.

"My life has become a circus and it's my fault," Pierre began, "but I can't let it control my life. My future."

"Why the sudden concern?"

"I know you told me the tape was destroyed, but I'm having a hard time believing that she won't show up when the time is right."

Hugh suppressed the urge to smile. "You have definitely made some interesting choices lately."

Pierre turned his head slightly, so their eyes connected. "Can I really trust you?"

The easy answer wasn't the truth. "You know you can."

"What's really going on with the North Korean deal. Am I going to see my money?"

"Most of it. Fisher fucked everything when the deposit was stolen, and it was never recovered." Hugh stood firm. "That falls on you. Fisher was your guy."

"I can accept that, but I need to know your confident the North Korean's destroyed the video."

Again, with the video. It was getting on Hugh's nerves. "I was told it was destroyed, so I'm not sure what else you want me to say?"

"Like the fish, I'm the only person I care about. I made a huge mistake trusting Beliveau, but I won't let the bitch bring me down. You need to find out if she has a copy."

"Let me ask you a question. If you knew you were going to play the fairy princess role, why didn't you have your security team search the room for electronics?"

"I told them to leave it," He admitted. "I wanted a memory. It's as much fun to watch as it is…"

Hugh interrupted. "I get it. I'm not surprised you wanted a copy."

The wind picked up and Pierre felt the chill. "Let's go inside and smoke a good cigar and enjoy a brandy."

Hugh didn't need to be coaxed.

Inside the living room, Pierre chose a comfortable armchair, while Hugh settled on the couch. A large mahogany table was between them. The brandies were served, and an ashtray held the unlit cigars.

Pierre picked up his drink. "What can you tell me about David Magill?"

Hugh had wondered when Pierre would bring him up. "Only what I hear on the news."

"My detectives can't find anything on this guy," Pierre whined. "It's like he was a virgin until he got married and hid in his bedroom until he was thirty. Nobody is this boring. There has to be something we can use against him."

"Do you want me to see what I can find out?" Hugh offered.

"Maybe," Pierre hesitated while he lit his Monte Christo, "but what I really want to know was who you met with at the Federal Coalition convention?"

ONE HUNDRED & 35

Mickey returned to the detention room and explained to the women that they were going to be there for awhile, so he offered to move them to a room with a bed and other amenities where they could be more comfortable.

Stacey was upset. "Why the hell do we need to wait to see my mother? Get her in here now!"

Mickey remained calm. "She's not ready to see you."

Suzanne had begun to figure it out. They hadn't broken into some warehouse where the owners call the police. These people didn't want the cops anywhere near this place. "We're not allowed to leave, are we?"

"Until I understand why you came prepared to cut through our fence or why you think your kids are here, I can't let you go."

"So, we are being held against our will," Stacey screamed. "What the hell do you do in this place?"

"You can ask your mother when you see her," He stayed in control. "Now, do you want to move to the room or stay here? Your choice."

Carol laid in her bed calculating the dates. If her daughter were eight months pregnant, that meant her son in law's legacy would live on through a second child. She hated Robert and never lost a minute of sleep when he smashed into a tree. The drunken bum got what he deserved. The only positive thing to come out of his marriage with her daughter was Joshua. Some how they conceived a genius. Could history be repeating itself?

The turmoil between Carol and her daughter confused Mickey. Their hatred to each other made no sense to him. Carol admitted that she was not cut out to be a good mother, but he could never understand the resentment she felt towards Stacey.

It made him flashed back on his own dysfunctional childhood. His memories were vicious and deeply rooted. He lived with his drunken father on the edge of the reserve until he was twelve. On most nights there was no food in the house, and he was left to fend for himself.

Mickey learned at an early age to be a survivor and he taught himself how to fish. The rivers were full of trout and it provided him with food most days. And then one night his dad came home with a female friend. She turned out to be a wicked person who had a plan for the young boy.

Mickey was cleaning his gear when they came home early, and his dad saw the fishing rod. He flew into a rage and accused Mickey of being a thief. He pulled it out of the kid's hands and snapped it. He tossed it on the floor. "Clean that crap up before I whip you with it!"

She laughed when she stepped on the reel and broke the handle. It was the last time Mickey cried. He grabbed what was left of the rod and scooted towards the door, but he got cut off by the new girlfriend. He held up the rod as a weapon. "Get out of my way!"

When she smiled, the color of her yellow teeth matched her nicotine stained fingers. This lady stunk. "Where do you think you're going? Your father promised I could play with you if I bought the beer," She held up a brown paper bag. "So, I bought the beer and you're not going anywhere."

Before he even thought about it, he shoved the broken rod into her face. A piece of fiberglass lodged into her eye. She fell to the

382

floor screaming in pain. Mickey was too scared to be sorry and he sprinted out the door.

His father grabbed the bag of beer and fell back on the couch. "Stupid bitch, I told you he was tough."

That was Mickey's last memory of his father.

Carol had decided what she was going to do with the girls and called Mickey. He came to her room, where she was still dressed in her housecoat and had a scarf wrapped around her hair. "Did you find out how they knew about the complex?"

"I don't think they knew much until they took the photos," Mickey surmised. "They'll never admit it, but we know Smith sent them in this direction."

"Do you think Smith knows we have them?"

"If he did, he'd be smashing down our door with a SWAT team?"

"So, what do you suggest we do with them? You know they can't leave. Stacey will go straight to the police."

Mickey thought about it. "I know I can't have a pregnant woman killed. She's your daughter."

"The organization before everything, Mickey," Carol reminded him. "We can never forget that."

"Then what's our next step?"

Carol looked out her window into the night. "I make them an offer they can't refuse."

ONE HUNDRED & 36

Curtis waited for Joshua in the cafeteria. The plan was to have some dinner and then make good on their agreement. Once on Level C, Curtis would reveal what he knew about the phone. He was confident his plan to get by security would work.

It was ten minutes to six.

Joshua was apprehensive now that it was time to deliver on the deal. When he arrived in the cafeteria his nerves made him pass on dinner. Curtis had no problem chewing on an order of chicken strips.

Joshua whispered. "Are you sure you have a plan to get by security?"

Curtis smiled confidently between chews. "You just be ready."

"Did you have any luck with my mom's phone?"

"We'll talk about it down on Level C," He stuffed the last fry into his mouth, "so let's get going."

It was now six.

The alarm was sounded right on time. Blue flashing lights in the halls meant there was a security breach on the property and all security personnel were required to provide support. The breach was on the south side, the same area the two women were found. The hallways would be empty.

"Let's go," ordered Curtis. "We have about three minutes before they figure out the alarm was a hoax."

The boys hurried to the elevator. Joshua swiped his security card and the door opened. He was nervous, but finally the door closed. Part one was over. "When we get on Level C, we'll go to my workstation. You'll be safe in there."

"Perfect."

The elevator opened and Joshua hurried down the empty hallway. The only people down there at this time of night were other recruits working on various assignments. They slipped inside Joshua's workstation and closed the door.

The room was a simple ten by ten box with all white walls and LED track lighting that cut across the ceiling. "Okay, I got you here. What about my mom's phone?"

"It was easy to locate."

"Why?"

Curtis knew Joshua was about to freak out. "It's inside the complex."

Joshua gasped. "Where?"

"In Mickey's office."

ONE HUNDRED & 37

Jonny emerged from his laboratory after living in there for almost a week. His little adventure with Cassie made him realize his dragonfly still needed to be tweaked. It was a good thing the cop didn't grab it. His attempt to impress her was stupid, and he knew it. After a week of long days, he was confident it was now perfect.

When Mickey got beckoned to the lab he was just as excited as the kid. The dragonfly was a key piece to the plan. When he walked in, Jonny had it out on display. The metallic blue insect looked perfect. Mickey stood over it and could only grin.

"What do you think?" Jonny asked.

Mickey nodded. "It's beautiful. You've done an amazing job."

"Thanks Mickey," Jonny beamed with pride. "I'm excited."

Mickey surprised Jonny. "Do you want to join me when we do field testing? I could sure use your expertise."

"Are you kidding," Jonny started to bounce. "I'd love to."

"You can't tell anyone. Your project is top secret."

Jonny nodded. "Not a problem."

Mickey leaned over to get a closer look. "You've done incredible work here. I'll let you know about the field testing."

Jonny was ecstatic with the idea of being involved with the field tests. It would be the first time he was off Gabriola Island since he was recruited four years ago. He decided to celebrate.

Cassie could sense his excitement. She erased her anger that he hadn't called since their night in the park. After a short talk they decided to share a pepperoni pizza and watch a Fast and Furious movie.

Jonny found the movie and hit play. "How's your project going?"

She had completely forgot about North Korea. "It's great now that Presley is gone. But I have some sad news."

"What's going on?"

"Mickey wants to begin field testing."

Jonny said nothing about the dragonfly. "What's sad about that?"

She had a hard time looking at him. "We'll be doing it in North Korea. I leave next week."

Jonny didn't know what to say. He was confused about his feelings for her. Like most teenage boys, he went silent.

Cassie looked up. It made him uneasy. "Are you my boyfriend?"

Before he could answer, she leaned forward and kissed him.

ONE HUNDRED & 38

It had been a crazy first few days for David Magill as the new leader of the Federal Coalition party. It was Friday night and he was exhausted but was relieved to know he'd sleep in his own bed tonight. When he walked through his front door all he wanted was to change into something comfortable and drink a cold beer.

He was greeted with a tight hug and a firm kiss. "Welcome home. I've missed you."

David hugged his wife back just as tight, but the guilt of spending the night with Cindy Austin flooded his conscience. It was a big mistake that he had to fix. "I missed you too."

"Want to share a beer?" Nina pulled him towards the kitchen. "I'll throw together some snacks."

"I want my own beer, but I'm going to head upstairs and change first." David climbed the stairs. "I'll be right down."

He walked into his closet and grabbed some khaki shorts and a summer shirt. While he dressed his phone buzzed. It was a message from Cindy. It was a happy face emoji with some hearts. "Shit." He deleted the message.

When David returned to the kitchen, Nina had prepared a plate of cheese nachos and there was a can of beer that he grabbed. "Let's go out on the patio. We need to talk."

Nina was startled, but not shocked to see a man wearing a suit looking through their bushes. "Is he your security guy?"

"That's one of the things we need to discuss. He's looking for cameras and listening devices." David explained. "We need to be careful what we say."

They toasted their beer.

It's nice to be home, if only for a short time."

The evening sun flickered through the pine trees and Nina adjusted her seat to get the sharp light out of her eyes. "You're not going to be here very much, are you?"

"We're expecting the Liberals to call an August election. I'll be travelling back and forth across the country for most of the summer. That's something we need to discuss."

"Tell me about your first few days," Nina was excited to hear about David's adventure. "What's it like to be the leader of a political party?"

"Busy is the best way to describe it," David took another sip of beer. "I'm amazed how organized my itinerary is. Everything is exactly as I was briefed."

"Not surprised to hear that," Nina knew what the organization was capable of. "When do you head out again?"

"You mean, we," David corrected her. "You're going to travel in the motor home with me."

"Seriously," Nina muttered. "When are we heading out?"

"In two days," David slapped a mosquito, "so you'll need to do some shopping."

"I like that idea," Nina smiled. "Did you see Ray at the convention?"

David shook his head. "I was told to ignore him if he approached me. That would have been awkward."

"They would never let him near you," Nina sounded confident, "but he's going to be trouble. I guarantee it."

"Why do you think he came?" David asked. "He had no idea I was there."

Nina never told David she was in contact with Ray. He'd freak on her. "Probably looking for his wife like a pitiful soul. I would have loved to have seen his face when they announced your name."

David didn't get the same satisfaction. "I bet he was. What's going on with Ray and his wife?"

"Ray's on a short leash with Tiffany. The man needs to get on with his life and get out of ours."

"That'll be tough considering he's a convicted felon." David felt a twinge of guilt. "That's not a good mark on your resume."

Nina was bored talking about Ray. "Tiffany seems to think Ray has a plan, so let's leave it to them."

"Good idea." David didn't want to ruin their limited time together. "Let's head inside to get away from the mosquitos."

They moved into the living room and Nina was happy to change the subject. "What's next on the political campaign?"

"We'll start with the Austin interview."

Nina sipped on her beer. She remembered the chirpy blonde reporter. "When is it?"

"On Wednesday night. It's a thirty-minute one on one that will officially launch our campaign."

Nina was bored talking about politics. "Anything else happen at the convention?"

"I saw Hugh Hutchinson in the hotel."

"The billionaire? What was he doing there?"

"No idea," David shrugged, "but I did see him leave with Tiffany."

"You're joking," Nina couldn't contain her excitement. "Does Ray know?"

"Who cares about Ray," David finished his beer. "I'm more interested in Hutchinson. If he was in the building, the deal must be done."

Nina's mind switched back to the reporter. She needed to keep an eye on the cute blonde. "Let's head up stairs."

"Sure. Let me just check my phone to see if I have anything important." There was another seductive message from Cindy. She wasn't going away.

ONE HUNDRED & 39

Carol paced inside her office waiting for Mickey to retrieve the two women. She told Mickey what she'd accept to spare them. He wasn't sure how to process her idea. It was about to be an awkward moment. As Stacey had a habit of doing, she had gotten in the way again. Its complicated things.

Mickey stopped by the security office on his way back to the detention room. He had security print a copy of Stacey's phone bill. He wanted to check her call history. When he scanned the first page there were eight calls to Sergeant Smith. He had a decision to make.

When he returned to the detention room both women looked exhausted. "You should have taken me up on my offer."1

"Fuck you. Does my mother have some time to see me now?" her voice was soaked with sarcasm, "because I'm tired of waiting."

Suzanne had a question. "Are we ever getting out of here?"

Mickey pretended to ignore Suzanne. "I have some questions for you, and I want the truth. How often do you talk to Sergeant Smith?"

Stacey wasn't intimidated. "Why do you care?"

I'm trying to keep you alive, but my patience is getting thin. "Answer the question."

Stacey was defiant. It was her nature. "What are you going to do?"

"Shoot you," he blurted before realizing he did, "so don't make the decision for me. How often do you speak with the cop?"

Suzanne's lips twitched. She was scared. "You'd really consider killing a pregnant woman?"

Mickey's eyes darkened. "Don't ask a question you don't want an answer for."

Suzanne now realized that coming to this place was a huge mistake. They had grossly underestimated the consequences if they were caught. And getting caught was their scheme to get inside. She pleaded with Stacey. "Tell him what he wants to know."

Stacey fell back in her chair. The baby was kicking. "He's investigating my son's disappearance and we talk regularly. But you already know that."

"What did you talk about today?"

"He thinks we're camping."

Mickey glanced at her belly. "Camping, in your condition? Should we expect a visit from the sergeant?"

Stacey shrugged. "I have no idea, but let's get to why we broke into this prison."

Mickey fought the urge to smile. Stacey was very much like her mother. "And what's that?"

"Is my son here?"

"No," Mickey handed Stacey her phone. "I want you to tell the sergeant you found nothing and are heading home."

Suzanne perked up. "Are we really going home?"

"Maybe," he taunted, "but I need to know what led you here."

Suzanne was anxious to co-operate. "Tell him what you know, or I will."

"Is my mother still here?" Stacey was strangely anxious to see her. "She doesn't even know I'm pregnant."

"You send Smith a message and I'll take you to see your mom. And before you consider sending something stupid, your phone won't work here unless I enter a code."

Stacey reluctantly picked up the phone.

Hey Mr. Smith

Everything is great over here. Tell Mary I appreciate the blanket she knitted for the baby. I'll call when I get back.

Mickey reviewed the message. "His wife actually knitted you a baby blanket?"

"She did," Stacey lied, "and it's more than my mother ever did."

"Speaking of your mother." Mickey began, "there are some things you should probably know before you see her."

ONE HUNDRED & 40

The President of the United States was the former governor from Colorado. The republican was elected in November and during his first six months in office he had kicked up quite the disruption in Washington. He quickly got a reputation that he wasn't going to follow the rules if they didn't suit him. In his short time, he had become one of the most detested politicians on the planet. He thrived on being the villain.

President James Tucker was relaxed, sitting in the back of his limousine thinking about the evening ahead. As a real estate tycoon who made billions back in Colorado, he always believed a great deal was one that made him a bunch of money and cost someone else their reputation. There were many who despised him for the way he did business and how easily he swept good people to the side. As the president, he planned to govern the same way. To rebuild America's economy, he was going to upset a few world leaders along the way.

It promised to be another interesting night if you were a republican supporter. The president was the keynote speaker at a dinner where people paid ten thousand dollars a plate to get a photo with him. People paid for controversy and Tucker was a master at creating it.

The concern the organizers had was who would be his target. What republican senator was talking behind his back or what governor was stepping outside his policy? Rarely did he stay on script or listen to his advisors. His team of speechwriters had touched on all the hot political points, but in the President's opinion, the speech wasn't controversial enough. It needed to be tougher. He intended to raise a shit storm and call out a traitor. He wanted everyone in the room to know who this person was, and the price you paid if you crossed him. It was another night in the presidency of James Tucker.

In the limousine with him, was his Chief of Staff. Drake Adams was a graduate of Harvard that got pulled away from a promising law career to work with the president. He was one of only a few of Tucker's original inner circle that remained.

Tucker got his attention.

"What can I do for you, sir?"

"I need you to confirm my attendance in Ottawa on July 1st and give the Prime Minister a reminder I need an update on the naval base."

"I'll send it out in the morning," Adams typed a reminder on his tablet, "and do you want me to attach an outline of terms you're willing to discuss regarding the base?"

"There terms are simple. He'll agree," Tucker countered sarcastically. "If he doesn't, I'll apply even tougher sanctions against his farmers."

"Do you really want to do that, sir?" Adams knew Tucker didn't like to be challenged. "We increased their tariffs only a month ago."

Tucker huffed. "Are you a fucking Canadian?"

Adams glanced out the car window at the White House disappearing in the distance. "You know I'm not."

"Then stop defending them. It's quite simple. People under immense pressure are easier to negotiate with. I want Elliot to feel immense pressure."

"I will get it ready, sir."

"One last thing" The president smirked. "Remind him about Cherie Beliveau."

ONE HUNDRED & 41

Sergeant Smith refused to acknowledge his phone while he had a quiet dinner with his wife for the first time in nearly two weeks. He was committed to being a more attentive husband. Helen had made his favourite five-cheese lasagna and he was enjoyed a second slice when his phone vibrated on the counter.

Helen grinned. "You can answer that, because I know you're dying to see who it is."

She was right, but he resisted. "They can wait. This is our time."

Helen loved her husband for so many reasons and one of those was what was happening at this moment. She knew it was killing the cop inside him not to check his phone, but he was trying to make up for all the missed dinners by being a good husband. "You need to save some space for dessert."

Steve maneuvered the last bite of lasagna onto his fork and shoved it in his mouth. "You made pie, didn't you?"

"Strawberry rhubarb," she boasted. "Made it today and I got ice cream."

Steve rubbed his belly. "I don't need the calories."

"We can walk it off after dinner." Helen gathered the dishes and put them in the sink. On her way to the fridge, she tossed him the phone. "Deal with it while I slice the pie. This way I'll get your complete attention back."

Steve felt a twinge of guilt and only took a quick glance to see who called. It was a text from Stacey.

'Everything is great over here. Tell Mary I appreciate the

blanket she knitted for the baby. I'll call when I get back.'

Helen cut two healthy pieces of pie. "Is it important?"

Steve re-read the text. "It's a message from Stacey Small. It doesn't make sense."

Helen put a piece of pie with a big scoop of vanilla ice cream in front of him. "What do you mean?"

"She thanked Mary for a baby blanket," He sounded confused. "Whose Mary, and what blanket?"

Helen felt for the young mother. "Why do you think she sent the message with the obvious mistakes?"

"I have no idea."

"It could be she's trying to get your attention," Helen suggested. "Something could be wrong."

Steve took a mouthful of pie. It was delicious. "I hope you're wrong, but she's over camping on an island when she should be home getting ready to become a mom, again."

"Answer her text with a message of your own. Tell her Mary is almost finished the booties. If she responds, then you know she's in trouble."

"Impressive, Mrs. Smith." Steve finished his pie. "A great wife, great baker, and now a great detective."

Helen grabbed Steve's phone and sent the response. "Let's go for that walk and we'll see if she responds. Grab your jacket. It might rain."

ONE HUNDRED & 42

After staying an extra day, Ray and Tiffany checked out of the Pan Pacific Hotel. The excitement of the convention was long gone and surprisingly, Ray hadn't thought much about his old buddy David. Tiffany kept him busy. They visited the sights of Vancouver and ate in expensive restaurants.

They spent the time getting to know each other. Ray learned Tiffany's favorite food was Sushi, while she found out her husband was a big soccer fan. They were simple facts that a couple married for six years should know about each other.

Six years equated to living under the same roof for seven months.

There was no mention of Tiffany's work. Ray decided he wasn't prepared to know the details of her career, or what happened on her date with Hutchinson. He could learn as they went along.

Tiffany worked with dangerous people who were capable of doing vicious things and she was part of that. The organization, as she referred to them, was in control of everything that took place at the Pan Pacific. When David's name was announced as the new leader of the Federal Coalition, it came as a shock. By the end of the night, Ray's surprise had turned to resentment.

While he served time, his ex partner was being groomed to become the next prime minister. Ray wasn't sure how he felt about that. He'd need to take some time to determine his choices. He knew his history with David could tarnish that shiny image. For now, his focus was the second chance his wife gave him.

They wandered hand in hand through the market, testing samples offered by the vendors. When they walked into a sweet-smelling bakery their breakfast was found.

Ray ordered two fresh fruit crepes and coffee and added a chocolate banana muffin to their tray. When their food was ready, they headed outside and found a table under a tree that offered some privacy.

Tiffany leaned forward and asked a question Ray was prepared for. "Are you going to be okay when Magill becomes prime minister? We obviously know your history with him and that leaves us exposed, and that's dangerous."

Ray knew not to raise alarms. "It's just that, history."

Tiffany took a first bite and licked her lips. "I'm just not sure if Carol will let you wander free. She's not one to leave loose ends around."

Ray ripped off a piece of muffin and stuffed it in his mouth. He chewed it nervously. "You can tell her I'll never say a word."

"I know you won't," Tiffany shrugged, "but you'll have to be careful."

Ray rubbed his chin. "Are you ever going to leave the organization. Is it something you'd consider?"

Tiffany couldn't answer him. "Do you like looking at boats?"

"I love boats," He smiled, knowing she avoided his question. "I've always wanted to sail the south seas."

Tiffany led Ray to a wooden walkway that angled down to a floating dock. There had to be over five hundred boats of all sizes and styles tied to the cleats mounted on the wooden beams. It was a busy place with fishermen unloading their catch into ice coolers destined for restaurants, while recreational boats lined up to take on fuel before heading out to Juan Du Fuca Strait

They stopped beside a tall cement pillar that held the dock in place and supplied power to the bigger vessels. Tiffany put her arms around Rays neck and looked like she was going to kiss him. "I heard what you asked me, and I'll answer it by asking you a question. Do you think you can handle the truth?"

Ray wasn't sure how to react but nodded anyway.

Tiffany was serious. "I need to ask you an important question and I want you to think before answering it."

"Okay, I'm listening."

Tiffany lowered her hands and interlocked their fingers. "Would you go back to prison for me?"

Ray locked eyes with his wife. "I'd take a bullet for you."

Tiffany was impressed by how quickly he responded. "Are you sure?"

"I love you."

They started walking again. "I have considered leaving, but I don't have a career where you simply give two weeks notice."

"So, can you get out if you choose to?"

They came to the end of the pier. "I do want too, and my way out is behind you."

Ray turned around and nearly choked on his own breath. Moored in front of him was a luxury yacht that he estimated to be about ninety feet. It was really one hundred and four. It's stream-line dark lines and wall of windows gave it a powerful presence next to the forty-foot sailboats. "Why am I looking at this magnificent boat?"

ONE HUNDRED & 43

The skies above Gabriola had turned dark and the wind gusts off the water caused the temperature to drop to jacket weather. Unrelenting sheets of rain and choppy water forced the coast guard to issue a small craft warning.

One of the few boats heading out was the SS Raven. The thirty-foot crusader had been hired out as a taxi service to retrieve some crew members from a freighter anchored two miles offshore. Sergeant Smith hitched a ride. In this weather the captain would enjoy the company.

Helen and Steve cut their walk short when the rain began. When they got home and there was no response from Stacey it was Helen's idea for her husband to head to the docks. They were both worried. His badge and a quick explanation got him a ride and the captain steered the SS Raven out into the open water. They were prepared for a bumpy ride.

After a bruising trip, the captain steered his boat to about fifty meters from the shoreline of Gabriola. In this weather he wouldn't risk getting closer. If the waves took it, his boat would be smashed against the rocks. Smith grabbed some binoculars and strained to see to the shoreline. The visibility was nearly impossible.

The captain shouted above the engine noise. "There's a dock about a half mile further. Do you want me to try and drop you off there?"

Smith nodded. "That would be great."

"I'll get as close as I can."

Smith yelled over the wind. "If you can get within a few feet,

I'll jump."

When they got closer, Smith saw an aluminum boat rocking violently against the dock. That meant someone was nearby."

The captain strained to see through his windshield. The rain and rolling waves were going to make it tough to get close. "We'll get one shot at this so be sure before you jump. I won't be able to cut the engine. You'll be on your own."

Smith understood. "I really appreciate your help."

"Hopefully, you find those women." The captain swung the bow of the boat and gunned the motor to fight the waves. "Get ready, because here we go."

Smith thought about Helen back at home, hopefully enjoying a second piece of pie. He realized how lucky he was. "I'll be ready."

The captain had years of experience in these waters. He pulled the crusader to within a few feet and never saw Smith leap off the side. He felt his boat jerk from the weight shift and gunned the motor to get back into open water. He wished the sergeant good luck under his breath.

The sergeant watched the boat disappear in the darkness and was relieved when he reached the solid wood of the pier. The cold wind was merciless, and Smith pulled his jacket collar up to protect his ears and neck. He worked hard to keep his balance on the teetering dock. The wood structure felt like it might be swept out to sea at any moment.

When he reached solid ground, he wiped his face and let his eyes adjust to the dim light. Any relief he felt being off the water was replaced by fear when he saw a shotgun aimed at his chest.

A man in his early sixties stood in front of him. He was wearing a camouflaged rain jacket and a Yankee ballcap. And somehow in this weather he was able to keep a lit cigarette dry in his lips.

Smith instinctively raised his hands. "Hold on. I'm just passing by."

"This is private property, so you need to turn yourself around and get back on that boat!"

Smith glanced back over his shoulder, knowing his ride was long gone. "I'm a police officer and I'm looking for two missing women. I need to cut through your property. I apologize, but I need to get to the road."

"I don't care who you are," the old man grunted, "turn around or I'll shoot."

Smith lowered his arms, "Turn around and go where? I sure as hell can't swim home."

The old man looked past Smith. His sixteen-foot aluminum boat was still bouncing with the waves. He held the shotgun tight as the rain dripped off the brim of his hat. "Why are you really here?"

Smith's tone was respectful, but the cold weather took a toll. "I need to find these women. They might be in trouble."

The old man didn't budge. "You should have taken the ferry like everyone else. This is private property."

Through the darkness, Smith eyed a greenhouse about fifty yards away. He had a hunch and motioned to the structure. "I don't care what you're growing on your property. I just need to get to the road."

"How do I know that?"

"I'll tell you what," Smith felt an opening. "If you let me by, I will make sure the police never bother you. You have my word."

The old man lowered his gun. "You can do that?"

"Yes, sir," Smith assured him. "I'll bet you're just growing some personal product to ease the pain in the joints."

"And a little for my nephews."

Smith stepped forward. "Can I ask you a question?"

"Maybe."

"What do you know about your neighbours on the other side of that fence line? Do you ever see anyone or talk to them?"

The old man shook his head to the disappointment of Smith. "I've never seen anyone."

Smith glanced at the old man's house. It reminded him of a hunting cabin. Log walls covered with moss and wooden shingles. There was an oil tank to run the stove and furnace. He wondered if this old-timer knew his property was worth millions to some developer. Or did he even care. "That's too bad."

The old man pulled a rolled cigarette from his pocket and lit it skillfully in the rain. "You should get going and find those girls."

Smith didn't believe that he had never seen anyone, but he'd worry about that later. "I will. Thank you."

The old man pulled his gun to the side. "Just so we're clear, you promised no cops?"

Smith arrived at the campsite twenty minutes later and was soaked to the bone. The weather wasn't backing down. He recognized Stacey's jacket hanging over a log beside the tent. Why would she be anywhere without her jacket?

He climbed inside the tent to get out of the rain and see if there was anything that would tell him where they might be. He spent the night waiting, before he finally fell a sleep.

ONE HUNDRED & 44

Before they left the detention room, Mickey ordered in some food and drinks for the women. While they ate, Mickey read Sergeant Smith's response. "This Mary must have a lot of free time. How well do you know her?"

Stacey hadn't read the reply. "Why?"

Mickey was suspicious. "She's knitting you some booties for the kid. Seems strange for a cop's wife to be so involved."

"I've never met her, but she seems like a great person," Stacey played along. "Now, when am I going to see my mother so I can go home."

"We need to discuss that."

Stacey's lack of sleep had her on edge. "You keep saying the same thing. What is it we need to talk about? Does she run this stupid place?"

Mickey's hesitation showed his hand.

Suzanne figured it out. "Her mother runs this place, doesn't she? That's why it's taking so long to see her."

It was like a bomb exploded and Stacey got a direct hit. Could it be possible? There was no way her mother could run a place like this. Or maybe she could? How well did she really know her? "Is my mother in charge?"

"I'll let Carol answer that," Mickey grabbed a wheelchair. "I thought you might need this."

Stacey sat in the wheelchair. "Let's go find my mother."

ONE HUNDRED & 45

Suzanne took control of the wheelchair and pushed it onto the elevator. Stacey was so exhausted that she fought to stay awake. When the elevator closed, Mickey turned to the women. "I need to emphasize that you listen to Carol."

Stacey tried to sit up. "Why are you scared of her?"

Mickey chuckled. "You'd be smart to leave your attitude outside her office. She is not someone you mess with."

Stacey scowled. "Isn't that a little dramatic? My mother isn't going to kill me. She might be a king-sized bitch but isn't a murderer."

Suzanne remembered the dead bodies the sergeant mentioned. "Maybe we should listen to Mickey."

"Listen to your friend and think of your baby. And don't count on Carol being a mother figure, because we both know that's not who she is."

The elevator opened and Suzanne pushed the chair into the hallway. "Which way?"

"Follow me," Mickey headed down the hall. "It's not far."

They arrived at a steel framed door painted blue that was designed to keep people out. Mickey scanned his card and the door unlatched. He held it open for the women. They entered slowly and looked around. They were nervous to see her.

Carol wasn't there.

The décor was nothing special for a boss. Steel framed furniture, an average desk and a few photos of scenery were spread around. The only indication that it was more than a place to hang her jacket was the wall of monitors. At that moment, they were all dark.

There was a couch and Stacey decided it looked more comfortable than the wheelchair. She didn't wait for an invitation to stretch out on it. Suzanne pulled up a chair beside her. "Any idea where she is?"

"Nope," Mickey retrieved some water from the cooler and handed them out. He looked at Stacey. "Do you need anything else?"

Stacey opened her tired eyes. "I'd love a hot bath, but the water will do."

Without any fanfare, Carol sauntered in, and went to her desk. She didn't acknowledge anyone until she was seated. "Look at you, Stacey. You've gained a few pounds."

That was a painful shot that Stacey ignored.

Suzanne tried to keep the tone civil. "You have quite the place here. It must have cost a fortune to build."

Carol smiled smugly. "I have a great capital acquisition team."

Stacey never took her eyes off her mother. She looked different. Her hair was styled, and her outfit was befitting a Fortune 500 CEO. She would have walked by her if they passed on a street.

The tension was building. Mickey took a seat to the side and became a spectator. Carol was now in control. He hoped the women understood that.

Carol looked at her daughter. "I see you're pregnant again. Is it his?"

Stacey glared. "Yes, it's Robert's."

Carol frowned. "I can only hope."

Suzanne saw the hatred firsthand. This lady was evil. "I'm sorry, I haven't introduced myself."

"I know who you are," Carol snapped. "The question I have is why are you here?"

Stacey struggled to pull herself up. "A better question is, where is Joshua?"

Suzanne joined in. "And Curtis, are they here?"

Carol didn't try to deny it. "Yes, they're here."

ONE HUNDRED & 46

The big night had finally arrived, and Cindy Austin was sitting in her dressing room getting her hair and make up done. Her thirty-minute interview with David Magill was being broadcast nationally, and by the morning would be debated in coffee shops across the country. This was her opportunity to show Dane and the industry that she was a serious reporter.

Cindy took a break from the questions that were sent over. The deal to get the interview was that she had to follow the script as written. No improvising was allowed. While her makeup was being applied, she let herself remember her time with David. It was an amazing end to what turned out to be an amazing day.

The sex was wild and exactly what she needed. But now she second guessed her decision to go to his room. Was there a connection or was it a simple one-night stand? David wouldn't respond to her messages, so she had no idea where they stood.

She knew being assigned dressing room D was not a mistake by the station. It was a subtle message from Dane. Room D doubled as a storeroom. He was going to do everything he could to remind her who was the boss. She didn't care. Nothing was going to break her spirit. Her sights were set on Wilson's anchor chair and tonight she'd get to feel how comfortable the seat was.

After trying on a half dozen outfits, she settled on a navy-blue business jacket with cream colored slacks. Her blonde hair was shaded to give her a mature look. She decided the cute blonde persona that Dane liked to bully was taking the night off.

The Magill caravan arrived forty-five minutes before the broadcast was to air. When David stepped out of his motorhome, he was greeted by a group of enthusiastic reporters that grew by the day. Nina gripped his hand as they walked to a barricade to answer a few questions.

A young reporter from Global spoke up. "What do you think about the opium crisis in Canada. Should the police do more?"

David shrugged. "Addiction shouldn't be a legal or police issue. It's a mental health problem and should be handled as one. Arresting a heroin user is doing no one any good and it's wasting millions of police resources."

"What else are you going to change?" a second reporter asked.

"Watch the broadcast tonight and you'll hear our platform and how we'll achieve it," David smiled at the cameras. "Thanks for coming and sorry, but I have to go."

Nina led him to the back entrance. A staff member greeted them and pointed towards Cindy, who was talking to her producer on the stage. When she saw David, she rushed over and gave him a friendly hug. Her hands were just above David's waist. It didn't go unnoticed by Nina.

Cindy gave Nina a respectful smile. She was checking out the wife. "I need to borrow your husband for a few minutes, if that's okay?"

Nina nodded, knowing she had no choice in the matter. The girl was perky with a cute smile. It was a combination that excited her. She stood back to stay out of the way, but she'd be watching.

Cindy gave David the five-dollar tour of the studio. She pointed to a camera that would face him for the entire interview. "This one is yours. You focus on me and we'll be good."

She gave David a wink that the wife couldn't see.

Nina pretended to be occupied checking messages on her phone. When she figured it was okay, she stole a glass of the reporter. She tried to understand why she felt so insecure around her. David had never given her a reason to feel jealous.

Cindy took her seat across from her guest and leaned forward. "Are you ready?"

"I am," he took a deep breath, "and how about you?"

"A little nervous," she admitted, "but once we start, I'll be fine."

"Good."

She gave his knee a quick rub. "I wanted to tell you that I really enjoyed the other night."

David smiled and hoped Nina didn't see that. "No more texts."

She pulled back. "Okay."

"Now make us famous," he said with conviction, "and give our country something to be excited about."

The producer took control of the studio and ordered everyone to their stations. "We're on the air in thirty seconds. This is the big time, so don't disappoint me."

Nina found an out of the way corner and sipped on a surprisingly good cup of coffee she was given by a staff member. She gripped the mug firmly. The last thing she wanted to do was drop it in mid-interview.

Cindy smiled and the countdown began. Before the show went live, Cindy leaned forward and patted David on the knee again. She wished him luck. Nina saw this and gripped her coffee tighter. David knew he was being watched and didn't react.

The red light on the camera was on, and Cindy began. "I want to welcome everyone from coast to coast. I'm Cindy Austin and I'll begin the evening by introducing the newly elected leader of the Federal Coalition party, and my special guest, Mr. David Magill."

He smiled confidently into his camera. "Thank you for having me, Cindy."

"Let's start with the night you got elected as the new leader of the Federal Coalition," She read from the script. "It's not an exaggeration to say you came out of nowhere to win."

"That was our strategy from the beginning. The timing was important, and we worked hard to keep it under wraps."

Cindy felt comfortable in Lane's seat and the cameras loved her. "I had the pleasure of meeting you at the convention when you stunned the party by winning so easily. The first thing most people said was how nice this man seems, but who the heck is he?"

David tried not to glance at Nina. "I'm a guy who cared enough to get involved, and lucky enough to have an amazing team behind me with the same vision on what has to happen in our country."

"And what is that?"

"We have to govern differently and that starts with changing the mindset of the people making decisions," David focused on the camera. "The priorities in this country are a mess and need to change."

"What would number one be on your list?"

"Education is where everything starts and gives anyone who wants it, the opportunity to be successful," David sipped the water in his coffee mug. "As we know, technology is where the world has gone, and we need to invest in our students so our industries can compete globally."

Cindy followed the script. "Let's discuss post-secondary. It costs a lot to get a good education, so what changes there?"

Everyone in the studio hung on his every word. "It will be free to all those who want to attend. We will eliminate up front tuition costs."

Cindy leaned back to feign being surprised. "How does this work. The money has to come from somewhere?"

David's passion played well into the camera. "It will be the government's investment in our future, and over time the students who take advantage of this program will pay a small tax based on their income. They won't leave school with massive debt, but they will have an obligation to pay the money back over their prime earning years. The bigger return for the country will be the industry and the jobs they create."

"That's definitely a fresh approach."

Cindy knew the audience would eat this up. She moved on, "What will be your policy on our military and the way they're treated? Any plans for our men and women?"

David looked frustrated. "The fact that you have to ask that question is embarrassing on so many levels. We hire, yes hire, these young men and women to go and fight for us and then feel good once a year when we buy a poppy. The soldiers who gave their lives must turn over in their graves by how their comrades are neglected."

"What are you suggesting?"

"Let's start with their health," David was well prepared and felt comfortable. "When our troops return from active duty, they will be required to attend a medical camp to be evaluated properly to see if they are showing symptoms of mental distress. This will happen before they can go home. It'll become part of the normal discharge process. No exceptions. Mental health concerns are real, and the families of our soldiers should not live in fear of the unknown."

"That's another amazing perspective, Mr. Magill," Cindy was as impressed as she pretended to be. "How will you tie this all together?"

David took another sip of water. It was hot under the lights. "It goes back to education. There are many small communities in this country without family doctors. The question is how many bright minds don't commit to medicine because of the cost? We should be encouraging those people, not discouraging them. The government needs to be proactive with these types of programs."

The thirty-minute interview flew by and social media was electric with the comments from across Canada. Even hardened Liberal supporters had to agree with Magill's fresh approach to old problems.

It didn't take Nina long to join her husband on the set. Cindy and David were thanking each other when Nina purposely took her husband's hand. "We should get going."

"In a minute." David responded tersely.

Cindy was smirking on the inside.

ONE HUNDRED & 47

Suzanne broke down into tears when she heard Carol admit that Curtis was close by and he was alive. The years of guilt evaporated instantly. She thought about Tom and how much the news would affect him. Hopefully, it would be the motivation he needed to get his life back on track.

Stacey reacted differently. "You took my son away! You're his grandmother and you stole him!"

Carol wasn't affected by her daughter's temper tantrum. She had seen it all before. She would give her another moment to get it all out. There was another announcement that would upset her even further.

She motioned for silence.

Stacey didn't back down. "What are you going to do, because your partner says we can't leave?"

"He's correct. You can't."

Suzanne started to panic. "Then what?"

Mickey stepped in before she answered. "I might have a solution that works for us." He looked at Carol. "They could fill avoid we have."

"You're referring to Detective Murphy?"

Stacey listened. Why were they talking about the detective? He was dead. Did her mother have something to do with that?

"Smith seems to talk freely with your daughter, so maybe she can be our ears with him."

Carol wasn't sure. "How do we know she doesn't just tell Smith everything. It's too risky."

Mickey glanced at Stacey. "If she doesn't, we'll kill the cop. His blood will be on her."

Carol didn't like it. "I want a bigger guarantee that she won't talk."

Stacey wasn't sure if Mickey was bluffing. Would he really kill Sergeant Smith? She scowled at her mother. "What else do you need?"

Carol zoomed in on her belly. "You won't leave here until the baby is born."

"Bullshit," Stacey's eyes ripped through Mickey. "I'm not agreeing to this."

Suzanne realized things weren't good and tried to change the focus. "What exactly do you do here. You don't seem like pedophiles or psychos, so why did you take our kids?"

Mickey answered the question. "We recruited them. They have skills and intelligence we need to execute our mission. And before you ask about what we do, don't."

Suzanne continued. "Our kids were only eleven when you took them."

Carol had no remorse for the pain she had inflicted. "We have a plan that we needed help to execute. It's like a car. I know I want one, but I could never build it. So, I find someone that can. Your boys built the car."

"What does Curtis do?" Suzanne knew she was trying to have a civil conversation with the person who destroyed her family. "I know he is good with computers."

"He's a genius with them, and he collects data for us." Carol wouldn't reveal more. She turned back to Stacey. "I'm thinking I don't like Mickey's plan. I can't have anyone, including my daughter, knowing who I am."

The tension intensified and Mickey rubbed his chin. He decided on a different approach. "Why don't we get the boys up here so they can see them. While that's happening, you and I can talk."

Carol didn't like it but agreed. "You'll have thirty minutes, so use it wisely."

Mickey headed to the door. "I'll go get them. And so, you know, they have no idea you're here."

While they waited, Stacey asked her mother a question. "Did Miss. Addison have anything to do with the fire at the school."

"If you're asking if she worked with us, the answer is yes."

"Did you kill her?"

"No," Carol lied with ease, "it was a bad accident. I actually miss her."

Stacey wanted to believe her mother. It would ease her guilt somehow. "Does Joshua know about his dad?"

"No. He never asks about the loser, so I thought I'd let you tell him."

ONE HUNDRED & 48

Hugh Hutchinson had purposely avoided any contact with the prime minister since the David Magill interview. The sit down with Cindy Austin drew over three million viewers and the response said the country was excited. The invasion of the Federal Coalition with a new way to govern the country was underway.

Hugh was on his way to meet the new political sensation and was excited to meet him. Like much of Canada, he was becoming a fan. He needed to learn more about Magill and how he could benefit Hutchinson Enterprises even further.

Hugh could only shake his head when he thought about Pierre's future. It was in the hands of a communist dictator and a high-priced hooker. Not the most secure position to be in. His days as the leader of the country were on the clock.

And then his phone rang. It was the prime minister. What a surprise. He decided to answer it this time. "Hello, Pierre."

Elliot sounded irritated. "Where have you been?"

"Taking a crap," It wasn't a total fib. "What's up?"

"Did you see the Magill interview?"

"It seems like the whole country saw it," Hugh shook his head at the stupid question, "but it's just one interview."

Pierre disagreed. "I can't just sit here and not respond. I need to do something."

"Like what?" Hugh questioned. "Don't start making reactionary promises. The media will eat you up."

Elliot knew Hugh was right about the media. "Then what?"

"His platform is built as a vision that he knows people want to hear," Hugh explained. "He's giving them hope that there is a better future."

Pierre wasn't convinced.

Hugh sensed his frustration, "To beat him, you'll have to play the long game. You need to get ready for a vicious fight."

"What are you doing today?"

Hugh decided to tell him the truth. It would be all over the media anyway. "I'm on my way to meet David Magill."

"Really?" Pierre sounded uneasy. "What are you meeting about?"

"Various topics," he was evasive, "and maybe I'll ask for position in his government when he gets elected."

"Fuck you," Pierre didn't see the humour. "It's your job to make sure that doesn't happen."

It was Hugh's job to make good business decisions. He wanted to end the call. "Relax for Christ sakes."

"Where is this meeting happening?"

"At the Ottawa food bank," Chuckled Hugh, realizing how that must sound to Pierre. "He wants me to help hand out food hampers why we talk."

Pierre scoffed. "How ridiculous is that?"

"It's a brilliant example of building a brand. Guess whose face will be on the front page of every news broadcast?"ghHugh Hufg

"I guess that could work," he sounded defeated, "but anyone can help out a charity."

"We're pulling into the food bank, so I need to go," Hugh hung up. "What a fucking idiot."

She squeezed his hand. "How's our prime minister doing?"

"Counting the days until he's unemployed," Hugh shrugged with a befuddled grin. "Magill will be the next prime minister."

Tiffany smiled. "Isn't that nice."

ONE HUNDRED & 49

Suzanne held Stacey and they waited nervously to see their boys. There were no words to explain this moment for either of them. But they had questions. How big was Curtis going to be? Would he be excited to see her? Those were Suzanne's questions. Stacey only had one. How does she tell Joshua about his dad?

Carol sat at her desk looking at documents like they weren't in the room. Suzanne tried to understand how she could be so calm with everything going on. This woman didn't seem to have any emotional latitude. In some medical circles, she might be diagnosed as a psychopath.

She decided to keep that diagnosis to herself. She tried to get Carol's attention. "What is it about the sergeant that has you so worried. Joshua's case is almost seven months old and he hasn't come knocking yet."

"He led you here and that's the concern," Carol told her, "and before you leave, I want to know how you ended up in my office."

"I can answer that."

Stacey squeezed her hand, an indication to stop talking.

"Let's just focus on now," Carol suggested. "Talk with your boys. See how well adjusted they are. Then we can talk about what I want you to do."

Stacey wouldn't stay silent. "Is that a shot to say you're a better mother than us, because we both know that's a load of crap."

"You really should consider anger management classes," Carol smirked, "because blaming me for everything wrong in your life is getting old."

Suzanne tried to intercept another train wreck between the two. "How long before the boys get here? I'm really nervous."

"They're on their way and remember to keep the conversations motherly."

"Coming here was such a bad idea." Stacey mumbled.

Suzanne disagreed. "You're going to see Joshua. That makes it a great idea."

"She's only letting us see them to get leverage on us," Argued Stacey. "She's not doing this to be a nice person."

Carol had heard enough of the whining. "It all changed when you married Robert. The only good thing out of that relationship was my grand son and possibly a granddaughter."

"Possibly? What does that mean?"

"It means that if she's as smart as her brother, I'll include her in my life."

Suzanne couldn't believe what she heard. "How could you say something like that to her?"

"I told you she was a monster." Stacey didn't hold anything back. "I can't stand being in the same room with her."

When the boys entered Carol's office the mood was like a foster child meeting their new parents for the first time. It was an awkward moment for everyone. Mickey had prewarned them, but it was still hard.

Suzanne stood and stared at Curtis. She hardly recognized him. He had grown so much and was muscular. "Oh, my god. Look at you."

"Hi mom," he said quietly. He couldn't hide from the guilt of running away. "It's good to see you."

Joshua knew his mom was pregnant when he joined her on the couch. He couldn't say anything about seeing her on the security monitor. Before they talked, Stacey grabbed him, and they hugged.

Carol watched the reunions with interest. The boys knew they couldn't discuss the complex, or what they do here. She made some tea and sat at her desk. She had a timer on her phone. She said thirty minutes and the boys wouldn't stay a second longer.

Joshua finally let go. "Where's dad?"

Stacey's excitement disappeared in an instant. She looked at her son. The inevitable question. "We need to talk about him."

Joshua saw her pain and didn't want to hear the answer. He looked at her belly. "Are you having a boy or girl?"

Stacey wiped the moisture off her cheeks. "You're going to have a baby sister, but I need to talk to you about your dad."

Joshua couldn't wait. "He's dead, isn't he?"

Stacey fell back onto the couch. She just wanted to close her eyes and go to sleep and never wake up. "Yes."

Joshua tried to be strong in front of his grandmother. "How did he die?"

Everything in the room stopped. Even Carol looked up to watch. She was enjoying the moment. The news would push Joshua away from his mother.

Suzanne buried her face against Curtis. It was unbearable to watch. She knew how hard this was for Stacey. What had been an amazing moment quickly changed.

It was exactly how Carol imagined it.

Stacey filled her chest and grabbed Joshua's hand. "He was driving home and hit a patch of black ice. He smashed into a tree."

"When?"

"Christmas Eve."

The thirty minutes passed, and Carol ended the reunion. "I need the boys to get back to work."

After some final hugs, the boys were gone. They never looked back.

Suzanne dried her eyes. "What's next?"

Mickey was out in the hallway. He had Stacey's phone. He sent a message to the sergeant.

'*The booties sound great. Can I meet you on the dock at 10:30 tomorrow morning? Something important to show you.*'

He hit send.

And then to add more excitement to the day, Stacey's water broke. She was going into labor.

Sergeant Smith had spent a cold night shivering in the girl's tent. They never returned, and the trails were deserted because of the weather. He caught the first ferry home to change and regroup. Then his phone buzzed. He responded.

'I'll be there.'

ONE HUNDRED & 50

Jonny waited in his room for Mickey to come and get him.
He only got a few hours of sleep, but he didn't care. Today was a special day. Mickey was taking him to help with the field testing which had him vibrating. This was a first. And today was the first time he'd get out of the complex and off the island since he arrived four years ago.

The black equipment case was packed with everything he needed. It was on the end of the bed. There were a few extra items that Mickey requested. A lot depended on today and Jonny fought some nerves. It had to go well today.

The dragonfly was his fourth assignment for the organization and was his best work.

Mickey popped his head inside the door. "Are you ready to go?"

Jonny grabbed the case. "Yes, sir."

Mickey was just as excited to get off the island. He needed a break. It was a busy time and the pressure mounted to get things done. And he couldn't listen to Carol and Stacey scream at each other anymore. Their hatred was intense.

They boarded the boat and Jonny took a seat in the stern, while Mickey stood at the bow talking with the captain. The boat pulled away from the dock and into open water. When the captain pushed the throttle, they skipped across the wavetops. Jonny saw the ferry head in the opposite direction.

They were greeted on the dock by a man that Mickey called V. He was older and Jonny tried not to stare at the rattlesnake tattoo that wrapped around his neck. The sharp fangs made it look dangerous.

Jonny wondered why he was there. He looked rough around the edges.

"Let's get in the van and head to the site," V suggested, "I have already secured the area. We won't be getting any surprise visitors."

Jonny climbed into the back and for most of their ride he gazed out the window. As they left the city, he realized how much he had forgotten about in his previous life. They passed a McDonalds and he remembered their fries. "Can we stop there on the way back?"

Mickey smiled. "If today goes well, then maybe."

Jonny estimated their drive was fifteen minutes before they pulled off the highway onto a secondary road. V slowed the van and turned onto a dirt path that didn't get a lot of use based on the potholes and tall grass. He parked the van beside an old barn that had seen better days. It leaned to one side and the red paint was gone from the rains and years of decay. Rodents and sparrows had taken up ownership.

V unloaded a table and small generator to supply power, while Mickey walked the perimeter of the property to be sure there were no curious neighbors. A hundred yards off in the field there was an old tractor that was nearly buried by overgrown grass. Jonny figured that was the spot where the motor had died, and the farmer just walked away. The only indication of recent activity on the property was a pile of beer cans beside a fallen fence. It looked as though teenagers used the farm as a place to drink beer and do target practice.

His eyes wondered over to Mickey who was returned from his tour. "Should I get the dragonfly ready?"

Mickey nodded. "Run everything through V. We need him to have a thorough understanding since he'll be the man operating it."

Never judge a book by its cover, Jonny thought. "Yes, sir."

V took a spot by Jonny and his sheer size overwhelmed the recruit. "I'll start by explaining the dragonfly and how I built it."

V listened and learned. Mickey had given him a heads up about what he'd be using, but this kid was years ahead of what was out there in the real world. The military, or a terrorist group, would pay big bucks for this technology.

Jonny fired up the operational software and ran through the control options. Once he was comfortable V was ready, he slid the laptop in front of him. He stole another quick glance of the snake. "Are you ready?"

V was excited to take it for a ride, "Let's get it airborne."

Jonny placed the dragonfly on top of a small steel box and the morning sun reflected off the metallic blue body. It was time to test it. Jonny changed the monitor to a virtual reality program and handed V some goggles. "This will make it easier. You will become the dragonfly."

V shook his head in amazement as he slid them on.

They stood and gawked at the gadget like some school kids. Jonny tapped a key and the insect came to life. Its big eyes opened, and the wings started to flutter. There was a lite humming sound.

V had a different perspective from behind the goggles. "This thing is amazing."

Mickey stepped away from the table. "Let's get going."

V felt a glass object in his hand. It reminded him of a die, but smoother. "What is it?"

"It's your link to the dragonfly. Now raise your hand slowly."

The cube got warm to touch. "What's it doing?"

"It's syncing to your brain."

V raised his hand and his view was like being in the cockpit of a jet. The dragonfly hovered above the desk, waiting for directions.

Mickey ordered. "Let's put it through the paces."

"The dragonfly is an extension of your thoughts," Jonny pointed out, "so what you think it should do, is what it will do."

V stepped away from the computer and looked out into the field. A second later the dragonfly headed towards the tractor. V easily landed it on what was left of the seat.

Mickey was impressed.

It didn't take long before V had a complete command of the dragonfly and had it doing everything it would need to do on its assignment. "How long before the batteries die?"

Jonny responded. "The wings are solar panels. It can fly forever."

"You're a genius kid," V landed the dragonfly back on the table. "What's next, Mickey?"

"The liquid release mechanism. Load some coloured water into the abdomen chamber. Exactly one ounce."

V was anxious to test it some more. "What's the target?"

Mickey pointed to a fence post fifty yards away. "I put a test tube on the top of that post. I want you to release the water into the bottle without spilling a drop."

V let out a sarcastic laugh. "You mean you want me to piss into the tube?"

"Just don't miss."

The wind picked up. It would make the challenge harder.

"What if I do?"

"Innocent people die."

On the way back to the ferry Mickey ordered V to drive thru McDonalds. Jonny got a Big Mac and fries.

ONE HUNDRED & 51

Tiffany was wrapped in her housecoat sitting on the end of the couch enjoying a latte. Ray was still upstairs, and she came down because she couldn't sleep, and she didn't want to disturb him. Mickey had sent her the details for her next assignment, and she had concerns. It could turn into a suicide mission if anything went wrong. So far, she had no answers.

She decided that a run up to the lake would be a good way to clear her head and she changed into her running gear before heading out the back door. When she got to the end of the trail, she sprinted the last few hundred meters to the shore. It got her heart rate beating.

Tiffany paced back and forth in the sand to catch her breath. She absorbed the scenery and never tired of the tall evergreens that dominated the shoreline. The parking lot that ran adjacent to the lake was empty at this time of morning and she used the open space to do her martial art training.

A rustling noise from inside the bushes got her attention. The morning sun made it impossible to see past the tree line. She kept her distance and continued her workout.

After her last set, she decided it was time for a hot shower.

The noise returned. This time it was closer, and she dismissed it as a bear. She was a trained fighter but getting caught off-guard by a black bear was something she wanted to avoid.

A human outline emerged from the bushes with their hands up in the air as though they were surrendering. The sun flickering behind the person blinded Tiffany and she instinctively got into a fighter's stance. "Who are you?"

"We need to talk." The voice was quiet and non-confrontational. Tiffany thought she recognized it.

"It's me."

"Holy shit, Laura," Tiffany didn't hide her surprise. "What are you doing here?"

"Waiting for the right time to find you," Laura lacked her usual self confidence. "I have to stay under the radar until I can clean up my mess in Washington."

Tiffany gave her a welcomed embrace. "I've heard stories, but never believed them. Let's go to my place and have some breakfast."

They kept their conversation light on the walk back. Both knew they'd have time at the house to get serious. When they walked up the back stairs Laura started to laugh.

"What's so funny?"

"Is your husband home?" Laura put her arm around Tiffany's shoulder. "Do I finally get to meet the mystery man?"

Tiffany remembered her lunch with Laura and her story about Ray. She had a problem that needed a quick solution. "He might be. He had a meeting, so he might have left already."

"It's six-thirty on a Sunday," Laura pointed out. "Are you trying to hide him from me?"

Yes, I am, was the truth. "I'll go find him."

Tiffany pointed to the coffee pot. "Help yourself. I'll be right back."

Laura grabbed an apple and poured a black coffee. "Don't take long. I'm dying to meet him."

Tiffany hurried up the stairs into her bedroom. She found Ray stepping out of the shower. "We've got a problem."

Ray wrapped a towel around his waist. "What's up?"

Tiffany held up a finger to her lips. She talked in a whisper. "Do you remember Laura Nelsen?"

Ray huffed. "Yes, I remember that crazy broad. How do you know that I know her?"

"Well, the crazy broad is downstairs right now. I work with her and she just showed up. She wants to meet my husband. She does not know that you're *that* Ray."

"You never stop surprising me," Ray pulled on his pants. "What is she doing here?"

"She needs to talk to me. And she wants to meet the man I love."

Ray continued to get dressed. "What am I supposed to do? She's going to remember me."

"Maybe not."

Ray pulled on a shirt. "I can tell you have something on your mind."

"I might," she whispered as she left the bedroom. "See you downstairs."

Tiffany returned to the kitchen and found Laura sipping her coffee with a suspicious smirk. Something was up. "What's the look for?"

She held up a picture she found in the living room and Tiffany knew she figured it out. "Are you kidding me? You're married to the asshole that I had lunch with."

"He's upstairs and he'll be down after he gets dressed."

"Your world never ceases to amaze me," Laura mused. "I have to admit, I'm looking forward to meeting the real Ray Cooke. The one that makes my friend happy."

Tiffany was skeptical. "You're not mad?"

"I have much bigger problems than being upset with your husband," Laura ran her fingers through her oily hair. She needed a shower. "Do you like the new haircut?"

"Not really," Tiffany grinned. "What's going on with you?"

Laura blew on her coffee. "Where do I start?"

"The beginning is always good." suggested Tiffany.

Laura explained how things went sideways in Washington. How she accidentally killed Detective Murphy, and then how her stupidity allowed Presley to escape. It was her biggest blunder ever.

"Didn't you realize Murphy was part of the organization?"

"So was Tracy," Laura reminded her. "I didn't know why Murphy was there and I wasn't taking any chances."

"What happened to Presley?"

"Wendell Presley is AWOL. I screwed up big time," Laura felt a sense of relief just saying it. "He dumped Murphy's body for me, but never came back so I could kill him. I guess he figured it out."

Tiffany laughed out loud. She was surprised by Laura's stupidity, and that's what it was. "You have no idea where Presley is?"

"Not yet."

Tiffany knew what was at stake if Carol acted on Laura's mistake. And she knew she would be complicit if she helped Laura cover her screwup. "Your biggest problem is that Presley knows he's a dead man if he surfaces. So, my guess is he won't until he has a plan to take you out. You've got a big problem."

"I know that," Laura stood firm, "but I'm not going to spend my life running."

"What do you want from me?"

Laura had thought about her options. "Do you remember our conversation at lunch?"

Tiffany nodded cautiously. "That was just dreaming out loud."

"Okay, let's make the dream come true."

Tiffany thought about the yacht. It could fit another passenger. "If Carol knew we were having this talk, we'd both be dead. I'm not interested in discussing a dream that has us ending up in coffins."

"I get it. I'm just trying to figure my life out. I screwed up."

"Do you have any ideas about finding Presley?" Tiffany was concerned. "because we both know he'll surface eventually."

"I know he will."

Ray interrupted them when he entered the kitchen with a towel wrapped around his head to hide his face in jest. "Have you seen my little sister?"

Both women burst out in laughter. Laura gave Ray a tight hug like they were long lost friends. "Good to finally meet the real you."

"Sorry about our lunch, but I'm sure Tiffany will explain that I'm actually a good guy."

"She told me all about you. You do play a great asshole though."

"Why don't you two go into the living room to continue your conversation? I'll make some pancakes for breakfast."

Tiffany had something she wanted to talk about and took advantage of Ray's offer. When they were alone in the living room Laura spoke softly. "I got a new assignment. I don't know a lot about it yet, but it's risky."

"Where is it?"

"In Ottawa with a high-profile target."

"Who?"

Tiffany shrugged. "No idea yet."

Laura realized she had left her coffee in the kitchen. "I'll be right back."

Ray was stirring the batter when Laura snuck up behind him and grabbed his ass with one hand and his balls tightly with the other. She had his full attention. "Are you still working with the cops?"

Pain was etched on his face and he could barely speak. "No."

"If you ever fuck with me again, I'll take these with me." She squeezed harder, before releasing her grip. "And oh, do you have any blueberries? I love them on my pancakes."

ONE HUNDRED & 52

Steve was only home long enough to change into some dry clothes, take a hot shower and eat the ham and eggs Helen made. She filled his mug with fresh coffee and joined him at the table. She had lots of questions.

Where did you stay last night? Who was the crazy man with the gun? Why are you going back there alone?

Lot's of concern from his wife.

Steve tried to answer them all without worrying his wife. "When I get into the office, I'll do a background check on the old timer, but I can't tie up resources to question two women on the dock."

Helen was rehashing what he told her. "Something doesn't add up. You stayed in their tent last night, so where did they sleep?"

Steve finished everything on his plate. "I will find out when I see them."

"How long will you be gone?"

He promised to be gone only a few hours and Helen knew it was an unintentional lie. He agreed to continue their discussion over dinner, and she would hold him to it. Helen knew that every day that he left for work was one day closer to them getting on a plane.

"When you get home, we can talk about our first holiday after you retire." Helen handed him his mug. "I'm thinking we go to Portugal first. I've read the seafood is amazing and the culture is very relaxed. It's just what we need."

The sergeant smiled. "I've heard they blend amazing ports"

"Yes, they do."

Helen was happy to hear Steve taking retirement seriously. "You be safe, and I'll see you when you get back."

Steve grabbed his jacket. "I have to get going if I'm making that ferry."

She walked him to the door. "Be careful, Sergeant Smith. I hope those two women understand how lucky they are to have you."

He gave her a kiss. "I love you and thanks for a great breakfast."

"I hope the girls have found something useful."

"Me too," He stepped out the door. "I love you."

"You've said that twice." She smiled.

"It's still not enough."

She closed the door behind him.

ONE HUNDRED & 53

Cherie Beliveau sat at a corner table of a small café that was a few blocks from where she lived. It was a very average neighborhood full of young families living in remodelled apartments that were now called condos. Not exactly where you'd expect a high-priced escort to be living.

She blended in with the others enjoying her morning coffee while she listened to some Taylor Swift on her headphones. The popular café was full of people drinking expressos while talking business, or those just enjoying their morning beverage.

One of those was a retired lieutenant who came in every morning and Cherie insisted on buying his coffee. It was her way of thanking him for his service, and she enjoyed his stories. She knew one day she might need him. The large black man was named Theodore, but everyone called him Teddy. He lived two stories above her.

Cherie had her real hair stuffed under a cap. There were no extensions or makeup today. She was just a plain looking neighborhood girl that lived two lives, one complicated and dangerous and the other as simple as it could get.

Her hundred thousand dollars from the North Koreans to play along was a nice bonus. And her copy of the video that only Eon knew about, was worth millions more. Once the election was called, it would be time to negotiate.

She was just about to leave when her phone rang. It was Hugh Hutchinson. What did he want? She smiled before she answered her own question.

Three months earlier, Cherie had attended a fundraiser with

the businessman and on the way home he insisted they stop by a nightclub he owned. After a quick drink in the main club, he took her to a private room with a bar and a bed. Didn't have to guess what went on in here. After another quick drink he had her lye on the bed on her stomach. It didn't take long. When he was done, he called her a cab. The life of an escort.

She thought about not answering it. "Mr. Hutchinson. What can I do for you?"

His voice was gruff. "I need to see you today."

"I'm not sure…"

Hutchinson cut her off. "Meet me at the Regency Hotel at two. And bring any copies of the videos you have with Elliot. And I mean all of them."

Hutchinson didn't intimidate Cherie. "Why would you think I have videos?" She was fishing. "There are no…"

He cut her off again. "Don't lie to me! Pierre told me you both liked to watch the show after you were done. So, bring everything."

"Why would I do that? What's in this for me?"

"I'll make it worth your while."

"And if I don't come?"

"I never took you for a stupid person. Don't prove me wrong. Two o'clock at the Regency. Room 505."

ONE HUNDRED & 54

Stacey was in a lot of discomfort when a nurse came into the office with a gurney and supplies. Once she was strapped in, it was off to the clinic to deliver a baby. Suzanne walked beside the nurse. It didn't surprise her that this place had a medical center. It seemed to be a self-contained community. She was impressed.

Carol had no interest in being with her daughter to witness the birth of her granddaughter.

The nurse had been instructed to do a complete genetic profile of the baby. Carol wanted to know if she had another genius on her hands. Another golden child. She locked her office door.

She called Mickey, who was off site doing a field test with Jonny. "How's it going?"

Mickey sounded excited. "It's better than we expected."

"No surprise there," Carol stifled a yawn. "And what about our friend the sergeant? What's going on with that?"

"Smith will be on the 10 o'clock ferry."

"Is everything in place?"

"Yes, we're all set."

"I'm going to bed," Carol yawned. "Let me know how everything goes"

"Yes, ma'am."

ONE HUNDRED & 55

Cherie entered her condo building and was greeted by Teddy, who was on his way to the corner grocer to buy something for dinner. His bright smile made her feel safe and they always took a moment to try and solve a world problem. Today it was the price of fresh produce.

For a man in his late forties, he kept his body in great physical condition. His thick chest and tattooed arms were an intimidating sight for anyone who didn't know him. For those that did, he was a lovable teddy bear.

"What's on the menu tonight?"

"I'm thinking I'll try and find some fresh fish. Maybe Atlantic cod. I'll sprinkle my special seasoning on it with lemon and it'll be amazing," He licked his lips. "Do you want to join me?"

"I can't tonight but thank you."

They said goodbye, and Cherie headed up to her condo on the sixth floor. It was a simple one-bedroom unit decorated with used furniture. The only piece she bought new was her bed. Keeping a simple profile was important to her plan.

She sat at her small kitchen table and flipped open her laptop. The call from Hutchinson had her on edge, and she wanted to check her security footage to make sure no one was in her place while she was gone. It came up empty. Good.

After making a turkey and cranberry sandwich, she went to a painting mounted on the wall. Behind the frame was a safe that she ignored. Any aspiring thief would assume that's where anything valuable would be kept, and they'd be wrong.

A tiny encrypted memory card was between the canvas and frame. Hidden in plain sight. She returned to her computer and took a bite of her sandwich before she got to work. She made a copy of each video that the prime minister insisted she make. That was his thing.

She felt that Hutchinson wanted more than the videos. He was getting her out of her place so it could be searched. This was one of those times why she bought Teddy so many coffees. Cherie ran up the two flights of stairs to his condo.

He opened the door. "Did you change your mind about dinner?"

She pretended to be disappointed. "I need a favor. Can I get you to keep an eye on my apartment for a few hours?"

"Yes, ma'am," Teddy was glad to help. "Is everything okay? Do you need me to talk to someone?"

"Only if they show up announced."

He understood. "Consider it done."

"One last thing." She handed him an envelope. "If I'm not back by three can you mail that?"

It was an envelope to the Ottawa Citizen. "Yes ma'am."

Hugh Hutchinson waited impatiently in his room for Cherie. She was late and he knew it was on purpose. There was finally a knock on the door and when he opened it, he hardly recognized her. All the Hollywood glitz and glamour were gone. The makeup and expensive outfits were replaced by a hoodie and sneakers.

She stepped past him and into the hotel room. "Are you slumming today? Not exactly a room suited for someone of your status."

He scowled. "It'll do."

She didn't want to be there any longer than necessary. "Let's discuss business."

"Did you bring them?" Hugh asked. "Give them to me and I'll

give you five thousand dollars. That's good money for a blackmailing hooker."

His quick offer told her he was worried, "I'm thinking that's a little low for something so valuable."

She pulled out the encrypted memory stick. "Everything is on this. The password is your birthday."

Hugh reached for it, but she pulled it back. "How do I know that is the only copy?"

"You won't until we settle on an offer."

He glanced at the bed. "My next offer will depend on how hard you're willing to work for it."

Cherie tried not to laugh. It would embarrass him, and she didn't come for a confrontation. "If you think I'm getting on my back, you're a fool."

Hugh pulled an envelope from his pocket and tossed it to Cherie. "There's the five thousand. That's the only offer you're getting."

Cherie caught the envelope and pretended to consider it. "I have a counter. It's higher and I know Pierre will agree."

Hugh listened. "What are you thinking it's worth?"

Cherie could sense that Hugh was nervous. It was time to push him over the edge. "Let me make a call."

Hugh didn't like it. "You don't need to make a call."

"It will only take a minute," She punched in a number on her phone. "Hey, Teddy, it's Cherie." She moved closer, so Hutchinson could hear.

"Hello, Miss Cherie," Hugh could hear Teddy's voice. "Is everything okay?"

"Do you still have the envelope?"

"Yes, ma'am," Teddy confirmed. "Do you want me to mail it?"

Hugh waved his hand wildly. He mouthed the words: '*What do you want?*'

"Hold on for a second, Teddy," Cherie looked at Hugh. "One million, or Teddy goes for a walk."

Like all good businessmen, Hugh looked for an edge, but he knew he was cornered. "Hang up the phone. You win, you bitch!"

She handed Hugh a business card. "There's a number on the back. That's the account I want you to deposit my one million."

"You want me to pay you one million dollars for a video with Pierre on it?"

She stuffed the five thousand into her bag. "And to keep my mouth shut about North Korea."

Hugh knew he was cornered. "The money will be transferred today."

ONE HUNDRED & 56

A black Escalade pulled up to the front entrance of the Royal Grande Hotel in Ottawa. Two men stepped out and after a quick conversation with the valet, they headed into the lobby. They walked to the front desk where a young Filipino woman, wearing a hotel issued wine colored blazer greeted them with a rehearsed opening line. "Welcome to the Royal Grande Hotel. How can I help you?"

"Good morning. Can you tell your general manager that Special Agent Kellan MacKay is here?"

She nodded and pointed across the lobby. "Mr. Singh will be right out. He'll meet you by the complimentary coffee station."

They thanked her and only had to wait a minute before being greeted by a short chubby man named Herb Singh. There was a ketchup stain on his cheek that both agents chose to ignore. They obviously interrupted his lunch.

"Hello Mr. Singh, I'm Agent MacKay and my partner is Agent Jackson."

Singh pointed to a small meeting room. "We'll go in here where we'll have some privacy."

Singh closed the door. "What can I do for you gentlemen. It's not every day the secret service comes knocking."

"We appreciate you taking the time to meet," MacKay stated. "I imagine you're busy, so we won't take much time."

Singh shrugged casually. "It does get busy, but it's my pleasure to help you anyway I can."

"As I explained on my call, President Tucker will be arriving here on June 30th, and he'll be staying for two nights. We're the advance team and that means we'll audit the hotel for security concerns."

Singh nodded politely, knowing it meant more work for him.

"The top three floors are designated for the president. He'll stay in the suite on the top floor but no one from the hotel will be allowed up there once we take over."

"Understood."

"Agent Jackson and I need to do a visual tour of the property if that's okay? That includes the room the president will sleep in."

"Absolutely," Singh obliged. "Anything you need."

"The last thing is a list of your staff," MacKay asked. "We will be doing background checks. And that will include you as well. Is that a problem?"

"I'll have HR forward you the list. Anything else?"

MacKay shook his head. "No, that will be good for now. We just need to do the inspection and we'll be done."

"I'll get you a key for the suite." Singh opened the door. "Just drop it off at the front desk when you're done."

MacKay shook Singh's hand. "The U.S. Government appreciates your co-operation."

They got off the elevator on the fortieth floor and went to the suite. The room was impressive in both size and amenities. The huge panoramic window had an amazing view but was a security nightmare. MacKay made a note. There was a well-stocked bar that was ready to go. The president's whiskey would need to be added. And with a few additions to the furniture that the president would request, this room would be fine.

MacKay looked at Jackson, "You check the bedroom. I'll do the bathroom. I need to use it anyway. Too much coffee."

While he relieved himself, he glanced around the room. It was a normal bathroom for a suite. There was an oversized shower, two sink stations and lots of towels. It had everything that Tucker required.

Then something got his attention. There was an X marked on the window frame with a pencil. It looked new. After a second look, the agent shrugged it off as leftover from a renovation.

ONE HUNDRED & 57

Sergeant Smith parked in the staff lot and displayed a badge number on the dash so it wouldn't get towed. He was the last foot-passenger to board the Queen of Coquitlam for the ten o'clock sailing to Descanso Bay. He hardly had time to find a seat before the whistle blew. The ferry pulled away from the pier and headed out on another thirty-six-minute crossing.

He checked his cellphone. He had hoped to find a response from Stacey. There was nothing new, so he settled in, and observed Gabriola Island off in the distance. He wondered what was waiting on the other side.

Steve thought about Helen and the effort she put into their marriage. She was always doing things for him and he was a lucky man to have her. Since he committed to retirement, she had found a renewed energy that was missing for years. Travelling to Europe was something they talked about since they got married and now it was only months away.

To pass the time Steve decided to wander down the steel staircase to the car deck. It was an opened air design. He made his way through the cars towards the stern. The winds off the water pushed the smell of diesel back through the ferry. The stench was unavoidable. He was going to turn back when he got a whiff of what he was sure was a joint.

Steve saw a scruffy looking man, with frizzy grey hair in an army jacket that stood at the back of the ferry. He was standing outside the chain barrier and one wrong move and he would fall overboard.

Smith shook his head at the stupidity, and realized it was now

447

his problem to deal with. The passenger had his back to the sergeant and the noise of the engines drowned out any verbal attempt to get his attention. Smith worked his way through the crowd that had gathered, mostly seniors on a day excursion to the island.

When he tapped the man on his shoulder, the only response he got was an irritated shrug. Smith had no interest in arresting him for smoking a joint, but he was concerned for his safety.

He tapped him again, this time harder. "You can't be smoking, and I need you to come back on this side of the chain."

He ignored the sergeant and continued to look out over the water. The man took another drag and gave Smith the middle finger. "Fuck off."

Smith flashed his badge and raised his voice. "You need to come to this side!"

The badge meant nothing to him. "I said fuck off."

Smith unhooked the chain. His impatience was starting to show. "Get your ass back on this side or you're going to jail."

The man turned to face Smith. "You said you owed me a favour."

Smith recognized him. "You're the guy who let me through his property the other night?"

He reeked of booze. "I am, so fuck off and let me finish my smoke."

Smith was deciding what to do with him. He didn't have time to deal with a drunk. Stacey was waiting. "You get on this side of the chain and I'll let you finish it."

"I have a better idea," The man took a last drag and flicked the butt into the waves. "My legs aren't what they use to be, so can I use your shoulder to lean on?"

Smith agreed if it would end the standoff. "What's your name?"

The man gripped Smith's jacket. "My name is Bjorn. I was in your jail once."

"Why?"

The man grinned maliciously. "I impersonated a prisoner. I was on a job."

What happened next shocked everyone. Smith never saw it coming. The man wasn't drunk. It was a con. And he was powerful and a skilled combat fighter. He used his leverage to pull the bigger sergeant over his smaller body and the sergeant fell into the water churning behind the ferry. Smith didn't have a chance and he never came up.

A lady screamed '*man overboard*' and others were already on their phones calling 911. The ferry captain witnessed what occurred from the bridge and sounded the emergency alarm. He ordered the engines to shut down immediately.

No one was ready to confront Bjorn, but he knew he was cornered. Then, without warning, he gave the crowd the middle finger and leaped into the water. He never came up either.

Helen Smith was looking at pictures of Portugal, when the there was a knock at her door.

ONE HUNDRED & 58

Mickey found the boys in the gym going through their workout. He let them finish their set before he interrupted them. "Hey, Curtis," Mickey eyed the door, "I need to talk to Joshua."

Curtis took the hint. "Be strong, buddy. I'll be back later."

Mickey took a seat and looked at Joshua, who hid his face in his towel. "I'm sorry about your dad."

When Joshua finally looked up, his eyes were swollen with tears. He jumped into Mickey's arms and for a rare moment, he was twelve. Mickey didn't know how to react, so he just held him. Was this what it was like to be a father?

"How come I never knew?" Joshua held on tightly. "Why didn't my grandmother tell me?"

Mickey had to be careful. He wanted to help Joshua work through this, but he knew he couldn't reveal the truth. "I'm sure she had her reasons. Sometimes life just happens, and we have to work through it."

Joshua trusted Mickey. "If you say so."

Mickey needed to change the subject, "Can we go inspect the animatronics?"

Joshua's expression changed. "That would be great."

They headed down to Level C and after clearing security, they walked to a large steel door that reminded Mickey of a bank vault. The difference was there was no money inside. What was in there was way more valuable.

There was no combination needed. Mickey stuck his index finger into a tube and a scanner verified his identification through DNA. A tiny needle took a small sample of his blood.

When Joshua was done, Mickey handed him a Kleenex to wipe his finger. The locks activated and the door swung open. "Let's go inside."

Motion sensors activated the LED tube lighting that was mounted on the two-inch steel plate ceiling. The walls were built of reinforced concrete with explosive inserts. If somehow, someone did manage to get inside without supplying a DNA sample or blowing up, the room would flood with seawater in one minute. Just enough time to say your prayers.

There were four polycarbonate plastic containers stacked upright against the wall. They looked like a row of coffins. Each one had an electronic keypad requiring a combination to open.

Mickey walked over to the cases with Joshua one step behind. "This is something out of a science fiction movie."

They both chuckled.

Mickey punched in the code and pulled the first one open. Even though he knew what to expect, the sight of the motionless body gave him the shivers. "This is incredible, but what's with the face? It looks like a mannequin."

"That's because it is. Once we input the person's genetics and program the facial recognition software, it will become whoever we want it to be. They will transform into a twin."

Mickey had a lot of questions. "What if the person is a hundred pounds heavier?"

"It will conform to the dimensions. That was one of the last pieces I had to figure out."

Mickey couldn't stop admiring Joshua's creation. "It's flawless."

Joshua thought about his dad and wondered.

ONE HUNDRED & 59

It was their second meeting in less than a week and it promised to be more eventful than the one in Ottawa. There would be no goodwill gestures for the public or smiles for the cameras. One man had a lot of power and the other was about to become the most powerful man in the country. They were meeting in Vancouver. To avoid the scrum of reporters out front, Hugh Hutchinson was brought in a back door and this time he was alone.

They met in David Magill's office and after they settled in, the two men started putting the pieces together to build a partnership. There was a lot to cover and much of it was detailed in the agreement Hugh had negotiated with Carol. Magill was assigned to tie up any loose ends. They talked about Hutchinson Enterprises and the goals of the Federal Coalition. After three hours, David was satisfied his party had a strong agreement with Hutchinson, and more importantly, the Liberal party had lost a huge piece of their infrastructure.

David stood up to stretch out his back. "Are you hungry?"

"I could use a sandwich?" Hugh nodded, "and a carbonated water. Lime if possible."

David sent in an order and after a few stretches returned to his seat. "I hear you're expanding into North Korea. You're working with Eon Kamahi."

Hugh shot David a sideways glance. "Is there any point of me denying it?"

David smiled, knowing he had the upper hand. "No, and you know that working with a communist regime goes against about a dozen trade restrictions under the International Trade Agreement."

Hugh knew it was Carol's idea to bring this up. It was her way of thinking she was in control. He wasn't happy being blindsided. "What do you want in return for my little indiscretion?"

David handed him a photo.

Hugh examined the face. "Who's the Asian girl?"

"That young girl is Cassie Chang, and she is a member of the organization."

Hugh held up his hands, looking confused. "Why are you telling me this?"

"She has created a food vapour that will feed the masses by simply releasing it into the air," David scrutinized Hugh's reaction. He hung on every word, "and we need to do field testing. North Korea is a perfect subject."

Hugh did what he did. He calculated the opportunity. "So, I'm clear. That young girl has developed a food product that people inhale to ingest dinner. It could revamp the food industry. She could be the first trillionaire."

"The organization has a different outlook. We think it could help end starvation around the world," David mused at Hugh's lust for money, "and starting in North Korea makes sense to us."

Hugh paused while he thought about his next question. "Why is the organization worried about the starving population in North Korea? Shouldn't all of their focus be on winning the election?"

David didn't agree. "The election is under control. We believe you should always make time to help others."

"Save the sermon for the congregation," Hugh refuted, "because we both know there is something much bigger going on here."

"Fair enough," David didn't want to debate the organization's long-term plan, "but back to North Korea. We want access to the warehouse Eon Kamahi has secured for you."

"Wait a minute." Hugh argued. "You're putting my entire crew

453

over there at risk if you get caught. Why do you need to test it there?"

"We're not testing it. The vapour is ready to be released in mass volume and we will begin in Pyongyang."

Hugh took a deep breath. He understood the bigger picture. "You're not only focused on feeding the starving North Koreans, you're planning an uprising."

David never responded to Hugh's accusation. "It looks like our lunch has arrived."

ONE HUNDRED & 60

After four hours of intense labour, an exhausted Stacey gave birth to a healthy baby girl that she named, Emma Roberta Small. Roberta was a tribute to Robert. It was the least she could do, considering the circumstances.

Suzanne stood in as the birth coach, and never left Stacey's side during the entire time. It was an exceptionally long day for both, and Stacey was now resting peacefully in a comfortable bed. Baby Emma was only a few feet away in a makeshift bassinet.

Suzanne was able to get a few hours sleep and when she woke up, she craved a hot coffee. The nurse on duty offered to take her to the cafeteria to get something to eat. It got better when the nurse suggested they go outside and sit in the garden.

Suzanne nearly spit out her French toast when a Cormorant search and rescue helicopter roared overhead. It wasn't much higher than the treetops when it banked sharply to head back over the water. "What's going on?"

"I heard someone fell off the ferry."

"That's terrible," Suzanne walked over to the bank and looked out over the ocean. The ferry was still anchored and there were at least a hundred boats helping with the search. "Any idea what happened?"

The nurse shook her head. "They won't release any details until they find the body. If they haven't found one by now, then it's a recovery mission."

Suzanne didn't realize how hungry she was until she finished everything on her plate. She enjoyed the casual conversation as much as the coffee. It had been a stressful day and a half, and it was nice to just relax for a moment and catch her breath. It didn't last long.

The nurse headed towards the building. "I have a meeting, so I need to go. I'll take you back, so security doesn't hassle you."

The hallways were busier than the last time Suzanne had walked them with Mickey. Everyone seemed to be so young, many looked to be the same age as Curtis. She wanted to say hello but knew that would be frowned upon. She thanked the nurse and went back inside Stacey's room.

The lab technician went to Carol's office with the results. Carol was on the couch reading a book and drinking some tea. It was how she relaxed. "Do you have what I'm waiting for?"

"Yes, ma'am."

"And?"

"Your granddaughter tested higher than her brother. She will have an extraordinary level of intelligence."

Carol showed no reaction. She dismissed the nurse.

Stacey was sitting up feeding Emma. It was the first time that Suzanne had ever seen her this calm. Being a mother does tend to change you. "How are you feeling?"

"Like I've been ripped apart," Stacey smirked, "but she's adorable. Where did you go?"

"I had some breakfast out in the garden."

"Outside?" Stacey looked surprised. "Did you escape?"

"I went with the nurse. I don't think she realized I'm a prisoner."

Stacey let that sink in. "Is that what we are?"

Suzanne shrugged. "I don't think we can walk out the front door without setting off an alarm. Your mom is big on security."

"I'm still trying to get my head around that she runs this place."

"It's actually very impressive," Suzanne said respectfully. "I would love to know what their end game is."

"Who knows or cares."

"When I was outside, I saw a helicopter fly over. It was really low."

"Were they looking for us?" Stacey joked.

"Apparently, someone fell off the Gabriola ferry. They were searching for a body."

Stacey's face sunk. "It can't be him."

ONE HUNDRED & 61

In all her years working for Mickey, Laura's visit to the complex today was her first time there. Mickey wanted the halls to his office cleared to be sure her presence was not detected. Mickey's elite team of problem solvers were not recognized as part of the organization, but they had their place. Outside of Mickey, only Carol knew of their existence. Her visit to Gabriola was necessitated on special circumstances.

Mickey was in his office when Laura was escorted in. She pulled off her hoodie and ran her fingers through her hair to loosen it up. She didn't know why she was there, but believed it had to do with Presley. She felt uneasy.

"This is quite the place. Does Carol know I'm on the island?" Laura asked cautiously. "I'm betting I'm not her favourite right now."

"You're right about that, but I'll deal with it."

"Okay," Laura tried to relax, "so why am I here?"

"Two reasons," Mickey started, "and the first is Wendell Presley. We know he's back in the country."

Laura perked up. "How?"

"A friend at border patrol called. He crossed into Ontario."

Laura literally licked her lips. "Will I get a second chance?"

Mickey hesitated. "He will be coming for you, so you've become the prey instead of the hunter. There is no way he can get to you here."

Laura got angry at the reversal of circumstances and wasn't going to stand for it. "I'm not hiding on this rock. I'll hunt him down."

Mickey didn't agree. "His ego will force him to come to you. I can't have a shootout between you two. We do things quietly."

Laura parked her emotion. Mickey was right. "You said there were two reasons I'm here."

Mickey took a seat and sipped his juice. "I have a new assignment. I need you in Ottawa for the Canada Day weekend."

Laura remember Tiffany saying she was headed to the nation's capital. "What's going on?"

"I'll send you the details, but I will tell you that you'll be taking some special training."

Laura's interest was peaked.

"Remember," Mickey reminded her, "do not reach out to find Presley. When it's time to deal with it, we'll get it done properly."

ONE HUNDRED & 62

Hugh was back in Ottawa after his meeting with Magill. The billionaire wasn't used to being the one on the outside looking in, but that's exactly where he was with the organization. He had no idea what Carol was creating, but he knew it was much more than winning an election. And it was beginning to scare him.

When the prime minister heard Hugh was back in Ottawa, he invited him over to his house. Hugh wanted to decline, but that wasn't an option if he wanted to keep his contracts with the government. He had to play nice for a few more months.

Pierre was in a feisty mood when he arrived. The prime minister had just finished up a meeting with his best strategists and they solved nothing. A bunch of overpaid thinkers and he was sick of them. They were hurried out the back just before Hugh arrived. Pierre needed some good news.

"How was your meeting with Magill?" Pierre got right into it. "Did you find out anything that justifies the contracts I give you?"

Hugh ignored Pierre. "Can I get a drink before you get going on another rant."

His tone startled Pierre.

"Pour yourself a drink too," Hugh suggested, "We need to talk."

"Is that so?"

Hugh picked up a copy of Stephen King's '*The Shining*'. He knew he needed to lighten the mood, "Are you trying to escape reality by dating Nurse Ratchet?"

"King's a master of horror and that's my life these days," Pierre tried to laugh at himself, "plus I like the Nicholson character in the movie. It reminds me of me when I'm with Cherie. A little wacky."

Hugh tossed the book back on the table. "I have nothing on Magill."

"How's that possible?" Pierre poured two generous shots of scotch. "There has to be something you're missing. Or maybe you're not looking hard enough."

Hugh ignored Pierre's accusation. He was getting used to them. "I've met with Magill and he's quite the man. He has a solid platform that people are buying into."

"This asshole is more popular than the Bieber kid."

Hugh could only smirk at the comparison.

"How was your meeting with him?"

Pierre moaned, "We have to slow him down."

"My suggestion is you ride it out and figure out how you can counter their platform."

Pierre didn't agree. "How do you compete with free education and everything else they're promising?"

"His popularity isn't a fluke. They've put a lot of time into creating a new image for the Federal Coalition."

Pierre slumped in his chair. "Do you think I have a chance?"

"As it stands now, no," Hugh replied honestly. "Magill is connecting with voters."

"What about his wife?" Pierre sounded desperate and that's because he was. "Anything nasty in her closet?"

"We don't exploit family members. The public will turn on you even more." Hugh answered sourly.

Pierre's frustration started to show. "I don't care what the public thinks. If there is something on her we can use, I want it. And if there is nothing, then create something."

Hugh wasn't comfortable with where Pierre was headed. "Have you talked with Cherie lately?"

"Not since you let her steal a million from you," Pierre couldn't resist the jab. "Did you at least get her on her knees?"

Hugh sipped his scotch and scowled. "Why are we talking about her?"

"Because you brought her up," He reminded Hugh, "and we need to find her."

"Why?"

"President Tucker is coming on July 1st and he requested her for a private party."

"How's this my concern?"

"She's gone AWOL. I was thinking you might know where she is. I'm a little nervous that she didn't hand everything over."

"She did," Hugh snapped impatiently, without really knowing, "and if you're concerned about the tapes then stop making them."

Pierre laughed. "If only my life was that simple. She's my addiction."

Hugh had made a copy of the tape for himself. It was an insurance policy because he knew his relationship wouldn't end well with the prime minister. "I might have someone even better than Cherie."

Pierre was easily distracted from his election concerns. He loved to talk about horny women. "Have you been holding out on me?"

Carol had given Hugh the idea. "I could get him two of the most gorgeous women he'll ever meet. He'll owe you big time."

"What are their names," Pierre bubbled with excitement, "and do they like to play games?"

Hugh stood up. He was ready to leave. "Just send me the details."

"Before you go, I have one more question." Pierre moved closer to Hugh. "I get the feeling you're holding out on me. Is this true?"

"Why would you ask me that?"

"You're a man who demands results and you're not getting any. At least none that benefit me. Maybe that's the plan."

Hugh already knew this would be the last time he got invited to this house. At least while Elliot lived there. It was only a matter of days before everything came out. Hutchinson Enterprises will release a campaign that threw his complete support behind the Federal Coalition. He shrugged as he walked past Pierre. "It's just been a bad week."

ONE HUNDRED & 63

Tiffany had returned home from the gym, where her team of trainers put her through a workout that most people would crumble under. She made it upstairs and walked over to the bed and fell face-first onto the pillows. The cool material felt good against her skin and she didn't want to move.

The first thirty minutes with her trainers was sheer hell. They had her focus on cardio and her lungs begged for oxygen after every sprint. Her exhaustion was excruciating, but she pushed through it.

Up next, she worked on her MMA skills. She loved the competitiveness in the octagon and the fear of losing motivated her to work harder than anyone else in the gym. It was in this same octagon six years ago that she got her cuts and bruises that she blamed on Ray.

She had hoped he would be home, but after a quick search, she was disappointed not to find him. She needed to talk about her latest assignment and the impact it would have on them. Ray had hinted over breakfast that he might go job-hunting, so she decided that's where he must be. She headed to the shower to wash the sweat and drips of dry blood from her body.

After getting dressed, Tiffany bounced down the stairs and into the kitchen to make a protein smoothie. She never saw the lingering shadow until she nearly walked into it. She intuitively got into a fighter's stance.

"Good to see your reflexes are still as fast."

"Damn it, Carol. What are you doing here?"

Carol put her hand on Tiffany's extended fist. "Relax. We need to talk."

Tiffany blew out a deep breath. "About what?"

Carol started looking through the cupboards, "Where is your tea?"

"In the one beside you." Carol was the one person who sent chills up Tiffany's spine. "Do you want something to eat?"

"Tea will be fine," Carol glanced at the blender. "but you make your drink."

Tiffany threw a bunch of ingredients into her mixer and blended them until they were edible with a straw. She joined Carol at the table. They had met only once before, but Tiffany knew the reputation of this woman. "Why are you here?"

Carol admired the open spaced kitchen. "Where is your husband? Will he be joining us?"

Tiffany sipped her smoothie, watching Carol with suspicion. "I have no idea. I was hoping he'd be here, but he must be out running errands. Why?"

"Have I told you how amazing you look? Going to the gym works for you. I was never one who enjoyed sweating."

Tiffany twirled the straw in the glass, trying to understand her visitor. She knew Carol didn't drop by to exchange pleasantries. "I don't want to sound rude, but why are you here?"

"You're not being rude," Carol answered. "I want to talk about Canada Day."

"What about it?"

Carol held her teacup in both hands. "The first thing we must discuss is your friendship with Laura."

Tiffany was blindsided. Friendships amongst Mickey's crew were discouraged. They could be your target one day. Laura must have said something to someone because she had been careful. "You know about that?"

Carol gave Tiffany a mock smile. "There isn't much that concerns my organization that I'm not aware of. Especially when the stakes are this high."

Tiffany forced an apologetic grin.

"Your resume of work with us is impressive, so don't screw it up. Everything we've worked for to this point is about to materialize and I cannot allow anything to interrupt us. You know you have a new assignment?"

"Yes."

"I know Mickey hasn't given you the particulars yet," Carol divulged, "and I'll let him do that. I'm just here to be sure that you're one hundred percent committed."

Tiffany nodded. "Absolutely."

Carol took a second to admire Tiffany's naked body under her dress. "With your female assets, you're perfect for this assignment."

Tiffany wasn't sure how she felt discussing *her assets* with someone old enough to be her grandmother. "Am I going to sleep with the target?"

"If it's necessary to secure access, but that's not so bad, is it."

"I'm not sure about that," Tiffany countered, remembering McKee.

Carol changed the subject. "How does your husband feel about your occupation? Is he okay with it?"

Tiffany thought before she answered. "He's accepted that I don't have a normal career."

"He must be very understanding," Carol suggested. "How would you feel about him joining us for one assignment?"

Tiffany was skeptical. "Doing what?"

"I need someone to replace Presley. It's just a small task. Nothing too dangerous."

"What would Ray get out of it?"

Carol sipped her tea. "Everything you took from him."

Carol's response surprised her. "Ray would like that. Let me talk to him."

"Do it soon," Carol ordered. "I need an answer."

"I don't mean to rush you," Tiffany stood up, "but I have to be somewhere in thirty minutes."

Carol patted her lips with a napkin. "How is Laura doing? She hasn't been herself lately."

"Is there something I should tell her?"

"No," Carol pursed her lips, "just be careful around her."

What did that mean? "I will."

ONE HUNDRED & 64

They met at the same restaurant on the water as last time. When Tiffany arrived, she found Laura out on the patio talking up the waiter. He pulled out Tiffany's chair and seemed relieved that she had arrived. There was a glass of wine on the table with her name on it.

The two hugged and Laura had a smirk on her face. "Our waiter with the nice ass is Seninio and he's Italian," She turned to him, who was trying unsuccessfully not to blush. "Can you give us girls some time."

Seninio was happy to give them some time. He needed a quick toke. This crazy lady thought his butt was her personal toy. Even though she was loud, she was very sexy, in an aggressive kind of way.

Laura turned her attention to Tiffany. "Hello, gorgeous. Thanks for coming on such short notice. I know you're busy."

"Not a problem and good choice for a restaurant."

"I loved the salad we had last time, especially when you almost choked on a tomato. Now I know why."

Laura didn't waste anytime asking all the questions she had about Ray. "Did you know he was working with the police? Did he really get busted with a kilo of coke? And the most important, how is he in bed? I hear older men are more passionate and understand a woman's body. No more wham, bam."

Tiffany chuckled. "The answers are no, yes and great. Now I get to ask you a question."

"Fire away," Laura was relaxed. The wine helped. "What do you want to know?"

"What did you do to get Carol upset?" Tiffany watched her friend's reaction. "She was just at my house and she told me to be careful around you."

Laura didn't seem concerned. "She's probably still upset about my Presley screwup."

Tiffany was surprised. "Does she know that Presley is alive?"

"Mickey must have told her because I never told anyone other than you."

"And you still haven't found him?"

"We know he's back in Canada so he's getting closer. Mickey thinks Presley will come looking for me. He's monitoring it."

"So, you think he's looking for revenge?"

"Absolutely," Laura insisted.

"If I were Wendell, I'd be more worried about Mickey," Tiffany countered. "Messing with that man is a bad life decision."

"We don't usually get do-overs in our business and I need to correct this."

Tiffany was surprised Laura was still alive. Her mistake was unforgivable in their line of work. She grabbed her menu. "Let's eat. I'm starving."

Seninio took their orders and was careful to stay out of arms reach from Laura. Once he was gone the conversation turned to work.

Laura started. "I'm told I'm in Ottawa with you."

"It's strange that we're both going to Ottawa. Our assignments have to be connected."

Laura agreed, "Any idea what the job is?"

"Based on Carol taking the time to come to my house, it must be a game changer," Tiffany grabbed a bun and put a slab of butter on it. "I'm waiting for Mickey to call me in for a briefing session."

Laura sipped on her wine. "Are you still considering retirement?"

Tiffany chewed on a piece of sourdough. She thought about the yacht moored in Vancouver. It was scheduled to depart the Monday after the long weekend. "Maybe."

"You know you don't get to retire from the organization. We've talked about this."

Tiffany conceded Laura was right. "I'm thinking about my options. I can't do this forever."

"If Carol finds out you're thinking..."

Tiffany interrupted, "Then I'll know you told her because I haven't told anyone else."

"Relax," Laura assured her, "your secret is safe with me."

Carol's visit reinforced the idea she needed to consider getting out. How to do that, or where to go to be safe was still a mystery. She'd never control her life if she stayed with the organization. What she didn't know was how Mickey might react and that was a concern. "Good."

Laura wondered why Tiffany would even consider a life on the run. "You really love that asshole, don't you?"

Tiffany tilted her head. "I really do, and having a normal existence is appealing to me."

Laura smiled. "I'm jealous."

"Have you ever considered it?"

"I love the work," Laura tried to commit to her laugh, "and most men are reluctant to be around women who kill people for a living."

Tiffany pursed her lips. "True enough."

"When are you considering this?"

Tiffany knew it would be stupid to reveal too much. "I'm not sure. It all hinges on surviving Ottawa."

"It must be hard to sleep with a target and then go home to your loving husband with poison on your hands?"

"That's a little melodramatic, but yes," mused Tiffany. "Our careers have violent endings and I'm thinking I want to change my future."

Laura reached for her friend's hand. "One last thing. You know they'll hunt you down? You might be committing suicide if you run and I might be the one chasing you. Don't make me do that."

"I think we need more wine."

ONE HUNDRED & 65

Suzanne snuck out to grab a breakfast tray for Stacey while Stacey fed the baby. She wanted to do a little exploring to see what this place was about. When they found her, she'd just play stupid and tell them she got lost. It would be easy to get mixed up in the maze of hallways.

While the baby snuggled against her chest, Stacey looked around her temporary residence. It was a small, but self-contained apartment with all the amenities someone would need to live comfortably. She wondered if Joshua lived in a place like this.

Suzanne wasn't gone long and when she returned, she had an escort. It was Mickey. He had the breakfast tray and placed it beside the bed. He handed Stacey the breakfast sandwich.

Stacey took a bite. It was delicious. "Thank you," She mumbled with a full mouth. "Can you pass me a hash brown. I'm starving."

Mickey took a seat. "I apologize for everything you've been through since you arrived. I'm hoping we have a solution you will both agree to."

Fed and no longer pregnant, Stacey was back to her impatient self. "What does my mother want?"

Mickey looked at them. He knew what he was about to tell them wasn't up for debate. "We want you to come work for us."

The shock on their faces indicated that neither saw that coming.

"Carol will explain the details, but if you agree you can go home and see your boys on a regular basis."

Stacey shook her head. "It can't be that simple. My mother will never let us go knowing what we know."

"But she will."

"How does she know I won't go to Sergeant Smith?"

"I have some bad news about Sergeant Smith," Mickey told them. "He got into a fight with a homeless guy on the ferry and he fell overboard. He's presumed to be dead."

Suzanne remembered the helicopter.

Stacey didn't believe him. "He was a big man. He was tough."

"If he was caught off guard, it wouldn't be that hard," Mickey countered. "They're saying it was a murder-suicide."

Stacey screamed, forgetting about Emma. "Don't lie to us to protect her. My mother had him killed."

Suzanne picked up Emma. "Tell Carol that she has a deal."

ONE HUNDRED & 66

Mickey left them to think things over. He'd let Suzanne settle Stacey down and think about his offer. They never asked what they'd be doing and that was good. He had no idea what Carol had in mind for them.

Carol was on the phone discussing campaign issues with David when Mickey showed up at her door. She waved him in. Mickey grabbed a water and waited patiently for her call to end.

Carol hung up. "How'd it go? Did Stacey resist?"

"Just like you said she would," Mickey nodded, "but she'll come around."

"Did they ask what they'd be doing?"

Mickey shook his head. "Stacey was too busy being angry at you. But I'm sure they're discussing it now."

"I'll give them the news," Carol changed subjects. "We have another concern."

"What?"

"They found a body washed up on the beach about a mile from here."

"Is it alive?" Mickey asked carefully.

"I'm told it is, but just barely."

"Is it Smith or Bjorn?"

ONE HUNDRED & 67

President Daniel Tucker enjoyed a French cognac with a cigar while he stood stoically on the porch of his cabin in the San Juan Mountains in Colorado. It was as though he was posing for a photographer, except there was no camera. He basked in his own power and admired the beauty of the sheer rockfaces that were defined by the lines of Aspen trees now in full bloom. It was some beautiful country.

The twelve-thousand acres of land had been in the Tucker family for almost a hundred years. This was where he came to get away from Washington. He chose it over Camp David.

Other than his secret service team wandering the vast property, he was alone on the porch. He had taken a few days to get away from the hectic pace before he visited China.

He had a few calls he had to make before he retired for the night. There was a tall blonde with endless legs waiting in his bedroom. He signalled a man named Nigel over. The tall black man wore a spotless white server jacket that was common in the south decades earlier.

"Yes, sir?"

"Freshen up my drink and bring me a secured phone," he demanded without even looking at the man. "And make it quick. I have a guest waiting."

Nigel wasn't sure if the president even knew his name. "Is there anything else that you require?"

Tucker handed him the glass. "Did I ask for anything else?"

Nigel returned with a fresh drink and a bowl of cashews that he knew were the president's favourite. Without acknowledging the extra gesture, the president grabbed the phone and waved Nigel away without so much as a thank you.

The first call was one he didn't want to make, but it was necessary because it was his wife. She was off on her little escapade to Hawaii with some friends he was glad he would never have to meet. When she answered the phone, her impaired tone immediately soured his mood. "What are you up to?"

Michelle despised her husband as much as he despised her, and their marriage was a contract of convenience. She negotiated a personal service agreement where she was required to be the perfect first lady when they were in public, and to use extreme discretion when they were not. She could do as she pleased if it didn't embarrass the oval office.

She knew he didn't care what she was doing. "I'm sitting here sipping on a mojito watching the waves roll in on a private beach that you're paying for."

Too bad your dead body wasn't rolling in the waves, is what he wanted to say. "That's good to hear, honey. I'm glad you're enjoying yourself. I called to remind you that we're flying to Canada, so you need to be in Washington for July 1st."

"I don't like Canada," she used her whiny voice to agitate him even more, "and the prime minister is a bigger pig than you."

Tucker was already bored. "What would you like to make the trip more bearable?"

"Better booze," she stated bluntly. "The vodka they served when I attended a dinner was not to my standards. And can you have them put me in a different hotel? I want to bring a friend."

Perfect. He planned on entertaining a friend as well. "Anything else?"

She loved to infuriate him. Rubbing him the wrong way had

become her life's work and she was good at it. "I have to go. My friend is massaging my shoulders and I need to concentrate. Thanks for the call."

He gulped his brandy and let the liquor burn down his throat. "You also have to be available…"

Michelle Tucker interrupted her husband. She was as bored as he was. "Why don't you just have your people contact my people like they're suppose to? Then you and I can meet in the middle? How about that?"

Tucker ended the call. He was furious at how easily Michelle could upset him. He let out his anger by whipping the phone into the bushes. The secret service heard the commotion and came running with their weapons drawn. When they realized he was just having another temper tantrum, they stood down.

Nigel ran from the kitchen and stopped at the end of the patio. "Are you okay, sir?"

"Just go get it!" Tucker yelled at him. "It's in the bushes over there."

Nigel wasn't sure what the president was referring to and was scared to ask. "What am I looking for, sir?"

"The damn phone," he snapped impatiently. "It slipped out of my hand."

"*It slipped* way over there?" Nigel knew he would be reprimanded for asking such a stupid question. "I'll go get it."

Tucker grabbed a handful of cashews while he waited for the phone. The clouds rolled over the mountain and it would only be minutes before the rain would start. "Have you found the phone yet?"

Nigel handed it to him and quickly disappeared.

Tucker had one last call to make. His wife wasn't the only one going to enjoy Ottawa. He lit his Cuban and took short quick puffs to get the embers glowing before he placed it in an ashtray. He punched in an access code that put him directly through to Prime Minister Elliot.

Pierre answered the call reluctantly. "Hello, Mr. President. How are you tonight?"

Tucker wanted to be quick. Upstairs was waiting. "I want to check on my special request."

"There has been a slight change."

"I don't like changes," snapped Tucker, "unless I make them."

Pierre despised the man's arrogance. "It is something out of my control, but I think you'll like the solution."

"What is it?"

"Cherie is away," Elliot wasn't comfortable with the topic, knowing the call was being monitored, "but her replacement will delight you."

"Is she a free spirit like the Beliveau girl?" A snapshot appeared on his phone. "Who the hell is this gorgeous creature?"

Elliot could hear Tucker panting, "She's requested that she bring a friend."

"She has a friend?" Tucker was fantasizing. "What's her friend look like?"

"She's a dark-haired version," Elliot felt like a pimp. "You'll love her too."

"You stay away from them," Tucker ordered. "I'll show these two girls a real good time."

Elliot had heard enough. "Is there anything else you need?"

"Yes, I want an update on Nanoose Bay," he reminded Elliot. "Where are we at with acquiring access to the naval base?"

"I'm working on it," Pierre lied. "It will take time."

"Make it happen," Tucker wasn't going to drop the topic. "It's a strategic counter to the North Koreans in the Pacific and I want my navy there."

Pierre was ready to hang up. "Like I said, I'm working on it."

"Work harder," pushed Tucker. "Based on the polls, you're not going to be the prime minister for much longer."

"The election's not over yet," Pierre snapped back, but without a lot of energy. He knew Tucker might be right.

ONE HUNDRED & 68

Suzanne steered Stacey's car into the driveway and when she turned it off, she realized they hadn't spoken since they left the ferry. They were both still in shock that Carol released them without any drastic conditions. There was something they didn't know.

Once Emma was fed and settled in her bassinette, Stacey turned on her computer and googled Sergeant Smith. It was true. "Oh my god! Some derelict attacked him on the ferry after an argument over a joint. They were both were presumed drowned."

Stacey shook in her chair and she couldn't stop. Tears dripped from her eyes and the guilt was unbearable. The sergeant had died trying to help her. She didn't think she had it in her to grieve anymore. Another man in her life was gone.

Suzanne stood behind her. "Has any of this sunk in yet?"

"I don't think it ever will," Stacey muttered. "It's been a crazy couple of days."

"Yes, it has. I can't believe your mother. I'm not sure if she's a genius like our kids or a wacko."

Stacey tried to laugh through her tears.

It was Suzanne's turn to get emotional. "We found our boys alive and that's a miracle."

"But Sergeant Smith is dead," Stacey moaned. "When does this all end?"

"I think we'll find out soon," Suzanne suggested, "because I don't think it will take long to find out what she wants from us."

Stacey agreed. "Should we go to the police?"

Suzanne shook her head. "I think we hear what Carol wants and

480

decide from there. For now, I'm going to tow the line so I can see Curtis. Remember Murphy was a cop and he worked for her. So, who can we trust?"

"Let's make some tea," Stacey suggested, "and see if we can come up with a plan."

"If it gets me close to Curtis, I'd consider almost anything. But we need to be careful. We both know your mom is a psychopath."

Stacey didn't disagree with her description. "I wonder when we'll find out what our new jobs are."

The back door swung open and a cool breeze whipped through the kitchen. The surprise startled them. They both looked at the door and before either could get up and close it, she stepped inside.

"What are you doing here?" Stacey asked.

Carol saw the kettle boiling. "Let's make some tea and talk."

ONE HUNDRED & 69

David was a few weeks into the campaign, and he sat at a desk in Vancouver. He was going at a hectic pace. His days were long, and his travel schedule was hectic. He never stayed in a city long enough to get comfortable. He would attend a rally or do a speech and then he was back into the motorhome and onto the next one. It was grueling.

Nina made a surprise visit and caught him rubbing his eyes. "You look exhausted. Do you want to go for a coffee?"

David knew he could use the break. "I'll even buy."

They snuck out the back door of the building like two delinquent teenagers. The Federal Coalition office was only a few blocks from English Bay, a popular beach waterfront where the tourists and locals liked to hang out.

Nina said. "Let's go to that coffee house near the beach. They make a great slice of banana bread and I'm hungry."

When they walked in, they were greeted by a friendly barista and the smell of fresh coffee beans. Nina excused herself to find the washroom and David stepped up to the counter.

While he waited for his order, he checked his messages. There was another one from Cindy Austin, with an explicit picture attached. He wanted to delete it but couldn't. They had spent some alone time in his office and things got out of hand when she climbed up on his desk. He couldn't resist her, and it was becoming a problem.

Nina joined him at a table and glanced out the window. The street was full of people heading to the water. She turned back to her husband. "Do you still think becoming the next prime minister is a good idea?"

David looked at her. "A better question is, do you still think it is?"

"I do," Nina didn't want to admit she was having doubts. She took a piece of the muffin, "but I do miss the privacy we had. I can feel people staring at us."

"We knew this was coming," he reminded her. And then his phone rang. He hoped it wasn't Cindy. He looked at the display. "I don't believe it."

"Who is it?"

He showed her the screen. "It's the White House."

"Why would President Tucker be calling you?"

"No idea. Should I decline it?"

"Just answer it." She responded impatiently.

He turned away from the table beside him and kept his voice down. "This is David Magill."

A female with a strong southern drawl was on the line. "I'm just confirming your identity, sir. Can you confirm you are Mr. David Magill, leader of the Federal Coalition party?"

He smiled into the phone. "Guilty."

"Can you please wait for the president?"

David smirked, realizing the President of the United States was calling him.

Tucker's voice was instantly recognizable. "Hello, Mr. Magill?"

David tried to steady his nerves. "This is a great honour."

"I bet it is, son." Tucker didn't even consider his statement egotistical. "I appreciate you taking my call."

"I'm with my wife enjoying a coffee."

President Tucker wasted no time with small talk. "Are you aware I'll be in Ottawa for your Canada Day celebrations?"

David sounded apologetic. "I wasn't. Can I do something for

you?"

"I want you to be available," Tucker ordered, treating Magill like he was a staff member. "We will need to talk."

"Can I ask about what?"

"Not on this phone."

David knew that Carol would object strenuously to the two men talking about anything. She despised Tucker. "I'm sure we can work something out."

"Good." Tucker sounded satisfied and ended the call.

One of Nina's assignments was to keep her husband focused. "You'll need to be careful around that man. If he's calling you, then you have something he wants."

"I understand that, so let's talk about something else."

Nina was happy to change the topic. "What's your schedule this afternoon?"

"Working on my speech, making some calls and then I have a short interview with Cindy," David told her. "Otherwise, I'm hoping to have an early finish today."

"Cindy seems to be around you a lot," Nina sounded irritated. "Why did they pick her?"

David rolled his eyes. "What's your problem?"

"I don't know," Nina lied. She knew exactly why, "but something doesn't seem right."

"Whenever I'm around her, you seem to get jealous," David wondered if his wife was suspicious. "She's just a reporter."

Nina laughed, but it sounded uncomfortable. "I know I'm over-reacting. Maybe I should invite her to coffee and get to know her. What do you think?"

He didn't think it was a good idea. "We should head back."

David's phone rang again. He recognized the number and answered it. "Hello, Hugh."

"Do you have a minute?" Hugh expected a yes.

"I have five minutes before I'm needed in a meeting," He winked at his wife. "What can I do for you?"

"I've reached out to my North Korean project manager."

"And?"

"He'll make it work. He needs to meet with the Chang girl to build an employment profile. We'll need to get North Korean approval."

"I'm sure you can make that work."

David hung up and before he could put the phone away, he got another message, with another photo.

Nina pulled on his arm. "Let's get you back."

ONE HUNDRED & 70

The conversations on local radio talk shows were a heated debate about the arrival of President Daniel Tucker coming to Ottawa. It seemed like everyone had an opinion of the man. There was a lot of hatred and distrust towards the president, but there was a section of the population that supported the man.

President Tucker had quickly become one of the most despised world leaders in his short term in power. The constant threats against his life were a security nightmare for the secret service. Even though his visit was still a few days away, the streets around Parliament Hill were already barricaded. There was a heavy police presence watching for anything that might pose as a threat.

The Royale Grande Hotel would host President Tucker and his travelling entourage. With the added workload, General Manager Singh had neglected many of his regular duties. That included staying on top of his messages. There was one that required his immediate attention. It was from Agent MacKay's office.

Singh finally found some time to have some lunch and grabbed a table. He took a seat to keep an eye on the lobby. While he gave the server his order, he saw a stranger in the lobby wearing a housekeeping uniform. It was a young woman and she loaded a laundry cart onto the service elevator. He made a mental note to introduce himself after lunch. A minute later he was distracted by some excellent clam chowder.

The housekeeper arrived on the fortieth floor and she was careful to keep her head down. She was prewarned about the cameras. She entered the Presidential suite and headed into the bathroom with a drill she had hidden in the cart. After cleaning up the sawdust she was back on the elevator.

On her way out the back door, she dumped her uniform into a laundry bin before hopping into a taxi.

Singh saw Agent MacKay's message. He responded with a short response. *'Everything is good and the top three floors are secured as requested.'*

ONE HUNDRED & 71

Joshua and Curtis shared a table in the cafeteria. They picked at a plate of nachos, while they waited for Jonny. Curtis grabbed a chip with only cheese, while Joshua found one loaded with jalapenos and black olive chunks. He scooped up some sour cream and shoved it into his mouth.

Curtis finally brought it up. "So, where are you at seeing your mom? For me it was kind of awkward. It's been three years since I left, and I felt guilty."

Joshua wiped the sour cream off his face. "I thought I would feel bad, but I didn't. I mean, I do miss her, but she has a new baby, so it looks like she's moved on."

Curtis grabbed another chip. "You have to wonder why Carol even let them see us?"

"We both know Carol must have a plan. Carol hates my mom, so she must need something from her."

Jonny slid into the booth and helped himself to a scoop of nachos. "I'm starving."

"You're always hungry," laughed Curtis, "and I can't remember the last time I saw you without smelling pepperoni pizza."

Jonny ignored him. "What's up with Mickey calling a meeting?"

Curtis shook his head. "No idea. Is Cassie coming?"

Jonny didn't mention North Korea. He had promised her not to say anything. "I haven't seen her lately, so I have no idea."

With Jonny's help, the nachos disappeared, and Curtis checked the time. "We should get going. Mickey will be waiting."

Mickey was watching a video when the boys entered, and he

pointed to three chairs he had setup in the middle of the room. His demeanour was quieter than the boys were used too. "Take a seat. We need to talk."

Curtis scratched an itch on his forehead. "Is Cassie coming?"

"She's on assignment off the island."

"When is she coming back?"

"I can tell you that she's doing what she loves."

The boys all knew what that meant, and Jonny cracked a thin smile. "So, why are we here?"

"The organization is moving forward, and we need to prepare for the future. And that means changes."

Jonny was scared to ask. "What changes?"

Mickey looked straight at him. "You're being transferred. We have a new project we need you to work on."

The disappointment was etched on Jonny's face. "Where am I going?"

"You'll be joining Cassie to help with her assignment, and then your off to Europe."

The disappointment was replaced with excitement. He was going to be with Cassie. "Can you tell me what I'll be working on?"

"You'll be making fireworks"

"Seriously? You know you can buy them at the store"

Mickey smiled. "You'll be making some very specific ones."

Jonny tried to understand the connection between food and fireworks.

Joshua figured it out. "That's how you're going to distribute the food particles without anyone knowing."

Mickey nodded. "Bingo!"

"When do I leave?"

"I need you to go pack your things. You're leaving tonight."

ONE HUNDRED & 72

Without waiting for an invite, Carol strolled in and made herself a cup of tea. She was familiar with the kitchen and grabbed a box of shortbread cookies from the pantry. She took a seat at the table, and from her perspective, this was just an ordinary get together. She knew the other two would be hostile if given the chance.

Finally, Stacey spoke up. "What are you doing here?"

Carol blew at her tea. "I thought I'd drop by and continue our conversation. I've had time to think and I know what I want from you two."

Stacey was ready to be confrontational. "You can't just barge into my house whenever it suits you!"

"Stop whining like a child," Carol grabbed a cookie from the box. "You two came looking for this and had no problem breaking into my place. So now we solve it."

The tension inside the kitchen was thick, and tempers were on edge. Suzanne tried to ease the pressure by pouring two cups of tea and taking the questions in a different direction. "You need to understand it's been a crazy two days and we're exhausted. We're trying to understand everything we witnessed."

"I understand it's a lot to digest, but you need to move forward," Carol stressed, "and I'm willing to consider a compromise if you agree to my terms. You can be more involved with your boys and even see them on a regular basis."

Stacey nearly spilt her tea she was so frustrated. "Why do you think you have all the power here? I'm not letting you control when I see Joshua!"

Carol showed no signs of backing down. "You'll do as I tell you or I'll make sure you never see the boys again. And if you consider talking about what you saw on the island, I'll make another decision."

Carol scared Suzanne. She knew this lady would hurt them without blinking an eye. "Are we in danger."

Carol sipped her tea. "Stop with the self pity. I'm giving you an opportunity to be involved in something meaningful."

"But?"

"But you put my organization in a precarious spot," Carol leaned forward, "and now we have decisions to make."

Stacey re-engaged her mother. "What decisions are you referring to?"

"Whether you'll stay quiet and work with us."

"There seems like there is only one choice worth considering," Suzanne decided. "What is it you want from us?"

Carol cradled her cup. "Why do you think I built the complex?"

Stacey didn't mask her sarcasm. "To impress us?"

"It's like I drove in the wrong lane of life when it comes to you."

"I'm not about to just agree with what you want. Why don't you tell me why you're really here?"

"Did you enjoy seeing your boys?"

Suzanne knew that the conversation was becoming a battle between the two, and their act was getting tiresome. "How long do you plan on keeping our boys?"

"As long as we need them," Carol took another nibble of her cookie, "and are you sure they even want to leave?"

Carol had hit a sensitive spot with Suzanne. "I'm sure Curtis would love to come home if you let him."

"I wouldn't be so sure. But let's get past that point. We all want them to be happy, so let's work on a deal."

"I'm confused," Stacey began, "why do you need to make a deal? You seem to have everything you need, so what can we offer?"

"You're right. I do have everything I need, but then I came up with an idea that solves a long-term issue."

Suzanne asked Carol. "And how do we solve that? I'm not sure what I could do to help you."

"Let's start with what you're both good at."

Stacey glanced at Suzanne. "What does that mean?"

They were interrupted by Emma, who was crying in the bedroom.

Before Stacey could go to her, Carol grabbed her arm and glanced back towards the bedroom. "That's what your both good at."

Stacey pulled her arm free. "Are you saying what I think you are?"

Carol responded calmly. "You both have proven you breed brilliant children and I need more."

"You are crazy!" screamed Stacey.

Carol finished her cookie. "Why don't you think about it, I'm going to see my granddaughter."

ONE HUNDRED & 73

Laura relaxed on her patio, sipping on a glass of wine while she listened to some blues on her headset. She was flying to Ottawa in a few hours, and for the first time since the fiasco in Washington, she felt comfortable where she stood with Mickey and the organization.

She still had no update on Presley since he entered Canada. The big man knew he had a target on his back and was laying low. She was confident he'd eventually surface and when he did, she would be ready.

Laura still hadn't received the final details for her assignment or who the target was. Everything was hush hush. This job was special on many levels and she was excited to know she would be working with her best friend.

When she heard Ray was coming along, she couldn't stop thinking about there conversation over lunch. Was Tiffany really considering leaving? The idea that she might be worried Laura.

Her peaceful time ended when her phoned vibrated in her pocket. It was from a BLOCKED CALLER. "Hello?"

"Are you alone?" It was a deep male voice.

She answered cautiously. "Who is this?"

"It's the man you tried to kill, and we need to talk."

"Okay," Laura rushed to a wall safe in her bedroom. "Where are you?"

Wendell teased her. "I hoped we could finish what we started in Washington before we got interrupted."

"Don't fuck with me," she challenged. "What does that mean?"

"We have some unfinished business."

Laura grabbed her pistol out of her safe. It was loaded. "Yes, we do."

"Is there still a contract out on me?"

"I'm not the one to ask," Laura remembered her flight, "and I'm getting ready to leave. What do you want?"

"Are you heading to Ottawa?"

Laura hesitated. "How do you know where I'm going?"

"Remember, I was part of the organization until it blacklisted me," He reminded her. "I know a lot of things."

Laura wouldn't debate the organization's decisions. "I don't have much time. Do you want to meet?"

Wendell laughed sarcastically. "So, you can shoot me? I don't think so. I'll find you."

He hung up.

Laura called Mickey and gave him an update.

"I'm glad he resurfaced," Mickey told her. "That means he's ready to try something."

Laura looked at her pistol. "I want to kill him so bad."

"You'll get your chance."

ONE HUNDRED & 74

Hugh Hutchinson tried to take a much-needed day off. Since his New Year's Eve party, it had been non-stop, and it was catching up to him. He didn't need to step on a scale to know he had put on a few extra pounds. The complications that Pierre added to his life were about to end, but he knew they'd be replaced by new ones. Welcome to the life of the rich.

Hugh enjoyed walking along his property and often wondered why he didn't do it more often. He held his phone in his hand. It was a habit he'd probably never break. He felt a message arrive. It was from the prime minister and his first reaction was to ignore it. What did he want? Hugh had no obligation but gave in to curiosity.

"Hello, Mr. Prime Minister. What can I do for you?"

Pierre sounded panicky. "I need you in my office now."

Hugh felt his heart rate increase. "What do you want?"

"Just get here," Elliot ordered. "We need to talk."

Hugh considered refusing but knew it would be a bad decision. "Give me some time."

An hour later he waited in Pierre's home office. He couldn't stop himself from wondering why he was there. Maybe Pierre wanted to berate him for changing sides. It wouldn't matter. It was a done deal, and it was the right decision for Hutchinson Enterprises. Their partnership was over, and their friendship was likely on its last threads.

Hugh sat and debated his doctor's orders to back down from the booze. A drink would be good right now. He knew where Pierre's brandy was. His phone buzzed. "I don't believe it." He muttered out loud.

Pierre walked in. "What don't you believe?"

"The North Korean money was just transferred into my account."

Pierre undid his tie and tossed his jacket on the chair. "Let's have a drink to celebrate."

This wasn't the Pierre he was expecting. "Why are you in such a good mood."

Pierre poured them both a drink.

Hugh was curious. "So, what's going on?"

The prime minister handed Hugh a glass. "I saw your campaign supporting the Federal Coalition. Impressive."

Hugh tried to gauge Pierre's mood. "I must tell you that I didn't expect this kind of reaction. I thought you'd be pissed."

"I was at first," Pierre sipped his drink, "but then I realized it was time to think about my future. You and I played a dangerous game with the North Koreans. We took a big risk."

"We did, but it's over now."

"At an expensive price. I lost a good friend."

Hugh wasn't sure where Pierre was going with this conversation. "It was a tragic accident."

"That plane crash was no accident." Pierre countered, his voice getting cold.

Hugh tensed. "Do you know something I don't?"

"There is a report that will never be made public without my okay," Pierre spoke slowly and very deliberate, "and there is a page in that report that indicates you were involved with the North Koreans in bringing that plane down."

Hugh went into full denial mode. "That's a pile of crap."

"Even if it is, if that report is released your support behind the Federal Coalition will kill their campaign. Your name will be mud."

Hugh forgot about his doctor's advice and gulped down his

drink. "You son of a bitch."

Pierre sneered, knowing he had the billionaire cornered. Revenge for Hugh's desertion was sweet. "I want the entire North Korean payment deposited into my account. It will allow me to retire comfortably."

This wasn't over. Hugh still had the video.

Pierre wanted to hear him say it. "Do we have a deal?"

ONE HUNDRED & 75

The room in the ICU was a non-cheerful thin blue with aging curtains that failed to keep the sunlight out. The tired conditions reflected the state of a health care industry that was grossly underfunded.

Room 307 was at the end of the hall, and there was a young police officer stationed at the door. Because of the bed shortage, there were two patients assigned to the room. The first was a young man in his twenties who had been critically injured in a motorcycle crash. Much of his body was broken and it was going to be touch and go if he even made it through the day.

In the second bed was the man they found on the beach. He was still unconscious and was hooked up to a respirator to help him breathe. The doctors had done everything they could, and now it was up to him to pull through. The next few days were critical for his recovery.

Looking uncomfortable in an old wooden chair beside him, with her head resting on the corner of the bed, was his wife. The last two days had been a roller coaster of misery for Helen. When she answered the knock on the door and saw the two officers, she fell to her knees before they even said a word. And then six hours later she got a call that her husband was found on a beach, alive. But just barely.

Steve Smith had serious head trauma and had swallowed a lot of seawater. The police said that he was still clinging to a log when the fisherman found him. The fact that he was able to escape the undercurrent behind the ferry and hold on to the log was a miracle.

Helen knew it was his desire to be with her.

A female detective popped her head in. "Hello, are you Helen Smith?"

She lifted her head off the mattress and nodded.

"I'm Detective Iman. How's our sergeant doing?"

Helen sat up. Her lower back ached from the chair. "Nothing new yet, but he'll pull through."

"And how are you doing? Is there anything you need?"

Helen gripped an over used Kleenex and wiped her nose. "I'm okay."

"Everyone at the station is thinking about Steve," The detective put a gentle hand on Helen's shoulder. "Do you want a coffee or something to eat?"

Helen appreciated her kind offer. "No, I just want to sit here and wait until he wakes up."

"Can I arrange you a ride home? You can take a shower and change," she offered, "and I'll stay here and keep him company."

Helen resisted the idea. "I want to stay."

"They'll bring you right back," the detective assured her. "You've been here for almost two days. Fresh clothes and real food will help you. You need to keep up your strength."

Helen agreed a shower would be good. "You'll call if anything changes?"

The detective nodded. "I promise. I'll get a car to take you home."

Helen pulled her cramped body out of the chair. "What can you tell me about the man on the ferry?"

"Not much to tell so far," The detective couldn't comment on the case, but she knew the wife of the sergeant deserved to know something. "I heard he was a loner that lived on the island. No motive so far. It might just be a random act by an unstable man?"

Helen disagreed. "No, that's not what happened."

"What do you think?"

"It has something to do with those missing children," Helen insisted. "Steve got a text yesterday from one of the mothers on the island. They found something and he was going to meet them."

"Who is this mother?"

"Her name is Stacey Small. Her son disappeared back in November when John Woodlands School burnt down."

The detective nodded. "I know the case. It was hard on your husband. What do you think happened?"

"Someone knew he would be on that ferry. He was set up."

"I'll run the phone records to see what we find."

Helen grabbed her purse. "And remember…"

"I know," smiled the detective. "I'll call you immediately if anything changes with the sergeant."

Helen gave the detective an appreciative smile. "I'll be back in a couple hours."

"Take some time," Iman offered. "I'll stay with him."

Helen put her hand on Steve's cheek and bent over to kiss him on his chapped lips. "I love you, baby. Please stay strong for me."

There was a dry whisper. "Portugal."

Helen's eyes widen. She leaned closer to her husband's mouth. "What did you say?"

"Take me to Portugal."

ONE HUNDRED & 76

Mickey put Joshua through a vigorous workout, knowing it would be their last time inside the squared circle for awhile. Joshua loved his time in the gym, learning skills he never thought would interest him until he came to the complex and met Mickey.

Mickey was amazed at Joshua's brilliance from day one and never thought of him as a kid. He was a young genius, who was the organization's future. When a recruit was vetted and brought into the organization, it was because they possessed a specific skill that was needed at that stage of development. No one until Joshua had brought the entire package.

Mickey pointed to the changeroom. "You go get cleaned up. Carol is expecting us."

Mickey stayed in the ring and did some intense shadow boxing to keep his skills sharp. He had a feeling he was going to need them. Wendell Presley was stuck in his head. Presley wasn't coming for Laura Nelsen; he was coming for him. Mickey was certain of that. The call to Laura was a reminder that he was back.

He finished his workout and leaned over the top rope. His sweat dripped freely onto the cement floor. When his body was rested, he climbed out of the ring and headed to the shower.

Joshua zipped up his gym bag. "Thanks for the workout."

Mickey tossed his gym gear into the laundry bin. "Your skills get better every time you get in the ring."

Joshua loved hearing Mickey's approval. "Why are we meeting with my grand mother?"

"She wants to review things before we head to Ottawa. Let me take a quick shower and we can head over."

Mickey was quick and they headed down the long hallway from the gym to Carol's office. He put his arm around Joshua's shoulder, like a proud dad after a big win. "Can I ask you something?"

Joshua tensed. "Am I in trouble?"

Mickey chuckled. "Never, but I need to get your help on something."

Joshua's nerves were replaced with curiosity. "I'd do anything to help you."

"Good to know," Mickey pulled out a small box. It was the same one Laura had brought back from Washington. "I need you to take this information and program it into the first animatronic. And you can not tell anyone. This is the most important thing we've done so far."

Joshua stuffed it into his gym bag. "I won't disappoint you."

When they got to Carol's office, she wasn't there. Mickey decided to wait and grabbed two waters from the cooler. He handed one to Joshua. "So, do you want to be a boxer?"

"I don't think so," Joshua shrugged with uncertainty, "but I enjoy hanging out in the gym."

"Fair enough. You do have some talent, but the fight game is a very tough life."

Joshua drank some water. "When was your last fight? Was it the one on the freighter?"

Mickey rubbed the scar tissue above his eyes. "There have been more."

Joshua loved hearing Mickey's stories. "Have you ever lost?"

He remembered a few fights that went the distance, and he would never forget the fight on the island with the Golden Eagles. "I've never been beaten, but I've taken some good shots. Boxing isn't to be confused with the street fights I talk about. Bare-knuckle fighting is extremely dangerous."

"Why did you do it?"

"It was survival for me. I was an Indian and sometimes that was enough for the other guy. But I was lucky to be good at it. Every fight scared me and most times I didn't want to, but there were times when I had no choice."

Joshua was on the edge of his seat. "Did you ever hurt anyone badly?"

Mickey remembered Frank. "Yes."

"Do you regret it?"

"No," Mickey admitted freely. "Sometimes violence is needed."

"Why?"

"To counter greed or power," Mickey explained. "There are some bad people who use intimidation and violence to get what they want. Have you ever heard of the Mafia?"

Joshua shook his head but made a mental note to research them when he got back to his computer. "Who were they?"

"Back in the 1980s, the Italian Mafia controlled the construction industry in New York through violence and extortion. If you didn't follow their rules you could pay a severe price. Sometimes the price was your life."

Joshua couldn't wait to read more. "How does that influence what we do?"

Carol walked in and interrupted the conversation. "We'll get to that one day, but not today."

Carol took a seat and poured a tea that Mickey had waiting. "Sorry I'm late. My meeting across the water took a little longer than I anticipated."

Mickey nodded that he understood.

She looked at her grandson. "How was your punching match?"

"It's called sparring," Joshua corrected her, "and it was great. I almost knocked Mickey out."

Mickey chuckled. "The kid is getting good."

"Just what I need. Another tough guy," Carol was already disinterested and handed them each a folder. "We have a lot to cover."

Joshua read the contents in under a minute and waited patiently for Mickey to finish. It was twelve pages.

She looked at them. "Is everything a go with our human copycats?"

"There are four that are ready," Mickey confirmed. "Joshua is still testing the support software, but we're not expecting any surprises. He has the Washington package."

Carol nodded her approval and handed Joshua a photograph. "Your first project will be to create this person."

Joshua studied the picture. "Who is he?"

"His name is Agent Kellan MacKay," Carol told him. "He's with the United States Secret Service."

"The secret service," Joshua got excited. "How cool is this."

Mickey said. "That package in your gym bag has everything you'll need to duplicate Agent MacKay."

Joshua put the photo in his bag. "Why are we duplicating a secret service agent? Don't they protect the president?"

Carol shut down Joshua's curiosity. It didn't matter that he was her grandson. Curiosity get's people killed. "Your assignment is to build it. We'll take it from there."

Joshua understood. "Is there anything else?"

Carol's face lit up. "I almost forgot. Your mom is coming to work with us."

ONE HUNDRED & 77

Ray and Tiffany checked into the Marriot hotel in the downtown district of Ottawa. While Tiffany dealt with the front desk clerk, Ray was cognizant of the strong police presence on the streets. He felt a little paranoid in the company of police officers. It was a side effect from his time in prison that he couldn't shake.

The desk clerk confirmed their booking. "Thank you, Mrs. Harding. Enjoy your stay."

"So, I'm Mr. Harding now," Ray mumbled as he grabbed the bags, "it seems a little excessive."

Tiffany was preoccupied thinking about her assignment. She still didn't know much, other than she was attending a meeting in a few hours with Mickey. Ray wasn't grasping the seriousness of their trip, and it annoyed her.

When they got to their room there was a king-sized bed on one side and some furniture placed strategically to utilize the space. There was a television mounted across from the bed and a mini bar that Ray eyed in the corner.

He tossed the bags on the bed and opened the cooler. "Do you want a drink?"

Tiffany was irritated with everything going on. She didn't like it when she wasn't in control and not knowing her assignment was wearing on her nerves. "Leave the bar alone. You don't drink before an assignment."

"Speaking of that, any idea when I find out why I'm here?"

"When they are ready, I'm sure you'll be contacted," Tiffany told him, "so why don't you find some sports on the TV. I have to get ready for my meeting."

Ray took the hint and climbed onto the bed. "Will I meet Mickey?"

"Not likely."

"What's he like? Does he have a last name?"

"He's a gorgeous man who commands respect. And we all just call him Mickey."

"So, he only has one name, like Sting."

Tiffany tried to ignore him. "You're being a pain in the ass. I need to meet with Laura, so can you please shut up."

Ray got up and paced the room. "I want to know what this Mickey expects me to do. Will it be dangerous?"

Tiffany didn't look up from what she was doing. "Everything we do has an element of danger. Just relax."

Tiffany gathered up what she needed and put it into a travel bag. She gave Ray a kiss on the cheek and headed to the door. "I'm not sure when I'll be back, so don't wait on me for dinner. I love you."

Ray switched on the television and found a Senator's hockey game. He decided he could use a snack, so he grabbed a soda and a bag of nuts. He'd worry about dinner later. He settled in on the bed to watch the game. "So, this is the life of a spy. Pretty boring if you ask me."

With the Senator's leading at the end of the second period, Ray was happy to hear his phone buzz. He grabbed it and read the text.

'Meet me in the pub in the lobby at four and don't be late. Carol.'

"Who the hell is Carol?" he mumbled out loud. He looked at his watch and saw he had twelve minutes. After he checked his appearance in the bathroom mirror, he headed to the elevator. It was time to find out why he was in Ottawa.

The Longwood Lounge was attached to the hotel lobby. When he stood at the doorway, he realized he had no idea what Carol looked like, but before it became a concern, a hostess greeted him. She pointed to a table in the back of the room. "She's waiting for you."

Carol pointed to the seat across from her. "Sit. We don't have much time."

No introduction. No nice to meet you. This old lady was all business from the time he took as seat. A waitress came over, but Ray waved her off. He didn't think he would be staying long.

Carol started. "I called you here to tell you what I want."

"Will I have a choice?"

Carol smirked. "Not if you're smart and I'm told you are."

Her compliment made him uneasy. "So, what is it you want from me?"

"Some legal advice."

Ray sat up in his chair. She had his interest. "What do you need help with?"

"I want to make a company disappear from the books."

"I'm not sure that's possible." He responded cautiously.

Carol's face tensed. "I'm not asking."

Ray decided to play along. He still wasn't sure who this lady was that was across from him. "What's the name of the company and are you the only shareholder?"

"I am, and the name is Liberty City."

Ray's expression showed his surprise, and then his anger. "Are you serious?"

"Yes, Mr. Cooke, or should I say Harding. I'm the one who sent you to prison. David and Tiffany were doing what I told them."

Ray clenched his hands and wondered what to do now. "Why would you do that? You ruined my life."

"You were doing that all by yourself. I just helped you get to the finish line." She snapped without any pity. "Now, here's the deal I'll offer you. If you can make Liberty City go poof, I'll get you a partnership in any law firm in the country. Seven figure salary with lots of perks. Do we have a deal?"

He leaned back and took a moment. Did Tiffany know this was why he was in Ottawa? "Sounds too good to be true."

Carol looked satisfied. "I'll get you everything you need. And there's one last thing?"

"What's that?"

Carol finished her tea. "Remember the name, Craven Ravenwood."

"Why?"

"He'll become an important person in your life."

ONE HUNDRED & 78

Protestors from all over the country had gathered at the Ottawa International Airport in anticipation of United States President Daniel Tucker. The crowds got louder and more boisterous as the arrival time for Air Force One got closer.

There was a group of about one hundred hard core protestors that were hired by an independent group that focused on discrediting the president at every turn. They were bussed in with specific instructions to be violent and disruptive. Their first assignment was to block the Airport Parkway with a human chain to disrupt traffic.

When the crowds outgrew the estimations, and the threat of violence was apparent, the Premier of Ontario ordered the military to assist with crowd control and intervene with anything deemed illegal. Violence was inevitable because taking back the freeway was now an order.

Back at the airport a second group from the bus pushed their way through the crowds towards the fence guarding the tarmac. They were armed with pipes and other weapons meant to inflict damage.

An eight-foot chain link fence with cement pillars was all that prevented the protestors from accessing the tarmac. The police were aware of the risks and sent a riot squad to defend the area. The fence wouldn't offer much resistance if the crowd surged, so the tactical squad took a position between the runway and the crowd. Armed with rubber bullets, they were ready to shoot upon command.

Air space for three nautical miles surrounding Ottawa International was now shut down to commercial air traffic in anticipation of Air Force One's imminent arrival. The atmosphere around the airport terminal grew louder when the president's jet could be seen approaching in the distance. Most of the protestors stopped what they were doing to pull out their phones to take a picture. When two F-18 military jets did a pass over, their sonic boom deafened most of the protesters for a second or two.

There was a noticeable air of disappointment amongst the protestors when Air Force One landed on the far runway and taxied passed them without parking where it was originally planned. The captain in charge of the president's jet was ordered to steer his plane into a massive hanger. Once inside, the doors were closed and protected by military personnel. The hanger would be home to Air Force One until the president departed Ottawa.

No one in the crowd anticipated what happened next. The protestors against the fence backed off when forty trained infantry men pointed loaded rifles in their direction. It was a smart decision. Rubber bullets hitting the right spot on the body can do serious damage. A few in the crowd had the scars to prove it.

A large garage door on the north side of the hanger slid open and a Black Hawk helicopter taxied out. It was less than thirty-seconds before it was airborne and on its way to Ottawa.

The president looked down at the crowd. "What a bunch of idiots."

ONE HUNDRED & 79

The trip to Ottawa on a commercial airline was a new experience for Curtis and Joshua. Once they were buckled in, both settled in for the three-hour flight. Curtis switched on the TV and decided on a Fast and Furious movie. Joshua had brought some books to read.

When they landed in Ottawa, Mickey hurried the boys out to a waiting van. He wanted to avoid any facial recognition software. He knew that both of their faces would be in the data base. Once the luggage was loaded, they were off to their hotel.

"You guys get everything setup. I need you operational within an hour. And don't forget that Carol has invited you to dinner."

Mickey exited the room.

Joshua mustered up the courage to address something that had him worried. "You never told me why you needed to get to Level C."

Curtis kept unpacking. "I was wondering when you were going to ask. I have to be sure I can trust you."

"You know you can," Joshua felt betrayed. "I trusted you when we were in the garden."

"True enough," Curtis agreed. "I have a plan for my future, and I needed access to a secured area outside the complex and the only way was from Level C."

Joshua stopped what he was doing. "Why are you worried about your future?"

"You were there when Jonny was sent packing. He had no idea it was coming."

"He was sent on assignment." Joshua countered.

Curtis frowned. "Who wants to be in North Korea? They eat bats and dead cats. He'll have a hard time finding a pepperoni pizza."

"So, what has this got to do with you going to Level C?"

"I'm not sticking around long enough to be sent to some god forbidden place," Curtis complained. "I want more out of my life than stealing money. Your grandmother is using us."

Joshua said nothing, but he couldn't disagree.

"Look at our moms and how messed up they are because of us," Curtis was on the verge of tears, "and it's all our fault."

"Carol said our moms are coming to work for the organization."

Curtis huffed. "Doing what? Cleaning rooms? Working in the cafeteria?"

Joshua looked disappointed.

"To answer your question," Curtis continued. "I installed a secured router because I need an internet account that no one can monitor."

"My grandmother will lose her mind if she finds out," Joshua reminded him. "Why do you need it?"

"To access bank accounts that Carol doesn't know about. I setup my own account that I deposit money into."

Joshua was impressed that Curtis had the guts to do this. "How much have you got so far?"

"Enough to live on for a long time," Curtis whispered. "Just over twenty million."

"Why are you telling me this?"

Curtis grinned. "Because when I leave, I want you to come with me."

512

ONE HUNDRED & 80

The boys looked sharp dressed in collared shirts with ties and slacks courtesy of Carol. She wanted them to impress whoever was coming to dinner. They climbed into the back of a waiting taxi and said little. The driver had the address.

After a few minutes, Curtis got the driver's attention. "Can we drive by the Parliament buildings?"

The driver shook his head. "The U.S. President is in town, so Wellington Street is closed."

When Joshua overheard the driver, he started to connect some of the dots. The U.S. president was in town, and he remembered that he been ordered to create a secret service agent. The two had to be connected.

The taxi stopped in front of Stanley's House of Beef and the boys climbed out and stood on the curb. A short, pot bellied man wearing a blue sports jacket approached them. "I'm Wiggins and you must be the boys I'm looking for. Follow me."

The boys followed Wiggins into the restaurant, and both were overwhelmed by the smells and noise. The aroma of beef captivated Curtis. "I'm having the biggest steak they got."

"You can afford it." Joshua whispered sarcastically.

Curtis glared at Joshua. "Back down, buddy. That isn't funny."

Wiggins ignored the boys little spat. "Follow me. Your table is ready, and your guests are waiting."

Once they were at the table, Wiggins said goodbye and left them to enjoy their dinners. The boys took a seat. Across from them was Carol, and a well-dressed man in his fifties that looked familiar.

Carol did the introductions. "These are the two young men that work for me that we were discussing. The blonde one is Curtis and the other is Joshua. Boys, this is Hugh Hutchinson."

Hugh forced a smile. These two kids can't be the brain thrust for everything Carol told him. They should be playing video games. "Carol tells me you've both done amazing things."

Curtis looked at Carol. "What can we tell him?"

The comment got Hugh's attention.

Carol answered. "Whatever you want. Mr. Hutchinson and I have struck a deal to work together."

Curtis wrote some numbers on his napkin and slid them to Hutchinson.

"What's this?" Hugh looked bewildered. "Does this mean something?"

Curtis reached across the table and put a decimal after the first two digits and a hyphen in the second sequence of numbers. "They should mean everything to you. The first one is your personal bank balance and the second is your account number."

Hugh wasn't sure if he was impressed or angry? "How did you do this?"

Curtis didn't mention that he was monitoring the account, waiting for instructions to drain it. "The question you should be asking is how do I stop it."

Hugh glanced at Carol. "Impressive kid." He turned to Joshua. "What do you do?"

Carol smiled. He's building your replacement. "Tell him about your animatronic beings."

When Joshua finished describing his project, Hugh was astounded by what he heard, especially because it came from a twelve-year old. "You're telling me you can replace a human being?"

"Pretty much," Joshua looked at Carol. "Can we order?"

Hugh thought about how this would benefit Hutchinson Enterprises. The options were endless, starting with payroll savings and work efficiency. "I agree with the boys. Let's order some food."

Everyone enjoyed dinner and the conversations were less formal, but once dessert was served Hugh got down to business. "I'm convinced we can do some great things, Carol. Pass me the contracts and I'm ready to sign."

After the contacts had signatures, Carol ended the meeting and instructed the boys to head back to their hotel.

Hugh stood up. "I need to get going as well. It was nice meeting you boys. Maybe one day you can use your talents at Hutchinson Enterprises."

Curtis smiled. You have no idea what my talents are. "Thank you. I'd like that."

The boys climbed into the waiting taxi, but before they pulled out Curtis told the driver to wait. He just got a text from Carol.

'Drain his accounts now. I have everything we need.'

Hutchinson left the restaurant and walked through the parking lot. Curtis intercepted him. "Excuse me, sir."

He was in a hurry and looked annoyed. "What's up?"

"Can I ask a favour?"

"That depends," Hugh kept moving towards his car. "What is it."

Curtis pulled out a fifty-dollar bill. "Can I ask you to invest this for me? Into one of your companies."

Hugh looked puzzled. "Why would I do that?"

"My mom would be very proud knowing I was doing business with someone like you."

Hugh took the fifty and examined it. "Sure, kid, I'll invest it for you."

"Thank you, sir." Curtis pretended to be appreciative. "I can't

515

wait to tell her I met you."

When Curtis jumped into the back seat, Joshua couldn't ignore his smirk. "You look like you won the lottery."

"That arrogant piece of crap is why I love my job." Curtis grinned. "I'm about to have some fun."

ONE HUNDRED & 81

A black Silverado pickup truck with a reinforced steel bumper pulled into the parking lot of the Holiday Inn in Kanata, which is twenty minutes southwest of Ottawa. Wendell Presley grabbed his duffle bag from the back of the truck and headed into the lobby. The entire time he was alert to the activity around him. Mickey knew he was back in the country and would have people tracking him down.

When he got into his room, he slid the chain lock in, knowing it would put up no resistance if someone really wanted inside. His plan for the rest of the night was simple. Take a shower and order in some dinner. It had been a long day on the road and tomorrow was going to be busy. It was retribution time.

He ordered a large meat lover pizza with some spicy wings and bribed the delivery driver with an extra twenty bucks to pick him up some beer and a bottle of tequila.

Thirty minutes later he was showered and eating a slice of pizza. A cold beer washed it down. The television broadcasted the news and Presley watched the story about the protests at the airport. "People are clowns. Did they really think they'd get close to the president?"

The next story kept his attention. He put his pizza down and turned up the volume. It was Cindy Austin doing an interview with David Magill. When it was over, he cracked open another beer. "Carol was right. Magill will be the next prime minister."

The tequila tasted good and before he knew it, he had drunk half the bottle. Add in four beer and he was not thinking straight. He was about to deviate from his plan and make a mistake.

He grabbed his phone and dialed her number. "Answer sweet

Laura. We need to talk," His voice was slurred, "and don't worry baby. I'm coming for you."

ONE HUNDRED & 82

After an enjoyable dinner with Carol and the two boys, Hugh decided he deserved some adult time and drove to Rascals nightclub. It was another business he had his fingers in, but the dividend check was not his sole motivation. This place came with benefits he didn't declare on his taxes.

This was the place he brought Cherie Beliveau after a fundraiser dinner. That was before she hooked up with Pierre. When he remembered how that relationship worked out, he could only write it off as a costly mistake. He did wonder from time to time where the hooker to the rich and powerful was hanging out these days.

Even with the Beliveau memory, he was in a great mood. What those kids talked about over dinner had him fascinated. The younger of the two was a prodigy with technology like Mozart was with music. What he described was years ahead of anything being developed or even considered in research labs and it would require billions in investment. Hugh was going to keep an eye on Joshua Small.

Hutchinson Enterprises had sent an advance team to North Korea to work with Eon Kamahi on locating warehouse space. He promised the diplomat that as a show of appreciation his company would supply fireworks for nightly celebrations. Kamahi accepted the idea as a nice gesture and got approval from his commander.

The last piece was to get Cassie and Jonny into North Korea. They were registered as interpreters. It ended up being as easy as making a generous money transfer into a Kamahi bank account. Now it was Carol's turn to start throwing favours his way.

Hugh parked his black Jaguar XE in his private stall and entered the club through a side door. He could feel the eyes of curious men and women watching him move through the room. There were times when the attention annoyed him, and there were times when he enjoyed the celebrity admiration. Tonight, it was the latter. He was ready to party.

He took a seat at a private table where a double Macallan and a bowl of exotic nuts was waiting. Before he could sip his scotch, he was joined by the club manager. Pinder was dressed a flashy sports jacket and white pants that looked to be a size too small. Red leather shoes finished the outfit.

"How are you doing, Boss?" Pinder asked.

"How's my investment doing?"

Pinder smiled. "Enjoy your drink. We can talk money another time."

Hip hop music was playing, and the dance floor was packed with mostly young people twisting their body parts in every direction. "Is my room setup?"

Pinder nodded. "Whenever you're ready."

"Good." Hugh looked at the group of women lingering near by waiting for an invite. "Send the ginger over. I feel like some spice in my life."

The filthy rich, which Hutchinson was a member, lived their lives like most people can't even imagine. For Hutchinson to invest his money and use his influence to keep the liquor board at bay, he had some special requests. One was that a private room would be attached to the club. It was his room and to be used by no one else. A bedroom with some added luxuries such as a stocked bar, sound system and hot tub. And there was a separate exit to avoid the crowds when he was ready to leave.

The idea behind the room was to allow Hutchinson to enjoy

some female companionship without all the baggage you dealt with after having sex. The awkward conversations, or do you have an extra toothbrush were situations he hated to be involved in. When he was satisfied, he sent them back into the club to have a couple free drinks while he disappeared out the back door.

The tall ginger wore a black satin mini dress with a cowl neckline that clung to her curvy body. She was easy on the eyes and apparently not shy. She slid in beside Hugh. "Thanks for inviting me over."

"And what is your name?"

"I call myself Red," she giggled. It was obvious that she'd been at the club for awhile, "and everyone in here knows who you are. I feel kind of special."

You should, is what he almost said. Her dress creeped up her thigh and he resisted putting his hand on it. "Now that's original."

Hugh waited until their drinks were empty before making his move. "I have a private room that would be more comfortable than being out here in this loud music. Do you want to head back?"

"I've heard about it," She leaned over and kissed him on the cheek as she put her hand on his crotch. "and I've always wanted to see it."

They stood up and Hugh put his arm around her waist as they made their way through the crowd. As they walked, his hand slid down and he rubbed her ass through the thin material. This crazy red head wasn't wearing any underwear.

Hugh poured them both a drink and turned on some mood music to match the soft lights. He handed Red her martini. "Let's take a seat on the couch."

Red had a better idea. "Why not on the edge of the bed."

Hugh took her up on the offer and it didn't take long before their tongues were entangled like a couple of teenagers at a movie.

After a few minutes of heavy kissing and adventurous hands, Hugh suggested they move onto the bed and get undressed.

Red was already pulling her dress over her shoulders when her opportunity appeared. Hugh climbed off the bed. "I need to take a piss. I'll be right back."

She pulled her dress back on her body, and once she was certain the billionaire was busy relieving himself, she opened the back door. There were two large men wearing ski masks waiting. Red didn't wait around to say goodbye. Her job was over.

When Hugh stepped out of the bathroom, he had no chance to defend himself against the two bigger men. They had the element of surprise and before he realized what was going on, he was gagged, and a needle was stuck into his neck. The medication knocked him out cold within a few seconds.

They loaded Hugh's limp body into a van parked in the back of the building. Before they left, the man with a snake tattooed on his neck left an envelope with $5000 in cash for Pinder on the bar.

Hugh's phone was buried and undetected under the pile of pillows on the bed. It was lighting up like a Christmas tree. He was getting an alert from his bank about some suspicious activity with his accounts.

ONE HUNDRED & 83

President Tucker's helicopter delivered him to the Parliament buildings. He was there to meet with the prime minister. There was another small, but just as boisterous crowd of protestors on Parliament Hill. The Parliamentary Protective Services was a branch of the police force designated to keep the parliament buildings and the members of government safe, and they had their hands full.

Tucker was escorted to Prime Minister Elliot's office. When the two world leaders were left alone, Tucker's brash personality kicked in. "Do you have anything good to sip on in this office?"

Pierre wasn't looking forward to this meeting. "I have some brandy."

Tucker popped himself down on a chair. "Well, get it out and let's celebrate our agreement."

Pierre grabbed the bottle he hid in the cabinet. "What agreement?"

Tucker sighed, showing his impatience. "The one that gives me control of Nanoose Bay. I came for your little celebration because I assumed it's done."

Pierre poured a bigger drink for himself. "I told you on the phone that my cabinet wouldn't support it."

"Are you shitting me!" Tucker was a man used to getting what he wanted. "You need to get this done. We both know the North Koreans are out of control with their nuclear weapons program. We can't trust that cheeseburger loving doughboy."

"We won't just hand over our naval base," Pierre remembered his agreement with the North Koreans. "Even if it's abandoned. There are protocols we need to follow."

Tucker stood up and wandered behind the prime minister's desk. He ran his fingers over the wooden piece of furniture. "How come your desk is so small? The one in the Oval office is so much bigger. And more impressive."

"I know you have a point, so what is it?"

Tucker mocked Elliot. "My point is your desk is like your balls. They're small."

Pierre bit his tongue. "Get out from there!"

Tucker continued to mock the prime minister. "Are you going to prove me wrong?"

Pierre pushed his way past the president to reclaim his seat. "What exactly do you want?"

Tucker sensed Elliot's hesitance. "I knew you wouldn't come through, so I made a deal with your successor."

"Who's my successor?"

"David Magill is a smart man. He sees the advantages of having me as a friend," Tucker finished his drink. "He understands politics and why my military support is important to Canada."

Pierre wondered if Magill had agreed to Tucker's demand.

Tucker helped himself to another drink. "You need to get your head out of your ass. The Russians and North Koreans are coming, and you better pay attention to the Middle East."

Pierre scrambled for an answer. "Wars aren't fought with armies anymore."

"Let's change the subject because I don't have much time."

"Let me guess. You want to talk about women?"

Tucker grinned like a greedy child. "Is everything ready to go?"

"I'm not a pimp, but I'm told they are." Pierre sounded jealous.

Tucker headed to the door that was surrounded by secret service agents. He turned to look at Pierre. "Do yourself a favour and make Nanoose Bay happen."

ONE HUNDRED & 84

Mickey climbed into a rental car and with the help of the dashboard GPS, he steered his way out of downtown and into the suburb of Old Ottawa South. The house he found was a red brick two story structure covered in climbing green ivy and white trim. A tall poplar tree shaded the small front yard.

Mickey greeted Vladimir on the front porch with a firm handshake. The two men first encountered each other on Gabriola Island, and it wasn't a friendly first meeting. It was twenty-six years earlier. Vladimir was a Golden Eagle gang member that arrived on the island to steal the hippie's pot plants. He was fight number two.

Years later their paths crossed again in a south end pub. After a cautious re-introduction, both men agreed to leave the past where it belonged. They played some pool and over the years Vladimir became a specialized contractor for the organization. That's why he was in Ottawa.

Vladimir, or V, took Mickey inside and closed the door. "How's that dragonfly kid?"

"He's good," Mickey said, "and he's heading out of the country."

Mickey followed Vladimir into the kitchen, and other than a small table with two laptops and a single folding chair, there wasn't anything else in the room. "You travel light."

V laughed at Mickey's joke, more out of courtesy than humor. "Let me show you my set up."

Mickey agreed with Vladimir's simple approach. Once the assignment was over, he'd pack up and disappear. "Is everything ready for tomorrow?"

Vladimir took his seat and Mickey stood behind him. V typed in a sequence of commands and the two monitors lit up. "We're good."

Mickey leaned closer. "What am I looking at?"

Vladimir pointed to the first monitor. "This is the view inside the Presidential suite. Remember, you're looking through the eyes of the flies. We have two positioned in spots where they won't be detected."

Mickey liked what he saw. "And, what about the dragonfly? Is it loaded?"

"Yes, it is," Vladimir confirmed, "and it's on the roof of the RBC bank across the street. I'll move it into position when we're ready."

"The entry through the bathroom is okay?"

"Absolutely, my friend. We've tested it. Everything is good."

"The girls will arrive at eight and Tucker should arrive thirty-minutes later," Mickey outlined. "The women are briefed on everything. Your job is to make sure we have eyes in the room."

"How are these girls going to be safe?" Vladimir's concern was sincere. "And how will they get their equipment past the secret service?"

"We have all of that under control," Mickey wasn't going to reveal that portion of the plan. "The girls understand the risk."

Vladimir nodded.

Mickey was ready to leave. "I need a favour."

"Anything you need."

Mickey handed Vladimir a photograph. "We need this man shut down."

"Who is he and where is he?"

"His name is Wendell Presley," Mickey explained, "and he's at the Holiday Express in Kanata. The address and his room number are on the back. We need it done tonight."

Vladimir grinned as he rubbed the tattoo on his neck. "Your

friend will have an accident."

"Tell your boys this man is not to be taken lightly," Mickey warned. "If he sees it coming, he'll put up a hell of a fight."

"Understood."

"One last thing," Mickey was curious. "How did things go with Hutchinson."

"Like clockwork. He's on his way to the complex."

ONE HUNDRED & 85

A black Suburban pulled into the Sheraton Plaza hotel and parked at the front entrance. Secret Service agent MacKay got out and eye balled the area before talking to the valet. It was a short conversation that ended when MacKay realized there was a crowd growing around him. People gathered hoping they'd get a glimpse of Tucker. They would all be disappointed.

The agent recognized the potential for a media circus and decided on a change of plans. After talking it over with the valet, MacKay took his advice and the two agents pulled back out on the road and drove into the service alley behind the hotel. MacKay hopped out and headed up to the fourth floor.

Tiffany and Laura were both prepared, but a little nervous. This was a huge assignment, and everything had to go as scripted. They had gone over ever detail with Mickey numerous times, and they were confident they could pull it off. If not, they were both ready to pay the price. Being shot dead by a secret service agent or spending their remaining years in a federal prison was the price if they failed.

When they met with Mickey, he emphasized that this would be their only chance to get this close to the president. This night was in the making for years, and Carol was locked inside her hotel room ready to watch everything unfold on her computer.

Laura pointed to the bedroom. "I can't believe that person in the other room is a robot."

"I don't think Mickey likes us calling it that." Tiffany laughed

Laura smirked. "I wonder if it can…"

Tiffany burst out with a belly laugh. It felt good. "It could be the perfect boyfriend for you. Once you're done with it you can store it in the closet."

There was an expected knock on the door, and their moment of fun was over. Their game faces were back on, and Tiffany disappeared into the bedroom. Laura checked her appearance in the mirror. She tucked in her sweater to highlight her thin waste and ample breasts. Her first job was to distract the agent. She opened the door and greeted him with a flirty smile. "You must be Agent MacKay?"

"Yes, ma'am," he responded politely. He tried not to stare at Laura's heaving chest. "Are you ready to go?"

"In a minute. My friend's in the bedroom," Laura told him. "Come on in."

MacKay did a visual inspection of the room. "We are on a tight schedule, ma'am."

Laura closed the door. "Can I get you something to drink?"

"No, thank you," MacKay saw a large blue duffle bag in the corner. "What's inside the bag, ma'am?"

"First, I'm Laura," she never took her eyes off the agent, "and it's coming with us. It's full of things your president requested. If you get my drift."

"I will need to inspect it before we go."

That was Tiffany's cue to enter the room. She was distraction number two. When MacKay saw this blonde goddess enter the room wearing only a tight white t-shirt, he forgot about the duffle bag momentarily. He was completely distracted by Tiffany's beauty and lack of clothing.

"What do you think, Agent MacKay?" Tiffany's eyes flirted with him and he looked embarrassed, "do you think your boss will approve?"

"You look amazing." was all he could mutter.

Their eyes locked and he couldn't look away. He was trapped without knowing it, and Tiffany kept his attention. She kept walking towards him. "Do you like what you see?"

MacKay never saw Laura come up from behind him and he didn't have a chance to defend himself. He was captivated by Tiffany. It only took a second for Laura to stick a needle into his neck. First his muscles were paralyzed, and then white foam dripped from the side of his mouth. The poison killed him quickly.

Neither woman showed any remorse when they dragged Agent MacKay's dead body into the bedroom. Tiffany stepped to the side. "I'll let Mickey know that part one is done."

Laura reached into the agent's pockets and pulled out his wallet and government-issued identification. "They'll be waiting downstairs, so we need to hurry."

Joshua's creation was already assuming the role of Secret Service agent, Kellan MacKay. He helped Laura strip the dead agent and he dressed himself in those same clothes. Once he strapped on the watch and slid on the wedding band, he was ready to take on the life as the leader of the president's security detail.

The women quickly changed into more conservative outfits for the drive to the president's hotel. With the help of the new Agent MacKay, they loaded the blue duffle bag onto a luggage cart and headed down the elevator. When they exited on the main floor, they knew the next few minutes were vital if the new agent would be accepted.

"What took so long?" the driver grumbled. He saw the duffle bag. "There was no mention of this coming along."

"Just load it," MacKay ordered. "I've already checked it and it's good to go."

The other agent was curious. "What exactly is in it?'

MacKay moved over and whispered in his partner's ear. "You've heard the stories?"

"Who hasn't?" the agent chuckled.

MacKay grinned. "Well, they're true, so let's get it loaded."

ONE HUNDRED & 86

Larry Chua was the Chief Financial Officer for Hutchinson Enterprises. He had known Hugh Hutchinson for almost twenty years and was Hugh's most trusted employee for nearly fifteen. Their personal lives rarely crossed, but inside the office they were inseparable.

When it came to the business operations, Chua was involved with every deal Hutchinson considered. He was the person that did the detail work for Hugh once the billionaire decided to vet an opportunity. Chua's loyalty to the company and to Hugh was never doubted.

He had noticed changes in Hugh's personality over the past few months. There were meetings Hugh was attending that he never mentioned to the CFO, and he was drinking more to ease the stress from whatever he was getting involved with.

Larry Chua had a troubled expression as he stood outside his boss's office. The biggest indicator that something serious was going on occurred at 10am this morning. There was a finance meeting that Hugh personally requested that he never attended. The frustration turned to concern when messages on Hugh's cell were never responded to.

The office door was locked, but he had a key and passcode. The luxuriously decorated space was the size of a tennis court with floor to ceiling mirrored glass. Hugh could see out, but no one could see him. It kept everyone on their toes.

Chua looked around, not sure what he expected to find. He

hoped something would solve the mystery of his missing boss, or at least point him in a direction. He finally wandered behind Hugh's desk and hesitated before taking a seat. He didn't feel comfortable, or worthy of sitting in the boss's chair.

Chua had an idea that he didn't like, but in desperate times he decided; what the hell. He placed his laptop on the desk and switched it on. After a minute of uncertainty, he typed in a sequence of account codes that gave him access to all of Hugh's personal and company banking information. He examined and re-examined the account's information.

Larry Chua, the CFO of Hutchinson Enterprises slumped back into his chair. "Oh my god, Hugh. What have you done?"

ONE HUNDRED & 87

The two women were so impressed by how easily the new Agent MacKay became the old one, that they quickly forgot that he was an animatronic being. He stepped right into his role as the head of the president's secret service detail without missing a beat. His partner, Agent Jackson suspected nothing, and it was business as usual. Their assignment was underway.

Jackson climbed into the driver's seat and snapped on his seatbelt. Everyone was buckled in. "Let's get these girls to work."

He drove the speed limit but pushed through a few yellow lights to get to the Royal Grande on schedule. There was a second team of agents that met them at the hotel entrance and after a quick debrief, they were escorted in. The bulky duffle bag on the luggage dolly garnered more than one curious stare from security.

MacKay led them to the elevator. When they exited on the fortieth floor, they had one last checkpoint to process before they could enter the Presidential Suite. For the third time, MacKay had to pull rank and explain the purpose of the blue duffle bag without another agent looking inside. The girls held their breath. It seemed to be an eternity before MacKay scanned his hand over a sensor to activate the locking mechanism on the door.

It swung open and the agent at the door pointed them inside. "Welcome to the Royal Grande, ladies."

Tiffany entered the magnificent suite first. As she walked by the agent at the door, she could feel his eyes glance at her ass. Laura received the same treatment. Everyone thought they knew why they were there, and the sexual tension was undeniable.

Mackay followed behind with the duffle bag in tow. They were the only ones in the suite, but MacKay reminded them of the security cameras. They were everywhere. The women surveyed the room. There was a transportable version of the Oval Office in the back that MacKay made clear was off limits. Where they stood was designated for guests. It was where the president entertained.

Laura eyeballed a large crystal bowl full of M&Ms on the table and couldn't help herself. She grabbed a handful and received a stern look from the agent.

Tiffany looked towards the bathroom. "Are there cameras in there?"

"Yes," MacKay confirmed, "but they will get shut down once the president arrives."

"How will we be sure?"

"The president will send us a signal to shut the cameras off when he's ready to play. It's the only time when no one has eyes on him."

Laura chewed on a M&M. "How do we know when that is?"

"The signal is when he tells you to pour him a drink. It's usually a double whiskey."

Tiffany continued to look for the two flies she knew were somewhere in the room. "It sounds simple enough."

MacKay wheeled the duffle bag into the bathroom. "I'll put this by the shower."

Tiffany grabbed her bag and headed to the bedroom. "I'm going to change into the gift the president sent me."

On his way out, MacKay winked at the women. "Good luck and have fun, ladies."

Laura snuck a few more M&Ms and poured two soda waters with lime. She watched Tiffany emerge from the bedroom wearing only a tiny stars and stripes bikini that Tucker insisted she wear. "Don't you look delicious."

"Did you put any vodka in this?"

"All in good time."

"I guess I should get ready too," Laura didn't use the bedroom and saw Tiffany looking at her. "What? He said there were cameras everywhere."

"Are you looking forward to meeting the president?"

Laura pursed her lips. "I'm ready to do my job, if that's what you're asking."

"Good."

"What does Ray think about you sleeping with the president? Does he even know you're here?"

"He knows I'm on an assignment. Why don't we stay focused on the job and forget about my husband?"

Laura knew she struck a nerve.

ONE HUNDRED & 88

Vladimir was alone in his workstation. He was miles away from the Royal Grande Hotel where all the action was, but that wouldn't stop him from executing his assignment. Jonny's technology gave him a clear view of the suite and it was his job to supply a live feed to Carol.

The dragonfly was scheduled to be activated at 9pm.

V sat at his table and watched the screens. He didn't expect Laura to change and it was a nice surprise that caught him off guard. He had never met the girls, but he knew what they were capable of, and he knew why they were there.

He sipped on his cola. It helped settle his stomach.

Vladimir was a lifelong criminal from the time he was twelve. It started when he would break into cars for spare change so he could buy a candy bar. As the time past, he grew bigger than the other kids and he could fight.

It didn't take him long to be recruited by the Golden Eagles street gang. Over time he became a full patched member who was selected to be their Sergeant of Arms. His job was to make sure that no one disrespected the club, and when required, remind people that they needed to pay their dues on time.

V had countless fights, mostly one-sided bouts against defenseless shopkeepers that couldn't afford the street tax. He was despised, but no one ever stood up to the six-foot-three bully. That was until that fateful night on Gabriola Island when a fourteen-year old Indian kid named Mickey knocked him out.

It was many years later before their paths ever crossed again and it wasn't a coincidence. Mickey came looking for him. Not to fight, but to invite V to join the organization. Mickey offered him the chance to change, and Vladimir was ready for a new life. His career as a gangster had worn him down, and he knew he was lucky to not have a bullet in his head. He shook Mickey's hand and accepted his offer.

The stakes were as high as they get and for the first time, he felt uneasy. He had never worried about the consequences of getting caught or letting people down when he was a young gang member. Aging changed that.

Vladimir wiped his hands and fired up the system. There was time to reassure the girls that they had backup. He navigated one of the flies to land on Tiffany's shoulder.

She almost swatted it off, but then gave it a wink. The fly winked back.

ONE HUNDRED & 89

When Daniel Tucker entered his suite, it was like nothing else mattered. The president marched past the women without even acknowledging their presence, which was not an easy task considering they were both wearing skimpy bikinis. Neither said a word, but both watched him closely.

The president went to his desk and glanced at a few messages while he loosened his tie and removed his jacket. It appeared that he was ready to call it a day. Without him saying a word, it was obvious by his mannerisms that he was a confident man. His golden blonde hair was neatly trimmed, and his clothes were expensive. His gold golf ball cufflinks were a gift from a PGA tour player from Colorado.

They were standing only a few feet from the most powerful man on the planet and it should have been intimidating, but it wasn't for either of them. They knew they controlled how the night would end. For now, they'd pretend to be playful playmates until they decided otherwise.

There could be no screwups. The only way out of the room was the same way they got in. And that was with a secret service escort. Tiffany was confident Agent MacKay had everything under control on his end.

Tucker finished at his desk and headed their way. Judging by the smirk on his face, they now had his full attention. "Are you Canadian girls ready for some fun?"

Tiffany stepped forward with open arms to greet him like an old friend. His eyes fixated on her breast that were ready to fallout of the small bikini top. "Can I get you anything to drink?"

"I'll take a double whiskey," Tucker embraced her hug, "and I see my gift looks great on you."

He said the magic password and the girls got busy, knowing the security cameras were turned off. Tiffany headed behind the bar and grabbed the whiskey. Before she pulled it off the shelf, she saw the second fly on the Jack Daniel's bottle. Seeing it there made her feel safe.

Tucker sized up Laura. "You look way better in person."

Laura smiled graciously. "So, do you."

"Why don't you get us started by getting me set up for a massage? And take the top off. This is a party and we're all adults."

Laura reached behind her back and undid the strap. She let her top fall to her feet. "There you go. Is that better?"

Tucker was giddy with excitement. "Definitely. Now let's get on with the massage."

Tiffany returned with his drink, while Laura setup the table.

He tasted the whiskey. "Not bad."

Tiffany put her arms around his neck. "Is it okay if I call you, Daniel?"

"You drop your top, and you can call me whatever you want," he giggled like a teenager at his first strip club, "but I prefer Dan."

It was Laura's turn to interrupt. She took the drink out of the president's hand and walked him over to the table. She had strapped on a massage belt loaded with oil bottles. "Let's get your shirt off and loosen up that belt."

Tucker was a willing participant, and his shirt was off in no time. He climbed up onto the table on his belly. Laura sprayed some oil on his back and started her massage. A local anesthetic was mixed into the oil to help numb the president's sense of pain.

The president was so relaxed that he didn't feel the tiny needle pierce his skin and take a DNA sample. While Laura's hands roamed over his body, he never noticed Tiffany disappear into the bathroom. She opened the blue duffle bag and injected the sample from Tucker into the animatronic president's mouth. That completed a big piece of their assignment.

Tiffany returned. "Why don't we both help with your massage. Your body seems tight."

Tucker closed his eyes and enjoyed the sensation of four strong hands working out the kinks. Laura took over the upper body while Tiffany worked on the bottom half. Everything was going as rehearsed.

Tiffany dripped some oil onto the president's feet and started rubbing it in. Her mind drifted to Ray. He loved getting his feet massaged. She wondered if he ever heard from Mickey about his assignment. Hopefully, he was safe.

"You girls should become Americans," Tucker laughed. "With hands like yours, I'm sure I could find you a suitable job in the White House."

Tiffany played along. "I heard it was hard to become an American citizen."

"I can get you in," He boasted. "We welcome foreigners with special skills. Especially when they look like you two."

Laura got Tiffany's attention without saying a word. She tapped her wrist to indicate the time. It was time for the next phase.

ONE HUNDRED & 90

By the time they finished his massage, the president was only wearing his gold Rolex. He gulped down the whiskey and growled as it burned his throat. "Fix me another and meet us in the bedroom."

Tiffany masked her disgust for the man behind a convincing smile. "I'll be right in."

She watched in stunned silence as the sixty-year old President of the United States, the man with his hand on the button, skip like a six-year old into the bedroom holding Laura's hand. How was it even possible that this clown could be the leader of the free world.

When Tiffany reached for the whiskey bottle, she saw the fly was still perched on the Jack Daniels. She gave the insect a quick wink and made no effort to cover her naked body. She poured a healthy second drink and put the bottle back. The fly was gone.

When she entered the bedroom, Tiffany started to laugh hysterically when she saw what was going on. She nearly dropped the president's drink. Tucker was in the middle of the bed on all fours. Laura wore a white cowboy hat and was on his back riding him like a bull. A picture would be worth millions to the paparazzi.

"Heehaw!" Tucker wailed.

After a few minutes of playing rodeo, exhaustion prevailed and the two collapsed on the bed. Tucker gasped for air, but he had a satisfied smirk on his face. "That was awesome."

Laura couldn't stop laughing. Boy, did she have a story to tell Mickey. "I need to pee."

Tucker fell back on the pillows. "Go ahead."

She winked at Tiffany. It was a signal to keep the old man

occupied. "I'll be right back."

Tiffany climbed up on the bed and leaned over the sweaty president. "Are you up for another rodeo?"

Laura closed the bathroom door and worked quickly. She unzipped the duffle bag and pulled out a smaller bag that contained everything they needed to finish the assignment. She set the pieces out on the bathroom counter and did a quick inventory before being satisfied everything was ready.

She sensed she was being watched and turned slowly. The metallic blue dragonfly was now on the windowsill. That was the last piece.

ONE HUNDRED & 91

The Ottawa Airport was a much calmer place than it had been the previous day. The protestors were long gone, and now security was bored watching the long lineups of travellers shuffling to make their flights. No one paid any special attention to a direct flight from Jamaica that just taxied to gate D.

In the line to get through Customs, there was a young lady with scorched red hair wearing an oversized pink t-shirt and cut off jeans. When it was her turn, she sauntered up to the customs booth. All relaxed and appearing bored. She received the look from the agent she expected.

The agent scanned her passport and asked the usual questions. And then this agent surprised her. "I love your hair. I wish I had the guts to do it."

"If you drink enough Jamaican rum, you'll do almost anything."

The customs agent cracked a smile. "Welcome home, Ms. Beliveau."

Cherie thanked her and then hurried to the arrival's terminal. Waiting behind the gate was a friendly face and she ran into his tight embrace. "Is it ever good to see you, Teddy."

He let her go. "It's great to see you too."

"How are you doing, my big black friend?"

Teddy's bald head glowed under the lights. "I'm good now that you're back. I miss our morning conversations over coffee."

He took her bag and within minutes they merged into the steady flow of traffic on Airport Parkway. They were headed to downtown Ottawa. "Am I taking you home?"

"Can you take me to the Sheraton Plaza?"

Teddy pulled his older Honda Civic up to the passenger drop off. "Do you want me to wait?"

She leaned over and kissed him on the cheek. "No, but thanks for picking me up."

Cherie stood on the sidewalk and let the cool breeze push her red hair in every direction. She was positive Pierre would have received an alert the minute she re-entered the country. That's why she called Teddy to pick her up instead of taking a cab. No trail for his men to follow.

She went inside and when she got to her floor, she located the room she was looking for. Before knocking, she took a deep breath to settle herself. Cherie had no idea what kind of reception she would get.

The door opened. "Look at you. A punk rocker."

Cherie forced a smile. "Hello, mom."

Carol stepped aside and let her in. "I love your hair."

"No, you don't. You hate it."

"How was your flight?"

"Too long," Cherie complained. "Do you have any wine in this room?"

"I can get some brought up." Carol offered.

"Forget it. I'll be fine with water," Cherie was drawn to the live feed that played on Carol's computer. "What's this? Are you watching porn?"

Carol shook her head. "It's a very important assignment that's underway."

"Holy shit!" She shouted. "That's the president. Who's the gorgeous blonde on top of him?"

"One of Mickey's agents."

Cherie knew who Mickey was, and what his agents did. "Are

you killing the president?"

"We're replacing him."

She continued to watch the screen. "Now there's two. Are they going to screw him to death?"

Carol closed her computer. "Let's talk about why you're back in the country."

Cherie took a seat on the couch. "I was wondering why you brought me back so soon. Aren't you concerned about Hutchinson finding out I'm here?"

"You shouldn't have blackmailed him," Carol responded matter of fact, "but he's no longer a concern."

"Why not?"

Carol joined her on the couch. "We decided to remove him from the public eye for a few days."

"What does that mean?"

"It means that when he returns from his little bender, you'll be his wife."

Cherie winced. "I don't want to marry that jerk."

Carol teased her. "Don't you want to be a billionaire?"

That got Cherie's attention. "What's that look like?"

"You're going to marry him and take over Hutchinson Enterprises. The Federal Coalition will award you lucrative contracts that you'll control. It will be a steady income for the organization."

"Why would Hutchinson let me manage his business?"

"When you're ready to take over he'll get very sick, and as the executor of his estate you'll assume control."

"You've got it all figured out," Cherie smiled. "You are brilliant."

ONE HUNDRED & 92

Tiffany took a deep breath to compose herself. The thought of having sex with James Tucker made her stomach twist. Her job for the next five minutes was to keep the president busy while Laura setup the final phase in the bathroom. Keeping him occupied shouldn't be too hard considering his excited state.

Tiffany pretended to be aroused and climbed up onto the bed. The president was lying on his back and he was ready. She took her time, counting the seconds, before she straddled him. "I've been thinking about this all day."

Tucker smirked like he was doing her a favour. "Climb on baby and enjoy the ride."

If was the hardest happy face she had ever faked. She wanted to spit in his face, but instead, buried her chin on his shoulder. She just wanted him to finish. It didn't take long to get her wish. The president climaxed and let out a high-pitched yelp that sounded like a pig before slaughter. Tiffany took deep breaths to relax her pounding heartbeat. Killing this man was going to be easy. "That was amazing, Daniel. Women are lucky to have you."

Tucker was spread eagled on the bed. His chest heaved. "Women around the world love me and what I do to them. And now you're on that list too, sweetheart."

Tiffany continued to play along. "Yes I am."

Laura returned to see Tiffany's disgusted expression. She had taken one for the team. "Why don't we get some drinks from the bar and take a few minutes to catch our breath?"

Tucker struggled to sit up. "Sounds like a good idea. Your friend here could use a few minutes. I wore her out."

Tiffany wrapped a robe around her body and headed out of the bedroom. "I'll make the drinks," She looked at Laura, who nodded. Everything was ready. "I'm having a real Grey Goose. Do you want one?"

Vladimir was speechless by what he had witnessed. Where did these women come from? There was no doubt that they were dedicated to Mickey. They had to be because what he was watching took commitment.

V steered the fly from the bedroom and into the bathroom. He landed it skillfully on the edge of the mirror. He now had a perfect view of the shower stall. It was ready to film the final scene.

The second fly was back on the Jack Daniels.

Tiffany handed out the drinks. She smiled cheekily at the president. "Do you want to play a game us girls enjoy?"

Tucker perked up. "What kind of game?"

"You play the commander of a women's P.O.W. camp."

He nodded. "I like it. Where do we play?"

Laura joined in. "It's more fun in the shower."

Tucker's grin widened. "I love that idea. Let's drink up and get wet."

Once the drinks were finished the three headed towards the bathroom. Laura stopped them at the door. "I heard you like to play with toys, so I brought some with us. I hope that's okay?"

Tucker looked suspicious. "What kind of toys?"

Tiffany put her arms around his neck and pulled him close. His nose was stuck between her breasts. "I like to wear a gas mask. Are you ready to punish me for being a bad girl?"

Tucker's eyes said it all. "Do I get to wear one?"

"Absolutely. You're in charge."

They entered the large bathroom, and three gas masks were lined up on the counter. Laura took control and handed them out. Only two had respirators. "We wear these to protect our eyes and mouth from the dangerous fumes."

Tucker was getting excited again.

There were six cans of whip cream inside the shower. "Those are the canisters of poison." Laura dropped her robe and slid on her mask. The other two followed suit. "Are you ready to punish us, commander?"

Tucker struggled to get the mask on, but finally with some help he was ready. "I can be a mean commander."

"I hope so," teased Tiffany. "Let's get inside and get this game going."

Laura checked the windowsill. The dragonfly was motionless, but it was ready. She also saw the fly on the mirror. Everything was now in place. "Let's have some fun."

Tiffany enjoyed the hot water splashing on her body. The smell and sweat from Tucker rinsed down the drain. The three naked bodies armed themselves with a can of whip cream in each hand. Tucker was prepared to play a game, and the girls were ready to play for real. Everyone was anxious to begin.

Tucker got it going and the three were spraying the whip cream wildly at each other. Everyone was laughing. Laura made sure her first shot was to the president's gas mask. It was a direct hit to his goggles and his vision was severely limited. Bingo!

President Tucker was spraying wildly and laughing like a drunken fool. "Can I lick the poison gas off your bodies?"

"You're the commander," Tiffany shouted above the noise, "so you can do anything you want."

It was time and the dragonfly was activated on the windowsill.

No one saw it. The wings flapped at 30 times per second, just like mother nature's version. V launched it and steered it over to the shower. It hovered above the waterspout and directly above the President of the United States. The moment that was dreamt about years ago was about to take place.

Vladimir waited for the signal from Tiffany. A simple thumbs up would activate the deadly gas. Tiffany turned Tucker around in the shower, so he was faced away from the door. He never saw Laura sneak out.

"I'm going to get some soap to wash your back." Tiffany lied to him. "Give me a second to get a cloth."

She stepped out and gave the thumbs up. Only the president was in the shower now. The dragonfly released the poisonous gas inside its abdomen. The assassination had begun, and now it was a matter of just time.

Tucker got impatient and stood up. When he couldn't sense the women were near him, he ripped off his mask. "What are you doing out there...."

The girls stood back and watched the poison take over. The effects it caused were terrible to see. Blood dripped from his nose and the water washed it down the drain. His eyes fell back into his head and were full of fear when he knew what was happening to him. He tried to speak but couldn't. When his legs gave out from under him, he fell onto the edge of the tiled soap dish, opening a huge gash on his forehead. Only a spot of blood dripped onto the tile. His heart had stopped pumping.

At 9:35 pm on June 30, Daniel James Tucker became the fifth President of the United States to be assassinated. When John F. Kennedy was murdered, there was public outrage and conspiracy theories that continue decades later. None of that would occur for

President Tucker. His death would never be reported on social media and there wouldn't be a state funeral. Only five people knew he was dead.

When the women had cleaned up and everything was ready, they sent MacKay a message. He instructed his team to enter the suite. They did a walk through and were careful not to interrupt the president, who was sitting at the bar fully dressed enjoying a whiskey. The ladies were enjoying their double Grey Gooses and tonic. Everything appeared to be perfect.

Vladimir was packed up. The dragonfly and the two flies had returned to home base. Before he left the kitchen, he looked at a memory stick in the palm of his hand. He wondered what a video of the President of the United States getting murdered was worth.

ONE HUNDRED & 93

What used to be the Cooke and Magill annual Canada Day BBQ with maybe twelve guests, had grown into a neighbourhood block party now that it was hosted by the leader of the Federal Coalition. A donation to a local charity got you a free t-shirt and a burger.

David tossed his apron onto a chair and headed to the house under the pretense that he needed to use the washroom. It was true that he needed to pee, but it was not his only reason. He needed some privacy. As he walked through the maze of guests, he shook hands and accepted well wishes. It was another reminder of how much his life had changed being in the spotlight.

Cindy had ignored David's warnings to stop contacting him. Her sexting got more aggressive and the photos were very explicit. He knew he had to end it, but he had crossed the line when he slept with her and now, she was in control.

He locked the bathroom door and dropped his shorts. He didn't need a drunk neighbor walking in. With his phone in hand he sat on the toilet. He sent a text to Cindy.

'You need to stop!!!'

He got an immediate response.

'u luv them.'

'Just stop!'

'Can u meet me?'

'I have a house full of guests.'

'Maybe I'll sneak into your bedroom. I need to see you.'

There was a knock on the door. David assumed it was a neighbor.

'I have to go.
,

"It's busy!" he shouted at the door trying not to sound annoyed, "but there is another bathroom at the top of the stairs."

"It's me."

"Give me a minute," David flushed the toilet and opened the door. "What's so important that it couldn't wait?"

Nina pushed him back inside the bathroom and shut the door. "I have something important to tell you. And no, it couldn't wait."

She didn't seem mad, so his secret was still safe. "What?"

"It's about Hugh Hutchinson," Nina said. "He's missing."

David shook his head in disbelief. "How does a billionaire go missing? He's always got someone with him."

Nina shrugged. "That's all I know."

"Do they know where he was last seen?"

Nina's tone got heavy. "The last thing in his calendar was dinner with Carol."

David knew that couldn't be a coincidence. "Maybe he's in a hotel with some hot woman?"

Nina didn't hide her disgust. "You need to get back outside to entertain your guests."

David nodded. "I'll just be a minute. I need to finish up in here."

Nina stopped at the door on her way out and smiled at her husband. "Say hi to Cindy for me."

ONE HUNDRED & 94

Getting out of the presidential suite was much easier than the years of work it took to get in. Once their drinks were finished, the president escorted the girls to the elevator. It was something the president had never done before, and it didn't go unnoticed by his security detail.

Agent MacKay was a few steps behind with the duffle bag loaded on a dolly. No one else was getting near that bag.

Once MacKay and the girls were loaded into the elevator, the president headed back to his suite. Before he called it a night, he pulled his chief of staff to the side and whispered into his ear. "I need you to do me a favour."

Drake Adams nodded. "Anything sir?"

"Go down to the lounge and retrieve my wife before she drinks all of the vodka. Tell her she can come up now."

Adams rolled his eyes and headed back to the elevator.

Agent MacKay personally gave the girls an escort back to their hotel. It was only the three of them now. When they pulled into the hotel parking lot there was a cargo van waiting. MacKay pulled up beside the van and popped the hatch. Two men grabbed the duffle bag and loaded it into their vehicle.

A few minutes later, Agent MacKay was headed back to the Royal Grande Hotel while the women stood inside the Sheraton lobby. Both were relieved to be back. Neither said a word about what happened earlier. What occurred was surreal. It was like something out of a Hollywood movie and the magnitude of what they pulled off still hadn't sunk in.

They had killed the President of the United States.

Tiffany said. "I'm going to head up to my room and get into the shower. I need to get Tucker's smell off my body."

Laura glanced around the lobby. "How about we go out for drinks to celebrate the holiday? You can even bring the old guy."

Tiffany chuckled. "Give me an hour. I need to talk to Ray, so why don't you come by my room. We can go from there."

"We'll drink expensive champagne and send Mickey the tab."

Tiffany gave Laura an embrace. "See you in an hour and it was great to work with you."

ONE HUNDRED & 95

Tiffany opened the door and threw her stuff on the bed, and that included the clothes she wore. She headed directly to the bathroom and turned on the water in the shower stall.

Ray had a game on the television, but as soon as she came in, he turned it off. He hopped off the bed and followed her. "How'd your assignment go?"

"It's over and I want to take a shower."

"You look exhausted."

"I am."

"Do you want me to join you? I can wash your back."

Tiffany smiled, but a tear was dripping down her cheek. "I'd love that."

Ray was concerned. "What's going on, baby? Are you okay?"

She pushed out a smile. "I'm just glad to be back here."

The water splashing over her body gave her some renewed energy. Ray gently massaged her shoulders. It was exactly what she needed. "So, tell me. How was your assignment? Did you get to shoot anybody?"

Ray chuckled but looked disappointed. "My assignment was having tea with Carol across the street."

"Are you kidding me?" Tiffany didn't hide her surprise. "You met with Carol?"

Ray shrugged softly as he continued to massage Tiffany. "What's the big deal?"

Tiffany considered why. "Carol meets no one unless it's personal. What did she want?"

"Not much really. She wants me to dissolve a company," Ray recalled, "but she also told me a name."

"What name?"

"Craven Ravenwood. She said he's going to be an important person in my life."

Tiffany looked panicked and shut off the water. "Get out and get dressed. We have to get out of here!"

Ray got worried seeing Tiffany's reaction. "What's going on?"

Tiffany already pulled on her pants. "Remember the big yacht we saw at Granville Island?"

"Hard to forget a magnificent boat like that. What's that got to do with this?"

"I was going to surprise you," She started, "I have us booked to sail on it tomorrow."

"You do?" Ray was confused, "How does this all tie together?"

"My surprise is I wanted you to run off with me so I can get out of this lifestyle." Tiffany packed their suitcases. "It would be just the two of us and no looking back."

"Who is this Craven Ravenwood that Carol mentioned?"

"He's the captain of the yacht."

Ray let that sink in. "How does she know him?"

"Exactly! How?" she replied, "now hurry up and pack. We have to get out of here."

ONE HUNDRED & 96

When Laura got back to her hotel room, the first thing on her list was to crack open a bottle of Silver Patron tequila. She poured herself a generous shot. She deserved it. That was an assignment that had pushed her emotionally. The adrenaline from the kill still pumped through her. She didn't have this kind of reaction when she killed Tracy.

She gulped down the tequila and the sting at impact exploded as it flowed down her throat. When her body was ready, she repeated the process. She looked forward to celebrating out on the town with Tiffany. And she was curious to learn more about Ray. She still couldn't understand the connection between them. Love was a strange drug.

After a cleansing shower, she slipped into a slinky satin dress that only allowed a tiny G string underneath. Maybe some lucky guy in Ottawa was going to win the Laura lotto tonight.

She tried to choose between style and three-inch silver heals, or comfort and a pair of ankle high black leather boots. Her decision was interrupted by a knock at her door. Every muscle tensed. She wasn't expecting anyone.

And then she remembered Wendell Presley was in town.

She pulled out a Glock 9mm from under her pillow and held it at her side as she approached the door. She checked the safety before she looked through the peephole. It wasn't Presley. It was room service.

A thin faced Filipino server in a white waiter's jacket looked impatient. He had one hand on the edge of the cart and the other was beside his leg. There was a bottle of Dom Perignon in an ice bucket on the cart. Someone wanted her to celebrate.

She opened the door enough to talk to him. "Who sent this to me?"

He appeared impatient. "I have no idea, ma'am. I'm just the delivery guy."

There was no billfold on the tray. "Do you mind stepping away from the cart?"

Her request caught him off guard. "Do you want the wine, or not?"

She pushed the door open and before he could react, a gun was pushed against his cheek. "Get the fuck in here!"

Her gut was right on. There was a steak knife in his hand. He weighed his choices. He didn't have any.

"I suggest you put the knife down or I'll put a hole in your face. It's your choice and you have three seconds to decide."

He was given bad intel. He was never told the lady would have a gun. Now he wasn't sure who was leaving in the body bag. He tossed the knife on the cart and pushed it inside Laura's room. The gun was never more than a few inches from his face.

Laura shoved him into a chair. "As you can see, I'm dressed to go out, so I don't have a lot of time for games. I need a name."

"You come sit on my lap and we can pretend that you never pulled a gun on me, you little slut."

The bullet blew a hole in the cushion one inch from his ear. "You might want to remember who has the gun. Don't ever think I won't kill you. Like I said, I'm in a hurry, so give me a name or my next shot will hit the bullseye."

"Fuck you, bitch!"

The gun fire and it was a direct hit, right in the crotch. He fell off the chair and screamed in agony. He was holding what was left of his genitals. "You crazy, bitch."

She needed him alive. She wanted a name. "One last chance."

He pled for mercy with his eyes. He struggled to speak. "I was told to kill the witness. They gave me a thousand bucks to kill you. They never said you'd be a commando chick."

Laura pursed her lips as she thought. "That's all they said?"

He squirmed in pain. "That's it. Now call me an ambulance. I'm going to bleed out."

She shot him one more time and he was dead.

He knew the code.

What did he mean, kill the witness? And then it made sense. She was a witness to the assassination of the president. Someone was getting rid of loose ends. She had to warn Tiffany. She grabbed the Dom Perignon and headed to the elevator.

Laura banged on Tiffany's room, but no one answered. She gave it three tries and got more frustrated the longer she stood in the hallway. She felt helpless. It was feeling she wasn't used to.

Did the piece of crap in her room come here first?

She pulled off her heels and sprinted down the four flights of stairs and burst into the hotel lobby. She stepped in the front of the line. "I have an emergency and I need a room key for my friend's room."

Sensing Laura' aggressive nature the clerk stepped back from the counter. "I can't do that."

Did you hear me tell you it's an emergency? I need a key."

The clerk waved off an approaching security guard. "What room is it?"

"4415."

The clerk punched in the number. She read the screen. "Mr. and Mrs. Harding checked out about fifteen minutes ago."

Laura shoulders slumped as she turned away from the counter. "I don't believe it. They're running."

She found a table in the lobby and popped open the Dom Perignon. She laughed and cried herself into a drunken bliss.

ONE HUNDRED & 97

Suzanne decided a trip back to Whitehorse was needed. She had to get her things in order, which included listing her home with a realtor and reuniting with Rupert. Her puppy stayed with a friend while she was away.

She understood that Carol's offer was really an ultimatum. Get on board or lose your son forever. That meant living closer to Gabriola. And funny enough she was good with her choice.

Now that she was back in her son's life, she had every intention of taking advantage of her second chance. He had been gone for over three years and was now a young man. His temperament had changed as much as his physical appearance. Curtis had an edge to his personality. Suzanne recognized it as a defensive mechanism to protect himself from being hurt again. She hoped over time she could tear it down and rekindle their relationship.

After some lengthy conversations with Stacey, it was decided that it made sense for the two to live together. At least for the short term until they recognized what their future looked like. Stacey could use some help around the house and the moral support would be good for both.

Suzanne had three hurdles to get over that she had not figured out. The first was how she was going to keep her pregnancy a secret from Curtis. Until she knew how all of this was going to play out, he could never know. The second was getting pregnant. She was going to need help with that, and her ex husband played a big roll in creating their son. There was no way she wanted to sleep with him again, but she would need his co-operation without him getting suspicious. That would need some thought. And then, how was she going to keep all this a secret from Tom. He had a right to know his son was alive.

She had some time to figure all of that out and for now, she tried to stay focused on packing up and saying goodbye to her northern friends. She'd never forget how supportive the Yukon communities were when her son went missing. Living in the land of the Midnight Sun was an adventure she'd never forget.

Since her return from Gabriola, Stacey had battled an endless surge of guilt that ate away at her. Instead of being overjoyed to find her son, she was tormented by the idea that it might have been her that pushed him away. She remembered the reunion in Carol's office. Joshua didn't run over to her shrieking with excitement, but instead she only got a courtesy hug. It seemed to be rehearsed. He was not the sweet boy she remembered prior to the fire.

Stacey hoped that her spending time with her son would help them to reconnect. If having a third baby would give her the access she desperately wanted to Joshua, then she was willing to go along with Carol.

If it was even possible, she hated her mother even more. But she understood her now. It was never about family or love. It was about control and Stacey accepted Carol had it all, for now.

Emma fussed in her new wicker bassinet. It was a gift from Suzanne. She was hungry and mom knew the routine. She picked up her baby and plunked herself down on the corner of the sofa. "Are you hungry again, my little angel?"

With everything in place, she let Emma get to work while she scanned her Instagram account. She found a posting about Sergeant Smith's attack on the ferry. It was hard to read and the guilt was back. It took a few attempts to get through the article without tearing up. She knew it was her fault.

The lunatic they mentioned in the story had no name and his body was never found. Stacey was convinced he was somehow connected to her mother. They must have felt Sergeant Smith was getting too close.

Stacey was suddenly in a hurry and after putting a fresh diaper on Emma she made a few calls. She had to pretend to be a florist before someone finally gave her Sergeant Smith's home address.

With Emma strapped into her car seat, Stacey had decided to take a big chance. She was about to ignore one of the biggest rules that Carol made clear. It was a huge risk, but her guilt pushed her to start the car.

She drove around the back streets for twenty minutes with no purpose other than to be sure she wasn't being followed. Paranoia had kicked into high gear. Her mother's reach and the lunatic on the ferry, everything was inside her head. What took place in the complex was proof of how far Carol was willing to go to protect her plan. The funny thing was that Stacey had no idea what that plan was.

When she was finally convinced that there were no bad guys following her, she turned onto Sergeant Smith's street. She slowed down to check addresses. There was his house. A two-story white and green bungalow with a cherry tree in full blossom in the front yard.

Before she could change her mind, she pulled into the driveway. She just sat there and let the engine idle. She didn't know what to do and looked back at Emma for an answer that wasn't coming. She decided she made a big mistake coming here.

Before she could back up, there was a tap on the driver's window that scared the life out of her. She turned slowly, hoping whoever knocked would just go away. It didn't work. A tall middle-aged woman stared through the glass at her.

Stacey rolled down the window.

The lady looked inside the car. "Can I help you?"

Stacey looked up. "I'm sorry, but I never should have come here."

"I'm guessing you're Stacey Small."

Stacey raised her eyes in surprise. "How did you know?"

"I'm Steve's wife and the baby in the back seat was my first clue. Did you come here to see Steve?"

Stacey nodded. "I feel so bad about what happened. It's my fault he got hurt on the ferry."

"Don't you blame yourself," Helen reassured her. "Steve's resting right now, but if you want to come in and talk, I'd enjoy the company. I have a lot of questions."

Stacey appreciated Helen's friendly gesture and the three of them headed inside. She had a lot of questions too. Helen led her to an enclosed porch that overlooked the backyard. Stacey saw a small vegetable garden against the fence and there was a cherry tree that was flowering. "Does the sergeant enjoy gardening?"

Helen giggled. "Heck no. He has trouble watering the grass. Gardening is my thing."

For some reason Stacey felt safe. It was the best she had felt in a long time. It was nice to have someone new to talk to. "My husband couldn't plant a rock."

They both laughed.

"Your baby is gorgeous. What's her name?"

"I named her Emma. It's from my German heritage. Specifically, after my grandmother, Amelia."

"Let me get us some iced tea and then you can tell me why you were parked in my driveway."

Helen returned a minute later with a jug of tea and some fresh biscuits. "Help yourself and then you can tell me what's going on."

Stacey poured herself a glass. "I had to come see for myself that he's okay."

Helen sipped her tea. "He's a lucky man and I'm sure he'd enjoy talking to you, but that's not possible right now. He needs rest."

Stacey understood and appreciated Helen welcoming her into her home. "Is there anything I can do to help?"

Helen looked at Emma sleeping peacefully. "I think you have your hands full, but can I ask you something?"

"Sure. What is it?"

"What really happened over on the island?"

Stacey wasn't sure what to tell her. How much did she know about her case? "We got trapped in some bad weather and stayed inside our tent until it passed. There was no Wi-Fi so we couldn't even contact someone. I was so pregnant that I could hardly move."

Helen played along and wondered why Stacey would lie to her. "So, you found no clues that might help locate your son?"

Stacey hated lying to Steve's wife. Her guilt was back. "It turns out we were on a wild goose chase."

Helen turned to look down at Emma. "When did you have the baby?"

Stacey felt the walls falling in on her. Helen wasn't looking for information. She was confirming what she thought she already knew. "When will the sergeant be back at work?"

"Never, if I get my way. They're bringing in a replacement while he's off." She stood firm. "I have to ask one last question. I need to understand something."

Stacey tried to appear in control but knew Helen would see the guilt in her eyes. "What's that?"

"Why did you send Steve the text about a blanket? We both know I never gave you one. I have to wonder what happened over there?"

Stacey was emotionally drained. She couldn't lie to this lady. It was all wrong. It was like deceiving her husband. "You need to understand the danger you could face if I tell you what happened."

Helen stood up. "You found your son, didn't you?"

Stacey's face fell into her hands and she burst into tears. "Yes!"

ONE HUNDRED & 98

Back in Ottawa in the Sheraton, the two boys were finishing a big dinner. Carol set it up to congratulate them for some great work. Curtis had a huge ribeye while Joshua ordered a plate of lasagna. Now they were waiting for dessert.

Their cheesecake arrived and Curtis dove in. "I wonder what's going on with your gramma. She's never been this nice."

"I'm just glad we get to go to see the fireworks festival tonight."

A ruckus at the front desk grabbed their attention. "Check out the lady in the sexy dress. She looks pissed about something."

Joshua watched her walk over to a table and open the bottle she was holding. "I hope she's okay?"

"Anyone that looks that hot will be fine."

Talking about women was not something the twelve-year old was comfortable with. "Let's finish up and get to the fireworks."

Curtis stuffed the last bite into his mouth. "I have something I want to tell you."

"What?"

Curtis waved his hand. "We can talk later."

ONE HUNDRED & 99

Mickey packed up his belongings and was eager to catch an early morning flight back to Vancouver. Everything that had to be accomplished in Ottawa was done. And it was done well.

There was still one outstanding item, and his name was Wendell Presley. The man was dangerous and still on the loose. Mickey was confident Vladimir's men would deal with him and dismissed any thought of getting involved. He zipped up his suitcase and grabbed a juice. He was ready for some holiday time.

He had promised himself that once the Canada Day assignments was completed, he would travel to his cabin and reconnect with his spirituality. It was something he wanted to do. Where he was headed, he wouldn't have technology. Just a fishing pole and the basic essentials.

He was headed to Flores Island that was predominately occupied by First Nations people from the Nuu-chah-nulth nation. It was also where Mickey was born, a secret that he shared with no one. He was taken from his bed when he was four. The thief was his drunken father, and taking the boy was his revenge for being banished from the tribe for pulling a knife on the chief.

Ten years later Mickey ran away from his father and moved onto Gabriola Island.

Carol had requested a meeting with Mickey before he headed to the airport. It was late, but he still had time. The hallways were empty and when he entered her room, he saw that it was only the two of them. Cherie had left to sleep in her own condo.

Mickey noticed a tray with finger foods setup on the table. It was a strange sight because he had rarely seen Carol eat. He didn't realize how hungry he was until he stuffed a mini sausage roll into his mouth. He grabbed a second and took a seat. "So, what's on your mind?"

Carol passed on the food. "I have a few things I want to clear up before you head out."

"The women did an amazing job with Tucker. The assignment was flawless," Mickey wiped his hands on a napkin. "We now control two key positions in Tucker's inner circle."

Carol didn't share his enthusiasm. "We still need to get command of Congress and the Senate. The only way to control the U.S. government is to control both parties. When we do that, we can have a big fireworks celebration."

Mickey agreed. "Speaking of fireworks, Cassie is setup in North Korea. They'll be doing a government approved show in Pyongyang. They're expecting up to a million in attendance."

"Did Jonny built fireworks that can distribute that much vapour food?"

"He's confident he did, and we have no reason to doubt that kid. But we'll have people in the crowd to monitor the results."

"There are hundreds of thousands of starving people in his country and their leader is a fat pig. I can't wait to take him out."

Mickey decided against a third sausage roll. "What about Hutchinson? Have you got that sorted out?"

Carol chuckled. "He's decided to get married and share his empire."

"You convinced Cherie that being a billionaire is a good thing?"

"I convinced her that being married to an animatronic being is every girl's dream. She'll control Hutchinson Enterprises before the end of the year. We'll let the newlyweds become old news before

Hugh has a stroke."

"Nice," Mickey moved on. "What else do we need to discuss?"

Carol rubbed her chin. "I need to figure out what to do with my other daughter. The evil one, and her new friend that can be just as annoying."

"I thought they agreed to be on board?"

"What they said and what they're thinking are two different things. They need to be watched." Her frustration was obvious. "I know they'll try and make trouble."

"Then why risk working with them? We should just remove them. They know too much about us to be wandering around on the outside."

"I'd have then eliminated in a second if they weren't so useful to me."

"How are they so useful that we risk being exposed?"

"Can you imagine us having another Joshua and Curtis in the organization? It will be amazing."

"True enough," Mickey stood. "I still haven't got a confirmation on the Presley situation."

"Do you trust Vladimir?"

"I have no choice."

"Then leave it in his hands," Carol recommended. "Now I need a favour. I need a lift to pick up a package."

"Now?

"Now."

Mickey changed his mind and grabbed a third mini sausage for the road and headed to the door. He checked the time. It was one-thirty-seven in the morning. "Let's go get your package."

Mickey exited the elevator on P3 and stepped out with Carol at his side. With a tap on his remote he located his SUV. It was at the far end of the lot. They walked side by side in the dimly lit parkade.

Carol strutted to keep up. "What do you think Presley wants from us?"

"He wants us dead. It's personal," Mickey explained. "We embarrassed him when he worked in the complex."

"Do you think money would solve it?"

"He didn't need to come to Ottawa to get money. He has something bigger on his mind."

"Does he want us both dead?"

Mickey kept walking. "Vladimir's boys will deal with him."

Carol walked to the passenger side of the SUV. "We can talk on the drive."

Neither noticed the black Silverado parked in the shadows at the other end of the lot. It was at least fifty yards away and the driver had backed in. They were ready for a quick exit. The engine started.

Mickey saw the steel bumper as he got into his vehicle. He wasn't sure if that was the truck the hotel clerk described in Kanata. With the distance and the lighting being poor, he couldn't see who was behind the wheel. He knew he had to get her out of there. "Let's go!"

Carol spotted the truck. "Is that him?"

Mickey put the vehicle into drive. "I'm not taking any chances!"

The parking garage was full of visitor vehicles, so it made the driving lanes tight. There were no shortcuts. When Mickey pulled out of the parking stall, he saw the truck ease forward. It was confirmed in Mickey's mind. It was Presley.

Mickey pounded the gas pedal. He only had one shot at getting out before the truck cut them off. The tires squealed on the slick cement and the sounds echoed loudly off the cement walls. It became obvious that a collision was unavoidable. It was Presley's plan all along.

Carol was in the direct line of the big steel bumper and unless Mickey did something quickly, she was in trouble.

"Get down!" he yelled. It was too late. "Shit!"

Mickey steered the SUV away from the truck, but it didn't matter. He saw the back of Carol's head as the truck came at them. She never said a word and prepared herself for impact.

The force of the heavier truck crushed the side of the smaller SUV and pushed it viciously against a cement pillar. Mickey could have reached out and touched the steel bumper, but his focus was on Carol.

Her motionless body was straddled over his lap and for the first time in a long time, Mickey was scared. He had failed to protect her. Above all else, that was his main purpose.

Carol moaned and gasped for air. She was having trouble breathing. Mickey turned her head to see the impact had literally torn her face apart. It was horrific to see.

Her eyes were full of pain, but she displayed no fear. Blood seeped out of her wounds. He knew Carol was about to die and he was helpless to save her.

Mickey looked through the shattered passenger window and saw Wendell's cruel sneer. He revved the engine and backed the truck away from the twisted metal. He saw that Mickey was still alive, so it wasn't over.

Mickey knew what Wendell was thinking. It was obvious that he was going to take a second run. He had to move quickly and pushed Carol's body off him. The truck smashed against what was left of the rental vehicle. It was another devastating hit.

Wendell backed the truck up. He was anxious to see the results of his work. He could only see one body inside the wreckage. And then, out of the corner of his eye he saw him. The son-of-a-bitch was alive.

A trickle of blood dripped down Mickey's face. He looked like a crazed wolverine. "Get out of the truck, asshole!" Mickey screamed. "It ends here and now."

TWO HUNDRED

The Canada Day fireworks festival on Parliament Hill was a spectacle of power and beauty that lasted for almost thirty minutes. The accompanying music made it a great show and it didn't disappoint the thousands who made their way to downtown Ottawa to wish Canada a happy birthday

The two boys enjoyed every minute of it and when it was over, they walked with the crowds on the large grass area back to the streets. They promised Carol they'd head back to the hotel.

As they approached their hotel a police car with it's lights flashing zoomed past them and turned into the underground parking lot.

Joshua looked at Curtis. "I wonder what's going on?"

Curtis shrugged as they walked into the crowded lobby. "Who cares. I want to party."

Joshua remember dinner. "What did you mean that you wanted to talk?"

Curtis ran his fingers through his hair and then put his hat on backwards. He was giddy. "It means that I hacked into Carol's computer. I know what she's up to."

Coming in the summer of 2021

Kids of Concern

The Continuation

What happens next?

<u>perrylogan.ca</u>

About the Author

Perry Logan

The Kids of Concern is my first adventure into fiction writing and I hope you enjoys the characters and storylines as much as I enjoyed creating them. Writing became a passion I never knew I had until I started typing and I hope I never stop.

I'm married with three grown children and two (so far) amazing grandkids.

Enjoy and follow your passion.